A DEADLY GAMBIT

Lucien Florian Nigellus. Vitala had never met him, yet he'd occupied her thoughts and shaped her studies for years. His biographical information painted a picture of an isolated man. Both his elder brothers were dead; his father had been forcibly deposed and imprisoned on the island of Mosar. He had no heirs and had not yet married. His only close relatives were an aunt, a female cousin, and a younger sister, none of whom were eligible for the throne. *He's crippled and alone,* Bayard had said. *Kill him, and you will spark a succession battle that will tear the empire apart.*

ASSASSIN'S GAMBIT

THE HEARTS AND THRONES SERIES

AMY RABY

A SIGNET ECLIPSE BOOK

SIGNET ECLIPSE

Published by the Penguin Group
Penguin Group (USA) Inc., 375 Hudson Street,
New York, New York 10014, USA

USA / Canada / UK / Ireland / Australia / New Zealand / India / South Africa /
China

Penguin Books Ltd., Registered Offices: 80 Strand, London WC2R 0RL, England
For more information about the Penguin Group visit penguin.com.

First published by Signet Eclipse, an imprint of New American Library,
a division of Penguin Group (USA) Inc.

First Printing, April 2013

SIGNET ECLIPSE and logo are trademarks of Penguin Group (USA) Inc.

ISBN 978-0-451-41782-4

Printed in the United States of America
10 9 8 7 6 5 4 3 2 1

ALWAYS LEARNING   PEARSON

For Sean and Ethan,
my Caturanga players.

ACKNOWLEDGMENTS

I offer my deepest appreciation to Alexandra Machinist and Claire Zion for believing in and championing this book. We've made our moves. Now we see how the board plays out.

Thank you also to Angie Christensen and JoAnn Ten Brinke, who understand the challenges of writing with children in the house. You've always been there when I needed you.

I write my early drafts in isolation, but much of the magic happens in the later drafting stages when I bring other people into the process. Many people helped make this a stronger novel. First, thank you to my romance critique group, Jessi Gage, and Julie Brannagh of the Cupcake Crew—you ladies are so talented! I can't tell you how much I look forward to our meetings, even if we're just having a chat. Nobody understands a writer like another writer.

Next, my SFF critique group, Writer's Cramp. Thank you to Barbara Stoner, Mark Hennon, Kim Runciman, Stephen Merlino, Steven Gurr, Tim McDaniel, Amy Stewart, Thom Marrion, Janka Hobbs, Marta Murvosh, Michael Croteau, and Courtland Shafer. And my online critique partners: Marlene Dotterer, Bonnie Freeman, Anna Kashina, Lisa Smeaton, Steve Brady, John Beety,

Heidi Kneale, Jarucia Jaycox Narula, Becca Andre, Bo Balder, and many others who reviewed individual chapters or the synopsis.

Finally, to five anonymous first-round judges of the RWA's Golden Heart® contest. I don't know who you are, but you do. You made a difference. Thank you.

PROLOGUE

His body moved against hers, chafing her skin. Vitala shifted beneath him and tried to remember his name. Rennic, maybe. Some spy in training from the practice floor who'd leapt at the opportunity to engage in a different sort of practice.

"Not much into this, are you?" he murmured, pumping away.

Right—she was supposed to act like she enjoyed this. And if she couldn't fool this Rennic fellow, she'd never fool the emperor. She moaned and writhed, convinced, as always, that such obvious fakery couldn't work. And yet it did. He quickened. The hard muscles of his arms tensed against her, and his rhythm accelerated. His eyes fluttered shut.

She ran her hands down his back.

Her mentor's words echoed in her head. *Remember the nature of the emperor's magic. If your timing is even a little bit off, he'll see the attack coming, and you will fail.*

She knew the difficulty of her task and the importance of getting the details right. She would practice until every move had the slick perfection of a well-played Caturanga game.

Rennic grunted, beyond speech. He jerked and gasped. The moment had come.

A touch of her mind and a flick of her finger, and from

out of nowhere a Shard glinted in her hand. She stabbed the tiny blade into the soft flesh of his back. He didn't react, probably didn't even feel it. Another touch of her mind, and she released the spell it carried—a benign white-pox spell, easily cured. Not the more fatal alternative.

With a grunt that could have been satisfaction or pain, he collapsed atop her, sticky with sweat.

She yanked the Shard out of his back, and he jerked in sudden awareness. He twisted and stared at the inky Shard, now daubed red with his blood. "You get me with that thing?"

"It's a good thing you're not the emperor," said Vitala, "or you'd be dead."

1

"Vitala Salonius?"

She set down her heavy valise on the dock's oak planking. The man approaching her looked the quintessential Kjallan—tall and muscular, black hair, and a hawk nose. He wore Kjallan military garb, double belted, with a sword on one hip. On the other hip sat a flintlock pistol with a walnut stock and gilt bronze mounts, so fine and polished that Vitala found herself coveting it. His orange uniform bore no blood mark but instead the sickle and sunburst—the insignia of the Legaciatti, which made him one of the emperor's famed personal bodyguards.

"Yes, sir. That's me," she said.

His handsome face broke into a smile. "My name is Remus, and I'm here to escort you to the palace. I'll get that for you." He hefted the valise with ease and gestured at a carriage waiting at the end of the dock.

She followed him, swaying at the sensation of being on dry land after two weeks aboard ship. Remus's riftstone was not visible. Most Kjallan mages wore them on chains around their necks, concealed beneath their clothes. The collar of Remus's uniform hid even the chain. He was certainly a mage—all the Legaciatti were—but she could not tell what sort of magic he possessed. Was he a war mage? That was the only type difficult to kill. She relaxed her mind a little, opening herself to the tiny fault lines that separated her world from the spirit world, and viewed the ghostly blue threading of his wards. He was well protected from disease, parasites, and even from the conception of a child.

They arrived at the carriage, a landau pulled by dark bays. At Remus's gesture, she climbed inside. He handed her valise to a bespectacled footman, who heaved it onto the back and strapped it in place. Remus, whom she'd expected to ride on the back or up front with the driver, stepped into the carriage and sat in the seat opposite her. Of course. The vetting process began here. He would make small talk, and she'd have to be very, very careful what she said to him.

The carriage lurched forward, and the Imperial City of Riat began to pass by the windows—wide streets and narrow ones, large homes and small ones, with the usual collection of inns, shops, and street vendors crammed into the available spaces. She spotted a millinery shop, a gunsmith, a Warder's, an open-air market with fresh, imported lemons. A newsboy with an armload of papers cried his wares from a corner. Kjallan townsfolk moved about the streets, buying, flirting, and trading gossip. The citizens caught her eye with their brightly colored, robe-like syrtoses, while slaves in gray flitted by like shadows. The city was pleasant enough, but unremarkable. Well, what had she expected? Marble houses? Streets lined with diamonds?

"I hear you're a master of Caturanga," said Remus.

"Yes, sir. I won the tournament this year in Beryl."

"The emperor was impressed by your accomplishment." His blue eyes studied her with a more than casual interest.

"I'm honored by that."

"And you're from the province of Dahat?"

Please don't be from Dahat yourself. It would be a disaster if he were looking for someone to swap childhood stories with. She'd been to Dahat, so she could provide a few details about the region, but she hadn't grown up there. "Yes, sir."

"How are feelings toward the emperor there?"

Her forehead wrinkled. *What sort of question is that?* "Citizens of Dahat have great respect for Emperor Lucien."

Remus laughed. "You think this is a loyalty test, don't you? Tell me the truth, Miss Salonius. Emperor Lucien likes to know how public sentiment runs throughout his empire. Platitudes and blind expressions of loyalty mean nothing to him. He wants honesty."

Vitala bit her lip. "I've been on the Caturanga circuit for more than three years, sir, longer than Emperor Lucien's reign. What little I picked up from my visits home is that while most of the citizenry supports him, there are some who disapprove of his policies and preferred the former emperor. I imagine that would be true in any province."

"Indeed," said Remus. "There are those who miss the old Emperor Florian and his Imperial Garden. Have you had the privilege of visiting it?"

"Visiting what?"

"Florian's Imperial Garden."

"No, sir. This is my first visit to the palace." Vitala was puzzled. He had to know that already.

"Ah," he said. "You should seek it out during your visit."

"That would be lovely, sir."

The carriage tilted backward. Vitala looked out her window. They'd passed through the city and started up the steep hill that led to the Imperial Palace. The carriage was navigating the first of half a dozen switchbacks. When she turned back to Remus, his eyes had lost their intensity. Whatever the test was, it seemed she'd passed it. "You are the first woman to win the Beryl tournament," he said. "Pray tell me who you studied under."

Vitala smiled. This was one of the questions she'd been coached on. "My father taught me to play when I was four years old and I showed an aptitude for the game. Within a year, I could beat my cousins. Later, I studied under Caecus, and when I'd mastered his teachings, I studied under Ralla." She droned on, feeding him the lies she'd recited under Bayard's tutelage. Remus leaned back and nodded dully. It seemed he'd lost interest in her. Thank the gods.

As the carriage crested the final switchback, Vitala craned her neck for a look at the Imperial Palace. Three white marble domes, each topped with a gilt roof, rose into view, gleaming in the sunshine. Next appeared the numerous outbuildings and walled gardens that surrounded the domes. A wide, tree-lined avenue directed them to the front gates.

Inside the palace, silk hangings of immeasurable value draped the walls, while priceless paintings and sculptures graced every nook. She'd never been anywhere so boldly ostentatious. What a contrast to Riorca, with its broken streets and ramshackle pit houses! How much of this had been built by Riorcan slave labor?

Two Legaciatti, both women, met them inside the door. Vitala studied them, curious at the oddity of female Kjallan soldiers. Bayard had told her that women made ideal assassins for Kjallan targets because Kjallan men didn't take women seriously. Ostensibly, that was true; Kjall was patriarchal, and women had little power under the law. But as she'd traveled on the tournament circuit, she'd learned the reality was more complicated. Most Kjallan men were soldiers who were often away from home. In their absence, their wives had authority over their households. Women and slaves were the real engine of Kjall's economy; few men had many practical skills outside of soldiering.

"Search her," ordered Remus.

One of the women beckoned. "Come along."

The search took place in a private room and was humiliatingly thorough. Vitala knew what they were looking for: concealed weapons or perhaps a riftstone. They would not find either. She didn't wear her riftstone around her neck; it was surgically implanted in her body, along with the deathstone, her escape from torture and interrogation if she botched this mission. Her weapons were magically hidden where none but a wardbreaker could detect them. And there were no Kjallan wardbreakers; only Riorcans possessed the secrets of that form of magic.

As she put her clothes back on, the Legaciatti emptied her valise, checked it for hidden compartments, and pawed through her paltry collection of spare clothes, undergarments, powders, and baubles. They found nothing that concerned them.

They repacked her things and led her up two flights of white marble stairs. The walls were rounded and concave; she must be in one of the domes. Her room was the third on the right from the top of the stairway. A young guard with peach fuzz on his chin stood in front of it, wearing an orange uniform but no sickle and sunburst. Peach fuzz. He looked familiar.

The young soldier lay on the cot, his wrists and ankles

bound. His blanket had fallen to the floor, a result of his struggles. His eyes jerked toward her, wide with fear, but when he saw her, he relaxed a little. He wasn't expecting a teenage girl.

"Miss Salonius?"

He shouldn't know her name. How did he know her name?

"Miss Salonius?"

And why did he sound like a woman?

Vitala blinked. The Legaciatti were staring at her in concern. "Miss Salonius?" one of them asked.

"I'm sorry." Gods, where was she? Marble walls. The Imperial Palace.

"You stopped moving. You were staring into space."

"Sorry, I was . . . never mind." Averting her eyes so that she wouldn't see the young man guarding her door, she stepped inside.

Vitala's room was a suite. Just inside was a sitting room with a single peaked window along its curved wall and a pair of light-glows in brass mountings suspended from the ceiling. The room was lavishly furnished with carved oaken tables and chairs upholstered in silk. A bookshelf on the far wall drew her eye. Among its contents, she recognized all the classic treatises on Caturanga and some she'd never seen before, as well as books on other subjects. An herbal by Lentulus. Cinna's *Tactics of War*. Numerous works of fiction, including the notoriously racy *Seventh Life of the Potter's Daughter*. Who had put a book like that into an otherwise erudite bookshelf?

On a table in the center of the room sat the finest Caturanga set she'd ever seen. Pieces of carved agate with jeweled eyes winked at her from a round, two-tiered board of polished marble. She picked up one of the red cavalry pieces. The rider was richly detailed down to the folds of his cloak. The warhorse was wild-eyed, his beautifully carved expression showing equal parts fear and determination.

Had Emperor Lucien set up this room just for her? No, of course not. He hosted many Caturanga champions. Probably all of them had been housed here.

The bedroom was equally fine, with a high, four-poster bed, silk sheets, and a damask down-stuffed comforter. The silk hangings were blue and red. Was that by design? Blue and red were the traditional colors of Caturanga pieces.

"You will reside here until the emperor summons you," a Legaciatta instructed. "Take your rest as needed, but you are not to wander about the palace. If you desire something, such as food or drink, ask the door guard. If you wish to bathe, he can escort you to the baths on the lower level."

Vitala nodded. "Thank you, ma'am."

The Legaciatti left, closing the door behind them. Vitala went to the window—real glass, she noted—and peered out. Below was a walled enclosure obscured by a canopy of trees, through which she caught glimpses of red, purple, and orange. The famous Imperial Garden? Looking up to take in the broader view, she noticed a patch of too-light blue in the sky and picked out the Vagabond, the tiny moon that glowed blue at night but faded almost to invisibility in the daytime. God of reversals and unforeseen disaster, the Vagabond wandered across the sky in the direction opposite the other two moons, and was not always a favorable sighting. "Great One, pass me by," she prayed reflexively.

Leaving the window and lighting one of the glows with a touch of her finger, she pulled *Seventh Life* from the bookshelf. Sprawling on a couch, she waited upon the pleasure of the emperor.

Vitala was not her given name. When she was born dark-haired, Papa named her Kolta: "blackbird."

She was eight years old when the stranger arrived. Mama and Papa took him into the bedroom to speak with him. They shut her out, but she pressed her ear against the door to listen.

"We've completed the testing," said the stranger, "and your daughter is exactly what we're looking for. Highly intelligent, physically strong, and coordinated. And, of course, she's black-haired."

Mama said something she couldn't quite make out.

"In the village, perhaps," replied the stranger. "But in the Circle, dark hair is an asset. She can pass for Kjallan. It will allow her to move in areas where others cannot."

More mumbling from Mama.

"The Circle is prepared to offer you compensation. Four hundred tetrals."

Papa gasped.

Mama raised her voice. "I'm not selling my daughter!"

"Of course not," soothed the stranger. "But Kolta will never reach her potential here in the village—not with the prejudice against girls like her. Why subject her to harassment and ostracism, when among the Circle she will be valued and revered? The money is our gift to you. A token of our thanks for aiding Riorca in its time of need."

Mama began to sob.

"Treva, he's right," said Papa. "It would be selfish to keep Kolta here. A half-Kjallan bastard will never be accepted—"

"You hate her!" cried Mama. "You want to be rid of her!"

"Madam," said the stranger, "consider the advantages to Kolta in joining the Circle. She will receive a thorough education, far better than anything she could get here. And she will be among her own kind. We have other half-breeds like her, dark-haired girls who know what it's like to be Riorcan but look Kjallan. For the first time in her life, she will have friends."

Mama continued to sob.

"Treva, think of it," said Papa. "Four hundred tetrals! You know what that money would mean for us. This man is right. The Circle can do far better for Kolta than we can."

Something unintelligible from Mama.

"No," said the stranger. "It must be now. She must begin her language training immediately, or she'll never speak with the proper accent."

A long silence followed, broken only by Mama's sobbing. There were soft words that Kolta could not make out.

The stranger was saying, "We find it's best if there are no good-byes."

The door opened, and the stranger stepped out. Terrified, Kolta hid in the corner between the wall and the door. But the door moved away, revealing her. The stranger stared down at her in surprise. "Were you listening, Kolta?"

She shook her head.

He knelt, bringing himself to her eye level. "Tell me the truth, and you will not be in trouble. Were you listening?"

She hesitated a moment, but nodded.

"And yet you do not cry." His mouth twisted as he lifted her chin with his finger. "My name is Bayard. I'm going to be your friend, Kolta. Would you like that?"

She was silent.

*"The people here don't treat you very well, do they?
They don't like dark-haired girls. But I'm going to take
you somewhere else. Somewhere you'll be loved, Kolta.
Do you want to be loved?"*

Her chin began to tremble.

*"Of course you do." He folded her into his arms, and
she began to cry. "It's what we all want."*

Lucien limped on his artificial leg through the doorway
into his office, fell into his chair, and leaned his crutch
against the wall. Four years he'd been emperor, and still
a shiver went down his spine every time he crossed that
threshold. He'd spent too much time in the opposite
chair, the one on the other side of the desk, facing a loud
and frightening father he could never please.

Septian, his bodyguard, a head taller than Lucien and
twice as broad, moved in almost perfect silence as he
took his customary place behind the chair and shoul-
dered a musket. He carried the weapon more for show
than for any real need; it would be a rare enemy Septian
couldn't handle with a sword or a knife or even his bare
hands. Lucien had been escorted by Legaciatti all his life,
but since ascending the throne, he'd become hyperaware
of them, especially Septian. The man rarely spoke, and
his face was impossible to read. What did he think of
Lucien? Did he recognize Lucien's head for military
strategy? Or, like Florian, did he privately roll his eyes at
what he perceived as a useless, crippled boy?

Lucien rubbed his forehead. His empire was fragile,
precarious. He had problems to solve. *Real* problems.
What his bodyguards thought of him should be the least
of his concerns.

Septian cleared his throat.

Lucien raised his head and saw the man standing in the doorway. "Remus. Come."

The Legaciattus entered, bowed his obeisance, and sat in the chair across from him. The door guards shut him in.

"What's the schedule today?" asked Lucien.

"You're seeing Legatus Cassian Nikolaos this morning."

Lucien made a face. "Pox. Is he waiting outside?"

"Yes, sir. And this afternoon, you were going to speak to the new recruits at the palaestra. Then there's the meetings with your advisors."

Lucien nodded. The morning would be a harassment, but the afternoon wasn't so bad. He liked public speaking, especially when the audience was young soldiers—it wasn't long since he'd been one himself. He'd seen action on the battlefield, and frontline soldiers tended to respect that.

Was there a gap in his schedule? His meeting with Cassian would not take all morning. "Remus, has that woman who won in Beryl arrived yet?"

Remus smiled. "She arrived by ship yesterday, Your Imperial Majesty, and awaits your pleasure."

Lucien brightened. "Have her ready to play by mid-morning."

"Very good, Your Imperial Majesty. Shall I send in Cassian?"

"Yes."

Remus left, and the guards admitted Legatus Cassian Nikolaos, Lucien's highest-ranking military officer. Cassian was a longtime friend of Lucien's father, the former emperor, and he was everything Lucien wasn't. Big, burly, whole—that is, possessed of all four limbs—and afraid of nothing. Middle-aged, he had decades of command experience behind him, and it rankled him to report to an emperor in his twenties. "Legatus," said Lucien, granting the man permission to speak.

"Your Imperial Majesty." Cassian bowed.

Lucien's eyes narrowed. The bow wasn't as low as it ought to be. It bordered on insolence, yet the slight was subtle. He would look foolish if he drew attention to it. "Have a seat." He'd tried several strategies for winning Cassian's respect. Flattery hadn't worked. Neither had pointing out the patently obvious holes in the man's proposed strategies. In the end, he'd given up and fallen back on the style he'd used with his equally intractable father, a tone of breezy, uncaring confidence. It didn't work either.

Cassian began, "Lucien, about the Riorcan rebels—"

"That's Sir or Your Imperial Majesty," snapped Lucien. "And I'm not going to decimate the Riorcans."

Cassian stiffened. "Sir, you've let their crimes go unpunished far too long. They flaunt their disrespect in a hundred tiny ways every day, and their Obsidian Circle sabotages our supply lines and assassinates our officers."

"I have a battalion combing the hills in search of the Circle. It's not easy to find. In the past year, we've found only two enclaves, neither of which had more than twenty people in it. And you know what my soldiers discovered when they broke in."

"Corpses," said Cassian.

"They killed themselves rather than risk interrogation. We know nothing about where their headquarters are or who's in charge."

"Sir, this is why you have to decimate the Riorcan villages. We can't find the Circle, but we *can* find the villagers who support them. Punish them, and that support will end."

"Cassian." Lucien paused, considering his words carefully. "You are one of Kjall's finest commanders, and I have a tremendous respect for your experience in the field. But you haven't been in Riorca. I have —"

"For two years!" spat Cassian.

"Two years longer than you have, and those years opened my eyes. Most Riorcans want nothing more than to live their lives and raise their families in peace. The rebels are a minority. Your opinion is noted, but my mind is made up. We will not decimate Riorca."

"Yes, sir." Instead of leaving, Cassian sat quietly in his chair.

Lucien eyed him narrowly. "You are dismissed, Legatus."

"Sir, about last night's state dinner . . ." He hesitated.

"Didn't like my speech?"

"Your oration was superlative and the food exquisite. But you deprived us of the court's brightest jewel, the imperial princess."

Lucien's mouth tightened. "Celeste chose not to attend."

"At your urging, no doubt."

"She is thirteen years old, Legatus, and she finds state dinners tedious." Indeed, he could hardly blame his sister for not wanting to spend an evening being slobbered over by older men looking to insert themselves into the line of succession. In Cassian's case, it was particularly disgusting, because he was already married. He would divorce his wife in a heartbeat if he thought he could remarry more advantageously. And while politically motivated divorces and marriages were common in Kjall, Lucien considered the practice repugnant.

"Perhaps she found them dull when she was a child, but she's a young woman now. Young women love to be the center of attention. Perhaps she would like to attend the upcoming dinner for the Asclepian delegates? I should be glad to escort her."

Lucien stared at him stonily. "No."

"If you should change your mind—" began Cassian.

"You are dismissed, Legatus."

Vitala paced nervously in her suite. The door guard—a new one, thank the gods; there must have been a shift change—had informed her the emperor would see her later that morning. Soon, the moment would come, the moment she'd spent eleven years preparing for. Could she seduce and kill Emperor Lucien?

Seduction was the easy part, but she'd never targeted an emperor before.

We know very little about his love life, Bayard had told her. *Only that he must have one.*

What if he liked only blondes or redheads? Gods, what if he preferred men?

She'd suggested to Bayard that she lose her first Caturanga game with Lucien. She'd seduced a Kjallan officer once with a similar technique. She played the part of a foolish bufflehead searching for a misplaced glove, which turned out to be under her chair. A little flattery and flirtation, a touch here and there, and he was hers. But soldiers were easy; an emperor was something else. Lucien was probably approached by beautiful, sexually receptive women on a daily basis. She had to make herself stand out.

You must win the initial game, Bayard had said. *He may lose interest if he thinks you have nothing to teach him. And we don't know how long it will take you to lure him into bed. This man is powerful. He has his choice of women. And he may be particular.*

Thanks for the encouragement, she had retorted.

We suspect he likes strong women.

How can you tell, if you know nothing about his love life? she asked.

Because the closest relationship he's ever had with a woman was with his cousin Rhianne, said Bayard.

The one who ran off to Mosar?

She was rebellious as a child, and Lucien was her partner in crime. Word is he misses her. We think the more you remind him of Rhianne, the more interested in you he'll be.

Fine. She would win the first game. But how to proceed from there?

Someone knocked at her door. "Miss Vitala? His Imperial Majesty will see you now."

2

Lucien Florian Nigellus. Vitala had never met him, yet he'd occupied her thoughts and shaped her studies for years. His biographical information painted a picture of an isolated man. Both his elder brothers were dead; his father had been forcibly deposed and imprisoned on the island of Mosar. He had no heirs and had not yet married. His only close relatives were an aunt, a female cousin, and a younger sister, none of whom were eligible for the throne. *He's crippled and alone,* Bayard had said. *Kill him, and you will spark a succession battle that will tear the empire apart.*

As she walked to the emperor's quarters, escorted by two Legaciatti, she glanced at the wall hangings and carved ceilings, relaxing her mind to see the magic anchored in them. Usually, magic dissipated quickly. A mage pulled a bit of magic from the Rift and used it to accomplish some purpose; then it drizzled away. But some mages—Warders—had the ability to anchor magic in the physical world. They could make it last. Anchored magics were invisible to most eyes, but Vitala could see them.

A blue glow infused the wall hangings; they'd been warded against parasites. The faint red line across a doorway she passed was an enemy ward, set to sound an alarm if someone crossed it with the intent to harm.

Each ward possessed a tiny contact point—literally, a hole in the Rift—through which the magic was anchored and made to persist. Vitala could see those contact points. And she could break them, sending their magic harmlessly back to the Rift.

Where were all the heat-glows? Since entering the palace, she hadn't seen a single one. They tended to be eyesores, but how did the imperial staff heat the palace without them? Perhaps the glows were hidden from view, inside the walls or behind the hangings.

Her escort slowed. Just ahead, four Legaciatti guarded a set of double doors. She'd reached the emperor's quarters.

"Vitala Salonius?" The door guard directed the question to her escort.

"This is Miss Salonius," one of her guards confirmed.

"The emperor is ready for her." They opened the double doors, and Vitala relaxed her mind to scan the threshold for wards.

There weren't any.

How could that be? Bayard had assured her they used enemy wards in the palace. She'd seen one already, across a different door. Was it possible they'd developed a ward she couldn't see? Would she trigger it if she stepped across the threshold?

One of the door guards raised an eyebrow at her. "Miss Salonius?"

"Sorry," she stammered. "I'm nervous."

He winked. "Don't be. He's not like his father."

Vitala's nerves sang as she stepped through the doorway, but nothing happened. There truly was no ward there. Why?

She was in a sitting room similar to the one at the entrance to her suite, but larger. She scanned the floor for wards and saw none. Then she lifted her eyes to a table at the far end of the room, where a man sat before a Caturanga board. Emperor Lucien.

She'd spent so many years studying this man and plotting to kill him that she felt a perverse and unwelcome intimacy with him. Having only a rough description of what he looked like, she'd constructed a mental image, which she saw was accurate in the broad strokes but wrong in all the details. He was taller than she'd expected, his build slim and muscular. As he struggled upright from his chair and slipped a crutch under one arm, she could not help taking in the most obvious fact about him, that he was missing the lower half of his left leg. She'd known he was an amputee, but it was different seeing it in person. She swallowed uncomfortably.

He wore a wooden leg of simple design, a straight post of polished mahogany banded in gold. He limped on it, supporting himself with a matching crutch. As he moved toward her, smiling broadly, she forced her attention away from his leg. He wore a fine syrtos of blue silk, over which glittered a jeweled loros, the mark of his rank. Like most Kjallans, he had a hawk nose. Coupled with the clean, masculine lines of his face, it gave him a commanding appearance despite his youth. His black hair, slightly mussed, dipped over his forehead—he needed a haircut—and his eyes, so dark they were almost black, regarded her with intensity and intelligence.

He didn't look like the sort of man who would enslave half her people and starve the rest with outrageous demands for tribute. He didn't look like the man who'd massacred her people at Stenhus. But one couldn't judge a man by his looks.

She sank into a submission curtsy, acknowledging their vast difference in rank.

He took her hand and lifted her up. "Vitala Salonius."

"Your Imperial Majesty," she answered.

He looked her over, and his eyebrows rose. He smiled appreciatively. "I've been looking forward to meeting you."

He led her to the table, and she gaped at the Caturanga set. She'd never seen anything like it, not even at the tournament in Beryl. The water piece, nearest her, was a clump of swirling blue mist—obviously magicked. Her hand moved unconsciously toward it, but, remembering her manners, she yanked it back. "May I?"

"Go ahead." Lucien leaned his crutch against the wall and lowered himself into a chair.

She picked it up. Underneath its pyrotechnic enchantment, the piece was made of stone. Perhaps carved agate, like the set in her rooms. The mist swirled over her fingers. "It's amazing. I've never seen anything like this."

Lucien grinned. "I have talented pyrotechnics on staff."

She set down the water piece and picked up the Traitor. Standing in the palm of her hand, he moved like a living thing, scanning his surroundings and tucking a dagger behind his back. As she turned him, he shifted the weapon from hand to hand, keeping it from her view. Curious, she relaxed her mind and spotted the contact point that held the enchantment in the physical world.

With her mind already in the proper state, she glanced at Lucien to view his wards. A fertility ward glowed purplish blue; there was nothing else. That couldn't be right. She looked again, convinced she'd made a mistake. No, she hadn't, unless the Kjallans had invented a new sort of ward she couldn't see. He had no wards at all to protect against disease or parasites. He wanted to avoid sir-ing bastards, but he didn't care if he got sick? That made no sense.

She forced her mind back to the physical world and set the piece down. "I'm speechless." She motioned at the Soldier, Sage, and Vagabond pieces, each of which was a hovering, glowing moon, one orange, one white, and one blue. "Those I fear even to touch."

Lucien picked up the brilliant white Sage, rolled it about in his hand, and set it down again. "They're quite safe—just harmless magic. Let's get started. My time is limited."

She sat. From the way the board was arranged, she would be playing blue and Lucien red.

"I've been so eager for a game," said Lucien. "You're the first woman I've played Caturanga with. Well, besides my cousin, but she hates the game. You, on the other hand—you won at Beryl!"

She nodded uncertainly, wondering whether he expected modesty or pride from her. "I've had excellent instructors," she said, and turned her attention to the board. She was playing blue, so the first move was hers. She chose a flexible opening, the modified Soldier's Gambit. It gave her an edge in gaining control of the middle top tier.

He responded with the Ilonian Countergambit. She smiled. He was *that* sort of player. It was an aggressive move that ceded her the middle top tier but claimed the outer edges from which he might make an end run. This was going to be fun.

She made a bid for the Sage's influence and won it, but Lucien made her pay for it with two cavalry units and a weakened center position. He also trapped her Tribune behind a mountain.

She bit her lip. So much for this being easy. He was

the emperor—far too busy a man to spend eight hours a day practicing Caturanga strategies, like she had. She ought to have the advantage. But he had a blazing intellect, and no doubt he'd had fine tutors. She tried a supply-line ruse; he saw through it and broke it. She skipped her Traitor into the back ranks, ready to wreak havoc, but he launched a counterattack that forced her to retreat and regroup. Exasperating!

She shook her head and grinned, thoroughly enjoying herself.

Lucien hovered over the board like a spring, tightly coiled and ready to explode into action. His eyes darted over every space, concerned and calculating, and when she made a good move, his cheeks flushed.

If she could only get her battalions around the water trap he'd set, she could bring her troops under the Soldier's influence. Her Traitor was well positioned to take advantage of the Vagabond, and she already had the Sage. But her Tribune was under threat, and she couldn't ignore that. *Gods curse it.* She leaned back in her chair, staring at the board.

Lucien smiled, tugging absently at his left earlobe.

Could she lure him with Pelonius? Maybe. He was neglecting the bottom tier a bit, focusing on the top. She made a couple of setup moves and offered her Tribune as bait. Lucien leapt to capture it. She made her end run, and he was left in a squeeze—the state in which any move he made could only harm his position. Frowning, he chose the move of least disadvantage. She moved in for the kill. Half a dozen moves later, the game was over.

"Excellent game, Your Imperial Majesty." She offered him her arm.

The emperor clasped wrists with her, still staring at the carnage on the board. "I don't believe it."

"You're a very fine player," she said. "I admire your bold style."

"How did you—? I thought you were going to—" He shook his head. "Your Tribune. That was a strategic sacrifice, wasn't it?"

"It was indeed. Pelonius's Mire, Your Imperial Majesty."

"Yes, I know Pelonius, but it's not normally played on the bottom tier, is it?"

"No, it's a top-tier strategy. I adapted it."

He shook his head ruefully.

Maybe Bayard was wrong. Maybe it had been a mistake to win—she'd embarrassed him. Worse, she'd gotten so caught up in the game that she'd forgotten all about seduction.

Suddenly, he laughed. "Three gods, that's the most fun I've had in ages. You *must* play me again." He scooped up the red pieces and began resetting them. "Hurry. I've got an afternoon appointment."

Relieved, she slid her blue pieces back to their starting positions.

"I've beaten the last two Beryl champions who came here," he prattled. "Though I'm not certain I earned those wins. I think they might have let me win."

"I doubt that, Your Imperial Majesty."

"Please, call me Lucien." He replaced the Soldier, Sage, and Vagabond in their respective tiers. "I'm glad you're not afraid to beat me. If I'm going to get better at this, I need someone who will give me a challenge."

"Your game is excellent," she said, settling back in her chair. "It would be an insult to you not to play at the best of my ability."

"I'll beat you this game. Or the next one." He rested his elbows on the table and propped his chin in his hands. "I dare you to try Pelonius on me again."

She smiled and reached for a cavalry unit, trying a different opening.

He tugged at his earlobe.

A heavy knock came at the door. "Your Imperial Majesty," called a muffled voice.

"Pox," muttered Lucien. "Come, Remus."

The double doors opened. Remus stared uncomfortably at Vitala. "Sir, we've had a message from Tasox."

"A signal?"

"No, sir. A message, delivered on horseback."

"What's the message?" asked Lucien.

Remus's eyes went to Vitala, his unspoken message clear. *Not in front of her.* He crossed the room and whispered in Lucien's ear.

Lucien grimaced. "Clear my afternoon." He turned to Vitala. "I'm afraid we'll have to play some other time. The guards will show you out." He struggled upward, placed the crutch under his arm, and followed Remus to the door.

Vitala felt strangely bereft. She'd enjoyed the emperor's enthusiasm and fierce energy so much so that for a while she'd half forgotten who he was—and why she was here. She hadn't made the least bit of progress in seducing him. And he seemed so pleasant, hardly the sort of man who would visit horrors upon her people. *Never forget,* she told herself as he disappeared from view. *This man has done terrible things, and you are here to kill him.*

The inside of the cave was cold. Kolta gawped at the people standing around her. Men and women, children and adults, yellow-haired Riorcans and dark-haired Kjallans. Except the ones who looked like Kjallans weren't really Kjallans. For that matter, neither was she. She shivered.

Bayard shoved her forward, gentle but firm.

The man beside the cup seized her arm and drew a knife. With a squeal of terror, she yanked at her captured arm, trying to flee, but Bayard held her still.

The man sliced her wrist, spilling a few drops of her blood into the cup. Then he ran his finger along the wound. The pain ceased. Though her wrist was still smeared with blood, it was whole.

Kolta stopped struggling. "You're a Healer."

The man with the knife smiled. "I am."

She'd heard of men with such magic, but never before seen one.

He took the cup and held it to her lips. "Drink."

She stared at the cup's contents and wrinkled her nose. There was a lot more blood in there than what her wrist had spilled. No way would she drink that.

"Everyone has contributed," said Bayard. "Including myself. Drink—one sip is enough—and you will be one of us. If you will not join us, you must return to your family."

She swallowed and stared again at the cup. She wanted to belong. She wanted to be one of these people. They'd been kind to her, mostly. They'd given her food every day, not just on the good days, and they had magical Healers. She screwed up her face and sipped.

Bayard took the cup from her lips. "You are one of us, now and forever." He raised his voice to address the crowd. "Welcome, Kolta, to the Obsidian Circle."

"Welcome," echoed the crowd.

"In honor of your joining us, I give you your new name," said Bayard. "No longer shall you be named for the shame of your birth, but for your purpose: to aid the Circle in returning Riorca to its days of light and happiness. Your name is Vitala, 'life-giver.'"

*   *   *

Lucien didn't send for her again that day. Vitala read, played Caturanga against herself, drank Dahatrian tea, and, in the evening, visited the imperial baths. The baths were warm, scented swimming pools, a luxury almost beyond her imagination. Bathing in the presence of other nude women was odd, but no one else seemed to be bothered by it. As for the tea, she'd asked for lemon balm, but the guards informed her that lemon balm was forbidden within the palace walls—Emperor Lucien's orders. She'd known the emperor hated lemon balm, but was surprised to learn he'd banned it.

Two days later, the Legaciatti delivered to her a letter from Emperor Lucien. The emperor had apparently inked it himself, since the signature at the bottom matched the writing. The loops and whorls of his hand were precise and clean. *My illustrious opponent,* he'd written, *I count the hours until we can cross swords again. As my apology for keeping you waiting, I offer you a gift: the Caturanga set in your rooms. I also invite you to a state dinner, tomorrow evening, honoring the delegates from Asclepia, which I hope will prove an enjoyable diversion. Remus has offered to escort you.* She sniffed. Remus again. Since he was part of Lucien's security detail, she was a little frightened of him. She'd have to be careful what she said in his presence.

She went to the Caturanga set, picked up a cavalry piece, and caressed it, her heart swelling with a fierce happiness. She'd never owned something so beautiful. In fact, she'd never owned anything at all. Her possessions belonged to the Circle. The sad thing was she would probably have to leave the set behind. Once she'd accomplished her mission—if she survived—she would need to leave in a hurry, and unencumbered.

What about the dinner? She had nothing to wear for

such an occasion. Aside from the requirements of propriety and fitting in, if Lucien was going to be there, she needed to look her best. She was on the verge of sending for Remus with a plea for help when a Riorcan slave girl arrived at her door, bearing an assortment of dresses.

Vitala had been in Kjall for years now, long enough that the sight of Riorcan slaves no longer shocked her. Still, she found it tremendously awkward, especially when the girl struggled to communicate with her in halting Kjallan, unaware that Vitala could have communicated in fluent Riorcan.

The slave girl helped her try on each garment. Vitala chose a silk gown in royal blue. The girl carried it away to be altered, and Vitala settled down to play a solo game with her very own Caturanga set.

After her initiation, they did not stay at the cave. They traveled to a new one, several days' journey away. There she joined a classroom with other girls, some of them her age and some a little older. All were dark-haired.

"Study hard, Vitala," said Bayard, "If you do well, I'll see you in a few years."

She clutched his hand. He was her rescuer, and he was all she had. "I don't want to stay here. I want to go where you go."

"This is not my enclave," he said. "And you are not ready for me."

Her tears did not move him. When he pried her hand away and shut the door behind him, she had no choice but to turn her attention to the hard-faced, matronly woman who was her instructor. "Welcome, Vitala," said the instructor. She knelt and pinned a bit of white cloth to the front of Vitala's tunic. On it was a foreign word, written not in the Riorcan runic alphabet but in the strange loops and whorls of the Kjallan language.

The other students all had similar bits of white cloth pinned to their clothes. Some of them had the same word as hers, while others had different words. None were familiar. "What does it mean?" she asked.

The instructor pointed. "This is the Kjallan word for commoner. *Today you are a commoner.*" She pointed at an older girl. "This is Arvina. Today she is a prefect's wife." She pointed to another girl. "And Ista is a tribune's daughter. They are your social superiors, and you must treat them accordingly. If you make a mistake, they will punish you."

Vitala wrinkled her forehead.

"Kjall is a rank-sensitive society, and the rules are taught to Kjallan children at a very early age. To fit in and pass for Kjallan, you must learn these rules until they are as natural for you as walking. Class, if you are seated and someone of superior rank walks by, what do you do? You may answer in Riorcan."

"Stand up," they intoned.

"May you greet someone of superior rank?"

"No," said the class.

"What do you do instead of addressing them?" She pointed at Ista, whose thumb was raised.

"Curtsy," said Ista. "A welcome curtsy if the difference in rank is small, or a submission curtsy if the difference is great."

The instructor drilled the class until Vitala felt dizzy and nauseous. There was so much to learn. So many rules!

"And from now on," added the instructor, "you will speak only Kjallan."

Vitala stiffened. "I don't know Kjallan."

The instructor smiled. "You will."

3

That evening, Remus arrived for her in his Legaciatti uniform. She'd expected him to wear some sort of formal syrtos for a state dinner, but what did she know? There were gaps in the Circle's understanding of the Kjallan aristocracy. When she arrived at the banquet hall, she discovered he did not look out of place. All the military men were in their uniforms, with ranks and insignias and medals boldly displayed.

She spotted Emperor Lucien immediately. He was in the center of the domed hall, unmistakable with his peg leg and crutch and the jeweled loros, and the enormous bodyguard shadowing him. Was that bodyguard always present? Vitala could just imagine him standing there in the bedroom while Lucien made love. Worse, that bodyguard was almost certainly a war mage, which meant she was no match for him. The emperor was in the company of three other men who spoke with him, their faces animated. A woman hung on his arm. Vitala's heart sank.

A slave showed her and Remus to a table. They were seated in a corner with six minor dignitaries, about as far away as they could be from the centrally located imperial table. Vitala greeted her dinner companions, who spoke to her warmly until they learned she was a commoner, and then lost interest. She snuck glances at the lady who'd sat down with Lucien. She wore a gown of sparkling silver that glittered when she moved. Silver was not a color Vitala could wear; it made her look washed-out. This woman's complexion was just dark enough to carry it off. Red-gold hair cascaded down her back, suggesting more than a trace of foreign blood, and her face was so flawless it belonged on a sculpture. Vitala was outclassed. She was attractive, she knew that, but she could not compete at that level.

A slave placed a bowl of soup in front of her. It was creamy and tasted of sea scallops.

"Those men with the emperor," she said to Remus. "Are they the delegates from Asclepia?"

"Yes," said Remus. "They want to build a dam on some river up north."

"And the woman? Is she from Asclepia too?"

"Yes."

"She's very beautiful."

Remus smiled, raising his eyebrows at her. "She's not the only beauty in the room."

Three gods, was Remus flirting with her? Interesting. Could she work that to her advantage and perhaps arouse some jealousy in Lucien? Maybe not. It might backfire. Remus was a high-ranking Legaciattus, and, for all she knew, he and Lucien had the kind of friendly relationship that precluded them from poaching each other's women.

After the dessert course was served, the light-glows were dimmed and the orchestra began to play. The first dance was reserved for the imperial party. The Asclepian delegates paired off with palace beauties, while Lucien hovered just off the edge of the dance floor with the Asclepian woman. She looked frustrated at having the only partner in the room unable to dance, even if he was the emperor. Vitala felt a pang of pity for Lucien. How did it feel to be a cripple surrounded by so many examples of physical perfection?

Perhaps she should reserve her pity for the Asclepian woman. Very likely she'd been thrown at Lucien as a bribe to help the delegation get what they wanted. Had she been forced into the role, or did she volunteer? Maybe she stood to gain as much as the men did from the construction of that dam.

No, the Asclepian did not deserve her pity. It could hardly be torture to sleep with Lucien. He was a handsome man, and maybe the passion he'd shown at playing Caturanga also manifested itself in the bedroom. As for the missing leg, Vitala found herself less put off by it than she had been initially, and more curious. What did it look like when not covered by his clothes and that bit of gaudy wood and gold?

The first dance ended, and more couples crowded onto the floor.

Remus held out his hand. "Dance, Miss Salonius?"

She smiled. "Certainly." Dancing would get her physically closer to the emperor, who was still hovering in the vicinity of the imperial table. Maybe he'd notice her. Though he seemed frustratingly focused on the Asclepian.

Remus's hand was warm and dry. He led her confidently onto the floor and wrapped an arm around her waist. He danced competently but without artistry or flair. Never mind. He was leading her closer to the imperial table. Surely it wouldn't hurt to inspire a *little* jealousy. She gazed adoringly into Remus's eyes as they passed Lucien.

For three rounds, they circled the floor. The dance ended and they retreated, flushed and exhilarated, to their table. It had emptied of the other guests, who'd probably left to seek more prestigious company. A slave refilled their wineglasses, and Vitala drank deeply. To her surprise, she found she was enjoying herself.

Remus scrambled suddenly to his feet.

Following his lead, Vitala set down her wineglass, spilling a few bloodred drops, and stood.

"Sit down, sit down," said Emperor Lucien. The Asclepian woman, still on his arm, gave Vitala an appraising look. Vitala was amused by her discomfiture. Kjallans were funny. Rank was encoded directly into their language, which had three separate grammatical forms: one for speaking to an inferior, one for an equal, and one for a superior. Thus Kjallans had to determine relative rank before opening their mouths. Usually it was easy to figure it out, because Kjallan men wore insignias denoting their rank, and Kjallan noblewomen, who derived their rank from male relatives, wore a bit of rank-defining jewelry. Vitala, who was at the bottom of the social scale, possessed no jewelry of that kind, so her rank was not evident.

Vitala and Remus sat. The emperor took one of the empty seats and directed the Asclepian woman to the other. The Legaciattus bodyguard lurked unobtrusively behind them as a slave brought more wine.

"Are you enjoying yourself?" asked Lucien.

"Very much, Your Imperial Majesty," said Vitala. "It's been lovely, though I fear I'm out of my depth in this company."

Lucien indicated the woman who accompanied him. "I'd like you to meet Nasica Vestinius. She's visiting from the province of Asclepia. Nasica, Vitala Salonius."

Nasica extended a perfectly manicured hand and wrist dripping with bracelets.

Vitala clasped wrists with her.

"Every year," said Lucien, "there's a Caturanga tournament held in the city of Beryl, and I invite the winner of the tournament to the palace. That way I can learn from the best. This year, Miss Salonius was our winner."

A look of surprise, perhaps even disapproval, flitted across Nasica's face. "I see. You play Caturanga?" She spoke in the diplomatic form of the language, which indicated she had no idea of Vitala's rank and was being careful not to offend.

"Yes, ma'am." Vitala corrected Nasica's mistake by answering her in the submissive. "My father taught me the game."

Nasica switched smoothly to command. "And your father is?"

"A soldier."

Nasica cocked her head. "What rank?"

"He was a squad commander."

"Oh." Nasica's gaze drifted away—she'd lost interest. "You must be very proud to have come so far. All the way to the Imperial Palace."

"Yes, ma'am."

Nasica said nothing further, and Vitala sat in awkward silence. The Asclepian woman outranked her, and that meant Vitala was not free to lead the conversation. Not that she could think of much to say.

Lucien rose irritably. The three of them stood, bowing their heads in deference, and the bodyguard handed him his crutch. "Please avail yourself of drinks and dancing for as long as you like." Lucien pointed at Vitala. "But keep your mind sharp. I hope to see you at the Caturanga board again soon."

He limped away with the beautiful Nasica at his side.

Lucien summoned her for Caturanga the following afternoon. When Vitala arrived at his rooms, the door was open, but a knot of Legaciatti stood within the doorframe, blocking it. Her escort made her stop where she was and wait. She obeyed but craned her neck to see what was going on.

Lucien stood in the center of the group, leaning on his crutch with one hand and resting the other on a kneeling man's shoulder. The kneeling man drew a magical red line across the doorway with his finger.

A tingle of apprehension crawled up Vitala's neck. The man was laying an enemy ward. That was why Lucien had his hand on him; attuning a ward required physical contact. There hadn't been an enemy ward before, but now there was going to be one. Why the change? Had something alerted Lucien to danger?

Since there was no doubt she would trigger an enemy ward if she crossed one, she'd have to break the ward before she passed through that doorway.

Lucien looked up and spotted her. His eyes smiled at her. "Vitala."

She dropped into her submission curtsy. "Your Imperial Majesty."

"Come inside. We're done here." He gestured, and the guards fell back to make a path.

Vitala relaxed her mind to find the enemy ward's contact point, but it wasn't there. No contact point. And no ward! Three gods, she'd just seen it placed! What had happened to it?

The guards closed in around her, urging her forward, and she had no choice but to pass through the doorway. Her heart throbbed as she stepped over the threshold, but nothing happened. The ward wasn't there.

Was the Warder incompetent? That didn't seem possible; a Warder knew when his wards were laid correctly. It had to have been deliberately mislaid, which meant the Warder was betraying his emperor.

Lucien limped across the floor to the Caturanga board. Poor man, he wasn't just hated by the Riorcans, but by his own people. Was the Warder acting alone, or were there others involved? *Gods curse it.* What right did these others have to move against Lucien? The man was *her* kill. She'd been training for this for years. And she had a reason to kill him—a *good* reason. What was this other plot about? Power?

Of course. These were Kjallans. This was nothing more than an old-fashioned attempt at a coup. Some brutish Kjallan cull wanted the throne, and the Warder was helping him get it. But who was the cull? The more she thought about it, the more unsettled she became. Her people were operating on the assumption that Lucien's death, without an heir, would throw the Kjallan Empire into chaos, possibly even civil war. But what if there was another man waiting in the wings, ready to step in and take control? There might be no war, no disruption at all.

And what if the new man was worse than Lucien?

"What's the matter?" asked Lucien.

Vitala blinked. "Nothing, sire." She sat down at the Caturanga table.

Lucien was playing blue, so he had the first move. "I'll have you know I read up on Pelonius and all its variations last night."

She smiled. "Then I'll have to be creative. I was surprised you had time to play today. Have the Asclepians gone?"

"Yes." He opened with Double Cavalry.

She answered with a battalion. Perhaps she should focus on the bottom tier this time. "I heard they wanted a dam built."

"They did. I turned them down." He moved one of his mountains.

She wondered if he'd slept with Nasica first. "Your Imperial Majesty, do you mind if I ask why? I apologize if my questions are impertinent. But it's a rare opportunity for me to see imperial politics firsthand."

He shrugged. "Ask away; I wish more people took an interest. The reason I said no is that it's bad for Kjall. We use the lower part of that river for transport, and the downstream farmers use it for irrigation. The dam would spoil it for both purposes." He made his move and leaned back in his chair, folding his arms. "The Asclepians are trying to grab a larger share of the river profits for themselves at the expense of everyone else."

"Then I'm glad you turned them down, sire."

He shrugged. "Kjall is struggling too much for me to even consider doing otherwise. But I'm sorry to lose the support of that family."

"With respect, why should you need their support? You're the emperor. They should be scrambling to earn yours."

"It's critical that I retain the support of my high-level commanders and the leading families."

Perhaps the imperial throne was not as all-powerful as she'd assumed. After all, his own men were plotting against him under his nose. She made her countermove. "Were the Asclepians the emergency that pulled you away the other day?"

"Oh no," said Lucien. "That was something else. Unrest in Tasox."

Her hand hovered over the board. "What sort of unrest?"

"Some out-of-work soldiers have turned to banditry

and are terrorizing the citizens. I've dispatched forces to deal with the problem."

Vitala studied the board. Lucien was an aggressive, innovative player, which made him difficult to predict. He was setting up terrain obstacles for her in the bottom tier, but he'd made a suspicious move with his Tribune that suggested he was about to make a run for the Vagabond. He'd left himself open in a few spots. She might just be able to get her Traitor across enemy lines. For now, she worked on getting her cavalry into position.

Three gods, she was supposed to be seducing him, and once again she was getting too drawn into the Caturanga. "Has Nasica gone home too?"

He chuckled as if at some private joke. "Yes." He moved his Tribune again.

Vitala grimaced. He was definitely making a bid for the Vagabond. Time to move her cavalry and block him. No, it was time to focus on her mission, not the gods-cursed game. Nasica was gone, so this was her opportunity.

She reached across the board for a cavalry piece and accidentally on purpose knocked Lucien's Tribune off the board so it landed near his foot. "Sorry." She reached for it. He moved to pick it up too, and their fingers met, but she didn't pull her hand away. His eyes met hers below the table. She parted her lips slightly and felt herself blushing—a natural reaction, and exactly what she wanted. She lowered her eyes and let go of the piece.

He sat up and set it on the board. She moved her cavalry piece, still blushing. His eyes were on her.

"I wonder," he said slowly, "if you'd like to come back later this evening."

"Very much, sire," she said.

"First let's finish this game." He neatly captured her

Traitor, which was one move away from getting behind his enemy lines.

"Yes, sire, but it's already over." With a Double Cavalry Strike, she captured his Tribune and a battalion.

His hands went up in shock. "Three gods."

He tried to recover, but it was impossible. Half a dozen moves later, she controlled all three moons. "Soldier's Sweep."

"Pox," he said. "I'd ask for a rematch, but . . ." He looked up at his bodyguard. "Septian?"

The huge man gave a slight shake of his head.

He looked into her eyes. "Well. This evening, then?"

"Yes, sire." She stared at his mouth and licked her lips.

He gazed at her for a moment. After an awkward silence, he said, "I look forward to it. Let me show you to the door." He slipped the crutch under his left arm. She walked with him, slowing her strides to match his swinging ones.

At the door, she turned and performed her farewell curtsy. When she stood, his hand ventured toward her face and pushed a stray lock of hair away from her forehead. He looked like he was going to say something, but apparently he decided against it. He smiled and signaled to the guards.

Her escort began to walk her back to her room. Gods, how easy that had been! She supposed she should have expected it. Lucien was a man who would be accustomed to women making sexual advances, even subtle ones.

She'd made progress. Now she just needed to finish the job.

Bayard returned a year later. Not for Vitala, but for Ista.

Vitala burned with jealousy. Ista. That poxy cull! The older girl was the smartest in the class, the instructor's fa-

vorite, good at everything. But Vitala was capable of anything Ista could do. Or would be in time. She couldn't help that she was younger.

Bayard took only the best of the fourth-year girls, and before Ista there had been two years where he didn't take anybody at all. Everyone knew he trained assassins. The other fourth-year girls left with different trainers. Some would be spies; some would be support staff. There was a role for everybody, but the assassins were the most important members of the Circle. They learned magic. They learned how to fight and how to kill. They were the ones who would make a difference, who would one day set Riorca free.

Vitala would show them. She'd be the best in her year. She'd study nights. She'd work harder than anyone else. Then when her four years were done, Bayard would come for her. And she'd show him how much better she was than Ista.

4

"The Kjallan infantryman." Lucien's voice rang out over the vast hall, returning to him in a slight echo. "My estimate of him was formed in Riorca when I fought by his side." He paused to let the words sink in. He was no soft aristocrat, but a seasoned war veteran. Eager young faces stared up at him from stiff, new uniforms, their eyes shining. "I know his patience, his fortitude, his grim determination. I have seen him march from dawn to dusk in wind and rain, bent under his soggy pack, and then form up for battle, his back straight, his strength undiminished.

"Today you join the finest fighting force in the world. You are well trained and well equipped, but that is not the secret to your success." He looked out over the crowd, making eye contact with a few individuals, who swallowed and blinked. "The secret to your success is your Kjallan heart. You were born to this legacy, as your fathers were before you, and their fathers before them. Your fathers did not sit idle, resting on the achievements of their forebears. Instead, they carved the Kjallan legacy on the breast of their enemies."

His eyes roamed the silent crowd. "You have much to live up to. I say this not to intimidate you—but, then, it is not the nature of the Kjallan infantryman to be intimidated. He conquers grasslands, hills, and mountains.

He sails the Great Northern Sea in all its capriciousness of wind and weather. He stands unflinching in the face of gunfire; he stands before the cavalry charge with bayonet in hand, straining to meet the enemy. He fears nothing, but, I assure you, his enemies fear him. Sons of Kjall, welcome to our country's most august tradition. It is time to write *your* legacy."

Cheering and foot stomping rose behind him as he stepped down from the podium. He clasped wrists with soldiers in the front row until his Legaciatti closed ranks around him and escorted him toward the door. "That went well," he commented to no one in particular.

"Indeed," rumbled a deep voice beside him. "Your Majesty is surprisingly eloquent."

Three gods, had Septian actually *spoken*? "Why do you say *surprisingly*?" he teased.

Septian's voice was humorless. "Because your father never possessed the talent."

It was true. Lucien was a better orator than his father. And no one ever acknowledged it unless they were baldly attempting to curry his favor. He smiled at the unexpected praise.

Pox. Remus was standing in front of his carriage. Lucien's smile faded. "Is there *another* disaster?" he called out.

"The same one as before," said Remus. "May I ride back with you?"

Lucien nodded wordlessly and climbed into the carriage. Remus stepped in after him. Lucien had barely settled before the vehicle jolted into movement. He reached down and massaged his stump where the peg leg attached. It often became irritated when he walked on it. "So, Tasox has taken a turn for the worse."

"Several of the larger groups of bandits have formed

an alliance and taken control of the town. They've run out the troops you sent and publicly staked the governor."

"What's our paper in Tasox? The *Tribune*?"

"They've shut it down."

"Who's leading the bandits?"

"A man named Gordian."

"Never heard of him. Is he a former officer?"

"A former prefect," said Remus.

Lucien slumped against the plush carriage back. What a mess. He'd have to send a whole battalion. Worse, the situation could spiral out of control if he didn't manage it carefully. "We'll send Blue Hawk."

"Yes, sire."

"Clear my schedule and send word. I'm going with them."

Remus stared at him. "Personally?"

"This will require a delicate hand. I need to be there."

"We'll be up half the night making preparations—"

"That was an order, Remus."

"Yes, sire."

Double pox. Clearing his schedule meant canceling his tryst with Vitala, and he'd been looking forward to that. Her come-on had been so obvious that he wondered what she wanted from him. A promotion for her father, perhaps? A rich gift? Once in a while he ran into a woman who wanted nothing more than the notoriety of having slept with the emperor, but he doubted Vitala was that type. She had a strategic mind; she was after something.

And who was he to gainsay her? She was no Nasica, trying to dam the river and starve her family's business competition. Vitala was a commoner, with a commoner's needs. Any favor she asked of him would be something simple. Indeed, he'd be happy to do her a good turn. He'd probably do it even if she didn't sleep with him. She was more deserving of imperial aid than most of the brainless aristocrats he made concessions to.

What a strange woman Vitala was. She had a hardness to her, a distance. His cousin Rhianne had been open-hearted and loving, and she kept no secrets—none that she wouldn't share with Lucien, anyway. But Vitala had layers. It fascinated him. He wanted to peel back those layers and figure her out. What did she want? What made her tick?

He thought back to the state dinner and what she'd looked like in that borrowed blue gown. Oh yes, he wanted to peel back some layers, all right.

Damn Tasox.

One day when Vitala entered her classroom, each table was covered with a strange, double-tiered structure. On each structure sat crudely carved blue and red game pieces.

"This is the game Caturanga," explained her instructor, after the other girls filed in. "The emperor's youngest son, Lucien, has become obsessed with the game, and we think it might benefit you to know how to play it."

Caturanga turned out to be a war game. The objective was to gain control of all three moons, the Soldier, Sage, and Vagabond, using foot soldiers, cavalry, and the so-called Principles, powerful pieces, such as the Tribune, that had special abilities. Terrain pieces could also be used either to speed one's own way or block the enemy's progress.

Vitala soon found her classmates were easy prey. They moved defensively, trying to protect their pieces while advancing slowly toward the objectives. Vitala moved boldly.

She sent her Traitor behind enemy lines. She pushed her cavalry straight into enemy territory. She learned to feint on one side of the board, then make a decisive strike on the other.

Soon none of the other girls wanted to play her anymore.

The stress of the game with Lucien had brought on a headache, and Vitala made the mistake of lying down. She fell asleep and had one of her nightmares. In it, the young soldier spoke to her, but she couldn't hear his words. He mouthed them, first calmly, then with increasing fervor and desperation, but no sound came. And she was too paralyzed to say anything back.

She awoke feeling hopeless and lost.

She checked her window. Good. The sun wasn't too low. She still had time to visit the baths and freshen up.

She stared at her hands and wriggled her fingers. Ten tiny contact points shone there, one on each finger, visible only to her. Warders were capable of an additional, little-known form of magic. Not only could they anchor magic from the spirit world in the physical world, but they could also do the reverse. They could pull an object from the physical world into the spirit world and hide it there. It could be done only with very small objects. Shards, for example, which were no larger than arrowheads. She had enough of them to kill ten people, but she hoped to need only one.

She wasn't looking forward to this kill. It was hard to reconcile the Lucien who victimized her people with the one who played Caturanga. The first was an evil tyrant; the second, almost likeable. She supposed it must often be thus. People behaved one way in one situation and differently in another. A Legatus might brutally stake a hundred Riorcans, then go home and be kind to his wife and children.

As long as she could stay focused and keep the visions at bay, it didn't matter whether she wanted to kill Lucien or not. Even if Lucien were innocent of all crimes—and he wasn't—he had to die, for the simple reason that he stood in the way of Riorcan freedom. Lucien was a strategic sacrifice, like the Tribune she'd offered up as bait during the first Caturanga game. If killing him meant more nightmares for her, more visions, so be it. He wasn't the only strategic sacrifice in this game.

Someone rapped at the door, and she nearly jumped out of her skin. "Come in."

The door guard admitted Remus, who clutched a single rose, deep purple in color. "Miss Salonius, I bear a message from the emperor."

Her stomach dropped. "Yes?"

"The emperor sends his regrets. He must travel tomorrow to Tasox and will be up half the night preparing."

"Oh." Gods curse it. She'd been so close.

Remus handed her the rose. "He desires your company, however, and asks if you will accompany him to Tasox in the morning."

She brightened. Going with Lucien to Tasox might be better than seeing him tonight. On a trip, his security should be lighter than here in the palace. Not only would that make her more likely to succeed in her mission, but it increased the odds that she might get away afterward without having to use her deathstone. After all, willing as she was to die for her cause, she was hardly *eager.* "I would be honored to accompany His Imperial Majesty."

Remus smiled. "I'll tell him the good news. We're

leaving with Blue Hawk battalion early tomorrow morning. A guard will come for you at dawn. Be ready."

Vitala ran an eye over the few possessions she'd brought with her. Lucien might be up half the night preparing, but all she needed was ten minutes. "Thank you, sir. I will."

It was not uncommon for them to move their location. The news would come suddenly. Vitala and the others would be told to pack their few possessions. In no time at all, the mountain sanctuary would be an empty shell, and its inhabitants would trek to the new place, by varying routes, in small groups of three or four.

During her fourth year, they moved five times. The fifth time, when she arrived at the new location, a familiar face was waiting for her.

"Bayard!" she cried, rushing into his arms.

"My dear Vitala," he murmured, "you've surpassed all expectations."

"You've come for me this time. Haven't you?"

"Yes, I've come for you," he said. "I'm to make an assassin of you, but I'm afraid this is the last time you'll feel such fondness for me."

"But you rescued me."

"For a purpose, and not a gentle one. The finest weapons are shaped in the hottest of forges, and I shall hone you into a blade so keen, so wicked, that the imperials shall weep to cross you."

They traveled to yet another enclave. There her instruction continued in Caturanga, history, and literature under new instructors, and she began new subjects. She learned to dance in several styles, some suitable for the ballroom, others for the bedroom. A stern matron spent endless hours teaching her to walk with good posture and just the

*right amount of sway in her hips. Another woman tutored
her in the care of her hair and skin, and in Kjallan fash-
ion.*

*Yet another woman began to teach her Rift affinity to
prepare her for soulcasting.*

And Bayard instructed her in combat.

5

The day broke muggy and wet, making for a dark and misty dawn. Vitala huddled in a borrowed raincoat next to the Legaciattus who carried her valise and stared at the array of soldiers who stood in perfect formation in the yard ahead, seemingly indifferent to the rain. Four magnificent gray horses trotted toward her, splashing mud on the gravel road. They drew a large, sleek carriage that she knew at once had to be Lucien's. It was cross-barred with gold, and the blue panels along its sides were inset with vivid, colorful paintings. As she stepped out of the path of the carriage and its escort of mounted Lega-ciatti, she squinted at the paintings, curious about the scenes they depicted.

Before she could make them out, the horses, blan-keted with brindlecat pelts, reined to a stop and waited, snorting, their heads held high. The carriage door opened, revealing a crowd of people. She heard Lucien's voice, followed by a young woman's laughter, and she froze. Had Lucien's excuse last night been a lie? Had he rejected her in favor of someone else?

The carriage began to empty. A uniformed Legaciatta stepped out first, followed by a kind-faced matron, a young woman smothered in a raincoat, and finally an-other Legaciatta. Vitala angled for a closer look at the young woman, but the Legaciatti blocked her view. She had the impression the woman was small or young, possibly just a girl. Could she be Lucien's sister, the imperial princess?

Lucien gestured to her from inside the carriage. "Get in."

Vitala glanced back to see if he was talking to someone else. She'd expected to ride with Lucien's support staff, not in the imperial carriage.

"Miss Salonius, ride with me," called Lucien.

Well, that was clear enough. Someone carried away her valise, and Vitala stepped into the carriage, trying not to get mud on the floor.

"Your Imperial Majesty," she said, making an awkward attempt at a curtsy.

He took her hand and helped her to her seat. "Please don't stand on ceremony."

Though the carriage was less crowded than before, they weren't alone—the bodyguard sat opposite them. That meant no assassination attempts in the carriage. She hoped Lucien didn't plan to while away the miles with lovemaking.

"Was that the imperial princess I just saw?" she asked.

Lucien smiled. "Indeed it was. My sister, Celeste. She wanted to see me off, so I had her ride with me from the gates."

What a relief. Not another lover after all. "Are the two of you close?"

His smile turned sad. "I'm nine years her senior. By the time she was old enough to talk, I was in training at the palaestra and the academy, and then off to Riorca. For most of our lives, we've been strangers. But she's all the family I have left, so I'm making an effort to get to know her."

The carriage rolled forward. Vitala peered out the

window at the now-marching musketmen on the right side of the road. "How can the soldiers keep up with us?" she asked Lucien.

"The infantry can't. We'll go ahead with the cavalry and establish a campsite. They'll catch up by evening."

She craned her neck and spotted the cavalry. The horses were just beginning to move, one line of them at a time, at a trot. If the carriage was pacing itself to match the cavalry, this would be a slow journey.

"I'm sorry we can't play Caturanga in here," said Lucien.

She nodded. The carriage was well sprung and the road was good, but nothing could smooth the ride sufficiently for a Caturanga board.

"I brought a set, though. For later."

"So did I," said Vitala. The set he'd given her, which she hoped she might smuggle away somehow afterward. "What's the emergency in Tasox? If I may ask, Your Imper—"

"Lucien," he corrected. "What's going on in Tasox is a man named Gordian has united several groups of bandits and taken over the city. He murdered the governor and the city officials."

"Three gods."

"Worse, most of the bandits are former soldiers— members of White Star and Red Eagle battalions, disbanded last summer." He shook his head. "It's tricky, because the men will not like killing their fellow soldiers. I felt the situation was touchy enough that I ought to handle it personally. You know what Plinius says— Have you read Plinius?"

She shook her head.

"'The only strategist is the man on the ground.' Meaning you must see the situation up close to make good decisions."

"What do you plan to do?"

"First, recapture the city. Then dispense justice."

Vitala bit her lip. That meant he was going to stake people. She'd seen staking victims in Riorca. The Kjallans left the impaled bodies up on the stakes for weeks to rot in the sun and serve as a grisly reminder of their power and cruelty.

"Perhaps we should speak of something else," said Lucien.

Vitala nodded.

"Tell me about your Caturanga career. People you've learned from, tournaments you've competed in. I want to know how you got to be so gods-cursed good at the game."

She launched into her cover story, a fabricated tale of a Caturanga-loving father who'd had no sons and taught the game to his eldest daughter, who'd shown so much promise she'd been passed along from one august tutor to another.

"I envy you," said Lucien. "All that time to study! I've never been able to learn the game as well as I'd like."

Vitala smiled wryly. "The Emperor of Kjall envies a nobody like me?"

"Don't call yourself a nobody. There are quite a few aristocrats who've had every opportunity available to them, yet they didn't do a gods-cursed thing with their lives. Whereas you had no advantages at all and wound up a Caturanga champion."

"Thank you."

"Besides," he said. "I envy you just for having a father who loves Caturanga. My father, the emperor, thought it a colossal waste of time."

"It's not given to us to choose our parents."

"Nor is it given to parents to choose their sons and

daughters, which for me is rather fortunate." He paused. "Vitala, is there something you want from me?"

She turned to him, perplexed. "Only the honor of playing Caturanga with you."

"But is there a favor I can do for you? I'd like to help you, Vitala. Depending on what it is you need." His fingers reached up and pushed a stray lock of hair out of her face. Her flesh tingled where he touched her.

Now she understood. He believed her interest in him was pragmatic. She wanted something from him, and he wanted to know what that something was before he committed. For Nasica, it had been the dam. For Vitala, it was . . . well. The true price he would not want to pay.

Was Lucien laying a trap for her? If she named something, he might become offended and send her packing. Or it could be the other way around. If she seemed to want nothing, he might become suspicious and wonder what trickery was involved, what price she might try to exact from him later.

"Sire," she said. "I don't want anything from you except . . . except your company. You've done so much for me already."

"What have I done for you?"

"You gave me the Caturanga set."

His eyes lit. "Right! I'd forgotten about that. I'm glad it pleases you."

She closed her eyes in relief. Gratitude, apparently, was a safe middle ground, neither arousing his suspicion nor risking his disapproval.

"Vitala." His eyes were soft and desirous. "You're very beautiful." He leaned toward her.

Pox. He *was* looking for a tryst in the carriage. With the bodyguard sitting right across from them!

But a kiss would be all right—wouldn't it? She parted her lips slightly.

He took them directly, needing no further encouragement. His mouth was warm and soft, assertive without being rough. So many Kjallans were sloppy kissers, especially younger men. Lucien was only twenty-two, but because he was the emperor, he'd probably been with a hundred women or more. His experience showed.

His hand slipped behind her neck, seeking skin, and she found herself worming deeper into his grasp. Gods, he was delicious. Her flesh prickled at his touch. A spike of heat and pleasure stabbed through her and settled in her groin, where it slowly spread. *Pox, pox, pox.* She'd let herself get attracted to her target. This was not good.

I hate this man. I hate him. I hate him. If she repeated it enough times, she might just get her body's ridiculous reaction under control.

Lucien released her. "Are you all right? You're tensing up."

"Yes. Oh yes," she said breathlessly. "It's just . . ." She turned to the bodyguard, who was staring at them, expressionless. Gods, this must be all in a day's work for him.

Lucien chuckled. "You don't like an audience."

Vitala nodded, her face heating.

"I'm used to Septian, but I can see how you wouldn't be." He shrugged. "We can do this later. If that's what you want."

"Yes, later," she said. "When I can have you all to myself."

Lucien grinned. "When we reach the campsite, you shall have me all to yourself. But do me a favor between now and then."

"What's that?"

"Tell me everything you know about the Cartasian Defense. Because if you don't change the subject fast, I'm going to have a cockstand all the way."

She laughed. The Cartasian Defense it was.

It was not long before Vitala learned Bayard had spoken the truth. She was rapidly becoming less fond of him and coming to dread her sessions with him in the training room.

Bayard crashed through her guard, spun around her, and with the flat of his wooden sword, delivered a stinging blow across her rear end. Vitala gasped in surprise and pain.

"Where was your defense?" he demanded.

Vitala stared at him.

"Don't stand there like an idiot." Bayard raised his weapon. "Inside guard. Now."

She braced herself for the attack.

"Stance, Vitala! Look at your feet."

Oops—she'd forgotten. Inside guard required a reverse stance, leading with the opposite leg. The moment she swapped the positions of her legs, Bayard rushed her. She parried his attacks, twisting and turning, but he drove her backwards. He swept her legs out from under her, and she crashed onto her tailbone.

"You're smaller and weaker than me." Bayard stood over her, waving his sword. "Can you afford to be slower, too?"

"I'm not that kind of assassin," said Vitala. "I don't kill with a sword."

"Wrong answer." Bayard hauled her up from the ground, delivering another stinging blow. "You're targeting an imperial. He's guarded by the Legaciatti, the finest warriors in Kjall. To handle a target that highly placed,

you need to be every kind of assassin. You have no idea what's going to happen, what you might have to be able to handle. Inside guard."

Ignoring the pain as best she could, Vitala assumed the correct guard and stance.

"Faster this time," said Bayard, "or you're going to be sore tonight."

6

At the campsite, servants collected poles and canvas panels from the baggage carts and began to erect the tents. Meanwhile, a fire mage coaxed some damp wood into a blaze, and a servant brought Vitala and Lucien mugs of steaming spiced wine.

"I could get used to this," said Vitala as she sat on a cushioned seat and wrapped her hands around the hot mug.

"Could you?" said Lucien. "Because I've been thinking. I want someone like you on the imperial staff, to teach Caturanga. First to me, and later to my children."

Vitala's eyebrows rose. "Really? But you don't have children."

He shrugged. "Someday I will."

"If you're offering me a position in the palace, I'll take it." The wine was strong, especially on an empty stomach, but Vitala drank it, anyway. "Given this talk of children, are you planning an imperial wedding?"

"I have no immediate plans. But I must produce an heir, if only to take the pressure off Celeste, and that means finding a wife. I don't want bastards."

Vitala suppressed a wince. That stung, however unintentional the insult. He could not know she was a bastard. "I thought it was traditional for emperors to sire bastards."

"If by *traditional* you mean commonly done, yes. But they foul up the succession. Did you know my great-grandfather was a bastard?"

"No."

"He murdered his half brother, the rightful heir, and claimed the throne for himself. I suppose I should thank him for it; it's because of him that I'm emperor. But it's dangerous to have too many potential heirs. People start having fatal accidents."

"Your father ended up needing all three of his heirs."

Lucien smiled wryly and glanced, perhaps unconsciously, at his missing leg. "Only because he was a sapskull, sending me and my brothers to Riorca all at once, where the assassins had easy access to us. And, yes, I am offering you a position in the palace. I'll confer with my advisors about payment, and they'll present you with a formal offer when we get back."

"Thank you, sire." A job in the Imperial Palace! Now she had more time to carry out her mission, if for some reason she was unable to perform it on this trip. She sipped her wine and watched the workmen swarm over the campsite.

The site was a large, grassy field, which had clearly been used for this purpose before. Large, circular bare patches told the story of fires once laid, while holes in the ground marked the locations of former tent pegs. Lucien's staff was raising tents, some of them small, others immense. Farther away, in a separate field, cavalrymen were untacking and airing their horses and putting them on hobbles to graze.

Remus approached them and bowed. "Sire."

"Yes, Remus?" said Lucien.

"We've had another message from Tasox." He glanced sidelong at Vitala.

Lucien sighed. "Very well. Is my tent up yet?"

"Partly, sire. It's usable."

"Miss Salonius." He picked up her hand and kissed it. "I'll send for you later this evening." He rose and limped across the field.

Vitala rubbed her arms and shivered, then scooted closer to the fire. She was glad to be rid of Lucien for a while. It was stressful being around him; she feared she would slip up and say the wrong thing. Gods, he'd offered her a job. A part of her was tempted to forget her mission entirely and just be the imperial Caturanga instructor.

Which was ridiculous. While she idled away her days in the palace, her people would be starved and massacred.

Still, what an opportunity to pass up. She needed another way to make a living. She'd thought her visions had stopped, but they hadn't. The door guard had triggered one simply by resembling the young soldier who was the subject of her nightmares. Lucien resembled him too, just not as closely. It was sheer luck that only the door guard triggered her visions, and not Lucien himself.

She wasn't the first Obsidian Circle assassin to experience visions, and she wouldn't be the last. But the others had all been removed from field duty. It could strike at any time; it made an assassin unreliable. And who could replace her? No one, not even Ista. No one else could gain intimate access to Lucien. She'd kept her problem quiet and spared her handlers from making a decision they wouldn't want to make.

Maybe after she killed Lucien, she would tell Bayard. But it seemed a shame. She had only one official kill, not counting the practice ones, while Ista had nine. At least Lucien would be a spectacular kill; an emperor was a more impressive target than the minor government officials and military officers Ista had gone after. Perhaps afterward she could step down and take a service role. Weapons trainer or something.

She sniffed. Gods, who was she kidding? She'd be lucky if she got out of this alive.

"It's all right, Vitala," soothed Bayard. "He can't hurt you."

Vitala stepped closer. Of course the soldier couldn't hurt her. He was tied to a chair. He strained at the loops of rope pinioning his limbs, but he couldn't break them. Since he was gagged, he couldn't even hurl insults at her.

He certainly wanted to hurl insults. He was sweating and red faced, his eyes bulging with hatred as he watched her approach.

She broke one of her contact points. A Shard materialized from the Rift, and she caught the tiny bit of obsidian neatly between her fingertips. What had happened to the man's comrade? There'd been two of them originally, a pair of unwise Kjallans who'd blundered into the enclave's sentries.

The soldier's chin jerked—he was trying to spit at her. Ineffective, since he was gagged. Poor man.

Bayard's voice grew sharp. "Do it, Vitala. No more stalling. You need me to give you some extra motivation?"

She gave Bayard a look of disgust. Then she jabbed the Shard into the soldier's throat.

Lucien's tent was a near replica of his rooms at home, with a sitting room up front, a door that led presumably to a bedroom, and furniture laid out in almost the same configuration. The bookcases and the magicked Caturanga set were missing, as were the wall hangings and the windows that overlooked the palace grounds, but a different Caturanga set sat on a table in the same spot—one of carved agate, similar to the one he'd given her.

Lucien limped across the room. The guards who'd escorted her filtered out of the tent, leaving only Septian, who lurked quietly near the door. She hoped he would stay there and not follow them into the bedroom.

"I've been thinking about you all afternoon," said Lucien.

She smiled. "Weren't you supposed to be thinking about Tasox?"

"Tasox—what's that?" He winked, then followed her gaze to the Caturanga set. "Would you like a game?"

Her mouth quirked. "Would you?"

"Gods, no. How about dinner? Are you hungry?" He gestured toward a covered tray that sat on a table.

She hadn't eaten since midday, but she feared she might throw up if she ate now. She forced a smile. "Actually, I'm feeling rather vulnerable right now. Too much Vagabond influence on the board, and my Principles are under threat."

He chuckled. "Are they really?"

"And there's only one answer to that. A bold move." She went to him.

He braced himself on his crutch to receive her. "You make a decisive strike, indeed," he murmured, and greedily took her mouth.

A decisive strike—if only he knew! She'd been a bundle of nerves all afternoon, stiff and anxious about the task that lay ahead, but now, in the warmth of Lucien's embrace, she felt herself relax. Lucien did not close his eyes when he kissed; rather, his dark eyes studied her, calculating. It was a little disconcerting to think that this time he wasn't analyzing the Caturanga board; he was analyzing *her*. And yet it pleased her to be, at this moment, the center of his universe.

She barely noticed when his tongue entered her mouth. He'd been teasing her with it, and now he took liberties. A delicious tingle ran through her, and she pressed herself closer to him, suddenly wishing the clothes were not a barrier between them—wouldn't his flesh feel lovely against hers? A soft sound purred from her throat, entirely unbidden. She wanted to devour him. She pushed a little too hard, and he stumbled backward.

She helped catch him.

"Careful," he chided.

His face was flushed, his eyes liquid with desire. "I'm not too solid upright. Shall we . . . ?" He gestured toward the bedroom door.

She nodded.

"I'd carry you, but . . ." He shrugged.

She giggled, feeling like she'd had too much to drink. Some distant part of her marveled at her absurd behavior. He had stumbled, but she was the one who was off balance. What was it about this man that her body responded to with such enthusiasm?

He's a tyrant. You hate him.

Her body wasn't listening.

He led her to the heavy leather tent panel that served as a bedroom door. He unfastened the panel, drew it aside for them to step through, and closed it behind them. Septian did not accompany them, thank the gods. However, the leather panel, thick at it was, would not muffle sound very well. She hoped it would not be an issue. If she did this right, there would be no struggle. And if there was a struggle, the bodyguard might still mistake the sounds of violence for lovemaking.

Lucien pulled her across the floor to the bed. She had

a brief glimpse of blue and gold—the color of his bed-sheets—and then his crutch was on the floor and he was on all fours atop her, kissing her and tugging at the belt of her syrtos. Upright, he'd been clumsy, but on the bed he was agile as a brindlecat. In an excess of enthusiasm, he nipped her lower lip, and she gave a surprised yelp of pain.

"Sorry," he breathed. "Am I going too fast? It's just ... gods, Vitala. I want you so much."

"Not too fast," she assured him. Really, the faster, the better. She started to help him with her syrtos, then realized she would be disappointed if he made love to her with most of his clothes on. She wanted to see him, *all* of him, before she committed the atrocity of killing him. She yanked him down onto the bed and climbed over him, reversing their positions. He was stronger than she, but he yielded, looking up at her in curiosity. "I want to see you," she explained, and wondered how best to remove his clothes.

He was still wearing the glittering imperial loros. It was a precious thing, a Kjallan relic, and she hesitated to touch it. Her hands moved toward it, then retreated.

"I'll do that," he said. He lifted the loros over his head, folded it carefully, and set it on the bedside table. He also removed his wooden leg, unbuckling a couple of leather straps that secured it in place, and set the device on the floor. Then he lay back, submitting to her once again.

She sat atop him, mesmerized. She could stare at his face all day. It was a study in contrasts—pale skin, black hair, and reddened, kiss-bitten lips. Those cheekbones— what god had gifted him with those? She touched a single finger to his cheek and traced a line down to his chin and the soft flesh of his neck. The lump in his throat bobbed, and his pulse fluttered. His dark eyes followed her, intent.

She began disrobing him, slowly and methodically, first untangling the knots of his two belts. She pushed the syrtos back, exposing his neck and chest. There was his rift-stone on its chain—the yellow topaz of a war mage. That stone was the reason she had to seduce him. Any other mage, or a nonmage, she could have killed more simply.

She wanted to touch it, but she knew better. Mages guarded their riftstones more jealously than they guarded their privates.

She continued undressing him. He lay tame under her ministrations, but a muscle jumped in his arms; he was struggling to remain still. She exposed his nether regions and found him erect and ready. But the sight of a hard cock was nothing new to her; she was more curious about his leg, the missing one.

He swallowed. "Go on and look. It's all right."

She peeled back the last bit of his syrtos. The stump of his left leg extended just a few inches below the knee. It was misshapen and ugly, mottled with red marks where the artificial leg and its straps had irritated it. She ran her hand over the area, and he winced.

She pulled her hand away. "Does it hurt?"

"No," he said. "It's just sensitive. Touch it if you like."

Her curiosity satisfied, she sat back up, looking over the whole of him. Except for the leg, he was a fine-looking man. Though he was not large in build, his body was hard and wiry and surprisingly well muscled. She wondered how that could be, given that the missing leg limited his exercise. Perhaps it was a gift of his war magic.

"Enough of you staring at me," he growled. His hands moved, almost faster than the eye could see, and her world flipped upside down. She was on her back again, and Lucien atop her. She marveled at his strength, but after a moment's reflection, she knew it shouldn't surprise her. Those were the war mage's talents—preternatural strength and speed. Along with the most dangerous ability of all, the gift of anticipation. A war mage could sense any attack before it came. To get past a war mage's defenses, one had to distract him to the point that he was oblivious to the outside world.

He began tugging off her syrtos, occasionally pausing to kiss her roughly, as if he couldn't decide what he wanted most—to look at her or devour her.

In less than a minute, she was naked on the bed. He looked her over, his eyes clouded with desire. "Gods, Vitala." He swallowed. "What do you like? What do you want?"

"You," she purred. "In me."

He paused, considering. Then he grinned. "No." He lowered his mouth to her nipple and did something with his tongue. She gasped. Her whole body contracted and she shuddered in sudden, intense pleasure.

He chuckled. "I think you like that."

"Lucien—"

"Shh." He worked her with hands and tongue, stroking and tasting. She writhed, utterly out of control, half-terrified at what was happening to her, half-consumed with yearning. She wanted him to stop. She wanted more. Lucien's hands moved farther south. "How about this?" he whispered. Her body shuddered again, and an involuntary moan escaped her. He'd touched her gently, ever so gently, yet the effect was profound. She was thoroughly wet down there.

This was ridiculous. She had to regain control. No

more of this . . . whatever he was doing. She reached for his erection.

He shuddered and pulled away. "Not yet," he scolded, kissing her in apology. "Or we'll have a very short night."

She reached for him again.

He dodged. *Gods-cursed war mage reflexes.* She glared at him. He grinned and moved downward along her body, keeping himself well out of reach. Then his tongue parted her, and such pleasure coursed through her that she did not dare move, lest it stop. He wasn't the first man to touch her there, but most men were too rough; they had no idea how sensitive she was. Lucien seemed to know the right amount of pressure to use. No doubt it was a skill born of practice; he'd pleasured many a woman before her. Why he should bother, she couldn't imagine. He was the emperor; he didn't need to be a good lover to lure women to his bed.

But, for whatever reason, he'd made the most of his opportunities. He sensed her rhythm and adjusted to it, sometimes speeding his strokes, other times slowing them or stopping them entirely, until she was ready to burst with frustration. Then he began again, and the pleasure mounted, greater than before.

As she began to buck, he gripped her around the hips. Then her world exploded and she thought of nothing but uncontrollable, shuddering pleasure. When it finished, she lay back, panting and sweating. She closed her eyes as her body throbbed gently. When she opened her eyes, Lucien was there, staring into them. He kissed her.

Three gods, she realized. *That was an orgasm.* She'd had plenty of sex, practicing for this very night, but never had any of her partners cared enough about her pleasure to bring her to orgasm.

The head of Lucien's cock nudged her opening, poised to enter.

She prepared herself mentally. The moment was coming when she would have to kill this man.

He pushed himself inside. And the vision seized her.

"Gods." The young soldier's eyes fluttered closed as he penetrated her. His dark hair, overlong, fell across his brow. She could feel his energy, his excitement, his masculine strength. His mouth found hers and kissed it eagerly. "Who are you?" he asked. "Tell me your name."

She said nothing. She lay still, submissive, waiting for her moment.

He sighed with pleasure, his hips moving. "You're so beautiful. Say something," he begged. "Are you a prisoner here too?"

She remained silent and motionless beneath him.

He smiled sadly and twirled a lock of her hair around his finger. "I don't understand. You offer yourself to me, but you won't talk. Have they cut out your tongue?"

"Vitala, what's wrong?" Lucien asked, waking her from the unwanted memory. He stilled. "Pox. I hear it. I hear it!" He rolled off her.

Vitala sat up, blinking back to full awareness. She heard it too. Shouts and the clashing of steel. Nearby.

"Septian!" cried Lucien.

There was no answer. By the sound, Vitala placed the action at roughly the entrance to Lucien's tent.

Lucien flung himself off the bed and hopped to a bedside table.

Vitala sat up in bed, trembling and confused. What in the Soldier's hell was going on? Had Lucien's enemies chosen this moment to move against him? And if so, what should she do? Fight? Do nothing?

Lucien fished a pistol and a wicked-looking knife from a drawer. He caught her eye and said, "Get my crutch."

His words ended her paralysis. She flung herself out of bed, grabbed the crutch, and shoved it at Lucien. Gods, they were stark naked, both of them. He would need the peg leg too, so she snatched it up, but Lucien was already in motion.

He scrambled across the bed on all fours, then, half hopping and half supporting himself with the crutch, made his way to the back of the tent. "Bring that here," he said. Vitala joined him as he knelt on the floor and jabbed the knife into the tent wall. He began to haul it downward, opening a gap. The leather was thick. He strained with the effort, gripping the knife with both hands, his muscles trembling. Without his war magic, he probably couldn't have done it at all.

He'd opened an arm's length of leather when a sword point stabbed through the opening. Vitala shrieked, and Lucien jumped back with a shout of surprise. He looked around helplessly. They were trapped. "Get under the bed." He yelled again, "Septian!"

Vitala heard someone unhooking the door panel—the intruders were close. She dove to the floor, still holding Lucien's wooden leg, and scrambled beneath the bed. She still had no idea what to do. Her job was to kill Lucien. These men probably intended the same. Should she just leave the task to them? But what were they going to do with her? Kill her, probably, since she would be a witness.

Should she fight? Naked as she was, she couldn't do much, not against men with guns and swords. With crippled Lucien as her only ally, the odds were impossibly long, especially if they'd already dispatched Septian, and she suspected they had. Or worse, Septian was among the traitors.

She heard the door panel open. She peered out from

under the bed, and several pairs of boots crowded into the room. A gunshot rang out, and a man in a Legaciatti uniform hit the floor. Blood welled from his forehead. More pairs of boots entered. Lucien's pistol clattered to the ground, useless now that its single shot had been fired. He had only the knife left. She counted six pairs of boots, and there might be more outside.

The boots shuffled forward. Steel clashed. Lucien moved with surprising agility despite having only his crutch. A man shouted in pain. There was more clashing, and Lucien fell with an anguished cry, clutching his right leg. From her vantage point, she saw his taut, ashen face, but he did not make eye contact or even glance in her direction. She realized with a twinge of shame that he was protecting her.

"Worthless cull," said one of the men. She recognized the voice as that of Remus, and her anger rose to the boiling point.

Lucien lunged with the knife and stabbed it into the leg of the man nearest him.

Chaos erupted. "Gods curse it, get that away from him!" roared Remus. One man stomped on Lucien's wrist, trapping his knife hand, and someone else kicked the weapon away. Then Remus was on top of Lucien, punching him in the face with his fist, once, twice, three times. Vitala winced with each blow. Lucien's breath was ragged. She could sense his fear, but he did not give his attackers the satisfaction of crying out.

"You horse fucker," snarled Remus. He turned back to his men. "Is Eustace dead?"

Someone laid a hand on the throat of the man who'd been shot. "Yes."

"He's naked," said a voice she didn't recognize. "Is there a woman?"

"Check under the bed," said Remus.

Vitala froze in terror. *Pox, pox, pox.* Two faces appeared below the edge of the bed and aimed pistols at her. "There is."

"Drag her out," said Remus.

Her hands itched to call a Shard. The men were putting their pistols away; they didn't expect her to fight. She could kill one man, maybe two, but all five? No. She hadn't a chance.

Two of the men grabbed her arms and hauled her out. One of them took the wooden leg from her. Among the traitors, she recognized only Remus and the Warder, but all of them wore Legaciatti uniforms.

The men stared at her naked form, and one of them gave an appreciative whistle.

Remus's mouth twisted in disapproval. "It's the Caturanga player."

"Let her go," choked Lucien, who was still on the floor, held down by two men and bleeding from his nose, his mouth, and his good leg. "This isn't her quarrel."

"She's a witness," said Remus. "Kill her."

Not a man made a move, even the ones holding her.

"We could fuck her first," said the Warder.

Remus gave Vitala a second, more appraising look. "I suppose. Someone has to stay with the riftstone, anyway. Make sure no one runs off with it."

"First watch," called two men simultaneously.

"*I'm* first, you culls," growled Remus. "Tie her up. Ankles together, wrists to the bedposts."

The men holding her pulled lengths of rope from their belts, shoved her onto the bed, and began to tie her up. She tensed the muscles in her wrists and ankles in hopes of getting a tiny bit of slack into the knots.

"Here it is," said Remus.

Vitala twisted her head around to see. Remus had found the folded loros and was holding it reverently to his chest. Was he claiming the throne for himself?

Remus strode to Lucien and leaned down. He grabbed the topaz riftstone that hung around his neck and yanked it away, breaking the chain. "Get him out of range of his riftstone," he ordered. "I'll stay with the Caturanga whore. Send someone to relieve me in half an hour."

"That long?" teased one of the men.

Remus gave them a thin-lipped smile. "Go."

One of the men took a length of rope, fitted it into a noose, and looped the noose around Lucien's neck. "On your feet, half man." He jerked cruelly at the rope.

Lucien rose to hands and knees and reached for his crutch.

Remus knocked it away with his foot, and the soldier who was carrying the leg picked it up.

"I can't—" began Lucien.

Remus kicked him viciously, eliciting a gasp of pain. "Move, Emperor!"

Lucien crawled toward the tent flap, leaving a smear of blood in his trail. One soldier tugged him by the noose while the others surrounded him, laughing and jeering and urging him on with well-placed kicks.

Vitala's heart ached for Lucien. Apparently killing him wasn't enough; they meant to humiliate him too. How unprofessional.

The soldiers left the tent, tugging their unhappy prisoner. Only Remus remained. He laid the loros on the table and began to unbelt his syrtos.

She taunted him with her eyes. *Come on and fuck me, Remus. I'm ready for you.*

7

Vitala watched closely as Remus set aside his double belts along with his sword, knife, and pistol. She hoped he would bare his chest and give her a glimpse of his riftstone. If it was anything but the topaz of a war mage, she could kill him before the sex and save herself some unpleasantness.

But he seemed to have no intention of doing so. He loosened his syrtos but did not remove it. And he had something on underneath—a mail shirt, which meant yet another layer below that.

Remus climbed onto the bed, knelt beside her, and checked the knots that bound her wrists to the bedpost. "I don't understand it," he said. "I've seen dozens of beautiful young women like you throw themselves at Lucien. And for what? Gifts? Money?"

"Dahatrian tea. Have you tasted the swill they brew outside the palace?"

Remus gave her a withering look. He untied and re-tied the knots, yanking them tight until she winced. "You think it's funny, joking about how cheap you are? Whore."

"And you're such a paragon of virtue," said Vitala.

He chuckled. Satisfied with the knots on her wrists, he moved down and untied her ankles. She willed the rift-stone to reveal itself on his neck, but it stayed hidden.

He pushed back his syrtos and pulled down his leggings, displaying his cock with a flourish, as if he expected her to marvel at it. He lay atop her, covering her body with his own. "Kiss me," he commanded.

She obeyed, without enthusiasm.

"Good girl," he murmured. "Relax, and you might enjoy it."

She hissed in pain as he entered her. She had some residual wetness and swelling from her encounter with Lucien, but it wasn't enough. Remus didn't notice or care. He thrust into her, occasionally fondling her breasts or kissing her. She tried to ignore it. *Mild discomfort,* she told herself. *It's mild discomfort, nothing more.*

She called a Shard into her right hand, maneuvered it into her fingertips, and angled its razor-sharp tip toward the rope that bound her wrist. Remus was oblivious. Though she had no leverage and couldn't exert much force, the Shard separated the fibers of the rope like an oar parting water. Her bonds loosened. With more room to maneuver, she cut through the remaining coils of rope, freeing her right arm. Though it ached from its uncomfortable position, she kept it where it was, pressed against the bedpost.

Now she had a problem. In her rehearsals with Bayard, she'd never been tied up. She'd always held her hand close to her target's body, usually resting on his back. That allowed her to strike with lightning speed—a necessity, along with distraction, for bypassing the war mage's gift of anticipation. But her hand was far away. Could she strike quickly enough to make the kill? It was a lot of distance to cover.

She'd lain passive as Remus kissed and pinched and penetrated her. Now she kissed him back, moaning deep in her throat. She moved her body in time with his strokes.

Remus chuckled, thrusting harder and faster.

She inched her right hand downward along the bed. When Remus's attention momentarily drifted toward her hand, she moaned as if in need and drew him back to her. Slowly, one finger's breadth at a time, she moved her hand.

Remus's body stiffened in a way she was well familiar with. She could wait no longer.

Vitala drove the Shard into the soft flesh of his hip and released the death spell. He began instantly to thrash. She scrambled out from under him, plucked the Shard from his hip, and kicked his flailing body away in disgust. She cut her left wrist free from the bedpost.

Remus twitched and seized, making little gasping sounds. His wide eyes stared at her; she had no doubt he was still conscious, but he couldn't speak; the spell had paralyzed his throat. Bloody froth leaked from the corners of his mouth. She was tempted to tell him, *Relax, and you might enjoy it,* but taunting was unprofessional. She scooped up her syrtos from the floor.

How much time did she have? Not much. Remus had said half an hour, but it was not impossible that the next man could arrive early.

Remus gave one final, convulsive gasp and lay still. Vitala threw on her syrtos, went to Remus's sweat-dampened corpse, and peeled the mail shirt and tunic back from his neck. There was his riftstone. Topaz. She'd made the right decision. She slipped the tiny stone up over Remus's neck. He'd also been carrying Lucien's rift-stone. She searched his clothes, found it, and pocketed both.

A shudder racked her. She sank to the floor and put her head between her knees, riding out a wave of dizziness. Her stomach lurched. Good thing she hadn't eaten anything. *Get yourself together, Vitala. There are more men coming. You want to go through this a second time?*

She got to her feet, still trembling, and armed herself with Remus's knife, sword, and pistol. She paused a moment to verify that the pistol was loaded. Remus's belt pouch was heavy with coins, so she took that too, along with the jeweled loros, which she tied up in a blanket. It would be quite a trophy to deliver to the Circle. The door flap to the bedroom hung open. She stepped through it back into the sitting room.

Septian's glassy, dead eyes stared up at her from the floor. Four additional corpses littered the room. One man had fallen partially onto a love seat, where he sprawled in a macabre imitation of a lounging aristocrat, with blood pooling beneath him. Did she have time to rifle the bodies and collect their riftstones? Some varieties of stone were hard to come by in Riorca.

Boots thudded on the grass just outside the tent. Vitala pulled the knife from her belt.

The man walked right in through the open door. "Remus?" he called.

It was the Warder. Which meant, thank the gods, he was not a war mage. *Come closer,* she willed him, fingering the knife, which wasn't as balanced for throwing as she'd like.

He spotted her and his eyes went wide. "Wait. Aren't you—? Shouldn't you—?" His hand went to his pistol.

Vitala threw her knife. She'd aimed for the chest, but it took him in the shoulder. He reeled and drunkenly aimed his pistol at her. She ran at him, knocked the weapon out of his hand, and swept his legs out from under him. He landed with a thud. She jerked the knife from his shoulder and slit his throat.

Her heart was racing. Her kill count had just risen by

two. She pulled the Warder's riftstone off his neck. That was three stones she could present to the Circle, not to mention the loros. The rest she would have to leave behind. She hurried out into the night air.

It was quiet outside the tent—surprisingly so. When she'd entered, there had been a tiny bit of daylight left. Now it was dark. She took a moment to reorient herself. The campsite had been laid out in a series of concentric circles. She was at the center of that circle, surrounded by the tents of Lucien's guards and servants. The tents were silent; she saw no signs of activity within. Scattered about were a few suspicious-looking lumps on the ground that she feared were corpses. Remus and his men had dealt with the servants first.

Beyond the tents was a ring of blackness, the wide perimeter that separated Lucien and the imperial staff from the rank and file of the battalion. Still farther, the distant specks of campfires were an ominous reminder that she had enemies on all sides. Lucien had encamped in the middle of his army, a security measure that in hindsight was ironic.

To the south, partially blocked by intervening tents, the plumes of a bonfire arced toward the sky. She should avoid it; probably it was where the Legaciatti and Lucien were. But could she really just leave? She didn't know Lucien's fate. She assumed they would kill him, but the plan could be something else, and she'd look unprofessional, even foolish, if she returned to the Circle and told her superiors, *I think he's dead, but I'm not sure.*

She had to be sure.

She ran back into Lucien's tent and stripped the dead Warder. She considered his mail shirt, but decided against it. She didn't have a man's size and strength, and the heavy armor would hamper her movement should she need to fight. She put on the uniform, folding parts of it to hide the bloodstains.

Back outside, she circled around to the south and headed for the bonfire, using the tents as cover. Her Legaciatti uniform might fool someone from a distance, but up close, anyone might notice it didn't really fit her. Plus the Legaciatti probably all knew each other by sight. As she crept closer, she heard voices and an occasional roar of laughter. Yes, they were definitely there.

She quickly identified two sentries. One of them was stationed on the far side of the bonfire and facing away from her. The other was facing her direction. Keeping a buffer of tents between her and the nearer sentry, she carefully skirted around him. Then she peered at the scene.

The bonfire was in the dark perimeter, just south of the tents, in a clear, open, grassy space with no cover. It roared skyward, sending a cascade of sparks dancing into the air.

"Get him! Get him!" someone cried.

A naked figure, dark against the orange glow of the fire, scrambled across the grass on hands and knees. Someone chased after him on foot, wielding a long stick with a glowing tip. He struck the crawling man with it. She couldn't hear much over the roar of the bonfire, but she could imagine the sizzle of burning flesh, and Lucien's agonized cry. The men laughed.

Vitala's teeth clenched. Those witless culls! Why couldn't they just kill him and be done with it? Her target was not dead, and not likely to be so anytime soon. If they hadn't killed him yet, it was probably for a reason.

Who was behind this? Remus seemed to be in charge of the men here, but he couldn't be claiming the throne for himself, or else he would have put the loros on right away to establish the rank. So who was the ringleader?

She perked up, watching in silence, as a uniformed soldier approached the northernmost sentry. "Florian's Imperial Garden," he said.

Vitala blinked. Gods, she'd heard that before. Remus had used that phrase when he'd escorted her from the docks in the carriage. It must be a code phrase that identified people involved in the plot.

The sentry let the man pass.

If there was a code phrase, the plot must involve a lot of people. What did this mean for Riorca and the Circle? Her purpose in killing Lucien wasn't to commit a random murder; it was to spark a battle for the succession that would destabilize the Kjallan Empire, perhaps even start a civil war. But was that really going to happen? Somebody powerful had organized this plot. That somebody was ready to step in and take the throne. There might be another party who would challenge that person—but there might not be. On the other hand, if Lucien escaped unharmed, he would certainly challenge the new man. That would almost guarantee a war.

Her mind sifted eagerly through the possibilities. This was like a Caturanga game—someone had made an unexpected move, the board had changed, and she needed a new strategy. She'd never relished the thought of killing Lucien, and maybe now she didn't have to. She could do more for her people by saving his life.

She counted targets. One, two, three ... eight, not counting Lucien. Plus the two sentries. She had her Shards, a pistol with a single bullet, and a sword. One at a time, she might be able to kill ten men, provided there were no war mages in the group, but all at once was ridiculous.

Lucien curled up on the ground, clutching his side. As she watched, he lifted his head and stared right at her.

Vitala ducked behind the tent she'd been peering around, her pulse racing. How had he seen her? It was dark, and she was hidden.

His riftstone. Of course. Mages were soul-bonded to their riftstones and could sense them. She was carrying the stone, and he knew it. By bringing it close to him, she had restored Lucien's war magic. He might help her fight, but in his condition, he couldn't be worth much.

Vitala needed a diversion.

She left her vantage point, recrossed the camp, and found a banked cookfire near one of the servants' tents. She lit a tent pole and laid it against the imperial tent. It was slow to catch, but soon flames licked their way up the walls. For good measure, she repeated the task, lighting the tent in two more places.

Satisfied, she crept back to the bonfire. While she hid behind a supply tent, a group of men ran past her in the opposite direction—Legaciatti, she hoped, heading for the burning imperial tent.

Back at her vantage point, she set down the blanket-wrapped loros and assessed the situation at the bonfire. She'd thinned their numbers significantly. Both sentries remained and two Legaciatti, who had Lucien lying on the ground at sword point and were craning their necks to look at the tent fire.

These weren't the best odds, but they were the best she was going to get.

The far sentry had ceased watching the empty field to the south and had turned to stare at the fire.

Painstakingly, Vitala circled round the bonfire, staying well out of its light and hiding behind tents when she could until she was behind the sentry. She drew her knife and crept forward, silent as death. When the sentry was close enough that she could smell his sweat, she drove her knife downward into his back, aiming for the kidney. He jerked convulsively. She grabbed him as he fell and slit his throat, grateful for the roar of the bonfire that covered the sound.

Now for the second sentry. She pocketed her bloody knife, straightened her borrowed uniform, and walked straight up to him. "Florian's Imperial Garden."

The sentry blinked at her, trying to figure out who she was.

She called a Shard, partially closed her fist over it, and held it out to him. "Remus said to give you this."

The sentry looked relieved. "He's all right? He got out?" He held out his hand. When their fingers touched, she stabbed the palm of his hand with the Shard and released the death spell. The sentry made a choking noise and sank to the ground, shaking.

"Hey! What's happening to him?" called one of the guards at the fire. Both of them were staring at her, as was Lucien, whose eyes were sharp and alert.

"I don't know!" she cried. "He's having some sort of attack. Help me with him!"

She'd hoped to draw one of the men away so she could fight them one at a time, but they hesitated to leave their prisoner.

"Is he breathing?" one of them called. "Loosen his collar!"

"Bring him over here!" replied the other.

Gods curse it, they weren't taking the bait. Which one was least likely to be a war mage? The smaller of the two, she decided. "I'm bringing him!" she cried. She dragged the dying man partway to the bonfire, then pulled out her pistol and shot the smaller man. He dropped to the ground.

The bigger guard pulled out his own pistol, but Lucien delivered a well-placed kick to his kneecap. The guard crashed to the ground, and the weapon went flying. Vitala drew her sword and charged.

In an instant, the bigger man was on his feet again, his sword leaping out to meet hers. His first stroke whistled toward her and she parried it, just barely. The sword whipped at her again, impossibly fast. *War mage.* And seduction was out of the question.

Vitala was a superb swordswoman, trained in techniques that compensated for her deficiencies in physical size and strength, but her light, quick movements that had been so devastating in the training room felt slow and clumsy next to her opponent's. She found herself driven back, one step after another, fighting off a rain of blows that were not only ridiculously fast but strong. Her arm ached fending them off.

She was no match for this man. She couldn't beat him, and she couldn't run from him either. The moment she turned her back, he would strike her down.

She made a desperate thrust at his groin. He shifted position to block it. Then his eyes went wide, his mouth flew open, and his sword arm went limp. Perplexed as to why he'd suddenly left himself open, she drove her blade into his chest.

As he fell forward over her blade, she saw the knife hilt sticking out of his lower back.

Her eyes went to Lucien.

"Come on," he said. "We have to go before they get back. Get my crutch and my leg. They're over there." He pointed. "I can't *believe* this. Gods-cursed traitors!"

Vitala fetched the crutch and peg leg for Lucien, then threw away her spent pistol and grabbed a new one off the smaller guard's belt. The guard's knife sheath was empty. Lucien had been given a choice, knife or pistol, and he'd chosen the knife.

Lucien strapped on the peg leg. "Clothes? Gods, I just want to kill them all."

"Here." She took off the Legaciatti uniform she was wearing over her syrtos and handed it to him.

He threw it on, flinging the belts into a crude approximation of the proper knots, and grabbed a boot off the smaller guard's corpse. "My riftstone," he demanded.

"Later," she said. "We're going to have to bind that gash in your leg."

"Do it," he said.

She wound the strip around his injured leg, pulling it tight to try to stanch the bleeding. He hissed sharply as she worked, but did not complain. She knotted the bandage and glanced in the direction of the imperial tent. The fire was still blazing; they hadn't yet gotten it under control. "Keep watch," she told Lucien. "Tell me if you see anyone coming back."

"Shouldn't we just leave?" said Lucien. "If we can get to the battalion commander—"

"No. He's one of the traitors." That might or might not have been true; she had no idea. She grabbed the smaller corpse, used her knife to quickly strip off his clothes, and tossed them into the bonfire.

"What are you *doing*?" hissed Lucien.

"Faking your death. Keep watch." She drew her sword, and with the strongest blow she could manage, severed the left leg at the knee. She tossed the corpse onto the fire. Greasy black smoke roiled upward.

"Three gods," choked Lucien, covering his mouth and nose.

"Let's go." She grabbed the blanket-wrapped loros and, with far less enthusiasm, the severed leg. She hauled

Lucien to his feet. "Can you walk?" With his one good leg injured, the prospect looked uncertain.

He took a couple of faltering steps, catching himself heavily on his crutch. He swapped the crutch to the right-hand side. "Maybe if I carry it over here."

"You're too slow," said Vitala, looping his arm over her shoulder so he could use her as a second crutch. "We have to get out of here fast."

They moved south into the darkness of the empty field. Supporting Lucien was less awkward than she'd thought it would be; perhaps his war-mage reflexes assisted him, granting him a certain grace, though he grunted softly with pain at each step.

Once they were out of easy visual range, she circled around to the east and then north, keeping within the ring of the perimeter that encircled the imperial camp. If the Legaciatti didn't fall for her trick, they would expect Lucien to flee toward the road, find transportation, and head south, toward the imperial city. Thus she had to take him in the opposite direction. Soon the northern campfires were near enough that they could see actual flames instead of just orange dots; they had reached the encamped battalion. She hoped this would go smoothly. Lucien was in a Legaciatti uniform, which ought to lend him an air of legitimacy. As for her, she wore only a syrtos. As a woman, she might be of interest, but should not be seen as a threat.

"We need to find the commander," said Lucien in a voice tight with pain. "He can help us. Look for a tent with—"

"No. I told you, he's one of the traitors. We need to get you out of the camp entirely."

"Pox it all, we have to stop them! We can't let them get away with this!"

"We can't fight them all. Too many."

"How do you know the commander's a traitor?" demanded Lucien. "Who and what are you, really?"

"I'll explain everything when we're safe."

They struggled past the pup tents of the infantrymen, past the occasional banked cookfire or donkey tied to a stake, and once past a group of men playing dice who stared at them curiously but did not move to stop them.

At the far end of the encampment, they reached a bean field.

Lucien asked in a hoarse voice, "Do you have any water?"

"No. Sorry." Pox, she'd fouled that part up. They had no supplies, and Lucien was badly injured. How long could he keep up? Already his pace was flagging. At least there was no pursuit yet. In time, there would be.

She set Lucien down in the bean field and dropped to the ground herself for a quick rest.

Lucien lay in the dirt, panting. "We're going the wrong way," he rasped.

"No, we're not."

"We need to get to the road. Find a carriage, get back to the palace." He rolled onto his side and groaned. "I need a Healer. I need to get back to Celeste."

"They'll look for us there. We need to stick to the fields. Besides, there won't be carriages at night."

"They'll look in the fields too," he panted. "It doesn't matter. We need transportation, and you never know what might come by. Give me my riftstone."

"Not yet." She scanned the horizon, looking for searchers.

"Give it to me," said Lucien. "That's an imperial order."

Vitala started to laugh, but when she turned toward

him, she found herself facing the barrel of a pistol. Despite Lucien's weakness, his hand was steady. Her mind raced as she tried to work out where he'd picked it up. Probably it was the weapon the war mage had tried to fire at her, the one that had gone flying when Lucien knocked him down.

"Give it to me," Lucien repeated.

"You wouldn't shoot me," she said.

He drew back the hammer. "Yes, I would. And I don't miss."

"If you want every search party in the area to converge on our position, pull that trigger."

His face was grim. "I don't know who or what you are, but if you're keeping my riftstone from me, you're not my friend."

"I saved your life. And, Lucien, I'm all you've got. You're wounded and crippled, and the people looking for you want you dead. Even if the sound of the gunshot doesn't bring a search party, you won't last a day without me."

After a moment, he lowered the pistol. "Please. I need the stone. It's my only defense."

"The stone works fine as long as it's close by. Stay near me, and there won't be a problem."

His face twisted in frustration and rage. "You godscursed—! What if we get separated? You're committing treason by keeping it from me. I'm your emperor!"

Vitala laughed. "You're not my emperor." He went silent, so before he could process that statement any further, she added, "You're nobody's emperor right now. You've been deposed."

"I don't care what those traitorous culls did. I'm still—"

"Shh," she hissed. "Do you hear that?" They fell silent. The wind carried voices—distant ones, but not too distant. She couldn't make out the words, but it might be a search party. "We've got to keep moving."

Still fuming, Lucien nodded.

She hauled him back onto her shoulder and trudged onward. The bean field seemed to go on forever. Beyond it was a hay field, and then another field filled with vinelike plants she no longer cared enough to identify. She stumbled on, exhausted, forcing one foot in front of the other. When she felt as if she could not take another step, she spotted an old barn with a partially collapsed roof. The rotting door swung open on its hinges. She dragged the nearly unconscious Lucien inside and laid him on the dirt floor. The barn was empty—no fresh hay or straw to spread over them for warmth.

She placed a hand on Lucien's arm. His skin felt clammy. Not good. She unwrapped the loros from the blanket. It was the blanket she wanted; the loros she dumped on the floor. She threw the blanket over Lucien. Then she crawled beneath it herself, pulled it tight around the two of them, and wrapped her arms around Lucien, hoping her body heat would keep him alive until morning.

8

When Vitala woke, sunbeams were spilling through the barn's collapsed roof onto the packed-dirt floor. Dust motes swirled in the beams. Lucien hadn't moved, but he was warm in her arms, and his chest still rose and fell.

She extricated herself from Lucien and the blanket. He still carried the pistol he'd pointed at her earlier, so she pulled it from his belt and tucked it into her own. As she headed out of the barn, her eyes fell upon the severed leg lying in the doorway, covered with flies. Gods, had she really carried that all the way here? She picked it up by a stiff toe, wrinkling her nose, and walked outside with it. Flies swarmed about her. She tossed the leg a short distance from the barn. She ought to bury it, but she didn't have any tools.

When they'd arrived, she'd been too exhausted to take note of her surroundings. The viny plants she'd tramped through last night were string beans, curling their way up wooden tripods. There were no people in sight, just empty fields in every direction, but a farmhouse squatted upon a hill, probably no more than half an hour's walk away. It seemed as good a destination as any. In her experience, most farmers were quite happy to sell supplies to travelers, and when she arrived at the farmhouse, she was not disappointed. She came away with a pair of waterskins, several wrinkled apples, bread, and cheese. When she returned, Lucien was still asleep.

She pressed the waterskin into his hands. "Drink."

His eyes fluttered open. He grasped the waterskin and gulped down about half its contents, then pointed at the second skin she carried. "Is that one for you?"

"No, I drank at the farmhouse. This one's yours too, but save it for later."

While he tackled breakfast, she went outside and, using Lucien's crutch and the heel of her boot, crudely buried the severed leg and covered it with a few inches of dirt.

Back in the barn, Lucien was struggling with his food. The sunbeams crept across the floor and caught the diamond-studded loros, which lay on the ground in careless folds. It lit up like a tiny, fallen chandelier.

"You saved the loros!" said Lucien.

"Yes." She was a little annoyed she hadn't thought to hide it, but it was inevitable he'd find out about it.

"Good. That will be a blow to Cassian."

"Cassian?"

"The man behind the coup."

"You knew about the plot against you?"

"No," said Lucien. "But, in hindsight, he's the only man with both the desire and the ability to pull it off."

"Who is Cassian, and what's he got against you?"

Lucien sighed. "He's the legatus in charge of the southern battalions. A nasty fellow, very ambitious. He wanted to marry Celeste, which would have put him next in the line of succession. With me out of the way, it will make him emperor. Do you remember what I told you about how my great-grandfather murdered the rightful emperor and took the throne?"

"Yes."

"Cassian is a direct descendant of the murdered emperor, so he probably sees himself as correcting history. With me out of the way, he'll force her into marriage. Which means we have to go back."

Vitala pursed her lips. What did these details mean for Riorca? Probably nothing good. Cassian's claim to the throne sounded strong, especially if he married Lucien's sister. "Are there others besides Cassian who might claim the throne?"

Lucien shook his head. "No. This plot has Cassian's stamp all over it. We must go back before he harms Celeste."

"That's ridiculous. We can't possibly return to the palace." Indeed, if there was no one to challenge Cassian and create a civil war except Lucien himself, it was all the more critical she get him out of harm's way. The girl could not be saved. And why was Lucien only picking at his food? "Eat," she commanded.

"I'm trying."

She folded her arms. "Are you too much of a snob to eat farm bread and cheese?"

"No," he said. "But I don't feel well, and I'm not sure I can keep it down. I've answered your questions. Now you answer mine. Who are you?"

"You already know."

"You're more than a Caturanga player. You killed that sentry with a death spell—I saw you do it. If you're a Healer, I could really use some healing right now."

"I'm no Healer. If I were, do you think I'd have dragged you miles across those fields last night when I could have healed the gash in your leg and saved myself the trouble?"

"I don't know a gods-cursed thing about you or your

motivations," snapped Lucien. "And how can you cast a death spell if you're not a Healer?"

"I'm not here to answer your questions," said Vitala. "I'm here to get you to safety."

His face clouded with anger and he reached for his pistol, but his hand found only an empty belt. His eyes went to her belt, where the weapon now rested.

"Eat," she said again. "We have to move, and you need your strength."

He managed to choke down a little more bread. She wrapped up what remained, along with the loros, and tied it all up in the blanket. A brief scouting foray outside the barn told her there were no search parties in view, and they set off.

Lucien was weaker than he'd been the night before. His face was pale, and he sweated profusely despite the chilly morning air. Limping heavily, he fell behind. Vitala asked if he would rather lean on her shoulder again, but he growled at her to leave him alone.

It was clear they would get nowhere on foot, so in spite of the risk, she led Lucien out of the fields and toward the road. They moved parallel to it, tucked away in the fields for cover, watching for wagons and carriages that might pass by.

She spotted a wagon piled high with carrots. "Stay here," she whispered to Lucien, and bounded out onto the road.

"Sir!" she cried, waving her arms as she stepped in front of the wagon. "My companion and I need a ride to Tasox. I have money." She held out a few tetrals from Remus's belt pouch.

The farmer pulled up his elderly bay team and frowned at her with deep suspicion. "I don't take passengers, and you don't want to go to Tasox. It's full of bandits."

"Sir, would this persuade you?" She added a few more coins to her offering.

The farmer shook his head and clucked to his horses.

Vitala stepped in front of her wagon, pulled out her pistol, and pointed it at him. "Get out."

"Ma'am!" He stopped the horses. "I— No! You'll strand me!"

"Take me and my companion to Tasox. We're driving your wagon there. You can be on the wagon with us, or you can be dead."

The farmer swallowed. "I'll take you to Tasox."

Still training the gun on the farmer, Vitala beckoned to Lucien, who emerged from the fields and limped to the back of the wagon.

The farmer looked horrified. "Your companion is *ill*."

"Injured," she corrected. But come to think of it, he did look ill. Pale and weak and sweaty . . . that wasn't normal for an injury. Was it? Her stomach twisted. Lucien wasn't warded. He could have contracted something.

Somehow, despite his weakness, Lucien managed to climb up the side of the wagon and collapse inside it.

"Don't break the carrots," the farmer pleaded.

Vitala put away her pistol and swung up into the wagon beside Lucien. A dozen carrots snapped beneath her. She looked up at the farmer, who, after a moment's stricken look, turned forward and clucked to his horses. The wagon jolted into movement.

She touched Lucien's cheek, which was warm. "How are you feeling?"

He screwed his eyes shut. "Like I got run over by a four-in-hand."

"I think you might have wound fever. You're not warded."

"Ridiculous. Of course I'm warded."

"I wouldn't be sure of that. Your Warder was one of the traitors."

Lucien lay still.

Fearing he'd lost consciousness, she shook him lightly. "What do you do for wound fever? How is it cured?"

"Haven't the foggiest," he murmured. "There's a Healer in Tasox. Get me there."

She wasn't wild about Tasox as a destination, given the unrest and the fact that it was the battalion's destination, but they had little choice. There wasn't anything else nearby except huge swaths of farmland. It was either Tasox or back to the Imperial City of Riat, and Tasox was at least in the right direction.

She placed a possessive hand on Lucien's back, as if by laying claim to him she could keep death away, and his breathing lengthened into the long, easy rhythm of sleep.

Lucien slept most of the way to Tasox. When he was awake, he was irritable and snappish, and sometimes not even lucid. Once he seemed to believe he was a soldier fighting with the White Eagle battalion in the mountains of Riorca. He spoke of slitting a man's throat.

That evening, while he slept, she unwrapped the crude bandage tied around his leg and found the wound swollen and red. It looked *wrong*, and it didn't appear to be healing at all.

"Will the bandits prevent us from entering the city?" she called to the driver.

"We'll bribe them," he said.

"You're aware the battalion is on the way there?"

"Yes, ma'am. That's why I'm in a hurry. No one will want to buy vegetables after the bloodletting starts."

"People need to eat, always," Vitala protested.

"If they're smart, they'll have stored supplies. Better to go hungry than get staked."

They arrived in Tasox the afternoon of the following day. A group of gaudily dressed bandits caught them at the entrance and demanded a "city access fee." The farmer paid it, and they drove on to an open-air market, where Vitala and a semiconscious Lucien disembarked. Even though she'd had to force the farmer at gunpoint to take them, she paid him for their passage. Perhaps he would keep his mouth shut if anyone asked about them.

Though called a city, Tasox wasn't as large as Riat; it was more properly a town. Vitala could see at a glance that it was well-to-do, or had been before the bandits took over. Kjallan cities housed their poor in rickety three-story apartment buildings, but she'd seen none of those on her way in. Instead, they'd passed rather nicer apartments, built in little squares around shared, central courtyards, as well as large, single-story villas.

The streets were clean and well maintained, but not bustling. Only about a third of the market stalls were open, and the queued-up customers looked nervous. They glanced about frequently, taking in the packs of bandits that roamed the streets—easily identified by their openly carried weapons—and, when business was concluded, disappeared furtively into their apartments and villas.

A bandit pack, seated on the edge of a public fountain and eating lunch, stared at her and Lucien. She had little doubt they would approach and perhaps harass her after they'd finished eating.

She beckoned to a street urchin. "Do you know Madam Hanna?"

The child nodded.

She handed him a tetral. "I'll give you two more of

these if you'll fetch her here immediately. Tell her I've got a man here with a Shard in his leg. Use those exact words: *a Shard in his leg*. Have you got it? Repeat it for me."

The child repeated the words, and Vitala sent him on his way.

Madame Hanna arrived, puffing and panting, fifteen minutes later, with the urchin and a Riorcan slave in tow. She was a graying woman in her fifties, a little overweight, with her hair pulled back from her face and tied at the base of her neck. She wore a silver chain around her neck and a collection of silver bracelets on her wrists.

"Aunt Hanna," Vitala greeted her.

Hanna's eyes briefly took her in—they'd never seen each other in their lives—and went to feverish Lucien. "You say he has a Shard in his leg?"

"Yes, ma'am."

"Let's get him back to the house. It's not safe on the streets."

Vitala paid the urchin, then lifted Lucien's upper body while the slave took his legs. Hanna guided them several blocks to one of the apartments surrounding a central courtyard. They went inside, and she shut the door behind them. A copper-colored dog with white markings trotted up to Vitala, waving its plumelike tail. It was carrying something soft and gray and unidentifiable in its mouth, which Vitala hoped wasn't a dead rat.

"I'm not a Healer," said Hanna. "I'm a midwife."

A quick glance gave Vitala the layout of the apartment. They were in a sitting room, which had a hearth and doubled as a kitchen, and there were two doors in the back that led to what she presumed were bedrooms. A third door led to the courtyard. The room smelled of herbs and home cooking.

The slave indicated one of the back bedrooms. Vitala helped her carry Lucien there and settled him on one of several empty cots. The dog padded after them and curled up on the floor at the base of the cot, still carrying its mystery object. "Is there a Healer in Tasox we could bring him to?"

"No," said Hanna. "Gordian's men killed one of them, and he's holding the other hostage."

Vitala stood, discouraged by the news. She doubted Lucien would survive without a Healer. "Can we speak to Gordian? Offer money in exchange for use of the Healer?"

"No. Do not approach Gordian. Who is this man?" Hanna pulled off Lucien's boot and began to undress him. The Riorcan slave moved to help.

Vitala glanced uncertainly at the slave.

"You can speak freely, child," said Hanna. "Glenys is one of us."

Vitala smiled. It was an ideal setup for a spying operation. Hanna looked Kjallan. Like Vitala, she was probably a half-blood, while Glenys was full Riorcan. A midwife and her slave could move freely about the village and would spend time in many households, learning much. Probably little went on in Tasox the two of them didn't know about.

"He's the Emperor of Kjall."

Hanna snorted. "Not funny."

"I'm not joking. That's Emperor Lucien. His men turned against him, and I barely got him out alive."

"I've heard no news of that."

"It only just happened," said Vitala. "And there's a battalion on the way here to deal with the bandits. I don't think they'll be looking for Lucien—they probably believe he's dead—but I don't know for sure."

Hanna ran her eyes over Lucien's sleeping form, taking in the wooden leg with its gold bands, his wasting body, his pale face and sculpted features. "Can he hear us?"

"I don't know," said Vitala.

"Let's assume he can." She laid a blanket over him. "We'll speak in the other room."

They left Lucien behind, shut the door, and moved to the sitting room.

Hanna took a seat, her bracelets clinking. "If he's the emperor, we should let him die."

"No." Vitala sat down opposite her. "I'm to bring him to the Circle in Riorca."

Glenys spread her hands. "Why? The Circle wants him dead."

"Not anymore," said Vitala. "There's been a coup. A man named Cassian has taken the imperial throne. If Lucien dies, Cassian will rule the country unchallenged. We need Lucien to raise an army and start a civil war, which will give Riorca the chance it needs to win its independence."

"That young man doesn't look capable of raising an army," said Hanna.

Vitala bit her lip. She had to agree; that was a sticking point. And yet something told her Lucien was capable of more than he seemed. "He's the best chance we have. Besides, I'm under orders." That was true; she *was* under orders. Just not those orders.

"What are you? Spy? Assassin?" asked Glenys.

"Assassin and wardbreaker." She lifted her hair and showed them the two hard spots on her neck where her obsidian riftstone and deathstone were implanted.

They came over and felt them, then sat back, exchanging a glance. Assassins were well respected in the Obsidian Circle. "All right," said Hanna. "I'll try to save him, but I make no promises. What does he know?"

"Only that I rescued him. He doesn't know I'm from the Circle."

"Let's keep it that way."

They returned to Lucien, who was still unconscious on the cot, with the dog keeping him company.

"What's your dog's name?" asked Vitala. "And what's that in her mouth?"

"Flavia, and that's a rolled-up bandage she likes to carry around. Do you know what's wrong with him?" asked Hanna.

"I think it's wound fever. His Warder was one of the traitors." Vitala pulled up Lucien's syrtos and unwrapped the bandage.

Hanna hissed at the sight. "Yes, that's wound fever."

Vitala bit her lip. "Will he die?"

"Probably not," said Hanna. "It's not streaky yet. But we need to get him warded before the sickness spreads any further. Glenys, get Antonius."

The Riorcan hurried for the door.

"Once warded, he shouldn't get worse," explained Hanna. "But curing the existing sickness may be difficult." She examined his back and sides. "He's got burns, too."

"Are they serious?"

"I imagine they're very painful, and they'll probably scar. But the blisters haven't broken, and that's a good sign. I'll put ointment on them."

"What can I do to help?" asked Vitala.

"Nothing yet," said Hanna. "But you'll have to nurse him back to health once I get some medicine and wards into him. Glenys and I must continue our midwifery. Do you understand? We could be called away at any time."

"Yes, ma'am. Of course."

"For now, I'll do what I can for him." Hanna left the room and bustled about the hearth, lighting a fire, putting a kettle on to boil, and mixing an herbal concoction. Vitala discarded the blood-soaked bandage, unstrapped and removed Lucien's wooden leg, and covered his lower body with a blanket to make him less recognizable. The former emperor's face was not well-known to the general population of Kjall, but his leg was distinctive.

The Warder, Antonius, arrived and was directed to the back room. He was an elderly man with a kind, wrinkled face. "The standard wards?" he asked.

"Yes, sir, including fertility," said Vitala. "The patient first, then me."

She liked to watch wards being placed, since, unlike most people, she could actually see them. She relaxed her mind as the Warder's fingers traced the symbols in the air, calling the magic from the Rift and anchoring it within Lucien's person and then her own. He was highly skilled and called forth what he needed with minimal hand movements. Vitala smiled at the perfectly formed blue and violet threading his handiwork left behind. She paid and tipped him with Remus's coin.

After Antonius had gone, Hanna brought the steaming kettle into the bedroom and set it by Lucien's bed. She poured some powder into the boiling water, stirred, and dipped a cloth into it, then removed the cloth with tongs and held it out to Vitala. "Let this cool for just a moment, then hold it on his leg. You need to soak the wound for fifteen minutes."

Vitala took the tongs. She waited until the cloth was cool enough to touch, then placed it on the wound.

Lucien groaned and shifted in his sleep.

Hanna left the room, and returned a while later with

a basin and a metal instrument that looked like a large set of tweezers. She took the tongs from Vitala and set them aside. "Hold on to him," she ordered.

Vitala gave her a questioning look. "He's unconscious."

"He may not stay that way."

Vitala pushed Lucien's arms into the bed, holding him down.

"No," said Hanna. "Go behind him. Pull his arms behind his back."

Vitala climbed onto the bed behind Lucien, lifted his upper body, and laid him against her chest. She twisted his arms behind his back and held them there.

Hanna used the tweezers to pry open the infected wound. Vitala winced and looked away.

Lucien, who had been deadweight in her arms, became a writhing, twisting force of nature. His arms ripped out of her grip. Something struck her on the chin. His arms flailed, and she ducked. The basin overturned.

"Be still! Be still!" Hanna shouted.

Lucien was yelling something incomprehensible.

Vitala tried to grab Lucien again, but he twisted out of her grip. She was afraid to try again. She was no match for magically enhanced strength.

Hanna righted the basin. "Lie down, you fool! I'm trying to help you!"

"What's going on? Who are you?" cried Lucien.

"Lucien, it's me!" Vitala circled around the room into his view.

He recognized her and quieted.

"You're in Tasox," said Vitala. "This is my aunt Hanna. She's helping you with your leg."

"Helping me with . . ." He looked at the leg wound, then at Hanna with her tweezers and basin. "What quackery is this? I need a Healer!" He tried to stand, but his injured leg buckled underneath him. Vitala caught him and maneuvered him back onto the bed. His voice sounded strange. Though his words seemed to be the product of a clear mind, she suspected they were fever induced.

"Shh," said Vitala, laying her hands on his arms and pushing gently to get him to lie down. "There is no Healer available. Of the two in Tasox, one is dead and the other is a prisoner of the bandits."

"Soldier's hell! When is the battalion getting here?"

"I haven't the slightest idea, but their arrival won't be a good thing for us."

"Pox it all," fumed Lucien. "Let's get out of here and move on to the next town. There are Healers in Worich."

"You'll never make it that far," said Hanna. "Not until we drain that leg."

Lucien paled. "Drain it?"

"You have wound fever," Hanna explained. "We have to drain the sickness out of the leg. Otherwise you'll lose the leg, and considering it's the only good one you've got left, I don't think you want that."

"Pox that. You're not opening up my leg. I'll kill you before I let you do it."

Vitala turned to Hanna. "He's not lucid—not rational. How about I take his riftstone out of range so he loses his magic? Then Glenys can hold him while you drain the leg."

Hanna frowned. "You shouldn't be on the streets. Not with Gordian's men out there."

"I'm not defenseless, and it won't take long. Will it?"

"No, but—"

"Don't go." Lucien stared up at her, his eyes cloudy and confused. "Don't take my riftstone."

"I'll stay, but only if you hold still for Aunt Hanna."

He winced but nodded acquiescence.

Hanna prodded at the open wound, and yellow fluid oozed out of it. She moved the basin to catch it.

Lucien howled in pain. He looked at what Hanna was doing, and his voice rose to an alarming pitch. "What's that yellow stuff? Blood is not yellow!"

"It's the sickness." Hanna continued to prod deeper into the wound, finding more yellow gunk. Bile rose in Vitala's throat. She'd never seen anything so disgusting in her life. "I'm getting it out so your leg can heal," continued Hanna. "Are you feeling better yet?"

Lucien's eyes glazed over. "Can't even stand up," he mumbled. "Gods-cursed horse."

Vitala and Hanna exchanged perplexed glances.

Lucien turned to Vitala and started, as if he'd just noticed her. He raised his hand gently to the sore spot on her chin. "Who did that to you? I'll poxing stake him—"

"You did that, you sapskull."

He looked shocked. "I couldn't have."

"It was an accident. Don't worry about it."

As if in apology, he kissed her on the chin. When she did not protest, he leaned in to kiss her on the lips.

She shoved him away.

As Hanna probed deeper into the wound, trying to extract every last bit of the foul-smelling stuff, Lucien's body stiffened and he gritted his teeth. He looked again at the yellow fluid draining from his leg. "Gods-cursed horse," he murmured, and suddenly he was deadweight in her arms.

"Out cold?" asked Hanna.

Vitala lowered him to the cot. "I think so."

Hanna clucked in sympathy. "Poor creature. It's for the best."

9

That evening, Hanna and Glenys were called out to attend a birth. Vitala stayed behind with Lucien and Flavia, following the orders Hanna had left her. Every four hours, she soaked the wound in boiled, treated water, packed it with powder, and bandaged it. To Vitala's discomfiture, they could not stitch the gash closed; it had to be left open until the sickness was gone. When Lucien woke, still delirious, Vitala plied him with medicine and water and, when he would take it, a little food.

By morning, Lucien was still weak, but the wound looked considerably less angry. He was aware of the dog and reached down from time to time to stroke her ears.

A few hours later, Hanna and Glenys burst in the door. "They're coming," said Hanna. "Down in the basement, both of you."

"Who's coming?" Vitala ran to the back bedroom. She would need help carrying Lucien.

"Gordian's men." Hanna pulled a rug aside, revealing a trapdoor. "Leave Lucien where he is; they won't want him. It's you and Glenys I'm worried about. They take young women. Better take Flavia too, in case they shoot animals for sport."

"How many of them are there? Do they have magic?"

"Don't fight them, child. Gordian will just send more." She raised the trapdoor and gestured to the ladder.

Glenys hurried down. Vitala grabbed her weapons and followed. The rickety ladder creaked under her feet. At the bottom, her feet dropped onto soft dirt.

"Here, take Flavia," called Hanna from above.

Vitala saw her handing the dog down, and her stomach tightened. She had no experience with dogs. Some of the Kjallan soldiers had them—great war dogs with bulging muscles, spiked collars, and mouths that bristled with teeth. Flavia wasn't a war dog. She seemed gentle, yet she was a sizeable animal nonetheless.

"I'll get her," said Glenys, stepping forward. She took the dog in her arms, to Vitala's relief, and set her on the dirt floor. The trapdoor shut above them, leaving them in darkness, but Glenys activated a light-glow that revealed a close space and shelves all around them. The shelves were stacked high with powder-filled jars, dried herbs, bandages, and food supplies. There was no furniture. Vitala sat cross-legged on the floor, half cocked her pistol, and rested it on her lap. Above, she heard a scraping noise as the rug was replaced over the trapdoor.

Flavia padded around restlessly, then curled up next to Vitala. Vitala recoiled, having never touched a dog before, but slowly relaxed; the animal obviously meant no harm. Tentatively, she reached for Flavia's head to stroke it the way she'd seen Lucien do. The animal's medium-length fur was coarse on the outside, but there was a softer layer underneath.

"You're not accustomed to dogs," said Glenys. "But our people used to keep them. Did you know?"

Vitala shook her head.

"The Kjallans slaughtered them, but a few survived, and the bloodline has been preserved. Few people are aware."

Vitala opened her mouth to reply, but shut it as, above

them, the door to the cottage flew open with a bang. Footsteps thudded across the floor.

Flavia leapt to her feet, but before she could bark or growl, Glenys seized her muzzle.

"Madam Hanna," said a man's voice overhead. "We need supplies."

"Whatever for?" she replied. "Haven't you got a Healer?"

"Gordian didn't like him." More banging as furniture was shoved aside and cupboard doors roughly opened.

"What do you mean, Gordian didn't like him? Is he *dead*?"

No answer. The footsteps crossed over their heads into Lucien's bedroom. "Who's this cull?"

"Never you mind," said Hanna. "Someone your men did wrong, that's who."

One of the men chuckled. "What's in the bowl? Soup?"

"Ain't for you," said Hanna.

A spitting noise. "Aggh, it's medicine."

More banging, more footsteps. There was a loud tromp as one of the men stepped right on the trapdoor, then a more welcome sound, that of the front door opening. "Thanks, Hanna. So obliging."

"You're nothing but thieves, you are!" she called after them. The door closed.

A few minutes later, the trapdoor opened, and Hanna peered down at them. "Well, come on up."

"What's the damage?" asked Glenys when they'd emerged from their hideout.

Hanna rifled through her cabinets. "Not bad. Our real stores are in the cellar. And they don't know what they're looking for. Look, they took the bandages but left this." She held out a jar of ointment.

Hanna and Glenys laughed.

Vitala asked, "What's in the jar?"

"Burn ointment," said Glenys. "Valuable and hard to get. They were sapskulls to leave it behind. So they killed the Healer?"

"Sounds that way," said Hanna.

"I never thought I'd say this," said Glenys, "but I'd welcome that battalion."

Hanna and Glenys were called out again that evening and had not returned by morning. Lucien's wound looked almost healthy at this point. Vitala wished Hanna would return and look at it and, hopefully, stitch it up. She didn't know what was delaying the battalion—they ought to have been here by now—but if the delay continued, she might get Lucien out before they arrived. It was time to move things along.

Lucien was getting his color back. He looked less like a corpse and more like the handsome young man she'd made love to in the imperial tent. Well, she supposed it was more that he'd made love to her. The memory of that night brought a flush to her cheeks and a disconcerting throb to her nether regions. Gods, what had happened to her? She'd been with many a man before Lucien, but never had her body responded the way it had to him. Was it his looks? His skill? His personality? It hardly mattered, considering what had happened afterward. She'd been worried that a vision of the young soldier might intrude and steal her consciousness, and that was exactly what had happened. If Remus and his soldiers hadn't interfered and forced her back to reality, there was no telling how far the vision might have progressed. She might have reached the ugly part, the part that made her start screaming, and what would Lucien think if he saw that? She couldn't risk sleeping with him again.

Still, nursing him back to health was less unpleasant than she'd expected. Now that he was stripped of his imperial uniform, he didn't look like an enemy. Tucked away in a back bedroom in Tasox, he wasn't the emperor who'd persecuted her people and presided over the massacre at Stenhus. He was just a man, and a handsome one at that. Even the dog seemed to like him. Flavia no longer slept beneath his cot but atop it, right next to him, and he often rested a hand on her or idly scratched her ears.

Vitala laid a hand on his cheek to check for fever and found it cool to the touch. She stared at his closed eyes, half wishing they would open. They were his most attractive feature, not their shape or color, which were ordinary, but their intensity. It was the intelligence that lay behind them that made them fascinating. She missed those eyes. Then there was his second best feature: his lips. Gods, but the man could kiss. She throbbed again at the memory, and in a moment of unthinking pleasure, bent down and brushed his lips with her own.

His eyes opened. She stood and turned away so he wouldn't see her reddening cheeks.

"Don't stop there," he said. "Things were just getting interesting." He was lucid now; she could tell by the sharpness of his voice.

"I was checking to see if you had a fever."

"Do I have one?"

"No."

"Maybe you should check again." He faked a cough.

It must have been his looks that had reeled her in, because it sure wasn't his personality. "You're not funny."

"I can't make you laugh, but I can make you blush."

Time to change the subject. "Gordian's men were here. They stole supplies from Hanna."

"When is the battalion coming into town?"

"They should have been here already. They're delayed."

"Why?"

"I have no idea," said Vitala. "I'd wager because of your disappearance."

"If Remus died in the fire, the traitors are leaderless and disorganized. They'd probably send back to Cassian for instructions before moving on. On the other hand, if Remus survived—"

"He didn't survive."

"How do you know?"

"Because I killed him."

"You lie. He's a war mage. You could not have killed him."

She pulled Remus's riftstone from her pocket and dangled it before Lucien's disbelieving eyes. It was important he know she was capable of killing a war mage. It would inspire an appropriate level of respect.

"It's not possible," he said.

"We killed that other war mage by the fire."

"*We* killed him. Two of us. And one of us was a war mage with really good aim. I watched you fight. You're good, but you could not have beaten him alone."

"Maybe not, but I did kill Remus."

"How?"

Vitala smiled. "Why would I divulge my secrets?"

He scowled. "What are you—Obsidian Circle?"

She was shocked that he had guessed so easily. But, then, it wasn't as if there were numerous well-known spy networks operating within Kjall. "I think the Obsidian Circle would have killed you, not rescued you."

He looked thoughtful. "Not necessarily. The Circle

would have reasons for wanting me on the throne instead of Cassian."

"Really? What reasons?"

"If you're not Obsidian Circle, why do you want to know?"

Vitala bit her lip, frustrated. She was going to have to tell him eventually. It would become obvious once he realized their destination was Riorca. And it wasn't going to be easy to transport him there without his willing cooperation. She had his riftstone, which gave her some leverage, but she couldn't rob him of his magic without taking it out of range, and how could she control him if she didn't stay close to him? She couldn't tie him up— he'd break the bonds. Chains would be conspicuous. And how would she get them on him in the first place?

No, force was not feasible. Her only option was to make him believe she was on his side.

She sat beside him on the bed. "Look, I'll explain what I can. Yes, I work for someone. An organization. I can't tell you what it is."

"Why not?"

She ignored the question. "My superiors knew of the plot against you. My orders were to get close to you and stay close, and if the traitors made their move, get you to safety."

"If you knew about the plot, you should have told me! There were steps I could have taken—"

"No," she said. "The plot was too big for that. Now that the traitors have made their move and I've rescued you, my orders are to bring you to my superiors."

He rolled his eyes. "And you can't tell me who they are or what they want."

"They want you back on the throne. If I'm not mistaken, that's also what you want."

"If you're my ally, give me my riftstone."

"My orders aren't to follow your instructions. They're to bring you to my superiors. And I don't trust you to cooperate unless I have some leverage."

His face twisted in frustration. "Look, Vitala. I can't operate like this. I need details or I can't strategize. You can't play Caturanga if you can't see the board. I need to know who these people are and how they plan to help me."

"I don't have those details. I'm not the brains of the operation; I just follow orders. You're going to have to trust me. Don't forget I saved your life."

"I'm grateful to you for saving my life, but it doesn't oblige me to follow you anywhere."

She smiled. "Now you see why I need leverage."

He opened his mouth to argue some more, but changed his mind and waved a hand in capitulation. "I'm hungry."

She headed toward the kitchen. "I'll get you something."

"Vitala?"

She turned with her hand on the door.

"If you're not the brains of the operation, you should be."

10

The next morning, gunshots and the sounds of skirmishing on the south side of town announced the arrival of the battalion. Vitala watched from the window as the soldiers marched past the apartment in formation on their way to the center of town. Their presence made her restless; she and Lucien were now trapped in the apartment until they departed. To keep herself occupied, she assigned herself the task of keeping watch. In the early afternoon, she spotted a small party of soldiers working its way down the street and knocking on the door of each apartment and villa.

Hanna barked orders. "You and Lucien, down in the cellar. Glenys, in the back bedroom with Flavia."

Vitala descended the cellar ladder first, then assisted Lucien, holding him steady as he grunted with each painful step. Hanna closed the trapdoor above them, leaving them in darkness. With a flourish of her hand, Vitala summoned a blue ball of magelight. Lucien settled against the dirt wall opposite her, wedged in between two sets of shelves. Vitala realized the space was so cramped they would probably wind up touching. She hadn't minded when it was Glenys and Flavia, but this was Lucien. She curled up tight, pulling in her legs to avoid bumping into his.

For a moment, Lucien looked disappointed. Then his

eyes gleamed, and he deliberately stretched his legs across the cellar and rested them against hers.

"Bastard," she hissed, kicking him.

"Don't be cruel. I'm injured." He pointed at his bandaged leg and dumped his foot practically in her lap.

Vitala laughed—she couldn't help herself—and tossed his foot off her lap. She flung her own legs into the shared space, denying it to Lucien. Gods, what had come over her? Why was she acting like this? It was hardly professional. "What are the soldiers doing?" she whispered. "Why are they going house to house?"

Lucien opened his mouth to speak, but then there was a rap on the door loud enough to have been delivered with a stick or the pommel of a sword. They fell silent.

The door opened. Hanna's voice was mild as warm honey. "Good afternoon, sirs."

"Good afternoon, madam." Footsteps rained on the floor over their heads. Vitala counted two soldiers. Chairs creaked as they sat. "I understand you're a midwife and herb woman."

"Yes, sir."

"You live here alone?"

"With a slave girl. And a dog."

"Is the slave at home? Kindly bring her out."

"Glenys, come," called Hanna. A door opened, and there were quiet footfalls, but no creaking of a chair. Vitala imagined Glenys with hunched shoulders and downcast eyes, the picture of a docile Riorcan slave.

"We're putting together a picture of what's happened here," said the soldier. "Did you know any of the bandits?"

"Not personally, sir. I know them only by reputation. Their leader is a man named Gordian. He was an officer in a battalion that was disbanded, and he came to Tasox with a number of men from that battalion, who proceeded to run up tabs at the local inns and taverns. When an innkeeper pressed them for payment, there was a fight, and they burned down the inn, which was a terrible tragedy. Two children were killed, and—"

"I know that part already," said the soldier. "Were all the bandits from outside Tasox, or were some of them locals?"

Hanna hesitated. "If any locals were involved, they were not people I knew."

"Failure to provide your full assistance in this investigation is a crime, madam. Think hard."

"Yes, sir. I am thinking hard."

"Where are the bandits staying?"

"I'm told that Gordian has taken over the council chamber, and that the Black Lamb and the Clay Platters inns and the northern bathhouse hold some of his men."

"How about food and supplies? Who provides them to the bandits?"

"Well . . ." Hanna sounded uncomfortable. "No one *provides* them, exactly. The bandits take what they want, without paying. Most of us have had things stolen."

"Including you?"

"Yes, sir. They've broken in several times and stolen medical supplies."

"How did you resist them when they broke in?" asked the soldier.

"I told them to leave," said Hanna. "But we're just two women here, and they had pistols. And our dog's not the aggressive sort."

Vitala, uneasy at this line of questioning, scooted close to Lucien, cupped her hand around his ear, and whispered, "Why are they asking about the stolen supplies?"

He whispered back, "Don't worry about it. They always ask these questions."

"But it sounds like they're blaming her for letting them take the supplies—"

"It's early information gathering—nothing more. If they have concerns, they'll come back later with mind mages for a full interrogation."

Vitala frowned. That almost sounded worse. It would be a disaster for Hanna to be interrogated by a mind mage. Mind mages could tell truths from lies, and Hanna had secrets—not only that she was an Obsidian Circle spy, but also that she was sheltering Lucien. "If a mind mage interrogates her, won't he find out she's hiding you?"

"She," he corrected. "Mind mages are women. And they can't force people to talk. All they can do is determine, when somebody does talk, if he spoke the truth. It's unlikely Hanna will be interrogated, and even more unlikely the questioning will turn in the direction of who's hiding in her cellar."

Vitala leaned back against the dirt wall.

"What about the man in the apartment next to yours? Felix is his name, I believe," the soldier was saying. Papers rustled. "Yes, Felix. Did the bandits steal from him?"

"Not that I'm aware of," said Hanna. "Felix and I rarely speak."

"What about the baker up the street?"

"Krys? He's had several break-ins."

Vitala leaned in close to Lucien again. "They're getting Hanna to rat on her neighbors. What if her neighbors rat on her? What if they don't like her and they make false accusations?"

Lucien shook his head. "The mind mages will straighten it all out."

Vitala's stomach twisted. That was what she was afraid of.

When the questioning was over, an unusually subdued Hanna let Vitala and Lucien up from the cellar. Lucien repeated his assurances—this was standard military procedure, they would use mind mages to sort out truths from fiction—but Vitala knew Hanna was thinking what she'd been thinking: that they could not afford to be subjected to such an interrogation.

"Begging your pardon, Your Imperial Majesty," said Hanna, "but you're not in charge anymore. You don't know how they'll proceed."

"I know well enough," he said. "This is how it's always done."

The following morning, Hanna and Glenys were called out to attend a birth. Vitala and Lucien, bored and stir-crazy, cobbled together a Caturanga board out of an old quilt and a set of pieces out of empty jars and bits of firewood. They played, stationing themselves at a table near the window to watch for soldiers, with Flavia lying across Lucien's foot. Lucien had a new strategy: he kept opening with the Vagabond's Gambit. A gambit in Caturanga meant offering up a piece in sacrifice in order to gain a more advantageous position—in this case, early control of the Vagabond. If Vitala captured the sacrificed piece, she accepted the gambit. She could also leave the piece where it was and decline. But she was curious. She accepted the gambit every time he offered it. She won the first game but lost the second. That was the first time Lucien had beaten her, and his crowing about it was so irritating that she challenged him to a rematch, accepted his gambit again, and beat him.

When they'd tired of the Caturanga, Lucien disappeared for a moment, then returned with what looked like a fireplace poker. He unstrapped his peg leg and used the poker to pry the gold bands off the dark wood. Vitala watched wordlessly for a while, fetching one of the mangled bands when it flew off the leg and skittered across the room.

"The gold is too conspicuous," Lucien explained.

"I agree."

"Also, we can sell the bands if we have to." After he pried the last one from the peg leg, he set to work on the crutch.

"I'm not sure that's a great idea."

"If we *have* to," he repeated. "We could melt them down. They're solid gold."

By the time he'd finished the task, his injured leg was bothering him, and he went to the back bedroom to lie down. Vitala stayed by the window, watching flies knock against the glass and clouds drift past. In the afternoon she heard activity in the distance—the shouts of soldiers, some kind of announcement made by a voice too far away for her to make out, and then, a little later, agonized screams. Her flesh quivered—it sounded like somebody was being staked. Multiple somebodies. Who were the victims?

Some hours later, Hanna and Glenys returned with flushed faces.

"Gordian is dead!" cried Glenys.

"And his lieutenants along with him," added Hanna. "Good riddance!"

Lucien emerged from the back bedroom, bleary-eyed, his hair mussed from sleep.

"The soldiers staked them?" asked Vitala.

"Yes, on Barley Street."

Barley Street was Tasox's main thoroughfare; Vitala had traveled on it on her way into town.

"Good," said Lucien. "Let's hope it's all over now."

But it wasn't. The battalion did not leave, and as the days passed, Hanna and Glenys returned from each birth pale and breathless, listing the new staking victims they'd seen. "The baker in Westmoon Square," Hanna said. "And that boy—the brother of the baby we delivered two sagespans ago."

"I don't understand," said Glenys. "How could he have been involved?"

"He must have been," said Lucien. "The mind mages would know."

"With respect, sire," said Hanna, "word on the street is that the mind mages are not being used."

A wrinkle appeared in Lucien's forehead. "Then the commander is a fool. Have you learned his name yet?"

"Tribune Milonius."

"Milonius? Tribune Donatus was in command when we left Riat." Lucien's eyes went to Vitala. "I thought you said the battalion commander was one of the traitors. If that's so, why would Cassian replace him?"

Vitala swallowed uncomfortably. "Perhaps he promoted Donatus to a higher position."

Lucien frowned. "Perhaps."

Vitala was impressed at how well Lucien was getting along with Hanna. She'd expected him to be a brat, snobby and domineering, but the man had manners. He praised the humble food Hanna brought him and thanked her for her attentions when she changed his bandages and treated his burns. Only one incident had been embarrassing, when Hanna had brewed some lemon balm tea and Lucien had shut himself in the back bedroom and refused to come out until the smell went away. Emperors had their quirks, but he wasn't as bad as she'd expected.

"Where did you get your dog?" Lucien asked Hanna one night at dinner, in between sneaking Flavia bites from his plate. "I have a suspicion about her."

"From one of our clients," said Hanna. "We delivered a baby for a young family, and they didn't want her after the baby was born. We didn't need a dog, but we didn't want to see her drowned, so we took her."

"Did they say anything about her background?"

Hanna shrugged. "Nothing."

"I believe she's a hunting dog. Not a hound, but a spaniel or a retriever. Watch this." He pulled the dirty, rolled-up bandage from her mouth and tossed it across the room. Flavia eagerly bounded after it, snatched it up, and brought it back. "Retriever."

"Lots of dogs play fetch," said Hanna. "It doesn't mean anything."

"She *looks* like a retriever. She's got the size and build for it. I grew up with dogs at the palace, and she strikes me as the hunting type. But her coloration is unusual. This white stripe across her body—I've never seen anything like it. She might be crossbred."

"Perhaps she is. We're not hunters, but we find she's good with our patients. She likes to stay with them, keep them company."

"Tell me about your business," said Lucien. "I know there's no Healer in town now, but there used to be. Why use these primitive supplies and antiquated methods when a Healer would be preferable?"

"Healers are expensive," said Hanna. "And most of them will not attend a common woman's birth unless there are complications. Herb women like me serve the townsfolk who are too poor to afford a Healer's services."

"How many cannot afford a Healer?" asked Lucien.

"What about an infantryman's wife? If he's sending most of his pay home, can she afford a Healer?"

He questioned her all evening about money and medicine, his eyes intense and calculating. There was no doubt he'd returned to his old self.

The next morning, Glenys and Hanna were gone when Vitala woke. When they had not returned by nightfall, Lucien, now reasonably agile on his crutch and peg leg, paced to the window and pushed the curtains aside. "Difficult birth, do you suppose?"

"I hope that's all it is," said Vitala.

But they weren't back the morning after. A complicated birth could last more than a day, but with the soldiers in town, the long absence was suspicious. And Hanna ought to have sent Glenys home at least once to send word or fetch supplies. Vitala tucked a pistol in the folds of her syrtos. "I'm going to look for them."

"How can you?" asked Lucien. "They didn't tell us where they were would be."

"I'll ask around. Someone must know where they went."

Lucien shook his head. "You shouldn't be out there on your own. I'll go."

"What?" Vitala laughed. "You're too recognizable! Especially with that." She pointed to the peg leg.

"My face isn't well-known," he said. "I could take off the leg and use just a crutch. The gold bands are gone."

"I appreciate your trying to protect me, but you'd be crazy to show yourself on the streets with the battalion there. Remember my orders to bring you safely to my superiors?"

He frowned. "Better to fail at those orders than wind up dead."

11

The next afternoon, the battalion formed for departure and marched by the cottage in a grim procession, the soldiers' footsteps thudding in unison against the dusty street. After their passage, the city was eerily quiet.

Vitala didn't like the idea of leaving without knowing what had become of her hosts, but she knew that if Hanna and Glenys could speak to her now, they would order her to go. The mission came first. She and Lucien packed bags of food and supplies from the apartment's stores, not stating the obvious: that it was unlikely Hanna and Glenys would need them anymore.

"Can you ride a horse?" she asked Lucien.

"Yes."

"We'll steal a pair of them. We can move faster that way."

"Where are we going?" asked Lucien.

Vitala sighed. "Let's not have this argument right now."

"Fine," he said. "We'll have it later."

"It's bad out there," she warned as she slung a pack over her shoulder and checked her pistol. She opened the door and stepped outside. The smell hit her like a coach-and-four; it had permeated the house, and to some extent they'd become accustomed to it, but outdoors it was far stronger. The sun was setting on the western hills, where it burned like a bloodred beacon, tinting the streets.

Lucien limped outside, his expression grave.

"I hate to say it," said Vitala, "but I think Barley Street is our best bet for finding horses." She followed the path she'd taken earlier, up the road and past the two staked men, who were now in an advanced state of decay.

"Gods," said Lucien, staring at the placards. "These men weren't bandits."

"No. The battalion staked anyone who assisted the bandits."

"Sapskulls. Don't they realize most of them were probably forced?"

"Don't ask me to explain their logic," said Vitala, heading onto the cross street. As far as she was concerned, it required no explanation. This was standard-issue Kjallan savagery. How strange that Lucien, the former leader of the Kjallans, did not understand that.

She covered her mouth as they stepped onto Barley Street, with its double rows of staking victims. They looked like grisly trees lining the roadside. Her stomach roiled, threatening to empty itself. She scanned the shops and buildings that lined the road. She and Lucien weren't alone. Other townsfolk flitted about the street like wraiths, darting into shops and emerging with stolen goods. A few were loading up wagons with possessions, preparing to leave town.

She pointed at a building. "There's a stable," she whispered to Lucien. She didn't know why she was whispering. The surroundings seemed to demand it.

She headed for it. Lucien followed, his breathing shallow and rapid. "Shouldn't we look for Hanna and Glenys?"

Vitala shook her head. She couldn't stomach the

thought of seeing the two women up on stakes. "I think it's obvious what must have happened to them. Let's get the horses."

"You get them. I'll look for Hanna and Glenys."

"Lucien, I could use some help—"

"You get them," he said firmly, and turned away, ending the conversation.

Excited whickers greeted Vitala as she entered the stable. The four animals were restless, almost frantic. Perhaps they hadn't been fed in a while? She looked around and saw an upper story loaded with bales of hay, with gaps in the floor above each stall.

She ascended to the upper story, grabbed a pitchfork, and pitched some hay through each of the gaps. The horses fell upon it greedily.

Which ones to take? Lucien should have come with her; he would be a better judge of horseflesh. After giving the animals a little time to eat, she saddled and bridled a sorrel gelding and a bay, and led them outside.

Lucien wasn't where she'd left him. She spotted him across the street, standing at the base of one of the stakes. She jogged toward him, muttering epithets under her breath and tugging the horses at a trot behind her.

"Look." He pointed at the placard. It read, GAVE MEDICINES TO THE BANDITS. At the base of the stake, half buried in the dirt, was a silver bracelet.

Vitala glanced up at the impaled corpse just long enough to verify that it was Hanna. Not as long dead as some of the others, she was still recognizable, though one of her eyes had been eaten away, and gobbets of flesh dangled from her cheek. Bile rose in Vitala's throat. On the adjacent stake, she found Glenys, with an identical placard. She felt her face flushing, and her eyes filled with furious tears. *Kjallan bastards.*

"Let's go," she said harshly.

"This shouldn't have happened!" spat Lucien. "Milonius didn't need to kill all these people. Certainly not Hanna and Glenys. They didn't do anything!"

"I know. It's awful." His reaction softened her anger. Didn't he know it always happened this way?

"It's *idiotic*," said Lucien. "Cassian has destroyed this city. And for no useful purpose."

"I know." She held out her arm and helped him up.

Lucien grabbed the nearest horse, the sorrel, and mounted by placing his wooden leg in the stirrup and pulling himself into the saddle. He sat there for a moment, blinking and rubbing his eyes, then seemed to make an effort to pull himself together. "Can you get me a riding crop?"

"You think you'll need one?" The horses looked lively enough.

"Not to hit the horse with," he said. "It's to serve as my other foot, in case the peg leg doesn't do the job. You'll see."

She handed him the reins to the bay, ran back to the stable, and fetched him a crop. He did not wave it about, but slid it down his left side and let the end of it dangle where his foot would be.

She struggled into the bay's saddle, feeling clumsy after Lucien's surprisingly graceful example. Her riding experience was limited. "You sure you can ride?"

"Of course. It's all in the knees."

Vitala leaned down to adjust her stirrups.

"Oh, gods. Look."

She sat up in alarm and looked where Lucien was pointing. A gold-and-white dog was sniffing around the base of the stakes. She watched in horror as Flavia whimpered a little, then lay down below the bodies of her owners. "Did you leave the door open?" she whispered.

"I thought I closed it," said Lucien.

Gritting her teeth, she steered her horse away from the scene. Lucien followed. After a moment, so did Flavia.

"I believe we've been adopted," said Lucien.

Vitala stared at the dark-eyed dog panting up at her. She had a high-stakes mission to accomplish; she didn't need a dog slowing her down. And yet she owed a debt to Hanna and Glenys.

Besides that, she had her suspicions about Flavia. Hanna's story about the dog's being abandoned by a local family did not ring true. If Flavia had been a cur off the streets, perhaps she might have been tossed aside like so much dirty straw, but Lucien had immediately identified her as a hunting dog. Hunting dogs had value. And Glenys had dropped hints about a lost Riorcan bloodline, now hidden away somewhere. Who else would hide and protect that bloodline but the Obsidian Circle?

Whether Flavia was a Riorcan hunting dog in hiding or not, the mission had to come first. "Can she keep up with us?"

"I'll wager she can," said Lucien. "A day or two from now, you may be asking, Can we keep up with her?"

Vitala looked back at Hanna and Glenys. They were Obsidian Circle spies. They had been prepared to die for their country. They probably expected to someday be exposed, arrested, and executed. Instead, they'd been the victims of pointless Kjallan savagery. It didn't feel right. If they were going to die, it should have been for a reason. Vitala's fingers itched to form the Riorcan blessing for them, but she could not do that in front of Lucien.

Instead, she said a silent prayer for them, the Sage's Peace, and laid heels to her horse.

She and Lucien galloped north with a dog at their heels, out of the graveyard that was Tasox.

Traffic on the road was light, and all of it northbound. Vitala sympathized with the departing Tasox residents. Who would want to stay? The corpses made the place unbearable, and as more people ventured out of their houses, the looting would get worse, possibly turning to violence.

A scraggly lot shared the road with them. Laden donkeys trudged beside wagons piled high with possessions: linens and chairs and bed frames, chests cinched closed with leather straps. Most wagons had extra horses tied to the back—fine horses of a quality not commensurate with the goods in their wagons. Stolen, perhaps, like her own mount. The families looked bedraggled and demoralized. Many seemed to be missing members. Here was a determined-looking father with two ragamuffins; there was a grandmother traveling with a woman close to Vitala's age, brushing tears from her dust-streaked face.

They camped that night by the side of the road, and were off again at first light. Unburdened by wagonloads of possessions, they quickly outpaced the other refugees, and by afternoon they had the road nearly to themselves. Flavia, as Lucien had predicted, kept up effortlessly, panting a little as she trotted alongside the horses. She'd lost her rolled-up bandage but often picked up a stick from the side of the road and carried that instead.

Lucien rode far better than he walked, his seat and posture flawless.

Vitala watched him admiringly. "You ride very well," she commented.

He nodded. "Been up on horses since I was four years old."

He rode on her left side, so she couldn't see his wooden leg. He looked so capable that she had to remind herself he was crippled. It was like seeing the man he'd been before he lost his leg. "So why do you need a crutch and a wooden leg?"

He shrugged. "More stability that way. I can get by with just the crutch when I need to, and I can walk on the leg without a crutch. But it hurts."

"Why does it hurt?" She'd known a Riorcan man, a member of the Circle, who used a wooden leg, and she'd never known him to complain of pain. He didn't use a crutch, not that she'd seen.

He looked at her with annoyance. "When I walk on that leg, all my body weight is on the stump. It's not meant to bear that much weight. I use the crutch to take some weight off it."

Maybe Lucien's wooden leg was poorly constructed. When they reached the Obsidian Circle headquarters, she would ask around and find that man with the wooden leg, see who'd made it for him. Riorcans were excellent woodworkers.

"Look." Lucien pointed to the road ahead, which forked, one branch heading north and the other east. "Decision time. Who do you work for, and where are we going?"

"We've been over this before. I can't tell you that."

"Because you work for the Obsidian Circle."

She shook her head. "No."

He snorted in anger. "You think this game of yours is funny? The Obsidian Circle killed my brothers. They cost me my leg."

"I know. It's not a game." Strange how those events

made her feel simultaneously proud and ashamed of her people. She'd been in training when those attacks took place. Her stomach had knotted when she'd learned that Lucien had been injured by the assassins but not killed. She was relieved that the target she'd been aimed at for years hadn't been taken away from her, but the partial failure had been a blow to Riorca at the time, especially since the assassins had all died in the operation, and the pressure on her to complete her training had become that much more intense.

"So," said Lucien, "when we get to that fork, you're either going to keep going north, toward Vesgar, or you're going to turn east toward Worich. If you choose north, I'm going to assume you're Obsidian Circle."

Her bay gelding chose that moment to swish his tail at a fly, and Vitala, annoyed more with Lucien than with the horse, rebuked the animal with a kick to the ribs. The horse tossed its head in affront. "And what if I'm not Obsidian Circle but my destination is still north?"

Lucien shrugged. "I'm listening. Explain."

"Gods, Lucien. I'm sick to death of this argument." She kicked her horse into a canter. Why did her plans never go the way she intended them to? If she'd just killed Lucien as ordered, her troubles would be over. She would ride home and be praised as a hero, even if the assassination didn't start the civil war they'd hoped for.

The problem was she was starting to second-guess herself. The more she thought about it, the more she feared the Circle would not see things the way she did. In theory, the Circle's purpose was to free Riorca. But for a lot of people, it was really more about killing Kjallans. What if she brought Lucien to the Circle and they decided they'd rather execute him than see him in command of an army opposing Cassian? Her efforts would have been wasted. Riorca would be no better off than it was before, and a man would die for no good reason.

Rhythmic hoofbeats behind her grew louder as Lucien caught up. "You seem touchy," he said. "Why? Guilty conscience?"

"I've been through a lot over the past few days," she said. "I've killed people. I've seen people killed. I've been—gods, never mind what all I've been through. I'm not in the mood to fight with you over this."

He spoke calmly. "I'm not fighting. I just want the truth."

She pulled up her horse. They'd reached the crossroads.

"Here's the truth, as much of it as I'm going to give you," said Vitala. "I'm going north. You can come with me, or you can go somewhere else. It's up to you."

He looked taken aback. Clearly he'd expected her to work harder to keep him with her. "What about my riftstone?"

"It stays with me."

His brows lowered. "That's not fair."

"Good-bye, Lucien." She sent her horse into a trot, taking the northern road toward Vesgar. To her irritation, Flavia did not follow her, but stayed behind with Lucien.

Vitala listened with increasing desperation for hoofbeats behind her, but they didn't come. Finally she looked back and saw Lucien and Flavia loping east, toward Worich.

12

She'd taken a risk. She knew that. Possibly a foolish risk, one the Circle would admonish her for. But what else was she supposed to do? She wasn't trained for this. She was trained to play Caturanga and to seduce and kill men, not kidnap them and haul them halfway across the country. This wasn't her area of expertise, and Lucien was no sapskull to be easily deceived.

She had to trust her Caturanga head. It told her that the board was better for Riorca with Lucien alive than dead. And surely Lucien would not leave his riftstone behind for long. He'd galloped away to call her bluff. When she didn't give in, he would come back. He needed her more than she needed him. She was risking only her reputation and standing with the Circle, but Lucien, a hunted man, risked his life.

She held her horse at a trot, not wanting to cover so much ground that Lucien couldn't catch up. He knew where she was. He could track her through his riftstone. Unfortunately, it didn't work the other way around. He could be following her right now, or he could be halfway to Worich. He could be lying dead on the roadside. She had no idea. If he wanted to, he could ambush her, though she doubted he would try. He knew she'd killed Remus, after all.

It was dusk when Vitala finally heard him cantering

up behind her. She hadn't realized how tense she'd been until she let her breath out and her whole body collapsed in relief. Her horse snorted, as if to say, *About time*.

But her relief soon turned to a fresh unease. If Lucien had ridden away and not returned, that would have been an embarrassing thing to explain to the Circle, but at least her role in these events would come to an end and she would no longer be responsible for what happened to him. Now the burden was solidly back on her. She held not only Lucien's fate in her hands, but possibly the fate of her entire country. If the Circle killed Lucien, his death would be on her conscience, Riorca would suffer, and she would never forgive herself.

Lucien rode alongside her in silence for a while, then said, "Your gambit is accepted."

Vitala chuckled, but her eyes swelled with unshed tears. This was the highest-stakes Caturanga game she'd ever played. She stretched her arm out to Lucien, and they clasped wrists. She glanced back and saw the dog was still with him.

Lucien grinned. "At least this way, I'll find out who you really work for."

"I'm not telling you."

"But I'll find out eventually, won't I?"

She nodded. "Eventually."

"So, you're heading north," he said conversationally. "Why am I not surprised?"

"Our enemies are south of us," she said. "Therefore, we're going north."

"And if we headed east, our enemies would be west of us."

Vitala smiled. "Eventually." She felt his eyes on her as they rode. She tolerated it for a while, but he just kept on looking. "Will you quit staring at me?"

"I see it now," said Lucien.

"See what?"

"The Riorcan in you."

"What?" Vitala turned to him, her surprise genuine, because she'd always thought she looked entirely Kjallan. "I'm not Riorcan."

"Based on your looks, I'd guess you're three-quarters Kjallan, one-quarter Riorcan. But if you're Obsidian Circle, you're probably half and half."

Vitala snorted. "I'm as Kjallan as you are."

He studied her again. "No, I don't think you are. It's subtle. I never would have noticed if I wasn't looking for it, but I see it now around your eyes, your mouth. It's part of your beauty, actually. A hint of the exotic."

Pleasure suffused her at the compliment—not that she hadn't been praised for her beauty before, but it meant more coming from him. She turned to thank him, but his eyes had gone glassy. He was looking straight at her, but without focus. "Lucien?"

No response. Lucien's horse slowed to a stop and tossed its head uncertainly.

Vitala turned her horse and reined up beside him. "Lucien?" Had his fever returned? No, surely not. He was warded now; she could see the threading. She placed a hand on his shoulder, which wasn't excessively warm, and shook him gently. "Lucien?"

His pupils contracted and he blinked. "What?"

"You went all strange just now. Like you couldn't see or hear me."

Lucien stared at her numbly, then wheeled his horse in a circle, scanning his surroundings. "We can't take this road. Not this section of it, anyway."

Vitala looked around, searching for whatever he'd seen, but there was nothing. Just a road and weedy farmland on either side. She saw no other travelers or even a house or barn. "But this is our route."

"We'll circle around and pick up the road farther north."

"Lucien, what trick are you playing?"

He frowned. "No trick. Didn't I say I'd go to your people?"

She didn't trust him; he had to be up to something. But when he took off at a gallop, circling wide around the field, she sent her horse after him, not sure what else to do.

A little over a mile later, they angled back and picked up the road again, with Vitala none the wiser about what they'd avoided behind them. She turned in her saddle and saw nothing but fields and road. At a loss, she sent her horse onward. In front of them, a cloud of dust resolved into a light carriage drawn by two grays. It passed by, creaking on its wheels. The driver, half-asleep on his box, lifted his cap at them.

"Was it rape?" asked Lucien, when the carriage was gone.

"What?" Vitala straightened in shock. Was he talking about Remus?

"Was your mother raped by a Kjallan soldier?"

Oh. "Gods, no."

"That's where most half-breeds come from."

"I'm not a half-breed," said Vitala. "And how rude of you to ask. I should slap you."

"Try it. You'll never land the blow." He grinned, taunting her.

Vitala gave him a dirty look. Why did he have to be a war mage?

"Look, I know why you're reluctant to talk," said Lucien. "The Circle and I aren't exactly friends. But I don't hold grudges, and if your people are willing to negotiate with me, I'll negotiate with them. The Circle is powerful. If they can put me back on the throne, I'll make concessions. Big ones."

"That's very interesting, but I don't know why you're talking to me about it," said Vitala.

Lucien rolled his eyes and fell silent.

In the town of Vesgar, they spotted a newsboy on a corner selling the *Imperial Herald* for a fifth tetral. Vitala bought one. She flipped it to the inner page, which had the most recent news, and read the headline EMPEROR LUCIEN MURDERED BY OBSIDIAN CIRCLE ASSASSINS. She glanced uncomfortably back at Lucien. At least there was no woodcut displaying his image.

His eyes narrowed, chiding her for drawing attention to him. He reached for the paper. "Go on and buy grain. I'll read."

"No, I'm reading it." Then she saw the smaller headline below it: IMPERIAL PRINCESS CELESTE WEDS CASSIAN NIKOLAOS. She bit her lip. "On second thought, you take it." She shoved the paper at him and hurried off.

When she returned from her errands, having bought food, grain for the horses, and warm blankets for Riorca's cold nights, an unusually somber Lucien handed her the folded paper. She felt she ought to say something to him—comfort him, perhaps? But what words could bring comfort? Anyway, they couldn't speak in the middle of Vesgar. They mounted and jogged their horses through the crowded streets until they'd cleared the city traffic, then sent the horses into a ground-eating canter. Vitala waited to speak until they pulled up their horses for a breather well outside of town. "What did the paper say?"

Lucien shrugged. "What I expected it to say. That Obsidian Circle assassins have murdered Emperor Lucien, and the imperial princess has taken a husband."

"Cassian."

Lucien nodded.

"You believe she was forced to marry?"

"Of course she was," snarled Lucien.

"How can you be sure?"

"She hates Cassian!"

"You said you didn't know her very well."

"I know her *that* well."

"I just want to consider every possibility," said Vitala. "Do you think Cassian . . ." She paused, trying to figure out how to word it delicately. "Do you suppose he consummated the marriage?"

Lucien was silent.

Vitala finally said, "I'm sorry. I shouldn't have—"

"It is against the law for Cassian to consummate the marriage," Lucien said softly. "At thirteen, Celeste is legally marriageable, but only for political purposes. He cannot take her to the marriage bed until her fifteenth birthday."

"I suppose that's some relief," said Vitala.

"No, it isn't. In stealing my throne and forcing my sister into marriage, Cassian has shown no respect whatever for Kjallan law. I have no reason to believe he'll honor this aspect of it. He hates me, and he hates her. She is in his power, and I fear he will inflict pain on her any way he can. I wish—" He looked over his shoulder, in the direction of the imperial city of Riat. Then he sighed. "Never mind."

Vitala rode in silence by his side. For the first time, a twinge of guilt throbbed within her for deceiving Lucien back at the camp rather than helping him to recover his throne. By forcing him into exile, she'd abandoned Celeste to who knew what fate.

Keep your eyes on the end goal, she reminded herself. She was here to free Riorca; that was all that mattered. Celeste was merely one more name in a long list of people who had suffered in pursuit of that goal. One day Vitala expected to be on that list herself.

She glanced back at Lucien, who was clutching his stomach as if he'd eaten bad fish, and frowned. It would be best if he could stop thinking about her, at least for a while. "So, why are they blaming your assassination on the Obsidian Circle?"

"Do you need to ask? You're always the scapegoat of choice."

"Not *me*. The Obsidian Circle."

Lucien managed a ghost of a grin. "I heard you."

Vitala waved away his baiting. Had this news reached her enclave? Unless their intelligence network told them otherwise, the Circle would take these lies at face value and believe her mission complete. Her stomach twisted. Had she completed her mission, she would have seen exactly the same headline, only it would be the truth. Would she have been proud of it?

She didn't feel proud now. "Stop playing games, Lucien, and answer my question. Why is Cassian blaming your so-called assassination on the Circle?"

"He has to blame it on somebody," said Lucien. "And the Circle is an easy target. Now he'll be able to justify his plan for Riorca."

Vitala turned to him, her throat tightening. "Which is?"

"Decimation."

"Of what? A village? An enclave?"

"Riorca," said Lucien.

"The entire country? *Why?*"

"Because he hates Riorca almost as much as he hates me and Celeste. And he's setting an example, same as he did in Tasox. This is what happens to people who cross him. Don't forget that Kjall is in economic crisis. There's a lot of anger, a lot of discontent, and he wants to focus that anger away from him and the imperial government. Riorca's a convenient scapegoat."

Vitala clenched the reins, causing the bay gelding to toss its head in irritation. She'd come within a hair's breadth of walking into a trap. Had she followed her orders to the letter and assassinated Lucien, this was what would have happened. No civil war, no freedom for Riorca. Instead, the worst sort of tyrant on the throne, and one in every ten Riorcans killed. Every last one of those deaths would have been her fault.

But she hadn't followed orders, so the situation was salvageable. Lucien was alive. She had evidence, physical evidence riding at her side, that the accusations against the Obsidian Circle were false. The Circle had saved Lucien, not assassinated him. She absolutely had to keep Lucien safe. Her people's lives depended on it.

"Your thoughts?" asked Lucien.

"Cassian's a right bastard," she spat.

Lucien snorted. "Besides the obvious."

"I'm glad I saved your life."

"Vitala, I'm loyal to my friends," said Lucien. "You rescued me at considerable risk to your own life, and that's why I trust you, even though my gut tells me you've been lying to me."

Vitala bit her lip. She couldn't keep her secret forever, and it was clear Lucien had already guessed it. He was just going to keep badgering her until she told the truth. "Look, what happened to my mother—it wasn't rape."

Lucien's ears pricked like those of a hound sighting its

quarry, and he kneed his horse closer to hers. "Did she lie with a Kjallan willingly?"

Vitala frowned. "Not exactly. I don't know what to call what she did."

"What happened?" asked Lucien.

"Do you know the Riorcan village of Iber?"

Lucien shrugged helplessly. "There are so many villages. . . ."

"It rebelled along with a string of other villages in the eastern foothills of the Ash Mountains, about twenty years ago."

"I was just a baby then," said Lucien.

"I wasn't yet born. Kjallan troops retook the villages. My father had been one of the rebels. He was maimed in the fighting and lost the use of his left arm. When Kjallans enslave a Riorcan village, they go through the populace and lay their death spells on everyone to trap them in slavery. And they execute anyone sickly or too crippled to provide useful labor."

Lucien nodded.

"The soldiers came to our door. My father tried to climb out a back window, but they'd surrounded the house and he was caught. My mother made a deal with the squad commander to save my father's life."

Lucien frowned, his expression darkening.

"The squad commander came to the house regularly. Sometimes he brought gifts—food, glows, medicines. It was a maddening situation for my father, but he had to put up with it. My mother was doing it for his sake, after all. When she became pregnant, they hoped my father's seed would predominate. Then I was born dark-haired, and they knew it hadn't."

"Why weren't you taken into the forest and exposed?" asked Lucien.

Her eyebrows rose. "You know about that?"

"I lived in Riorca for two years. Of course I know about it."

Vitala frowned. It was supposed to be a secret, that Riorcan parents exposed or otherwise disposed of dark-haired babies, as dark hair was a sure sign of impure blood. Kjallan law forbade it, but infants died often enough of natural causes that without mind mages to ascertain the truth, it was near impossible to prove that a family had killed one on purpose. "They would have exposed me, but the Kjallan squad commander would not permit it. He was reassigned to another battalion when I was two years old, and I suppose my parents could have killed me then, but by then my mother had become attached to me."

"Did you ever meet your father? The squad commander?"

She shook her head. "I suppose I would have seen him as a baby, but I have no memories of him."

"When did you join the Circle?"

"When I was eight years old," said Vitala. "I wish I'd joined sooner. My father—the Riorcan—hated me. My siblings wouldn't play with me, the villagers threw stones at me ..." She shut her eyes. She didn't like to think about those days.

"What's your role in the Circle? Spy? Assassin?"

"You don't need to know that," said Vitala. "My task is to bring you to the Circle in one piece."

Lucien smiled and motioned at his left leg. "Too late."

"Without any additional body parts missing."

Vitala's gelding tossed his head and sidestepped, a sign that his energy was returning. Vitala took the cue and sent him into a canter. Lucien followed, and they rode past several way posts in silence. When they slowed the horses for another rest, Lucien said, "Thank you for telling me the truth. I'm glad you're from the Circle. I want to make a deal with your people. Our interests are aligned."

"What sort of deal?"

"I need three things to retake my throne and recover Celeste. First, an army. Second, an intelligence network. Third, supplies for my troops. Food, clothes, ammunition."

Vitala's forehead wrinkled. The Obsidian Circle could not provide all that. Yet she didn't want to discourage him. Not until she'd delivered him to headquarters.

"The army I can manage on my own—" continued Lucien.

"How?" she blurted.

He glanced at her sidelong. "I have resources. But an intelligence network can't be established overnight. That's why I need the Circle. I also need supply lines set up from Riorca."

She raised her eyebrows. "What's in it for the Circle?"

"Freedom," he said. "Isn't that what your people want?"

Vitala twisted in her saddle. "You would free Riorca? Entirely free it? No more enslaved villages, no more tribute payments?"

"If Riorca puts me back on the throne? Yes."

"What about Riorcan slaves in Kjall? Will they be freed too?"

Lucien frowned. "Freeing all Riorcan slaves at once would devastate Kjall's economy, and it will already be suffering for losing the tribute payments. I'll speak to your leaders about it, but I can offer no guarantees."

Vitala nodded. That was disappointing, but his honesty about not being able to deliver absolutely everything suggested he was speaking in earnest. Maybe a schedule of staggered release could be worked out for the existing slaves. At any rate, the logistical issues couldn't dampen her spirits much. Imagine, a free Riorca! There needn't be a bloody rebellion, one probably doomed to fail; all her people had to do was help Lucien defeat Cassian. They could do that. Couldn't they?

But what was their assurance that Lucien would keep his promises? This could be a ruse on Lucien's part. He might accept Riorca's aid, use it to win back his throne and his sister, and then leave Riorca enslaved. Once he was back in power, what was to stop him from doing what he pleased? He'd never shown any predilection before for wanting to see Riorca freed.

Any arrangement made with Lucien would have to be based on trust. She was beginning to trust Lucien, a little bit, but could she trust him to the astonishing degree required for this plan?

13

In the evening, after she'd untacked the horses, Vitala spotted the distant Ash Mountains through the haze. Those mountains alone separated Riorca from her aggressive and much larger neighbor, and they were not much of a barrier. Centuries ago, Kjall had been a tiny nation on the southwestern coast of the continent of Issyv, home then to many small kingdoms. Kjall had swallowed up its neighbors one by one until the entire land mass south of the mountains was the Kjallan Empire. And then it had swallowed Riorca.

But Kjall wasn't invincible. Several years ago, Lucien's father, Emperor Florian, had tried to extend the Kjallan Empire overseas by attacking the island nation of Mosar. Florian's overreach had been a costly failure, leaving Lucien to pick up the pieces of a diminished empire. The debacle had emboldened Vitala's compatriots at the Obsidian Circle. If one could bloody the lion, could not one stab it in the heart and end its tyranny altogether?

Just over those mountains lay Vitala's homeland. And yet Riorca didn't feel so much like home anymore. It was a country that had never wanted her. A chill breeze ruffled the prairie grass, raising goose bumps on her arm. She was going to need warmer clothes. The wind was descending out of the north, rolling down from the mountains and curling about her toes, though whether it meant to welcome her back or warn her away, she could not tell.

Her bay gelding and Lucien's sorrel had finished their grain. She unclipped their nose bags and gave their hobbles a final check. With a good night slap on the shoulder for each animal, she turned to walk back to the campsite, only to run straight into Lucien.

"What do you want?" she said, flustered at being taken by surprise. He was staring at her with an odd expression. "Is something wrong?"

"You looked cold. I brought you a blanket." He held it up, not offering it to her but inviting her to come closer so he could wrap it around her.

She had a feeling that invitation involved more than just a blanket. Hair rose on the back of her neck, yet she stepped forward into the blanket's embrace—and into Lucien's arms. He drew her into him, surrounding her with warmth.

One of his hands cupped the nape of her neck, while the other tilted her chin upward. She parted her lips slightly and, without hesitation, Lucien covered them with his own. In the Imperial Palace, Lucien had smelled of lavender from the baths. Now he smelled earthier, horsier. His tongue teased her lips open, and his kiss was sweet, faintly reminiscent of the cheap ale they'd shared at a roadside tavern that afternoon.

She wrapped an arm around his shoulder, pulling him closer. His other hand, lightly callused, came up to stroke her face and neck as he deepened the kiss, then moved downward and lighted on her breast. His thumb found her nipple through the fabric of her syrtos and slid back and forth, sending little jolts of pleasure through her. Then it moved farther downward.

The young soldier.

She thrust him away. She couldn't afford to do this. It would only lead to trouble, to another vision. To problems she couldn't explain.

He blinked at her, surprised and hurt. "Is something wrong?"

"I'm sorry," she said. "I can't do this."

Lucien's mouth twisted. "Was it false, what happened between us in the tent? Were you acting on orders—spying on the emperor by sleeping with him?"

"It's not that. Look. Something happened—" The words caught in her throat. "I can't talk about it."

"Something happened when?" His brows rose in alarm. "Do you mean something happened in the tent, after they took me away? But I thought . . ." He hesitated. "You said you killed Remus."

Vitala shook her head. "I can't talk about it." She hurried away before he could ask any more questions.

Sweet pleasure flooded her as her lover moved inside her. His face was blurred, hard to make out, but she knew it had to be Lucien. He leaned down and kissed her. She moved with him, drowning in the sensations—

And awoke, flaming between her legs. She opened her eyes to darkness broken only by the faint orange glow of the banked campfire. She poked her head out of her bedroll just enough to see the stars up above, an act that exposed her to a gust of frigid night air and set her whole body to shivering, not that it helped at all with the other problem. By the stars' position, she could see it was several hours until dawn; she needed more sleep. In the state she was in, that wasn't going to be easy.

She sighed and crammed herself deeper into her bedroll, resigned to an hour or two of uncomfortable sleeplessness.

She heard a low moan and poked out her head again.

Flavia slept soundly, curled up in a ball, but on the other side of the campfire, Lucien thrashed in his bedroll. He moaned again. Vitala had a disturbing thought: could he be having the same dream she'd been having? Did that ever happen, shared dreams?

"Can't," he murmured thickly, followed by another round of thrashing. "No water. I need it."

No, not an erotic dream. That was a nightmare. She pitied him. She'd had her share of nightmares after Tasox too. What was that business about water? She considered waking him, but decided to leave him be. It would pass, and by morning he probably wouldn't remember it.

He gave a strangled cry. With a violent wrench, he rose from his bedroll and looked around, wild-eyed and frantic.

"It's all right," Vitala called to him.

He turned, fixing on her like a terrified rabbit.

"You were having a dream," she said softly.

Slowly, the fear drained away, to be replaced by embarrassment. "Did I wake you?" He ran a hand through sweaty, mussed hair.

Another spike of longing ran through Vitala. *Pox.* Just what she needed, Lucien looking handsome and beddable when she was too aroused to sleep. "No. I was already awake." Then, to head off any questions about what had been keeping her up, she added, "I've been having nightmares about Tasox too."

"Oh." He shook his head and collapsed back onto his bedroll. "That wasn't about Tasox."

"The attack by the Legaciatti?"

He chuckled darkly. "No."

"You said something about water."

He shuddered. "Never mind what it was." His bedroll rustled as he shifted position, and then went still.

She nestled back into her own bedroll. She wished she could invite him into her bedroll. It would be warmer that way, and they could comfort each other, stave off the nightmares. But it wasn't possible, given her problem with the visions.

Or was it? That night in the tent, she'd had a problem only when he'd entered her. What they'd done before had been fine. More than fine; she'd enjoyed it, and she could pleasure him in a similar way. The problem was going to be explaining that to him, telling him what she wanted and did not want, and hoping he didn't ask for an explanation. But then he'd already inferred there'd been some ugliness in the tent after he'd been dragged away. If she let him assume that was the reason for her preferences, she wouldn't have to tell him about the young soldier and the visions.

She flung the bedroll open and dragged herself out into the night air.

"Vitala?" Lucien's eyes were soft and dark in the moonlight.

She picked her way across the campsite, shivering in her chemise.

"Aren't you cold?" he asked.

"Extremely." She rubbed her arms. "Aren't you going to offer me a warm place to sleep?"

Wordlessly, he opened his bedroll.

She slipped into the snug space. Lucien wrapped his arms about her, entangled her legs in his, and closed the bedroll except for one small corner, leaving them in total darkness. "Better?"

"Still cold."

"Let's see what I can do about that." His lips feathered against hers in the darkness, and his hands slid under her chemise.

In the dark confines of the bedroll, Vitala could see nothing, and she knew him too little to predict where his hands would go. Her body prickled, sensitized to his touch. He disrobed her without urgency, removing the layers that separated them and pressing his hot skin against hers.

Aroused from her dream and impatient for more sensation, Vitala pressed her bared breasts against Lucien's warmth, and he reached for them with his hands. He deepened the kiss as he rubbed her nipple between his thumb and forefinger. She shivered.

"I hope you're not cold now," he said.

She felt like she was burning up inside. "Not at all."

He shifted, struggling in the tight confines to bring his mouth to her breast. The bedroll wasn't large enough for two people, and when he pressed her against the straining fabric and did something deliciously naughty with his tongue, she melted in his grasp, surprised to discover that instead of feeling trapped or constrained, she just felt excited. Her nether regions throbbed, and she gripped him possessively with her legs.

In response, he shifted again, this time positioning himself to enter her. Alarmed, Vitala stiffened.

He went still. "Are you all right?"

"Not exactly," Vitala stammered. She'd come very close to forgetting herself. "Something did happen in the tent."

Lucien lowered himself to her side and kissed her. "Don't apologize. It's not your fault."

"Can we do . . . something else?"

"What did you have in mind?"

Vitala's cheeks warmed. "Maybe what you did before in the tent."

Lucien chuckled. "Liked that, did you? I don't think there's enough room in this bedroll. But I can make you happy another way." His exploring hand worked its way downward. His finger found the nub that was the center of her pleasure and circled it with exquisite gentleness. Vitala pressed herself into him. "You're wet for me," he said, covering her mouth with his own.

As her body moved in an involuntary rhythm, Lucien's hard length pressed against her hip. He had gone unsatisfied that night in the tent, and Vitala did not want that to happen again. As she took him in her hand, a growl pulsed from his throat. She knew how to bring a man efficiently to his peak, but Lucien was building her pleasure slowly, and she matched his pace, reveling in every moan she could elicit from him. They fell into a rhythm, a dance of give-and-take shaped by the fluttering of their pulses, the quickening of their breaths, and the movements of their bodies.

It was a dance, she realized with some surprise, that she enjoyed. Before Lucien, pleasuring a man had been nothing more than a dull, even mildly unpleasant task, a means to an end—sometimes an untimely end, in the case of her partner. But if sex with Lucien was a new and different experience, that didn't mean anything. She wasn't emotionally involved. He was attractive, and he was good in bed—there was nothing more to it than that—and she was no longer on a mission to assassinate him. Why shouldn't she enjoy him while she could?

Pleasure seeped languidly through her, from the core of her body into the farthest reaches of her fingers and toes, building from a trickle to a delicious and almost unbearable torrent. Lucien gripped her and drove her through a release that pulled a cry from her throat, turning her limbs to liquid and her mind to glass. He finished alongside her almost simultaneously, drawn into his peak by the excitement of hers.

Afterward she slept, snug and warm in Lucien's arms, and did not wake again until dawn.

Vitala was not aware of exactly where the border was between Kjall and Riorca, but when she rode into the thickly forested village of Nihenny and saw the pit houses, she knew she'd crossed it. The houses were squat, sunk into the ground to take advantage of the earth's natural warmth. Some of them rose no higher than her head. A crude stairway led down to each home's front door.

In Riorca, there were "living" villages and "dead" villages. In dead villages, every Riorcan citizen had been infected with a death spell that would kill them if not held in abeyance daily by a Kjallan Healer. Kjallans lived among the Riorcans, directing their daily work, and Riorcan culture was nearly obliterated. The enslaved Riorcans wore Kjallan dress, spoke the Kjallan language, and, like the Kjallans, were made to honor the Soldier above the other two gods, though Riorcan theology viewed the Three as perennially squabbling equals.

Nihenny was a living village, poor because of the crushing tributes but with its culture intact. There were no Kjallans about, and the villagers wore Riorcan peasant tunics. Pigs rooted in the streets but fled as their horses approached, disappearing into the forest that loomed on both sides and stretched overhead, the high branches grasping like claws. The stairways of the pit houses were crumbling and most of the roofs were missing shingles, but the roads were in good repair. That last part was to the Kjallans' credit; they meticulously maintained roads in case they needed to move their troops somewhere in a hurry.

In the central square, Vitala saw evidence of Kjallan presence—two stakes mounted in the ground, quite old, since the corpses they'd once supported were now heaps of bones lying in the dirt. The villagers did not challenge Vitala and Lucien as they rode, but scurried out of their way, sending them nasty looks.

Vitala sympathized. She and Lucien looked Kjallan—indeed, between them they were three-quarters Kjallan—and the horses they rode were a clear sign they didn't belong here. There were only a few places in Riorca where grain could be grown to support horses, and all of them had been claimed by the Kjallan occupiers. For these Nihenny villagers, who eked out a living cultivating spinefruit in the forest, Kjallans on horseback meant nothing but trouble.

"They hate you as much as they hate me," whispered Lucien, pulling his horse up alongside hers.

Vitala shrugged. "They don't know who I am."

"Has it occurred to you that you make a better Kjallan than you do a Riorcan? These people don't want you."

Though his words pained her, she could not deny their truth. She'd found more acceptance among the Kjallans she'd met on the Caturanga circuit than she'd ever experienced among her own people—the Circle excepted, of course. "You couldn't pay me to be Kjallan."

"Are we so terrible?"

"Yes. Look what you've done to this village. Your tributes are crushing it."

"Was it better off before we arrived? You don't know."

Vitala rolled her eyes. "Of course it was better off when it didn't have to pay tribute."

"That's your assumption," said Lucien. "But you don't know, because when this village was taken, you weren't born. I wasn't born either. I wasn't the one who ordered the taking of Riorca. Nor was it my father. It was *his* father, and it happened before my father was even born."

She sniffed. "That's not a lineage I'd be proud of."

"Are you proud of yours?"

Her cheeks flamed. Furious, she kicked her horse into a trot.

He cantered to catch up with her. "I'm sorry, Vitala. I shouldn't have said that. The point I was trying to make is I had nothing to do with this. I was born to it, as you were born to be what you are."

"It isn't fate, Lucien. You made choices. You held the imperial throne for four years. You could have helped Riorca during that time."

"No, I couldn't have."

She snorted.

"Vitala, you don't understand the complexity of managing an empire. If I'd begun my reign by freeing Riorca or even lowering the taxes, when I was having trouble just paying the troops their wages, I'd have been out on my ear in less than a month."

"So you were out on your ear after four years, having accomplished nothing. What good was that?"

"At least I spared your people from what Cassian will do to them, if only for four years."

"You're no better than Cassian. What about Stenhus? That village was massacred on your orders."

"Stenhus rebelled, and I ordered in troops to put down the rebellion. That was my job, Vitala. That's what emperors *do*. I could hardly have ignored an uprising."

"But after your troops put down the rebellion, they massacred half the citizens!"

Lucien looked pained. "I had been emperor less than half a year. I trusted the judgment of the battalion commander, Secundus, and gave him the authority to handle the situation as he saw fit. If you must know, I was furious over the unnecessary brutality, and I later removed Secundus from command. And the reason I went to Tasox personally to handle the bandit situation was because I didn't want something like that to happen again."

They'd passed the last set of pit houses of Nihenny and reentered the forest, which the Kjallans had meticulously pruned back from the road. Vitala laid heels to her horse, forcing an end to the conversation. The problem with Lucien was that the more she listened to him, the more he made sense.

14

Lucien clucked encouragement to the sorrel gelding as it picked its way up the rocky mountainside. With so many loose stones on the path, this was the perfect place for the creature to pick one up in its hoof, and the last thing he needed in this remote wilderness was a lame horse. He was also on the lookout for wolfsign. While Riorcans exterminated any wolves that descended into the lowlands, there were still packs in the higher elevations that might see a horse as a tempting meal.

Vitala's bay was struggling up a steep rise just ahead. Lucien hoped she knew where she was going. This morning, after several days of winding their way through the twisty forest, they'd emerged from the tree cover into this desolate, rocky landscape in the middle of nowhere. Flavia, at least, was taking it in stride. She'd run ahead of the horses, guessing at their path, and was waiting for them to catch up.

Most Kjallans who visited Riorca saw it as wild and primitive, but Lucien knew better. Though it was sparsely populated, with its forests intact, Riorca was as fully cultivated as Kjall. When his people had first conquered it, they'd driven out the Riorcans along the southern border, cleared the forests, and established farms. But what crops they could convince to come out of the ground at all grew to half height, anemic and sickly. His people, starving, had abandoned the settlements in desperation.

Riorcan soil was unsuitable for farming, at least by Kjallan methods. But the Riorcans knew how to coax a yield out of it. Spinefruit grew in the shade of the forest, never in direct sunlight. The plants were fragile and the fruit slow to mature—a tiny green spinefruit took two years to reach its full size and turn yellow, and during its green stage, it was poisonous. Riorcans cultivated spinefruit bushes all throughout the forest, planting and fertilizing and weeding them by hand. The forest looked wild, but it wasn't. It was an enormous farm. It had taken his people some time to understand that.

Two years of living in Riorca had lessened his contempt for the Riorcans and replaced it with a grudging admiration. They were a tough, rugged people, impossible to fully subjugate. His people had occupied Riorca for generations, and still pockets of rebellion persisted, not to mention the gods-cursed Obsidian Circle. Riorcans were pragmatic and often ruthless. Vitala, despite her Kjallan looks, was a perfect example of her race.

His sorrel, a little more agile than Vitala's bay, catapulted up the rise, landing him beside Vitala on the rime-encrusted path. "I just love Riorca at this time of year," he commented. "It's so wonderfully windy and frigid."

She eyed him narrowly.

"And then there's the food. Spinefruit and dried fish. Every single day."

Her lips puckered just a little. She was amused and trying not to show it. He was getting to her little by little. She was like a spinefruit herself: hard and spiny on the outside; soft on the inside. It was getting past the spines that was the challenge.

His horse halted abruptly, having nearly collided with Vitala's. She'd stopped to stare at a featureless cliff face. He stared at it too, trying to see what she was seeing. "Are there code words there or something?"

She looked up as if startled. "Yes, for those who know how to read them." She clucked to her horse and turned left. Flavia, who'd run ahead in the wrong direction, corrected course and scampered past her.

Lucien followed, apprehensive. He was taking a huge risk following Vitala into the hands of the people who hated him most. But if he wanted to retake his throne, he needed the Circle's resources. And they needed him too. While Vitala seemed to be lying about a few things, he didn't think she would outright betray him. Not to his death, else why would she have saved him in the first place?

The enclave had moved since her last visit, but if Vitala had read the signs correctly, this narrow canyon was their current location. She walked her horse straight into it. Lucien hung back a moment, then followed. She couldn't blame him for hesitating; the canyon was a natural ambush point.

"Wait here," she said. "Give them a moment to recognize us."

Lucien gazed about him in all directions, silent.

She couldn't see the lookout, but by now the enclave was surely aware of them. "We should be safe now," she said, and urged her horse farther into the canyon.

The hoofbeats of Lucien's horse echoed hollowly behind her.

As they rounded a curve, an opening appeared in the cavern wall, large enough to admit a horse. She entered it, followed by Lucien. Three shadows passed across the mouth of the cave, cutting off their retreat. Obsidian Circle agents—she was among friends.

"Vitala . . ." murmured Lucien.

"It's all right." She hopped off her horse. A man and a woman came forward and took the reins of both geldings. "We're home."

Lucien climbed carefully from the saddle, lowering his crutch to catch himself.

"He's with me," Vitala told the three men, who formed a rough circle around Lucien. "A friend. He's not armed."

Another man appeared at the other end of the cavern. "Vitala, is that you?"

"Bayard!" As happy as she was to see a familiar face, a knot formed in her gut. She was not at all certain that her old mentor would approve of the way she'd handled this mission. Still, she had to project confidence. She strode to him boldly and clasped wrists. He looked good. His blond hair was graying a little—fading, almost—but he was lean and well muscled, no doubt still spending much of his time in the training room.

"Congratulations are in order," said Bayard. "Your mission was a success."

"Actually," said Vitala, "about that . . . I have someone to introduce you to." She glanced at wary-eyed Lucien.

"I always said you were my star," said Bayard. "I knew you'd be the one to get the job done. It hasn't started the war we were hoping for, but give it time."

Vitala said, "I didn't kill Lucien."

Bayard's forehead wrinkled in confusion. "Our sources say he's dead. Are you saying it wasn't you?"

She turned and indicated Lucien. "I mean he isn't dead. Cassian tried to kill him in a palace coup, and I rescued him. He's standing right there."

Bayard turned and stared.

"I have a proposal for you," said Lucien. "One that could save Riorca."

Bayard gaped and signaled his men.

"No!" cried Vitala. "He's on our side! He came willingly!"

The three agents grabbed Lucien and flung him to the ground. Flavia barked furiously.

"Quiet that dog, or I'll quiet it for you," said Bayard.

"Flavia!" she called, uncertain the dog would respond, since Lucien was the one who snuck her food from his plate and threw sticks for her to retrieve. But she came immediately, pressing against Vitala's leg and looking up with a whine.

Bayard smiled grimly.

Vitala grabbed his arm as he stalked toward Lucien. "Listen to me! Lucien is our ally. Cassian's men tried to kill him. Their plan was to blame the assassination on the Obsidian Circle and punish Riorca by decimating it. All of it, Bayard. The entire country!"

Bayard turned to her. "Where did you hear this?"

"From Lucien," she said, wincing at how weak that sounded.

"Ah." Bayard turned away and strode to where Lucien lay pinioned by three guards, his face pressed into the rocky cave floor. "Bind his hands."

"Are you listening?" Vitala grabbed Bayard's shoulder and turned him to face her. "We can't allow any harm to come to Lucien. We need him alive to prove that the Circle is innocent." She turned to Lucien, whose wrists had been yanked behind his back and were being tied together. "I'm sorry. This wasn't supposed to happen."

Lucien coughed, expelling a mouthful of dirt.

"Prove it to who?" asked Bayard. "Cassian's lackeys?

You must realize Cassian will oust the existing battalion commanders and replace them with his own men. He may already have done so."

"There are ways to get the word out," choked Lucien. "I have an idea—" One of the guards kicked him in the stomach, and his words ended in a gasp.

Anger boiled within Vitala. Her fist curled instinctively as if to produce a Shard. She advanced toward the guard, who, catching the look in her eyes, backed away.

Bayard stepped between them. "Gudrik, do not harm the prisoner again. Vitala, control your temper."

Vitala stared balefully at Gudrik, then turned to Bayard. "Lucien will be our ally in figuring out how to thwart Cassian. He has the connections, he has the knowledge, and he's as motivated as we are to see the man removed from power. If we help him take back his throne, he'll free Riorca."

Bayard laughed. "Is that what he told you? He'd free Riorca? Vitala, did this man put something in your food?"

Gudrik and the others chuckled.

"It's the truth," rasped Lucien.

"Vitala, that was a wild promise of desperation," said Bayard. "This man is out of power. He knows that Cassian sharpens a stake for him, and he'll say anything to save himself. What has he ever done for Riorca? Nothing."

Vitala could hardly contradict him; Bayard had zeroed in on the flaw in her argument. Yes, Lucien had not helped Riorca when he had the opportunity. Yes, his motives were questionable. But her gut told her that the Caturanga board had changed more than Bayard realized, and Lucien was more trustworthy than the Circle gave him credit for. An alliance with Lucien was chancy, but less so than Bayard believed, and the rewards were potentially so great that it was a risk worth taking. "Bayard, what if he's telling the truth? We can't squander this opportunity. It could save Riorca. And what's the alternative? We do nothing, hiding away in our caves while Cassian decimates our people?"

"We don't do *nothing*," said Bayard. "We interrogate this man. If he's truly the former emperor, he's the richest source of intelligence we've ever had within these walls. Gudrik, clear a room."

"Yes, Bayard."

Vitala grabbed Bayard's arm. "No! There's nothing to be gained by an interrogation. Make a friend of Lucien, and he'll tell you everything you need to know. But if you hurt him, you may forever spoil any chance of our forging an alliance with him."

Bayard removed her hands from his arm and gestured to the remaining guards, who hauled Lucien to his feet. "This alliance you propose has no value to the Circle, but the information this man carries does. Vitala, I have the utmost respect for you as an assassin and field agent. But we're in enclave headquarters, and I give the orders here."

Lucien found himself half dragged, half carried through a hallway of rough, damp stone. He turned his head, trying to catch a glimpse of Bayard and Vitala behind him. They were arguing furiously, Vitala continuing to plead for his freedom, but it didn't seem to matter; she had no power here. Gods, why had he trusted her?

The hallway ended in a natural cavern, rather like an air bubble blown into the rock. Indeed, the entire compound seemed to be a natural cave system, unaltered by any stoneworker but simply cleared out, equipped with crude doors, and furnished. Although *furnished* was an exaggeration in this case; the room contained only a single crude, wooden chair. Streaks of green, gray, and ochre stained the craggy walls.

The guards shoved him into the chair. They bound his arms to the seat back and his right leg to the right chair leg. They stared at his wooden leg for a moment, uncertain what to do with it, and finally just left it free.

"Leave us," ordered Bayard. There had been only a handful of guards to begin with, but during their walk to the interrogation they'd picked up several more, as well as a few men and women and a teenage girl in Riorcan peasant tunics. They looked like civilians, but they had to be Obsidian Circle agents of some kind. Whoever they were, they left at Bayard's order, along with all but two of the guards, whom Bayard gestured at to stay. Someone slipped a loop of rope around Flavia's neck and led her away. But Vitala folded her arms stubbornly when Bayard told her to go, which was a relief. Her presence, he felt, extended him a sort of protective aura.

Bayard began stripping off his outer tunic.

"Look," Lucien said quickly. "This isn't necessary. We may have once been enemies, but we'd be fools to nurse old grudges when we can accomplish more by working together. My interests and the Obsidian Circle's are aligned—"

"What would you know of the Obsidian Circle's interests?" Bayard cast an accusatory look at Vitala, who frowned at him, rejecting the insinuation that she'd been airing Obsidian Circle secrets.

"They are common knowledge," said Lucien. "You seek Riorcan freedom."

"And you seek to recover the Kjallan throne," said Bayard. "These goals are not the same."

"We have a common enemy in the usurper Cassian, who stole my throne and plans to decimate your people. Help me regain my throne, and I will free Riorca."

Bayard snorted. "Empty promises born of desperation. You don't know our true interests."

"Then tell me what you want. I'll—" Lucien cut off his own words, because his magic told him the blow was coming, even though Bayard was too skilled a combatant to telegraph it physically. He couldn't dodge the blow entirely, not tied as he was, but he twisted his head, and Bayard's callused knuckles glanced off his chin instead of breaking his nose.

"Bayard!" cried Vitala. "Stop!"

Lucien's chin throbbed dully with a pain he knew would worsen later. He worked his jaw, verified it wasn't broken.

Bayard leaned over him in a classic pose of intimidation, his hands resting on the arms of the chair. Lucien's flesh prickled at his nearness. "You think this is a negotiation? It's not. It's an interrogation. From now on, you will be silent except when you are answering my questions."

"Bayard, this is—" he began, then stopped as his war magic warned him again. Bayard grabbed him by the hair and yanked his head back. Lucien twisted frantically, using the full force of his magically enhanced strength to try to free himself, but Bayard, wise to the tactics of war mages, moved with him, using the grip on his hair to track him rather than hold him still. Lucien knew where the blow would come from but could do nothing about it. It smashed into his nose with a sickening crack. His mind reeled, and his vision fuzzed around the edges, darkening almost to blackness. Then there was shouting, and Bayard's hand was torn painfully from Lucien's hair. Lucien shook his head, then regretted the motion, as it set everything to throbbing. He tasted blood and opened his eyes—no, they were already open. His vision was returning. He coughed, spat out a mouthful of blood, and tried to make sense of the blur around him.

Bayard was on the ground and Vitala was on top of him. He thought his eyes must be playing tricks on him, because the scene was ludicrous. Bayard was so much bigger than she; he could have flung her off easily. But he lay passive and still, taking shallow, frightened breaths. Looking closer, Lucien saw that Vitala held something tiny and dark to his throat. A trail of blood tracked its way down the man's neck.

The shouting hurt his ears. He could hardly make sense of it. The guards were shouting at Vitala. Bayard was shouting at the guards. But Vitala was silent, her mouth a hard, thin line.

"Get back! Get back!" cried Bayard. "She's got a Shard. Don't threaten her!"

A Shard? Lucien looked closer. Was that the tiny black thing piercing Bayard's throat? Her knife and her two pistols sat at her belt within easy drawing range, yet they were untouched. When she'd wanted a weapon, she'd reached not for one of them, but for this Shard.

"Vitala . . ." said Bayard placatingly.

"I'll kill you," snarled Vitala. "You touch him again, and I release the death spell."

The hair rose on the nape of Lucien's neck. He'd never seen Vitala like this. When she'd fought at the bonfire, she'd been cool and dispassionate. Now her whole body trembled with rage. On a ship in a storm, he'd seen a hawser pulled so tight it quivered and hummed under impossible strain, until finally it broke. Vitala was like that hawser, poised just shy of the breaking point, tense and fragile and dangerous all at once.

"Haven't we been friends?" said Bayard in a tremulous voice. "Did I not save you from a family you hated and bring you someplace better?"

Vitala spat in his face.

A lump bobbed in Bayard's throat. "All right. I'll end the interrogation. Someone will see to Lucien's injuries—"

"A Healer," said Vitala.

"Yes, a Healer will see to Lucien's injuries. Let me up and take that Shard out of my neck, and we'll discuss this later, when our tempers aren't running so high."

"You have to promise me he won't be harmed. If you hurt him again, I'll kill you." She looked around the room, catching the eye of the two guards, both of whom recoiled from her gaze. "I'll kill anyone who hurts him."

"I promise," said Bayard. "He will not be harmed. Let me up, Vitala. Please."

Vitala removed the tiny, dark object from Bayard's throat, hid it in her fist, and stood. Bayard got up next and brushed himself off. "Well?" he snapped at one of the guards. "You heard the orders. Fetch the Healer for Lucien." He turned to Vitala. "Go and calm yourself. I'll do the same, and we'll discuss this later."

15

Vitala lay on the bed in her room, staring at the cracks in the wall. As a child, she had often done this, stared at the cracks in the wall and made up stories about them, imagining them to be animals and people and places. But those were different cracks, in a different location. The enclave had been in this cave for only a couple of years, and she'd spent most of that time on the Caturanga circuit. These were not her old friends. What could she make of them? The nearest one looked like a broken window, the one near the corner like a human face. The one by the chair looked like a bloodstain, spreading and spreading until . . .

She squeezed her eyes shut. What was wrong with her? Could she see nothing but destruction and ruin?

"Are you all right, Miss Salonius?" piped a timorous voice from the girl in the chair.

"I'm fine." It had been Bayard's idea to have her watched by a twelve-year-old. He knew Vitala wouldn't do anything crazy in the presence of a child. But the girl didn't know that, poor thing. She was an assassin in training under Bayard's tutelage and named Estelle, if Vitala remembered right. She was cute and innocent; it would be a few years yet before the ugly part of her training began.

Vitala sighed and rolled over onto on her stomach,

propping her chin on folded arms. She'd never before noticed the enclave's bleakness. Raw stone walls; crude wooden furniture. When an enclave moved, it typically left any furniture behind; the Circle possessed little in the way of pack animals, and carts could not navigate the rough mountain paths. Lumber was plentiful in Riorca, and support staff would quickly build new furniture at the new location, but the hurried, uncaring construction showed. The chair Estelle sat on was creaky and bristled with splinters. The legs on Vitala's bed were so uneven that she could rock the structure back and forth. The Imperial Palace had spoiled her, not only with its beauty, but with its sense of permanence. Here everything was temporary, neither valued nor cherished.

The door handle clicked. *Bayard.*

Estelle scooted to the edge of her chair in eager anticipation of her rescuer, while Vitala stared at the door with dread.

He entered. "Estelle, thank you. You may go."

The girl leapt from her chair and fled through the open door.

"Vitala." Bayard shut the door. "I'm sorry about earlier. We both acted rashly."

That was her cue to return the apology, but she only regarded Bayard stonily. She would not apologize for defending Lucien, nor for stopping Bayard from an ill-conceived act that might have spoiled Riorca's chances for a better future.

After a moment of awkward silence, Bayard said, "I've spoken to the prisoner."

Vitala gasped. "You promised you wouldn't—"

He held up his arms. "I said I wouldn't touch him and I didn't. I only wanted to see what questions he would answer voluntarily, and he was quite forthcoming."

"I told you. He was forthcoming because he's not our enemy."

"Mm." Bayard shook his head slightly. "He's not our friend either, but I didn't come here to argue about that. Shall we debrief? I heard a few details about what you've been through from Lucien, and it sounds like you've increased your kill count." He smiled. "Ista will be envious."

Vitala waved her hand, denying that. "Isn't her kill count nine already?" She took a deep breath and told the story of her mission, beginning with the day she met Remus on the docks of the imperial city. Bayard listened without apparent emotion at first, but his eyebrows went up at her description of the fighting in Lucien's tent and at the bonfire, particularly her encounter with Remus. The events at Tasox shocked him. The news of the town's near destruction had not yet reached the enclave.

"Your tale is astonishing," said Bayard. "I'm sorry for the loss of our agents in Tasox."

"I know." Vitala felt a pang, thinking of the sweetly indomitable Hanna and Glenys. "And their deaths were so senseless. Lucien grieved for them too."

"I'll speak with the enclave leaders about getting someone else out there quickly."

"There's something else about them. The dog was theirs, and because of some hints they dropped, I believe it may be a Riorcan dog."

"We've no Riorcan dogs, not any longer. The Kjallans wiped them out."

"Glenys said the bloodline had survived, hidden away. Will you make inquiries with the other enclaves, see if Flavia is one of those survivors?"

He shrugged. "I'll ask around. It sounds like you had six kills on this mission, all of them incidentals. Remus, the Warder, the two sentries at the bonfire, and the two Legaciatti guarding Lucien. Am I right?"

She nodded. "Yes, six."

"Did you collect any riftstones for us?"

She made a face. "Only the Warder's." She pulled it from her pocket and placed it in Bayard's hand. "I would have taken more, but we were in a hurry."

"I understand," said Bayard.

Vitala's heart twisted at his look of disappointment. She'd spent so much of her life trying to please this man. Later, that desire had worn off—so she'd thought—but it seemed some small part of her still wanted to make him proud. Then she remembered something. "Wait. I have the loros."

"The imperial loros? You're joking."

"No. It's in one of the saddlebags."

"How did you carry it such a distance without attracting thieves?"

Vitala shrugged. "It was just in the saddlebag. Nobody knew."

Bayard shook his head in wonder. "I'll fetch it directly. Well, you've gone from one kill to seven in a single mission. Or perhaps eight. I'm wondering if I shouldn't count Lucien. You didn't kill him, but you did bring him to us, and I think that may be the greater achievement. It's obvious you could have killed him at any time, if you'd chosen to."

"Don't count Lucien," said Vitala. "Leave it at seven." Counting Lucien as a kill might make it look as if she were giving up on him, which she had no intention of doing.

Bayard frowned. "Very well. Now, about this morning—"

"Listen," said Vitala. "You've got to let Lucien go.

Stop treating him as a prisoner and open negotiations. He claims he can raise an army—"

"I find that hard to believe."

She shrugged. "Either he can do it or he can't. If he can't, then he's a powerless fugitive and no threat to us. If he can, then he's an ally of great importance."

Bayard shook his head. "Lucien is not and never will be an ally to Riorca."

"His interests and ours are aligned—"

"Vitala!" His voice grew sharp. "You are not thinking clearly, and the reason is obvious. You did what an assassin is never supposed to do. You fell in love with your target."

Vitala blinked at him, shocked at that possible truth. *Was* she in love with Lucien? No, surely not. She was sleeping with him, and she found him attractive, but that wasn't love. Or was it? How would she know, when she'd never been in love?

Bayard spoke gently. "We all know how it happens. You studied this man for years. Fixated on him, as an assassin must. For nearly a decade, he occupied your thoughts, and then you finally met him. You were nervous and excited, and you mistook your intense feelings—"

"No." She shook her head. "That's not what happened. I'm not in love with Lucien." Bayard's words cut deeply. They couldn't be true. She'd always prided herself on her professionalism. She would never allow personal feelings to cloud her judgment.

"He was too crippled to overpower you physically, so he came at you another way—charmed his way past your defenses, made an ally out of you, got you to plead his ridiculous case. He's a clever boots, I'll grant him that—"

"Bayard—"

" — but he's not worth an iota of our respect or consideration. He's poison, Vitala, toxic as an undergrown spinefruit. For what he's done to you alone, I'd gladly beat him to death."

"Bayard, you cannot!"

"I've promised not to touch him, and I'll keep my word. But maybe you'll change your mind later, when his influence over you begins to wane. I think you'll soon realize how much he's lied and taken advantage of you."

"What about Cassian and his plan to decimate Riorca for our supposed assassination of the emperor? At the very least, we must prove him a liar by producing Lucien alive," said Vitala.

"Do you believe Cassian will call off his plans for decimation if we prove that Lucien lives?"

Vitala considered. "No. But it's not Cassian we're trying to reach. It's the Kjallan people. If we show them the truth, they'll know Cassian lied to them, that he seized the throne under false pretenses. They may refuse to carry out his orders, maybe even rise up against him."

"Mm," said Bayard. "I think Kjallans like the lie. They want someone to blame their troubles on, and vilifying Riorca has always been Kjall's favorite sport. How many people can even identify Lucien on sight? We might be accused of producing a false emperor."

"I'm sure there are people who know Lucien well and could vouch that he's the real man."

Bayard shook his head. "There *were* such people. Cassian will remove them from power, discredit them, or have them killed."

Vitala bit her lip in exasperation. Every solution she produced, Bayard found flaws in. "What can we do?"

"Consider this," said Bayard. "The Circle had trouble stirring up rebellion under Lucien's rule. He was a status quo emperor; he neither improved our situation nor made it worse. Our people are suffering, but they're not suffering so badly that they're willing to risk their lives and their families in rebellion. Cassian, on the other hand, is aggressively targeting Riorca for punishment. It's a deflection tactic so that the Kjallans turn a blind eye to other abuses, and our people will not stand for the random, ruthless executions of decimation." Bayard's eyes glinted. "Vitala, I think we shall finally have war."

She stared at him, horrified. "Is that what you want? An emperor worse than Lucien, one who will drive our people into such despair that they'll throw their lives away in rebellion?"

"They won't be *throwing them away*." Bayard folded his arms. "You've never had any illusions about the Circle, Vitala. You know that our goal is to free Riorca, whatever it takes. Our methods may not be noble or honorable. We're fighting an enemy far more powerful than ourselves. Honor is a luxury we cannot afford."

Vitala lowered her head. She knew this was true; she'd accepted it long ago. Why else would she have agreed to devote her life to dealing out death? "I know. What will be done with Lucien?"

"I've summoned the leaders from two other enclaves. They'll be here in a few days, and we'll discuss what to do with him. This is too big a decision for a single enclave to make."

"May I make my case to the other enclave leaders for allying ourselves with Lucien?"

"I wish you wouldn't," said Bayard. "It will do you no credit. But if you insist, you may speak on his behalf."

"Thank you."

He nodded. "Before I go, there's one more thing I must ask of you."

"What?" asked Vitala.

"I understand you're carrying Lucien's riftstone, which means his war magic is still active from proximity. As you know, we have no proper facilities for keeping prisoners. All we can do is restrain Lucien and place guards over him, and I'd feel better about that if we could at least deprive him of his war magic. I need that riftstone."

"What are you going to do with it?"

"Send it to another enclave for safekeeping."

Vitala shivered. While she was certain Bayard was not lying when he said Lucien's fate would be discussed and decided in a meeting of enclave leaders, she was equally certain that Bayard had no intention of ever freeing Lucien or accepting him as an ally. So where did that leave her? Where did it leave Lucien? If she let the riftstone go, it severed too many options. Lucien would lose his magic permanently; she'd never be able to recover the stone.

She reached into her pocket, pulled out a broken chain with a yellow topaz riftstone, and placed it in Bayard's hand.

His hand closed over it. "Thank you," he said gently.

It was Remus's riftstone.

Vitala spent the next few hours staring at the cracks in the wall and thinking. One thing she knew for sure: she couldn't let the Circle's shortsightedness spoil Riorca's best chance for freedom.

Approaching footsteps startled her out of her reverie, and she looked up to see Ista scowling in her doorway. "Kill count *seven*? What'd you do, take out Lucien's entire personal guard?"

Vitala smiled, flushing with pleasure at the backhanded praise. Somehow Ista still intimidated her, though she shouldn't. They were equals now, both proven and accomplished assassins. They had much in common. Ista, like Vitala, was a dark-haired Kjallan/Riorcan half-breed, rejected by her family and village. She was shorter than Vitala, but just as appealing to men if not more so, with her curvier, larger-breasted body and an outgoing personality that captivated her victims. Bayard said Vitala and Ista were different types, that Vitala would appeal more to aristocrats and Ista more to commoners, but from what Vitala had seen, Ista was capable of seducing any man she chose. If Ista had possessed Vitala's Caturanga skills, she would likely have been the one assigned to kill the emperor.

"It was complicated," Vitala answered. "I didn't actually kill Lucien. I rescued him from a palace coup, and I killed four Legaciatti and two sentries in the process."

Ista looked closely at Vitala's hands. "And you used only three Shards?"

Vitala nodded. She wiggled her fingers, relaxing her mind just enough to see the contact points for her seven remaining Shards. Sometimes she forgot that they weren't invisible to absolutely everyone; other ward-breakers, like Ista, could see them or even break them. She'd actually used only two during the mission. The third missing Shard was the one she'd pulled on Bayard.

"I heard the former emperor is imprisoned here," said Ista.

"Have you seen him?" Vitala asked eagerly.

"No. They won't let me in."

Vitala nodded, unsurprised. Obsidian Circle assassins were rarely permitted to show themselves to enclave visitors; they needed their anonymity preserved. It made for a lonely existence—the assassins had only the enclave staff and each other. For that reason, it was sad that she and Ista had never struck up a friendship. The difference in their ages had been a barrier. Ista was four years older and had been so much more advanced in her training. She had ignored Vitala, just as Vitala now ignored younger girls like Estelle. Later, when they had both been fully qualified assassins, they'd kept their distance through a petty rivalry that now seemed silly.

"I just got back from a mission." Ista grinned. "Kill count: ten."

Vitala's eyebrows rose. She looked at Ista's fingers and counted only nine contact points. "Congratulations. Who was the target?"

"Governor of the village of Malham. I have to debrief tonight, but . . ." Ista looked at the ground a moment, uncharacteristically shy. "Do you want to meet for breakfast tomorrow? I can tell you about my mission, and you can tell me about yours. I'd like to hear why you rescued Lucien instead of killing him."

"I'd enjoy that." Vitala's throat tightened with emotion. She had long wanted to make peace with Ista, but lacked the courage to extend the first overture.

She ought to have done it herself years ago, because it was too late now. Vitala would be gone from the Circle by morning.

16

Vitala stalked purposefully through the caverns of the enclave. One of her best Caturanga strategies was to make aggressive moves early, before her opponent had a chance to settle in to the game. In this too she had to move quickly, before Bayard realized the danger of keeping Lucien here in the enclave, where she was capable of breaking him out.

She anticipated some trouble, but less so than if the Circle had any real prison cells. The Circle's policy was simply to execute anyone who wandered too near its enclaves; thus they had no holding facilities and their means of detaining Lucien would be makeshift and crude. He'd probably just be in a room with a couple of guards in front of it.

She rounded the corner, and her heart sank. The guards were Rodmar and Hodd. Not close friends by any means, but she'd sparred with them on a few occasions. She'd been hoping for people she didn't know.

They straightened at her approach, and Rodmar swallowed nervously.

"Miss Salonius," said Hodd with a nod of greeting. "With respect, we cannot allow you access to the prisoner. Bayard's orders."

"I know. Bayard sent me to find you. He wants to see you in the training room."

The men exchanged glances.

"I can't leave my post unless he sends someone to relieve me," said Hodd.

"I'll relieve you."

Hodd stared at her with obvious suspicion, and Vitala felt a pang of sympathy for him. While the Obsidian Circle had no official system of ranks, an informal hierarchy had nonetheless formed, and assassins were near the top of it. To challenge her was akin to disobeying an order from a superior officer.

"You'd better go," she added, allowing a little menace to creep into her voice. "Bayard doesn't like to be kept waiting. I'd hate to see anything happen." She curled and uncurled her fist in a gesture reminiscent of Shard summoning.

The guards' eyes followed the movements of her fist.

"Maybe we should both go," said Rodmar.

Coward, Vitala thought.

Hodd shook his head. "No, stay at your post." He gave Rodmar a look, which Vitala interpreted as *You keep an eye on her and I'll fetch help.*

Vitala exchanged places with Hodd and he walked off, his back very stiff, as if he half expected a knife in it. He turned the corner. Vitala waited until she judged him out of earshot, then launched herself at Rodmar.

His arms went up to block her—he'd anticipated the attack—but his reaction was poorly planned. He reached for his flintlock, but halfheartedly, as if in his mind he'd already judged her the victor. She had her Shard in his arm almost immediately. "Do not move," she whispered. "Do not make a sound. Or I release the death spell."

"Get off him!" Hodd commanded.

She looked up. A pistol was trained on her from the far end of the corridor, held in Hodd's trembling hands.

"Get off him," he repeated, "or I'll shoot."

"If you pull that trigger, he dies," said Vitala. "I've got a Shard in him."

"You'll die too."

Vitala snorted. "From a pistol at that range?"

Hodd shuffled forward.

"Stay where you are! One more step, and I activate the death spell!" cried Vitala.

He stopped, emotions warring on his face. Then he lowered his pistol, turned, and ran. Going for help, no doubt. She hoped he ran straight for the training room, because Bayard wasn't there.

"I'm sorry for this," Vitala said to Rodmar. "I'm sure the Healer will be here for you soon." Rodmar shut his eyes tight. Vitala pulled the pistol from his belt and shot him in the foot.

As he lay howling on the ground, she burst through the cell door, which like all Obsidian Circle doors had no lock, and glanced about, taking stock. Lucien was the room's only occupant. He lay with his back against the wall, his wrists and ankles bound with rope. She knelt at his side and sliced through his bonds with a knife.

"Crutch and leg," said Lucien, pointing.

She fetched them from where they lay against the wall.

He strapped on the leg and stood, wincing, though the injuries Bayard had inflicted were gone. Probably he was just stiff from being tied. "Weapon?" he asked.

She loved that about Lucien, that he accepted new situations instantly and did not ask idiot questions like *What's going on?* or *What are you doing here?* She handed him her pistol. "Use it if you have to, but try not to kill anyone."

He took the weapon and looked it over.

She reached into her pocket, took out his riftstone, and shoved it in his hand.

His eyebrows rose in surprise. "Thank you. But aren't you coming with me?"

"Yes," she said, moving for the door. "But if we're separated, get yourself clear and don't worry about me. Move fast."

He limped quickly after her. The corridor was empty except for the still-wailing Rodmar, but that wouldn't last. At the end of the corridor, she turned right, taking the back route. She'd mapped out her escape route in advance, even walked it a few times. But the enclave was small, and its caverns crossed and recrossed one another like a latticework. They would not get through it without being seen.

"Vitala!" cried a voice she dreaded.

She risked a glance behind her. Bayard was there with Ista and several guards. *Pox.* Vitala could outrun them, but Lucien couldn't.

"Faster!" she hissed, but he was already moving rapidly, running almost normally and no doubt calling upon his war magic to enable him to do so. She positioned herself behind him, acting as a human shield. Bayard and the others would shoot at Lucien, but they might hesitate to fire on her.

"Vitala, stop this!" cried Bayard. "Don't be foolish."

"Turn left," she whispered to Lucien.

He swung neatly into the passageway, and she followed, still shielding him. Just ahead were the stables. If they could get to their horses, they had a chance. On the back of a horse, Lucien would have no speed handicap.

Bayard and the others pelted toward them, their footfalls growing louder as they closed the distance. Then, to Vitala's astonishment, Lucien reached back, grabbed her

by the syrtos, and yanked her to the floor. Almost simultaneously, she heard the crack of the pistol behind her
and the whine of a bullet overhead. Lucien fired his pistol
back at them, and there was screaming and a cacophony
of gunfire. Lucien contorted his body, almost impossibly
it seemed, avoiding bullets. The air was full of smoke.

Then he was back up, limping swiftly down the corridor. The pistols were empty.

Vitala feared to look back, but forced herself to do it
even as she scrambled to her feet. As the smoke began
to clear, she saw a downed man on the floor. *Bayard.* Ista
was at his side, tending to him. The guards were still in
pursuit, but they were hanging back, perhaps not too eager to engage her up close. Good. If they were afraid of
her, so much the better.

She hurried after Lucien into the stables. The horses
were tacked and ready to go, just as she'd left them. She
hauled them out of their stalls by the reins, shoved Lucien onto his sorrel, and climbed onto her bay. The
guards had not followed her into the stable, which made
her suspicious. Perhaps they were setting up an ambush.

Vitala set heels to the bay and galloped toward the
cavern exit in a mad scramble of hooves. Lucien's horse
catapulted after her. The sunlit chasm loomed ahead. As
she emerged from the cavern into daylight, she spotted
the guards—and the muzzles of their pistols, aimed in
her direction. She leaned low over her horse's neck, ut-
tering a quick prayer to the Soldier, and heard the sharp
report of the pistols. Lucien yanked his horse to the left,
then back to the right. Vitala didn't feel any bullets con-
nect. But then everything went wrong.

Her horse staggered, tripped heavily, and staggered
again with a terrible groan. The ground lurched toward
her, then retreated. She flung her feet out of the stirrup

and jumped clear of her horse, twisting her ankle as she landed. Her vision filled with the contorted faces of the guards, fearful but determined, as they rushed her. She took a few limping steps. Then Lucien's chestnut gelding swept in front of her. His arm was outstretched. She grabbed it, and he swung the horse around, using its momentum to help toss her onto the back of the saddle. Then they were off at a gallop.

Bouncing awkwardly on the saddle's cantle, she looked back. The guards were jogging after them, but in a desultory way; they could not outrun a horse. Her poor bay was still staggering about.

She wrapped her arms tightly around Lucien, not wanting to think about the image that kept pushing its way into her head: Bayard lying flat out on the ground while Ista tended him. She closed her eyes. Some decisions could never be unmade, some actions never undone.

When they'd ridden long enough that it was clear there would be no pursuit, Lucien pulled up. "We need to rest the horse."

Vitala slid down. Stiff muscles and a bruised bottom from where she'd been banging against the saddle protested as she landed. She embraced the pain, welcoming its distraction.

Lucien hopped down beside her.

"Gods," she moaned. "Why'd you have to shoot? I told you not to kill anyone!"

"I didn't kill anyone," said Lucien. "I shot him in the leg."

"Are you sure? He was on the ground."

"Of course he was on the ground. Nobody takes a bullet in the leg and keeps running."

If Lucien was correct about where the bullet had struck, Bayard had a good chance of surviving. But it depended on the exact location of the wound and how quickly a Healer reached him. She'd chosen to shoot the guard outside Lucien's cell in the foot because while it was a disabling and painful wound, it would not kill him. But a man could bleed out from a leg wound.

"I had to shoot him," said Lucien. "He fired at you."

"He was firing at *you*."

"Wrong. Why do you think I yanked you to the ground?" He pulled the reins off the sorrel's neck and started walking, leading the sweat-soaked animal.

Vitala stepped forward and took the sorrel's reins, figuring it would be easier for her to manage the horse, since she didn't have to also manage a crutch. "But your war magic works only for you. If a bullet were aimed at me, you wouldn't know where it was coming from the way you would if it were aimed at you. Right?"

"No, I can extend it to people close to me. Animals too. Those last shots were aimed at the horses—did you see me steer my horse out of the bullet's path?"

"The Circle has war mages, and they can't do that."

"War mages vary in how effectively we can use our magic."

Vitala nodded distractedly. She couldn't stop thinking about Bayard.

"The woman stopped to take care of him," Lucien added softly.

"Lucky for us," said Vitala. "She was the most dangerous one among them."

"Really? Why? Is she a mage?"

"She's what I am. An assassin." Except Vitala wasn't that anymore. After what she'd done, the Circle would never take her back.

Lucien tugged at his earlobe, his eyes bright with curiosity. He wanted to ask her more, that much was obvious, but he seemed to decide against it. Instead, he said, "You did the right thing."

She shook her head. "I don't know."

"Really, you did."

"And where do we go from here? The Circle was all I had." Her voice shook. Any moment now, she might burst into tears.

"I know a place we can go. Why don't you let me guide us for a while?"

She laughed, though her throat was so tight, it almost made her choke. "Do you even know where we are?"

"No. But if you can get me to the village of Vorst, I can take things from there."

She shrugged helplessly. "And where are we going from Vorst?"

"The White Eagle encampment."

Vitala shuddered. The home of a Riorcan-stationed Kjallan battalion—not a place she was enthusiastic to visit.

"It'll be all right," said Lucien. "You'll see."

Vitala said nothing. It was of little importance where she went. She was an assassin who'd gone rogue. The Circle would send people to kill her.

"What do you suppose will happen to Flavia?" asked Lucien.

"I couldn't get her out!" cried Vitala. "It was hard enough just freeing you. If I'd tried to rescue both of you at the same time—"

"You misunderstand me," said Lucien. "I don't blame you at all. You made the right tactical decision, and if I'd been in your position, I'd have done the same. But you know your people better than I do. Will they harm her?"

"They won't. She'll be fine with the Circle." Especially after what she'd told Bayard about Flavia having belonged to Hanna and Glenys, a pair of Obsidian Circle spies who'd died for the cause. "I daresay she's safer right now than we are."

"Hey." Lucien held out his hand, showing her his rift-stone. "Thanks for this."

17

It was late afternoon and the sky was overcast when Lucien pulled up the sorrel in the rocky foothills and pointed to a plateau ahead. "There. Do you see him?"

"See who?" She squinted.

"Up on the cliff, at the far end."

At first she saw nothing, but then movement caught her eye. There was a man there, a sentry, shifting from one foot to another. She couldn't make out any details, but from his outline he looked Kjallan.

"That's one of mine. Let's move out where he can see us." Lucien kneed the sorrel forward, out of the tree cover and into the open.

"One of yours?"

The distant sentry stilled as he sighted them. Then a ball of blue magelight sputtered into existence over his head and rose upward.

"One of White Eagle's. And he's signaling. Perfect."

A tiny storm of magelight followed as the signal made its way across the encampment, relayed from one person to another.

Lucien's eyes were bright with excitement. "Won't be long now."

In the distance, she heard hoofbeats. Sorting them out, she counted half a dozen or more separate animals. Bushes rustling along the edge of the plateau betrayed the riders' presence as they descended from the high ground. "You're sure this is safe?"

"Fairly sure," said Lucien. "If not, you can handle them. Can't you?"

She snorted. *Six at once?*

Lucien grinned. "I'm teasing."

The riders, who'd temporarily vanished onto a switchback, suddenly appeared on the low ground, galloping toward them. Uniformed soldiers, eight of them. She clenched her fist, wishing for the security of a Shard between her fingertips, but held back from summoning one. Her six remaining Shards were all she would ever have now, and she would have to save them for true emergencies. Without the Circle, she had no way of replenishing her supply.

The riders surrounded them, leveling muskets at their chests. The leader spoke. "Who are you, and—" His eyes widened. "Three gods!" He stared at Lucien for several long seconds. "Your Imperial Majesty—is it really you?"

"It's me, Quincius," said Lucien.

Quincius's face lit up like that of a child whose first puppy had been placed in his arms. He dropped his musket into the saddle holster, leapt off his horse, and dropped to one knee. The other soldiers scrambled to do the same. From their faces, it was evident that most of them recognized Lucien and were equally stunned and happy to see him. "Sire, we were told you'd been murdered by the Obsidian Circle."

"Obviously, I wasn't. Cassian betrayed me so he could force Celeste into marriage and seize the throne; he laid the blame on the Circle. The Circle is not responsible at all; in fact, they helped me escape. I would be dead now if not for their assistance." Lucien gestured at the soldiers to stand.

Quincius rose, looking puzzled. "But the Circle—"

"They're on our side now. I'll explain later."

Vitala raised an eyebrow at Lucien, but he ignored it.

"My companion here is our liaison from the Obsidian Circle," Lucien added.

The soldiers looked at Vitala with new interest and more than a little suspicion.

Lucien's tone turned teasing. "Quincius, what are you doing leading a patrol? Haven't you learned how to delegate?"

The soldiers exchanged glances, and their bodies tensed.

"Ah," said Quincius. "I'm afraid I've been demoted. Emperor Cassian—I mean, the usurper—sent a new tribune to take command of White Eagle."

Lucien's eyes hardened. "Who?"

"Antius."

"Did Cassian send anyone with him?"

"No. It's just Antius, sire."

"You have new orders, Quincius. Remove Tribune Antius from command and bring him before me. Can this be done without bloodshed? Will the men obey you in preference to Antius?"

The soldiers nodded vehemently.

"I want it done immediately, before he can react to my presence," said Lucien. "Go."

The soldiers grinned and remounted their horses.

The trail up the mountainside was steep and narrow. Vitala and Lucien rode in the middle of the procession, their sorrel struggling at a canter under its double load. After several switchbacks, the trail opened onto a series of terraces. The battalion's encampment appeared to be a permanent one, with crude buildings instead of tents. Dirt ramps connected the terrace, and simple fortifications lined the cliffs. A signal tower rose from the tallest terrace.

The soldiers huddled to confer. "Antius will be in the command center," said Quincius. "We'll spread the word among the men first, make sure there's no confusion that might lead to violence. Eonus, you speak to First Century. Pullo, you take Second Century . . ."

When he finished doling out the assignments, the men galloped off, leaving Quincius alone with Lucien and Vitala.

"Where's the command center?" asked Vitala.

"The highest terrace," said Lucien, pointing. "Near the signal tower."

She kept an eye on it, knowing that if trouble were to arise, it would come from there.

The camp began to stir. Soldiers, most of them on foot, began to converge on their position. Some were uniformed, others seemed to have been off duty, but each of them looked eagerly up at Lucien. Vitala received a few stares as well. At first she felt intimidated, but she soon accepted that the soldiers were no threat as long as she was with Lucien.

"We'd best act now," said Quincius. "Antius will have noticed the activity."

Lucien nodded. "Do it."

Quincius assembled a squadron of twelve officers and dismounted some of the patrolmen to supply them with horses. Then the squadron galloped off toward the tallest plateau. Vitala listened intently for the sounds of violence, but she heard and saw nothing. After what seemed an eternity, but in truth could have been no longer than the time it took to brush and saddle a horse, the squadron returned, escorting a gaudily uniformed prisoner.

Lucien turned to Quincius. "Any casualties, Commander?"

"No, sire. He surrendered to our numbers."

"Good." Lucien gestured to Vitala to get off the sorrel. She hopped down and turned to steady him as he dismounted. He took up his crutch and limped to Antius.

Antius's hands were bound, yet he dropped quickly to one knee. "Sire, I—"

"You will speak only when spoken to," said Lucien. "You're Cassian's man. Are you not?"

"Begging your pardon, sire, I am Kjall's man. Cassian appointed me to this position after your tragic . . . assassination." He swallowed uncertainly. "It's wonderful to see you alive. An honor, sire."

Lucien's eyes narrowed. "You knew nothing of Cassian's plot against me?"

"No, sire." He shook his head vehemently. "It's a shock to discover I've been lied to."

"If you are indeed innocent, then I'm sorry for this. But I don't think you are, and I cannot trust my enemy's handpicked man." Lucien grasped the chain that hung around Antius's neck and yanked it free. The yellow riftstone dangled from it, glittering like a miniature sun. Lucien handed it to a junior officer. "Take this far away from here."

"Yes, sire." The officer mounted and rode off.

"Execute him, Quincius," said Lucien.

"By the stake?"

"No, the sword. Make it honorable."

A chill crept over Vitala. She had never seen this side of Lucien. It was unsettling, yet it didn't surprise her. It was consistent with his Caturanga play; he had never hesitated to sacrifice a piece in pursuit of a larger goal. Horrified as she was, she was also pleased with him. Lucien was demonstrating the strength he would need to win a war in which he was the underdog. He was quite right that Antius could not be trusted. He could not afford either to send Antius home to Cassian, bearing news of Lucien's location, or allow him to stay here. Even imprisoning him would have been risky.

Tribune Antius's face flushed with anger, but he showed no fear as the soldiers led him away.

"You." Lucien beckoned to a nearby soldier. "What's your name?"

The man stepped forward and pressed a thumb to his chest in salute. "Sigilus, sire."

Lucien handed him the sorrel's reins. "Sigilus, take this faithful creature to the stables and see that he's well tended to. Do not ride. Walk him there."

"Yes, sire."

Lucien commandeered two fresh horses from the squadron, one for himself and one for Vitala. They mounted and rode on through the camp, past crude barracks buildings and storehouses and up the packed dirt ramp to the tallest plateau. Here the buildings were larger and finer than below.

The signal tower spiraled upward in the center of the plateau, and just beside it squatted a low building with a doorway framed by two White Eagle standards.

"The command center," Lucien announced as they dismounted from their horses.

He led her inside. The building was windowless and a little dreary, but glows kept it lit and warm. Maps, papers, inkpots, and quills were scattered over a large table in the center of the room. Lucien shuffled through the materials, taking stock. "Are you hungry? Would you like to rest? There are living quarters through that door there. They were Antius's, but we're going to take them over."

Vitala turned to him in surprise. Apparently, he intended for them to remain lovers, and publicly so. "What will the men think of that?"

"I don't care what they think."

She was not averse to sharing a bed with him, but how long could she sustain such a relationship, given her problems with the visions? He might tolerate her limitations for the time being, but he would not put up with them forever. In his raw, unembarrassed sexuality, Lucien was *normal*. And she was not.

His mention of rest had brought a great weariness upon her, an exhaustion that was more emotional than physical. The reality of what she'd done—left the Circle and defected to a Kjallan battalion to consort with the enemy—was overwhelming. "I'd like to rest."

"Go on, then. I'll see that you're not disturbed. I need to read Tribune Antius's correspondence, especially anything from Cassian." Lucien began to arrange the papers on the table into piles.

"There's something you need to know," said Vitala.

His head popped up. "Yes?"

"White Eagle has been infiltrated by the Obsidian Circle."

He stood silent, considering. "Do you know who the infiltrators are?"

"No, but we have spies in all the Riorcan-stationed battalions. That means the Circle will soon know where the two of us have fled to."

"And what will they do about it?"

"Send assassins."

"For me or for you?"

"For me. Possibly for you as well. It depends on whether or not they like your being a thorn in Cassian's side."

A line of worry appeared in the center of his fore-head. "All the more reason we should stick close to each other. We have a little time, don't we? They'll have to get the information back to headquarters, make a decision."

"Yes, we have a little time."

He waved her toward Antius's living quarters. "Get some rest. Later we'll discuss this at length. We have an advantage, after all—you know how these assassins operate."

Vitala smiled humorlessly. "I do."

That night, Vitala slept so deeply she could barely claw herself back to consciousness in the morning, while the only indication Lucien had slept was the mussed covers on the bed. When she'd retired, he'd been cramming information like a mage candidate awaiting his soulcasting ceremony, skimming through documents and poring over maps. At suppertime, he'd summoned a group of officers to the command center and questioned them for hours. Now, at breakfast, he was back to the cramming, so absorbed in a sheaf of letters that he seemed barely aware of her presence.

As if reading her thoughts, he glanced up. "You need to have a look around camp."

She nodded. "I need to learn how an assassin might gain access."

He called to the door guard and requested a man named Kryspin, a weathered-looking squad commander with broad shoulders and a patch over his right eye. Lucien ordered him to give Vitala a tour of the camp.

She followed Kryspin out of the command center. Squad commander—that was her father's rank. Kryspin, like her father, must be common born, with no magic, since only a highborn officer could afford the magical training needed to become a prefect, tribune, or legatus. He would have joined the army as an enlisted man and somehow distinguished himself to earn the promotion. What if he actually was her father? It was possible; he was old enough. Vitala banished the thought. *I really don't want to know.*

He led her first to the signal tower next door to the command center. She climbed the spiral stairs to the platform at the top, where two sentries stood watch, one facing north, and the other facing south. Leaning on the railing, she drew in crisp morning air and analyzed the scene, picking out the approach points to the camp. South of her were the Ash Mountains, which she and Lucien had crossed on their way to the enclave. They were not the steep, craggy, snow-covered peaks that rose in parts of eastern Kjall, but low, smooth mountains. *Tired mountains,* she thought. Easily navigable, they would not present much of a barrier to invading Kjallan troops.

She circled around. To the north, she spotted the characteristic pit houses of a Riorcan village only a short ride away, surrounded by forest. Farther still was the mottled gray expanse of the Great Northern Sea. From here, it looked calm, but that was an effect of the distance. Up close, it would be turbulent and dangerous. "What village is that?" she asked.

"Tinst," replied Kryspin.

"Is it living or dead?"

"It is a dead village, miss."

When she finished observing her greater surroundings, she descended the signal tower and Kryspin showed her around the upper terrace, pointing out officer's quarters, the infirmary, the stable, a dusty training field, and several crude storehouses for weapons and grain. He was polite and businesslike in his conversation, but she caught him staring at her a few times and realized he had to be curious about her, as all the men were. Who was she? What did it mean that Lucien had arrived at the camp with her in tow?

"What do you think of Lucien?" she asked as they descended the packed dirt ramp to one of the lower terraces. "I mean, what do the soldiers think of him?"

"It's *Emperor* Lucien, ma'am, and any man here would give his life for him."

"Why?"

"He's a brilliant commander, and he cares about his men."

"I know he's brilliant, but Lucien wasn't a popular emperor. After all, he was deposed by his own bodyguards—"

"Now, ma'am, that ain't fair—" began Kryspin.

"But it's true. Kjall as a whole is not loyal to Lucien, but you say the men of this battalion are. And clearly that is so, because the officers here instantly accepted Lucien's command, despite the fact that Cassian—I mean, the usurper"—Lucien had spread the word last night that Cassian should henceforth be called by that name—"will consider that treason. Why does White Eagle trust Lucien when the rest of Kjall does not?"

"Miss," he sputtered, "those folks in Riat don't know tomtit about Lucien. They never gave him a chance. Lucien came here when he were just sixteen years old—just a boy, miss!—and we didn't like the idea of being commanded by a young man barely into his bumfluff, and that were before he lost his leg. But appearances is deceiving. We've never seen a commander like him, and we'll not see one again."

"How is he different from other commanders?"

"Most commanders just holes up in their quarters

and send orders out, but Lucien's always out with the men, looking at things, figuring things out. He don't fight directly, of course, but he goes on scouting expeditions to study the terrain so he can put us in the winning position. Back then, he knowed every man in the camp by name. He don't now, because there's been some changes, but he'll know 'em soon. And he keeps them alive."

"Through superior strategy?"

"That and sticking his neck out for us. You know the rebellion at Echmor?"

"I've heard about it." Echmor was a Riorcan tragedy. Some years ago, at the Circle's urging, the village of Echmor had rebelled and refused to pay its tribute to Kjall. Two Kjallan battalions had been sent to quell the uprising. The Circle and the villagers thought they had the upper hand, but the Kjallans had won. Now Echmor was a dead village.

"White Eagle was one of the battalions sent. The rebels was entrenched along the foothills of Mount Banough. You know the place?"

She shook her head. "Not well."

"Orders came in from the legatus that we was to march to a place where the roads meet in the foothills and join forces with Blue Lion battalion, but Lucien, he'd sent scouts and he knowed the Riorcan rebels was dug in all over the high ground and well armed. If he marched us into the valley, we'd be cut to pieces from above. So he signaled back that it were a bad meeting place and we should go in over the far side of Mt. Banough and come in from up top. Then we'd have the high ground, and we could take out the rebels easy."

Vitala bit her lip. Had the Circle failed at Echmor because of Lucien?

"So," continued Kryspin, "he made the signal, but the legatus weren't listening to no kid, even if he was the emperor's, and he signaled back to stick with the original plan. The legatus weren't a sapskull, mind, but lots of Kjallan commanders have never fought in the mountains, or if they have, not *these* mountains. So Lucien broke the chain of command and signaled the tribune in command of Blue Lion, tried to get him to take the route over the pass, but the tribune weren't going to disobey orders. So Blue Lion battalion went to the spot where the roads met, on the low ground, and Lucien brought White Eagle in over the mountains." He shook his head. "It weren't an easy march. Snow and winds to freeze your cods off—pardon my language, miss—but we made it. And when we got there, we picked off the rebels like shooting apples off a fence. Blue Lion got cut up, but they'd have been worse off if we wasn't winning the battle for them. So, now you see, miss, why there's nothing we wouldn't do for Emperor Lucien."

"Did Lucien get in trouble for disobeying orders?"

"Yes, ma'am, but his father was the emperor, and for that reason he weren't removed from command, but I heared his father gave him hell for it, calling him a coward, which he weren't, miss."

"Of course not. It was just good sense." Three gods. The rebellion at Echmor might have been successful if not for Lucien. At least this time he was on *her* side.

Kryspin grinned. "I'm glad you see it that way, miss. I'm glad you understand Emperor Lucien, because lots of folks doesn't." He pointed at his head. "He's just got more up here than they does, that's all." He halted before a series of long, low buildings. "These here is the barracks for Fourth Century. Do you know how the battalion is organized, miss?"

"No, sir, not very well."

"Well, it's ten centuries, with a prefect in command of each one—there's the prefect's residence, right there." He pointed at a smaller building. "I'm in Fourth Century," he added, swelling with pride.

"Very good," she said, and followed him as he headed for another terrace. She pointed to a terrace he appeared to have passed by. It was different from the others, dotted with tents rather than stone buildings. "What's on that terrace?"

"Oh." Kryspin's cheeks colored. "That's no place for a lady."

"But what is it? I need to know the whole camp, sir, not just certain parts of it."

He avoided her eyes. "Well, in them tents is the camp followers, miss."

"Oh. Thank you. That's very important, actually." If the Circle sent a female assassin, she would almost certainly infiltrate the battalion as a camp follower. "Can you tell me anything about the women there? Are they Kjallan or Riorcan? Do they stay on their own terrace, or are they allowed into the camp proper?"

"Um." Kryspin rubbed the back of his neck. "Some is Kjallan, some Riorcan. And they're supposed to stay in their own terrace, but . . ."

"But what?"

"I'm not the person to talk to about this, ma'am. I don't know much about them."

Vitala suspected he knew quite a bit about the camp followers, whether he visited them or not, as did virtually every man in the camp. But she let it go. There would be others who would speak more freely.

Kryspin led her toward the next terrace. "How is it, miss, that you came to be liaison to the Obsidian Circle?

'Cause the Circle, they don't trust outsiders, especially Kjallans. They kill anyone who stumbles onto one of their enclaves. Lost two good men that way once."

"Oh, I'm not Kjallan."

He stared at her. "But—" He gestured vaguely at her, as if trying to indicate her hair without directly pointing at her.

"I know I look Kjallan, but I'm half-and-half. Kjallan father; Riorcan mother. I was raised Riorcan."

He continued to gape at her for a moment. Then he turned and headed for the next terrace, leaving her to scramble to catch up. "Fifth Century," he said, his tone terse and businesslike. "Prefect's residence."

Vitala sighed as she followed him. Kryspin didn't know it, but he'd just answered her most urgent unspoken question. Lucien might have accepted her, despite her Riorcan background, but if this man was any example, the soldiers of White Eagle battalion would not.

The lower terrace stank of refuse and excrement. Until now, Vitala hadn't truly noticed and appreciated the cleanliness of the rest of the camp. There must be some kind of work schedule such that the soldiers removed and disposed of waste, swept the paths, mended their uniforms, and polished the weaponry. But the rotation didn't apply here.

Kryspin had oversimplified when he'd implied the camp followers were all whores. In fact, the lower terrace was a fully functioning village, with food vendors, laundresses, liquor sellers, cooks, boot menders, and an herbalist. One section of the terrace was reserved for soldiers' wives, and from there she heard the squalling of babies. The marketplace was subdued rather than bustling. But there was more variety here than she'd imagined.

It was midday, and hardly any of the women were about, nor any soldiers. She paused to examine a crudely lettered sign that detailed one woman's prices, and then another across the road with very different prices.

Someone behind her spoke in halting, thickly accented Kjallan. "Wrong side."

Vitala turned. The speaker was a Riorcan woman of indeterminate age—she had a look of youth about her, but with her weathered face, she might have been as old as forty. "What do you mean?"

The woman pointed. "Kjallans, that side. Riorcans, this side. You on wrong side."

Vitala blinked, absorbing this. Apparently, the women were segregated. Now she understood why the prices on the right side of the road were higher than those on the left. The Kjallans were able to charge more. She switched to fluent Riorcan. "I'm not Kjallan. And I don't live here."

The woman also shifted languages. "Are you a half-blood?"

"Yes, ma'am."

The woman frowned. "Then you belong on the other side." She turned to leave.

"Ma'am," called Vitala, hurrying after her, "I'd like to ask you some questions. I'm . . ." She lowered her voice. "I'm from the Obsidian Circle."

The woman glared at her. "If you truly were, you'd never say it out loud." She walked off, her back very straight.

Vitala swallowed. Some liaison she was.

"She's jealous, hon," called another voice, this one in fluent Kjallan.

Vitala turned. A dark-haired woman had poked her head out of a tent on the other side of the street. "Jealous of what?"

"*You*. Look at you." As Vitala approached, the woman framed her face. "So young, so pretty. You'll fetch a good price. That Riorcan filth will have to sleep with three men to earn what you could make with one."

Vitala stared at her. Hadn't she heard Vitala say she was herself Riorcan? No, she hadn't, because Vitala had spoken those words in the Riorcan language. "Actually, I'm not—"

"Come in, come in. Are you new here?" The woman beckoned her into the tent.

Vitala stooped under the entryway and sat down beside the woman on the blanketed floor. A sheet hung from the ceiling separated the tent into two "rooms." On this side, the only furnishing was a plush bedroll. The other side was hidden from view. "Well, yes, but—"

"I can set you up, show you how everything works. Get you the best men, the best prices. You're warded, aren't you? Ten percent of your earnings, that's all I ask."

"No!" cried Vitala. "That's not why I'm here. Emperor Lucien sent me here to ask some questions."

"Oh." The woman looked impressed. "If His Imperial Majesty would like, I can find him someone very special—"

"Please just answer my questions. Can anyone take up residence in this terrace? Kjallan or Riorcan? Are there any restrictions as to who can strike a tent here?"

"Any woman can set up camp here. No men, of course."

Vitala nodded. "Are there rules and restrictions? May the women join the soldiers on the upper terraces, or must the soldiers come here?"

"The soldiers come here. We're not allowed on any other terrace."

"Thank you. Rules and restrictions?"

"Any woman who assaults a soldier gets staked—even if he hits her first, so pick your clients carefully. No weapons. No Riorcans on the Kjallan side of the street. No Riorcans at the market except after the sun passes Spyglass Rock. No Riorcans at the west or northern latrine—"

"Why so many restrictions on the Riorcans?"

"We don't go in their places. Why should they go in ours?"

Vitala let out her breath in exasperation. These were impoverished women in desperate circumstances, selling their bodies to survive. And they couldn't find any common ground? If there was ever a situation for them to band together, this should be it.

She changed tacks. "Do you have any idea what sorts of Riorcan women come here?"

The woman gave a crude laugh. "Ugly ones."

Vitala frowned.

The woman shrugged. "I don't know. Ones who can't make a living no more, I guess. Families dead and what-not."

"Probably the same reasons as the Kjallan women. Don't you think?"

The woman snorted. "It's different. Kjallan women sleeping with Kjallan soldiers—we're helping the cause, in our own way. The men need us. But the Riorcans? They're consorting with the enemy. They're not just whores; they're traitors."

Traitors. Like herself. The word stung, but Vitala needed this information. "Please." She swallowed the lump in her throat. "Tell me more."

18

Two days into his stay at White Eagle, Lucien was finally beginning to feel he had a handle on things. Antius's correspondence had mostly dealt with routine matters, supply caravans, and discipline and transfers of young officers, but often he could read between the lines and determine from the tone who was a Cassian supporter and who accepted the usurper's rule only grudgingly. There was also the lay of the land to study, specifically where each of the usurper's battalions was stationed. Cassian had moved several of them since seizing the throne, and some of these were telling moves, though they didn't tell him quite everything he needed to know.

He'd placed each battalion's flag on the map and was calculating distances and march times when Quincius burst into the command center.

Lucien growled at him. "Curse it, Tribune, you made me lose count."

"Is it true, sire? About the woman you brought with you?"

"Is what true?" He stared at the map. What did it mean that the usurper had moved Red Fox battalion to Phiath? What could he possibly hope to gain by that?

"That she's Riorcan."

Lucien looked up. "Of course she's Riorcan. I said she was our liaison to the Obsidian Circle."

"That's— We didn't know she was Riorcan, sire."

"Now you do." He moved Red Fox from Phiath to Argentum. Could that be the final intended destination? From there, they would have an unimpeded path to western Riorca.

"Sire! This doesn't concern you at all?"

"No." Honestly, looking at the map, it was the least of his concerns.

"But Riorca is our enemy!"

Lucien shook his head. "The usurper is our enemy."

"Sire, I must object to your sharing a room with her, especially at night. It isn't safe. Consider what the men must think—"

Lucien straightened. "Tribune, is it your place to tell me whom I can and cannot spend time with?"

Quincius lowered his eyes. "No, sire. I'm only worried. There's not a man in this camp who wouldn't lay down his life for you. Do not devalue our loyalty by taking foolish risks. There are other women—"

"Whom I sleep with is my own business, Tribune. Vitala is trustworthy. She's saved my life twice."

"She's arousing suspicion, sire. She's been running all over the camp, questioning people. She even consorted with the prostitutes on the lower terrace. What do you suppose that means?"

Lucien shrugged. "That she had questions for them."

"Don't you think it looks suspicious?"

"No." Indeed, it was perfectly natural behavior for someone trying to prevent an infiltration and assassination. She was a Caturanga player—of course she would want to familiarize herself with the board. The prostitutes were part of the environment; she would not ignore them just for reasons of propriety. He picked up the marker for Red Fox again. Maybe they weren't headed for Argentum at all. Maybe they were headed for the fort at Rakum.

"Are you aware that she's left the camp, sir?"

Lucien blinked at him. "What?"

"She headed down the switchbacks a little while ago. The sentries didn't stop her because you said she was to be allowed to move freely. She can't have gone far, because she didn't take a horse. I only found out minutes ago."

He set down the Red Fox marker. "Pass the word to Glabrio. Bring my horse."

Though Quincius urged him to take an escort, Lucien rode alone. He wouldn't be going far, and whatever Vitala was up to, she would respond better to just him than to a pack of guards. He'd neglected her of late, not deliberately, but he had so much information to absorb and little time left. The usurper's army was on its way to Riorca to carry out the decimation plan, that much was clear. It was only the exact route he was unsure of.

Vitala would understand. She knew he was playing this game to win, and sometimes that meant he needed to focus on one thing and drop everything else. But perhaps he hadn't considered how she might feel after having just betrayed her own people. She needed companionship, and he hadn't offered it.

He leaned back in the saddle as his horse trotted jarringly down the switchback. She couldn't have left the camp permanently, not on foot. More likely she'd gone to look at something, perhaps the access points to the encampment through which an infiltrator might approach, or had simply felt the need to be alone. But it was ridiculously unsafe for her to leave the camp when there was an assassin, or multiple assassins, on her tail. He'd have words with her about that.

He pulled up his horse. A little trail, badly overgrown, wound its way off the switchback, heading upward to a small, unoccupied terrace. The ground was too rocky to show footprints, but he had a good feeling about it. He turned his horse onto it.

He coaxed the animal forward through the spiny bushes and ascended a small rise. At the peak of it, he spotted Vitala. She was sitting at the edge of the terrace beneath a scrawny mountain tree, her arms around her knees, facing away from him.

He clucked to his horse to close most of the distance, then hopped down and pulled his crutch from the saddle holster. She had to have heard him by now, but she hadn't turned. Foolish. How did she know he wasn't an enemy? "Vitala, what are you doing out here?"

"I'm in no danger, Lucien. Go back and study your maps."

He limped toward her over the uneven ground. "What about the assassins? If you leave the camp, you must notify me and take an escort."

"I don't take orders from you."

Gods-cursed woman, this was for her safety. Did she think he gave orders to amuse himself? He circled round to look her in the eye, stare her down if he had to. "In this camp," he began angrily, then saw the half-dried tear tracks down her face and bit his lip. "Did something happen?"

She laughed bitterly. "You mean, did something happen besides my breaking you out of an Obsidian Circle enclave and making myself a traitor and an outcast and betraying the only friends I've ever had?"

Something shivered in his chest. "I'm sorry about that. I meant, did something happen more recently?"

Vitala shrugged. "No," she said softly.

Liar. "What is it?"

"It's nothing. I told Kryspin I was Riorcan, and he spread it all over the camp. Now everyone looks at me differently. They point at me and whisper. Gods know what they call me behind my back. And a camp follower all but called me a traitor. But it's nothing I didn't expect."

Lucien's hand tightened around his crutch. "Kryspin, that sapskull. I'll have words with him—"

"No, he's done nothing wrong. I never meant my ancestry to be a secret. I just— I don't know. I was hoping people would react differently. But that was silly of me." She waved a hand, dismissing him. "Go back to your maps and win this war. That's what I rescued you for."

"No."

She gave him a withering look. "You're not going to win the war?"

"No, I'm not going back to my maps. I don't take orders from you either." He lowered himself to the ground and sat beside her. When she scooted aside to make room for him, he moved with her, closing the gap, and slipped an arm around her shoulders. She was stiff and trembling. What a deceiver. She'd been playing tough, like she didn't need anyone, but it was all an act. "If I look at one more map, my head will explode. Why don't we just sit here for a while?"

"Lucien—" Her flesh quivered against his, and she didn't finish her sentence.

Her reactions were so perplexing. "Do you not like to be touched, Vitala?"

"I—I don't know," she stammered.

Odd answer. She either liked it or she didn't—how could she not know? She seemed to like it when she was in bed with him. But then there had been that ugly business in the tent with Remus. And maybe no one had ever before held her to comfort her. "Well, do you want me to move my arm?"

After a moment's hesitation, she shook her head.

Taking that as permission, he tugged her closer, pulling her almost onto his lap—already her trembling was subsiding—and pressed his face into her hair, inhaling her scent. Gods, she was beautiful.

Before he'd been deposed, he could have almost any woman he wanted for the asking. He'd taken full advantage of that privilege, bedding countless young beauties as well as older, more experienced women who'd been more than happy to teach him the finer points of pleasing the female sex. Those women had slept with him because he was the emperor, not because they cared for him. Now he wasn't emperor anymore. Could he earn the love of a woman on his own merits? Surely he could apply his strategic mind to more than just Caturanga and winning wars. He could use it to win a woman. *This* woman. Much of her heart remained closed to him, but he'd find a way in.

Vitala's shoulders began to shake again, and he realized she was crying. His hand curled into a fist. He wished Kryspin were here so he could punch him in the face. And that camp follower too. Who did she think she was?

Instead, he kissed Vitala's hair. "I'm sorry about the way the men are behaving. We'll work on them. We'll bring them around."

"It's not really that," she said. "It's that I don't belong here—or anywhere. In Riorca, people hate my Kjallan half; in Kjall, they hate my Riorcan half. I had a home in the Circle, where there were others like me, but now I don't even have that. I have nothing, Lucien. I have nobody."

"I've been called many things, Vitala, but never have I been called a *nobody*."

"I don't mean you. I mean there's no group where I belong."

"We'll make our own group. You belong with me." He'd never spoken words more true. She *did* belong with him. For all the women he'd been with, he'd never found a more perfect companion for himself than Vitala. And so what if she was half Riorcan? What an empress she would make! If he were still emperor.

"I appreciate that, but . . ." She waved her hand. "You have a war to fight, papers to read. That's why when I started feeling sorry for myself, I came here on my own. So I wouldn't disturb you. I sacrificed my position with the Circle for a reason: so you would win this war and free Riorca, as you promised. You'd better keep that promise, Lucien."

"I will."

"I'll kill you if you don't."

He pressed his face closer to take in more of her intoxicating scent. "And what will you do to me otherwise?"

She smiled.

He was getting to her. Little by little.

"Lucien . . ." She hesitated, biting her lip. "Obsidian Circle assassins don't live very long."

"Well, it's a risky profession." It didn't concern him much. She wasn't an assassin anymore.

"The oldest assassin in our enclave is Ista, and she's twenty-four. She's unusual to have survived that long."

"Only twenty-four?" He'd assumed they lived longer than that.

"Lucien." Vitala glanced around them as a breeze ruffled the dry grasses on the rise. "Can we go back to the command tent? I have something to show you. And I think we're being watched."

"We're definitely being watched." He didn't go anywhere around camp without being discreetly tailed by a bodyguard. "And I have something to show you too." He placed his hand on what he wanted to show her.

She punched him, which he richly deserved.

In their bedroom, Vitala removed her heavy woolen cloak. Lucien, after shedding his, also unstrapped his wooden leg. He sat on the bed, rubbing his reddened stump.

Vitala picked up the wooden leg from the floor, wondering why the device caused Lucien so much pain. The leg was all wood except for the leather straps. The top, where it attached to his body, dipped into a carved hollow contoured to fit his stump. This hollow was padded but too slight to distribute pressure across a broad area. "This isn't well designed."

"So you say. It's the best wooden leg money can buy," said Lucien.

She traced the uneven wear patterns in the padding and frowned. It wasn't right that Lucien's leg should hurt him all the time. There had to be a better solution.

"That wasn't what I wanted to show you," said Lucien.

"In good time." Vitala put the leg down. She sat on the bed beside him and lifted her hair. "Feel my neck."

Lucien complied.

"No, here." She directed his hand.

His fingers found two hard lumps, right next to each other. He pressed on them, and she winced. "What are these?"

"One of them is my riftstone."

"Three gods!" he said. "So that's where you hide it!"

"The other is my deathstone. It has a death spell embedded in it, which I can release with my magic at any time. All Obsidian Circle assassins from my enclave have deathstones. This is why your people have never been able to interrogate one of us."

He traced the deadly bump with his finger. "You trigger it with your *magic*?"

"Yes. So, tie us up, chain us, gag us—it makes no difference. An Obsidian Circle assassin can kill herself whenever she chooses, and will do so when captured. Shall I demonstrate for you?"

"No!" he said.

"Kidding. The point is, I never expected to have much of a future. A long time ago, I dedicated my life to helping Riorca win its freedom, and whatever it costs me, I'll pay it. Even if it means betraying the Circle. Even if it means having no home, no acceptance, no place to go."

He wrapped his arms around her. "If we win this war, you'll have a place with me. Always."

She leaned against him, sighing with unexpected pleasure. Lucien could be exasperating sometimes, and she didn't always agree with him, but with him she felt appreciated, even loved. Not as a weapon she could be forged into, but as a person. She'd never had that, not with the Circle or with anyone at all. If she could have her way right now, she'd spend the afternoon with him, just shut herself up with Lucien and forget the outside world, but her problems and his were too pressing. She could not stop turning them over in her mind. "How do we win this war? We have only one battalion and no support from the Circle. How many battalions does Cassian have? Thirty?"

"Twenty-six. The odds are not on our side. But he

won't send all of them. He won't repeat Florian's mistake of leaving Riat and the Imperial Palace unguarded."

"He'll need to send only a few to have us vastly out-numbered."

"I'm going to persuade more battalions to join my cause. We'll improve the odds. But I still need the Obsidian Circle, and they're a mystery to me. How can I win them over? You know them better than anyone."

"I can think of only one way. Free Riorca *now*. Bring your troops to the dead villages, run out the overseers, and release the slaves from their death spells. And free the living villages from the burden of tribute payments."

He blinked at her as if he hadn't even considered that possibility. "You realize that freeing Riorca will greatly upset the usurper?"

Vitala smiled. "Isn't that a side benefit?"

"Yes, but timing matters. I don't want him coming af-ter me too early. Still, he's already on the way to deci-mate the populace. If freeing Riorca is what I need to do to win the support of the Obsidian Circle, let's stop wast-ing time and do it."

She raised her eyebrows. "Do you mean it? Free Riorca? Not sometime in the distant future, but now?" She could barely dare to hope he was serious. She'd ded-icated her whole life to freeing Riorca and had expected to die someday for the cause. She'd never thought she'd see it happen.

"Yes, I mean it."

"Right this minute?"

"We could ride out as soon as tomorrow."

"I don't believe you actually mean it."

Lucien hopped to the bedroom door, opened it, and spoke to a guard. "Pass the word to Quincius. Tell him to prepare the battalion. We march tomorrow to free the Riorcan village of Tinst."

Vitala's heart surged. Could it be this simple? No, of course it wasn't. They still had a war to win, a war in which they were ridiculously outnumbered. But this was a first step, a real first step toward what she'd worked for all her life. She felt light on her feet, as if a huge burden had been lifted from her—and suddenly spending the afternoon, or at least an hour or two, with Lucien seemed within the realm of possibility. In fact, given the desire rapidly pooling within her, she was beginning to think it was a necessity.

Lucien closed the door and hopped back, grinning. "There, we've made our Caturanga move. Let's hope it was the right one. *Now* do I get to show you what I wanted to show you?"

"You're really going to free Riorca?"

"Yes! Did you not hear what I said to the guard? You realize it won't be all at once. It'll be one village at a time, starting with Tinst."

"Get on the bed," said Vitala.

Lucien straightened in alarm. "Why?"

She circled, placing herself between him and the door. Gods, he was a fine-looking man, the way he filled out that syrtos so perfectly, without a hint of coarseness. The look of surprised innocence on his face added an extra dollop of charm. "Because I'm going to have my way with you."

"This sounds promising," he said.

"Get on the bed."

"I'm not accustomed to being ordered around."

"That's exactly why you need it, Emperor," said Vitala. "If you don't want to play, I'll go find something else to do."

Lucien scrambled onto the bed. "All right, I accept your gambit. Now what?"

"You do exactly what I say and nothing else." She unbelted his syrtos, and when he reached to do the same for her, she pushed his hand away. "No."

He gave her a sly look but acquiesced.

When she had him naked except for his riftstone, she ordered him to the back of the bed and sat him upright. "Here are the rules," she said. "You can't use your hands. Grip these posts with them to remind yourself to keep them still." She directed his hands to a couple of upright posts on the headboard. "If you cheat and use your hands, the fun stops. Got it?"

"You're still dressed," he pointed out.

She was, but that was part of the point. He might be complaining, but he was excited; he'd gone from half-mast to full arousal. She scooted back so he couldn't reach her with any part of his body, and unbelted her syrtos. After dropping the belts to the floor, she parted the garment's fabric, slowly revealing her breasts, and one of Lucien's hands came away from the posts.

"No," she scolded, covering herself up.

"This is unfair." He shifted uncomfortably but returned his hand to the post.

She resumed her tease, watching the muscles bulge in his arms as he fought temptation. This time he didn't move. She dropped the syrtos entirely and went to him. The moment her mouth was in range, Lucien's hungry lips met hers. She arched her back, letting her breasts dangle against him. Easing closer, she rubbed his tight muscles with her hands and massaged the knots out of them.

He groaned in pleasure and frustration. "Gods, Vitala. You're torturing me."

"I'm going to make you happy. Be patient."

He growled, and his arm muscles tensed and relaxed, but he remained still.

She moved downward, licking and nipping at his neck, then his chest. Lucien was firmly muscled, with a solid, hard body. Nonetheless, he was certain to have his vulnerable spots. She toyed with him, finding his sensitive places, his ticklish places, the places that made him groan. He was tightly wound, like an overtuned harp string, and she played him gently, driving him to greater heights of frustration and arousal, careful not to send him over the edge.

Finally, she dropped her head into his lap and took him in her mouth. It was what he'd been waiting for, and the tension in his legs and body melted as he received the stimulation he craved. He moaned something—her name, it sounded like—and she slowed her pace to draw out his pleasure longer. His hands came down to stroke her hair, her shoulders, her back. He was breaking the rules, but she didn't care. She'd tortured him enough, and now she would give him what he wanted.

"Faster," he muttered, and she complied, having sensed his need just before he voiced it. His hand tightened at the back of her neck. She slipped a hand beneath his cods and cupped them gently in her hand. His moment of crisis was near. Sensing both his desire to thrust and his restraint in not doing so, she drove him harder with mouth and tongue. He cried out, and a moment later his climax was upon him.

His seed spent, Lucien sagged glassy-eyed against the headboard. Vitala snuggled up against him while he rested.

"I am never going to forget the day I decided to free Riorca," he said after a while. "I should have done this sooner."

"You should have," she agreed.

He smoothed her hair, working out a tangle. "And now it's my turn to have my way with you."

Vitala chuckled, tracing an idle finger on his chest. "I don't know. I think I wore you out."

Lucien looked down at her, eyes glinting. "You think so?"

Seeing the challenge in his gaze, Vitala scrambled away from him, laughing, only to be pounced on, flipped over, and pinned by a lover who suddenly seemed more brindlecat than man. His golden riftstone dangled between them on its chain, warm and alive.

"And now," he said, "what set of rules shall I come up with for you?"

19

The next morning, the camp was a flurry of activity. Preparations had begun the moment Lucien had given the order from his bedroom door, and the battalion would depart by midmorning. While Vitala remained with Lucien in the command tent, going over some of the particulars about Riorcan villages, all around her were the sounds of bustle and activity—horses whinnying, squad commanders barking orders, the clatter of furniture being broken down and wagons being loaded.

Lucien gathered up a sheaf of papers from the command center table. "There's something you didn't tell me last night. You showed me your riftstone, or at least where it was implanted, but you never said what it was. What sort of mage are you?"

"I'm a wardbreaker."

"What is that? I've never heard of it."

"It's what it sounds like."

He shot Vitala a look of disbelief. "You can *break wards*?"

"That's right."

"But wards are invisible," said Lucien.

She smiled. "Not to me."

He set the papers down. "Really? I'm standing here, and you can see my wards? What do they look like?"

"I don't see them all the time. I have to do something

with my mind to see them—relax it, sort of. And they look like splashes of color from the spirit world. You've seen the spirit world, haven't you?" He had to have seen it, since he was a mage; to soulcast into a riftstone, one had to open the Rift and peer inside.

"Yes, I've seen it." His forehead wrinkled. "Ordinary colors?"

She nodded. "Not the strange ones." In the spirit world, one saw things that made no sense: impossible shapes, impossible colors. It had frightened her during soulcasting, and she had no desire to ever look upon it again.

"So what sort of stone is your riftstone?"

"Obsidian, of course."

"That's impossible. Obsidian—" Lucien paused as a guard poked his head inside the command center.

"Sire, the squad wants to know if they can come in and pack up your things," said the guard.

"Not yet," said Lucien. "I'll tell you when."

The guard nodded and shut the door.

"Obsidian can't be soulcast into," Lucien continued. "It's been tried."

"The Circle can do it."

"How?"

"I don't know."

Lucien rolled his eyes. "Well, tell me about your soulcasting process. You obviously went through it."

"Tell me about yours," she said, annoyed at his probing.

"All right." He shrugged. "It requires other mages. I had six Warders, good ones, who opened the Rift for me and placed my stone inside. Then I had to go in after it—not physically, but spiritually, the way we're trained to do in our Rift-affinity exercises where we separate mind from body. I had to find the stone and spiritually . . . enter it. I felt like I was lost in the Rift for hours, but they said afterward it was only a few minutes. And now part of my soul is inside the stone, and will remain there until I die."

"That was essentially how I did it," said Vitala. "Except it was five Warders who opened the Rift."

"But why were you able to soulcast into obsidian when no one in Kjall has been able to?"

"I truly don't know. The Circle's structure is not like what you have in Kjall. It's distributed, and information is limited to those with a need to know. This protects our secrets. I have an obsidian riftstone, but I have no idea what was done to the stone to make it possible for me to soulcast into it."

"How is the Circle structured?"

"Each enclave operates independently," said Vitala. "There's no leader, no central authority. The enclaves communicate, share resources, and sometimes join forces on a project, but they don't always use the same methods. Assassins from other enclaves may operate differently. For example, the assassins who attacked you"—she indicated his missing leg—"were male war mages. I'm a female wardbreaker. Not the same at all."

"But that means your information on how Obsidian Circle assassins operate isn't very useful. All you know is how *your* enclave operates, and the assassins may come from elsewhere."

"That's correct. But since my rescuing you offended my enclave personally, I think they'll be the ones to act. If they fail, we may see more attempts, perhaps from other enclaves."

He nodded. "Are all your enclave's assassins wardbreakers?"

"Yes, and all women. All solo operators."

"So they'll infiltrate through the camp followers. Fine. I'll set an edict that no new camp followers will be accepted on White Eagle grounds, and if any man sees a strange woman in the camp, he's to report it immediately."

"That's a good start, but I think you'll find it hard to enforce."

"This is a military camp; I can enforce anything. Our wards will be useless. Won't they? The assassin will just break them." Lucien straightened, his gaze suddenly becoming intense. "Wait. Couldn't an infiltrating assassin kill you by activating your deathstone?"

"No, the deathstone is attuned to me. No one else can activate it."

"Isn't ward-breaking an odd sort of magic for an assassin? I understand it gets you past our wards. But beyond that, it's hardly lethal. War magic would seem the better choice."

"Ward-breaking *is* lethal, at least in my hands." Vitala reached into her pocket and pulled out her eighth Shard, the one she'd used to threaten Bayard but still hadn't activated. She handed it to Lucien and explained about the death spells embedded in the Shards, which could be released by breaking a ward, and how she could call other Shards into her hand out of thin air.

Lucien fingered the Shard, turning it over and over in his hand. He tugged at his ear. "This is what you used to kill the guard at the bonfire."

"One just like it, yes."

His eyes met hers. "But how did you kill Remus? I don't care how effective these are or how well they're kept hidden. No war mage is going to let you stab him with one."

Vitala swallowed. "We have a special technique for war mages."

"What special technique?"

Vitala took a seat at the table. She'd dreaded explaining this part. "There are two ways to defeat a war mage, aside from sending a war mage of one's own. The first is to overwhelm him with attackers. The other is to distract him at a critical moment."

Lucien nodded.

"We use distraction," said Vitala.

He shrugged. "I don't find that credible. It's hard to find a distraction powerful enough to affect a war mage. Say, for example, I'm reading this letter." Lucien picked up a paper from the top of the sheaf and waved it at her. "No matter how interested I am in its contents, no way is it going to—"

"We use sex," Vitala blurted.

"What?"

"During sex, there's a moment . . ." She stammered. "There's a moment when the man is highly distracted, and that's when we strike. It's, you know . . . um . . ."

"When he climaxes? Three gods." He propped his elbows on the table and rested his chin in his hands, looking unhappy. "So that's how you killed Remus. During the sex act."

She curled up on her chair, pulling her knees into her chest. "Yes."

"That's what you didn't want to talk about. In the tent after they took me away, he raped you. And then you killed him."

"Yes."

He laughed, a brittle sound. "Well. I daresay he deserved it."

Vitala was silent. He did deserve it, but that wasn't the point.

"How do you learn this technique? Do you *practice* it?"

"Yes. We practice." Vitala darted a glance at Lucien. What thoughts hid behind that unreadable expression? He was no dummy. He would be putting two and two together, realizing she had slept with him in order to kill him, that she must have done the same with other men before him. And she had nothing to say in her defense. There could be no apologizing for what she was.

"Well," said Lucien, avoiding her eyes. "I think I'd better check on the battalion and make sure we're on schedule. Perhaps you should see to your horse?"

The dismissal pained her, but it also came as a relief. She could hardly bear to be in his presence right now. Vitala unfolded her legs and left the command center.

The following morning, she rode through the village of Tinst beside a silent Lucien. Since their discussion, she felt he'd been avoiding her. Either that or he'd been too busy with the preparations for departure to talk to her. But if it were the latter, why ignore her now, when they were traveling? When it had been just the two of them, fleeing to Riorca, he'd been outright chatty. Now he was taciturn, his expression guarded, and she had no idea whether it was because his feelings toward her had changed or because they were riding in the company of Quincius and the other high-ranking officers and had no privacy. She missed him, and to her surprise she missed Flavia too and wondered how she was coping back at the enclave.

Lucien had spent half of yesterday afternoon plotting

a route through Riorca that would lead them through
the maximum number of Riorcan villages in the shortest
amount of time, and give them access to the other
Riorcan-stationed battalions. The first stop was Tinst, the
village so close it could be seen from White Eagle's signal tower.

She'd never been in a dead village before. She'd expected poverty and demoralization, but she hadn't realized the village would also be depopulated. Fully a third
of the houses were abandoned. The streets were empty
too, and if she didn't know any better, she might think
the village deserted. The only Riorcan she saw was a
man patching a hole in a pit-house roof, who, when he
saw the battalion, climbed down hastily and disappeared
into his home.

She knew the real reason the streets were empty. It
was because the villagers spent the daylight hours at
work in the forest where they cultivated spinefruit, collected mushrooms, and harvested lumber. They would
surely be less than eager to return home with the battalion present, but they had no choice. Like all residents
of dead villages, they were enslaved by death spells that
had to be put into remission every evening by a Kjallan
Healer. Without the attention of the Healer, they would
die a slow, painful death.

At the center of the village, Vitala and the others
came upon six large houses built in the Kjallan style,
aboveground with central courtyards. They were quite
unsuitable for the climate. Central courtyards were supposed to be for growing a garden, but no Kjallan plants
could be grown here. Old habits died hard, she supposed.
Smoke curled from the chimneys, and the homes were
decorated, manicured, and in perfect repair. Surely these
were the homes of the Kjallan overseers. Her guess was

confirmed when one of the doors opened and a Kjallan man stepped out, shivering in his syrtos, to salute the passing battalion. Soon others joined him.

"Grab them," ordered Lucien.

A squad of men ran at each house. Some seized the unresisting Kjallans standing on the doorsteps, while others barged indoors to look for more.

Within minutes, the soldiers had the Kjallan overseers and their families assembled on the road before the battalion.

"Prefect Quincius!" one of the overseers cried. "Have we done something wrong?"

"My rank is now tribune," Quincius corrected mildly from where he rode on Lucien's left side. With a flick of his chin, he indicated Lucien. "Kneel before your emperor, Mercurius."

The Kjallans turned to Lucien. Their eyes went wide as they took in his wooden leg, and they dropped to their knees. Mercurius's jaw moved, as if he itched to say something, but he held his tongue.

"Speak," said Lucien.

"Your Imperial Majesty, we thought you were dead."

"I'm not dead, only betrayed by the usurper Cassian." He raised his voice so that the entire battalion, now forming in columns behind him, could hear. "By my order, the village of Tinst is no longer under your leadership. This evening, when the villagers have returned from their duties, I shall address them. As for you . . ." He looked down at the prisoners. "You have committed no crimes, so you may either stay in our custody temporarily, until it's safe for us to allow you to return to Kjall, or to stay and take up new roles with White Eagle. Mercurius, you are a Healer, are you not?"

"Yes, sire."

"We would value your services in White Eagle. But if you choose to return to Kjall, you will do it without your riftstone. I cannot have you providing succor to the soldiers of my enemy. All of you will make your decisions by morning." His eyes flicked to Quincius. "Tribune, the battalion is yours."

Quincius swung his horse around and gave orders to his prefects and squad commanders. The battalion erupted into activity, setting up camp in the village streets and establishing one of the Kjallan houses as a holding area for the overseers.

The encampment formed rapidly. Once it was established, the afternoon passed slowly for Vitala, while the soldiers of the battalion played dice games and gnawed on strips of dried spinefruit. She was impressed at how orderly the camp was; each century seemed to know where to position itself relative to the others, and the end result was a tight grid with Lucien's command tent in the center. The camp followers had set up their tents a slight distance from the battalion. Vitala had discussed with Lucien not allowing them to come at all, to eliminate the possibility of infiltration, but after some argument they'd agreed it wasn't feasible. The men would balk at being denied such comforts, and morale was important. Besides, with no source of income, the women might starve.

As the afternoon wore into evening, the Tinst villagers began to filter in from the woods. No doubt many of them had hesitated on the edge of the forest upon seeing the battalion encamped in their village. The battalion offered the possibility of decimation—surely rumors of that prospect had reached them by now—but hiding away and succumbing to the death spell was no palatable alternative, so they turned up in groups of two and three.

The soldiers directed each frightened-looking group

into an open space in the center of the village the soldiers had cleared for the purpose. Engineers had pulled apart an abandoned house and used the lumber to construct a podium, from which Lucien would address the village. The Riorcans huddled together, darting occasional glances at the encamped battalion and at the podium, speaking to one another in low whispers.

When the sun set, the villagers were still arriving, and the soldiers lit a pair of bonfires on either side of the podium large enough to shed some light, but not so big that their roar would drown out Lucien's words. Then Lucien mounted the podium, and silence fell.

"Riorcans," he began.

He had a good voice for oratory, Vitala discovered: not deep, but clear and powerful.

"I am your emperor, Lucien Florian Nigellus." He paused for reaction, but there was none, except for the crackling and spitting of the fires. He held up a letter. "In my hand, I hold the latest orders for White Eagle battalion. These orders were not issued by me, but by the traitor who now commands the Kjallan military, the usurper Cassian."

Hundreds of pairs of eyes fixed on the letter in his hand. Vitala was as surprised as anyone; she had not known orders had arrived for White Eagle.

"These orders call for the decimation of the village of Tinst. We are to select one of every ten men, women, and children by lot to be executed by the stake."

In the near silence that followed, Vitala heard someone quietly sobbing.

Lucien looked over the crowd, pausing to make eye contact with individual villagers. "These orders will not be carried out." His words were punctuated by an explosion of sparks from the bonfire. "This is what I think of these orders." He stepped off the podium, walked to the rightmost bonfire, and fed the paper to the flames. Then he mounted the podium again. "People of Riorca, long have you suffered, first under my great-grandfather's rule, then my grandfather's, and finally my father's." He leaned forward over the podium, and the Riorcans in the audience mirrored the gesture, leaning toward him. "Countrymen, these orders are *vile*. They are inhumane. And do you know why the usurper issued them? To punish Riorca for murdering me. When here I stand before you, alive and well!" He gave a bitter laugh. "The usurper attempted to kill me, and he blames my supposed death on Riorca. But this is no surprise to you. As Riorcans, you are accustomed to being blamed for things you did not do, punished for crimes you did not commit, and forced to labor while others lay idle and enjoy the fruits of that labor. Is this not true?"

Vitala watched the crowd as Lucien continued to speak. They were a worn, demoralized people who had barely reacted to his opening words. But as he went on, chronicling and excoriating the Kjallan abuses of the past, she began to see signs of life—a pair of bright eyes, an encouraging murmur. They were skeptical, but they warmed to him, blinking awake from long, unwanted dreams. Lucien engaged them well; his voice had an intensity that compelled attention, and he actively sought eye contact with his audience.

"No more!" cried Lucien, pounding the podium as his oration neared its conclusion. "Today, my Riorcan brothers and sisters, I ask your forgiveness for the crimes of the past. Riorca shall suffer these injustices no longer. As proof of my good intentions, I offer you a gift. Though, in truth, it is something that belongs to you by right, something taken from you by force that shall now be returned to you. I speak of your freedom." Several villagers gasped, and Lucien paused to let the words sink in. "Standing on either side of this podium are the Healers of White Eagle battalion. In a moment, I'm going to ask you to form lines before each of them, so that they can remove your death spells. Your former overseers are in custody and will be returned to Kjall. Ladies and gentlemen, Tinst is now a free village."

The Riorcans greeted these words with a ragged cheer.

"Now, I must warn you," said Lucien, "there will be some hard times ahead."

Every eye rose to meet his. They knew there had to be a catch, and here it was.

"In freeing Riorca—and Tinst is but the first of many villages White Eagle is about to liberate—I have all but declared war on the usurper Cassian. He will send troops to oppose me. Though you are a free people of whom I make no demands, I cannot win this war without your support and cooperation."

Heads nodded hesitantly throughout the crowd.

"I do not ask you to fight for me—that is the battalion's job—but the usurper will move quickly to cut off our supply lines. Without supplies, my troops will starve, and the usurper will reclaim and re-enslave this village. Yet Riorca, when not saddled with crushing tributes, is a rich land, fully capable of supporting its population and supplying my troops as they fight this war on its behalf. Villagers of Tinst, can I count on your support?"

"Yes!" many cried.

"Stand up and get in line to have your death spells removed," said Lucien. "And then we shall celebrate. My men have brought food, and we have musicians. Are there any Riorcan musicians in the crowd?"

A few heads nodded.

"After your spells are removed, fetch your instruments and join the others. But first, hear White Eagle's salute to the liberated village of Tinst. White Eagle!" He turned and gestured to Quincius.

For a moment, nothing happened. Then the ground shook beneath Vitala's feet as a thousand Kjallan boots, all around her, hit the earth at the same time. "HURRAH!" came the soldier's cry, so loud and so primal, emerging out of the darkness, that Vitala's hair stood on end. There was a ringing clash as their swords struck one another in unison. "HURRAH!" Finally came the ear-shattering blast of muskets firing, and the accompanying flashes of orange. "HURRAH!"

Vitala's flesh felt electrified. The soldier's salute wasn't merely a gesture honoring Tinst; it was a demonstration of power—power that was now acting for Riorca instead of against it. To witness it was exhilarating. Having never admired him more, she felt a fierce desire to run to Lucien and embrace him, but she refrained. He'd stepped down from the podium and was surrounded by his officers and by Riorcans who wanted to look on him, touch him, as if he were a god come down from the sky.

She brushed tears of joy from her eyes. She'd dreamed of this moment, offered herself up as a sacrifice in order to help to bring it about, but never expected to see it with her own eyes. Their work wasn't over yet, not by a long shot; they still had the usurper to deal with. But even if they lost the war against Cassian, at least the Riorcans would die free.

The musicians struck up a tune, and Riorcan couples headed into the open area to dance. Vitala looked about for a partner. Lucien was busy, and anyhow he was not able to dance. She spotted a Riorcan fellow eyeing her;

he seemed too shy to approach her. She took him by the hand, gave him an encouraging nod, and let him whirl her into the crowd.

She danced for over an hour, turning often to glance at Lucien. Always he was surrounded by admirers, Kjallans and Riorcans, with whom he clasped wrists and conversed, seldom smiling but nonetheless making himself approachable. She had a feeling he wouldn't have danced even if he'd had two good legs; to dance with commoners would have diminished him in their eyes. Happily, there was no such restriction on her.

The celebration was still in full swing when Lucien excused himself and headed for the command tent in the company of his officers. Vitala excused herself as well, bidding farewell to the young, pock-faced Kjallan soldier she'd been dancing with, and hurried after him.

Lucien's party separated, with the officers going to their own tents and Lucien to the command tent he shared with Vitala. The guards admitted her as she followed him, and she found Lucien in the bedchamber, stripping off the outer layers of his military uniform.

His eyes met hers. "I think that went rather well."

Vitala reeled as if drunk. "You're a gifted orator."

His eyebrows rose. "Thank you. It's good to have that acknowledged."

The formality of his speech stung. He was still imposing distance between them. Too bad—she'd never been more attracted to him than she was right now. "Surely you've heard it said many times."

He sat on the edge of his cot and began working loose the intricate knots of his sword belt. "Not as many as you might think. And when subordinates praise me, I assume they're just trying to curry favor."

"But when you're emperor, everyone's a subordinate."

Lucien smiled. "Now you see the problem. But you're an exception. You're not a subordinate. You're— Well, I don't know what you are."

Vitala smiled. *That makes two of us.* "Did you really tear up the orders from Cassian?"

Lucien chuckled. "No, I wrote those up myself. We haven't received orders from Cassian yet, and, besides, they'll arrive by signal, not by letter."

She stiffened. "You lied about the orders?"

"We know they're on the way."

She allowed that was probably true, and she didn't mind a little stagecraft for the crowd. But if he'd so casually lied about the orders, was the rest of the speech also peppered with lies? His words had so affected her. She hadn't considered that they might be just an act, another bit of strategy well executed. "Did you mean what you said in that speech, Lucien?"

"Of course I meant it."

"Including the part about asking forgiveness for the crimes of the past, about there being no more injustices under your watch?"

Lucien tugged off his boots. "Some of the sentiments were overblown, but the gist is true."

If she'd been drunk before, she was rapidly sobering up. "The sentiments were overblown?"

He shrugged. "A little."

Vitala fumed. "Is this all pragmatics for you, then? I don't believe you care a whit about Riorca and how it's suffered over the years. I believe you're just flattering and seducing the locals so they'll provide your army with food and supplies."

He stared at her in bewilderment. "I didn't flatter them—I set them free. Are we in this war to win or not?"

"Yes, we're in it to win!" She shook her head. "It's just . . . your words were so moving. I couldn't help thinking you actually meant them. I *wanted* you to mean them."

"Vitala, old wounds can't be healed in a day. I'm helping your country. Don't ask me to love it."

"It would be nice if you stopped hating it."

"Vitala, *look* at this." He jabbed a thumb at his maimed leg. "You expect me to love the people who did this to me? And you! They turned you into an assassin who seduces men and kills them. It's disgusting. It's horrifying! What amazes me is that *you* don't hate them!"

"They didn't force me to be what I am."

"Did you *ask* for the job?"

Vitala burst into tears. "Riorca is what your people made it. Do you think the Circle would even *exist* if Kjall hadn't enslaved my country?"

He gave a sigh of exasperation. "So it's Kjall's fault."

"Yes, it is! If you hate me, if you hate what I am, blame yourself for it. Blame Kjall. We Riorcans only did what we had to do."

He was silent, and for a while all she could hear were the sounds of her own choked weeping. Finally, she climbed into her cot, pulled the covers over herself—no way was she going to undress in front of him—and reached up to deactivate the light-glow, which plunged them into darkness.

"I don't hate you," said Lucien softly.

"Never mind," said Vitala. "It's not important." But it was.

His footsteps padded across the room toward her, and he knelt by her cot. She felt his warm breath on her face. "Can I make a deal with you?"

She screwed her eyes shut. Her sobs had ceased, leaving her in the desolate, empty state that followed. "What deal?"

"I don't have to love your country, and you don't have to love mine."

"Fine. I accept."

A warm hand touched her cheek, and she instinctively turned toward it, opening her eyes again, though she could see nothing in the darkness.

Then she felt the prickle of his heat, the promise of his lips as they hovered a breath above hers. "I don't love your country," he said. "But I love *you*."

She hesitated. Then, in response, she kissed him.

He rose from the floor to deepen the kiss, climbing on the bed and then on top of her, framing her face with his hands and stroking her neck. "I enjoyed watching you dance this evening," he said. "I was glad you took part — otherwise all the women would have been Riorcan, and there weren't near enough to go around."

"I'm Riorcan too."

"They didn't know." He paused. "I was jealous of all your partners."

"You needn't be. I wished every one of them was you."

He smiled and reached under the covers, where his hand encountered her syrtos. "Did you really get under these covers fully dressed?"

She laughed. "Yes."

"Let's fix that," he said, tugging at her belt, "and then I'll show you how much I love you."

20

As Vitala and Lucien rode at the head of the battalion, now on its way to the village of Echmor, a messenger galloped up to the troop column. Vitala watched as Lucien unfolded the message, studied it with unblinking eyes, then grimaced and folded it up again.

"What does it say?" she asked.

"Two things. First, it's the orders we expected from Cassian. We're to decimate the villages of Tinst, Echmor, and Rynas."

"I thought you said those orders would arrive by signal." She poked him in the arm, teasing.

"They did arrive by signal, at White Eagle headquarters. Then a runner delivered them to us on paper."

"So that's one thing. What's the other?"

"We've captured the signal tower at Turos Tor."

Vitala glanced around at the marching battalion. "We have? What does that mean?"

"The day after we arrived at White Eagle, I dispatched two squads on horseback to capture the signal towers at Emwar Pass and Turos Tor. All signals from the interior of Kjall pass through those towers. Once I have them both, not only will I be able to intercept all communications from Cassian, but I'll also be able to send false signals in Cassian's name."

"Three gods," said Vitala, astonished at the power

that would grant them. "What signals are you planning to send?"

Lucien shot her a sly grin. "I'll figure it out when we capture the other one."

That evening in the command tent, Vitala sat with Lucien as he scratched out a letter with his quill. Their argument the night before, rather than driving them apart, had drawn them closer together. He didn't have to love her people to help them, and it was a relief to have it known, at least behind the closed doors of the command tent, that she possessed no fondness for Kjall either. The burgeoning alliance between Riorca and Lucien's army wasn't a love match, and it didn't have to be. Riorca didn't have the resources to save itself; neither did Lucien. But if they worked together, however uneasily, they just might save each other.

How she and Lucien felt about each other was something else. Lucien had outright told her he loved her. He knew her history, some of it, and hadn't rejected her, which she regarded as a miracle. Unfortunately, there were still some things he didn't know, like her problem with the visions. He was being patient in the bedroom and seemed content with activities other than intercourse, but how long could that last? Not forever. Their relationship could only be temporary.

Lucien finished his letter and folded it up.

"Who are you writing to?" she asked.

"My cousin."

"Queen Rhianne? How are you going to get a letter to Mosar? Won't Cassian intercept it?"

"I'm sending it to her best friend, Marcella, under Quincius's name," said Lucien. "Marcella will send it on to Rhianne."

"You're certain Marcella won't betray you?"

"Yes."

"Do you think Rhianne might aid us against Cassian?" His cousin had recently been crowned queen of Mosar, a wealthy island nation, though it was small compared to Kjall and battered by a recent war. A war with Lucien's father, in fact, which didn't help Lucien's case.

Lucien shook his head. "I doubt Mosar has any aid to spare, and King Jan-Torres is no friend to me. But Cassian is claiming I'm dead, and word may have reached Rhianne by now. I hate the thought of her grieving."

She smiled, touched by his concern, but at the same time, she felt a hollow ache in her chest. She had no family members who would miss her if she died.

One of the door guards poked his head inside the tent. "Sire, there's a man here who wishes to see you."

Lucien frowned. "Can it wait until morning?"

"Perhaps, sire. The man says one of his squad mates is hiding a woman, not one of the usual camp followers. Shall I dispatch the prefect on watch to deal with the situation?"

"No, this can't wait until morning. Send him in."

The young soldier entered the command tent, nervously running a hand through his hair. He bowed his head, knelt before Lucien, and recited, "Matho, Second Century, Green Squadron."

Lucien clasped his wrist and pulled him upright. "Matho, I don't believe we've met. Are you new to White Eagle?"

"Yes, sire. I joined early this spring."

"Very good, and which of your mates in Green Squadron, Second Century, is the one hiding the woman? Would it be Protus, by chance?"

Matho blinked, startled. "Yes, sire."

"Show me to Protus's tent." Lucien rose, grabbing his crutch.

Vitala grabbed his arm. "Let me go instead of you. If the woman is an assassin, let's not give her access to you."

He plucked her hand off his arm and checked the pistol at his belt. "I thought you said the assassin would be after you, not me."

"Could be both of us. Why make things easy for her?" Vitala wrapped her sword belt around her waist and began to tie the knots.

"Why let her take us on one at a time? Besides, the woman probably isn't an assassin at all, in which case this is a simple disciplinary matter."

"Lucien—" she began, but he headed out through the tent flap as if he hadn't heard her. Two bodyguards moved to flank him.

Vitala trotted after him. "Wait. I'm able to sense assassins through their wards. Let me do that before you send anyone into the tent."

Lucien halted, and his eyes lit. "How do you sense them?"

"Relax my mind and feel for the contact points that conceal the Shards. But walk slower."

He continued at a slower pace, and Vitala softened her mind, letting the edges of her vision blur. The real world grayed into dimness, as in the faded moments before sunrise, and the colorful undercurrent of the spirit world sprang into view, soft blues and purples and greens. Usually she didn't see so many wards at once, but she was in the midst of so much tightly packed humanity that her surroundings swirled with them. Yet she sensed nothing in range that suggested an assassin with Shards. "Nothing yet," she said. "Tell me when we're getting close to the tent."

Lucien took her hand and led her through the maze of squadrons.

"It's up here, sire," called Matho, pointing. "The one with the green circle on the side."

Vitala sharpened her mind just enough to spot the tent with the green circle, then relaxed it again to see the wards inside. "No assassin," she said. "At least, no one with Shards. And judging by the wards, there's only one person in the tent."

Lucien's forehead wrinkled. "Shouldn't there be two?"

"Well, there could be another person who's not warded. I doubt it, though." No one went without wards in Kjall or Riorca, not by choice.

"Could the second person be dead? Can you see a dead person's wards?"

"No, wards dissipate when their hosts die," said Vitala.

Lucien shrugged. His bodyguards shadowed him as he approached the tent. "Protus," he called. "Come out."

A disheveled-looking soldier appeared at the tent flap and blanched at the sight of the emperor and his entourage.

Lucien exchanged a glance with Vitala. "Let's go inside."

Vitala, Lucien, and the two bodyguards squeezed uncomfortably into the interior of a tent meant to house only two.

"Where is she?" Lucien asked.

Protus's eyebrows rose in poorly feigned surprise. "She?"

"Do not lie to your commander, Protus," said Lucien.

Protus cast an angry look outside the tent. "I don't know, sire. I'm not even the one who brought her here. It was my tent mate, Matho. He's trying to frame me because he thinks I stole his grain ration three days ago—"

"No more lies, Protus." Lucien's voice was unusually quiet. He was one of those men, Vitala realized, who raised his voice in passion when arguing a point but lowered it when truly angry. "You're already getting the lash. How thoroughly and accurately you answer my next question will determine whether or not you also get the stake. Who is the woman, and where has she gone?"

The soldier turned beleaguered eyes on each of Lucien's companions, wordlessly begging for support. When he found none, he stammered, "Sage's Honor, sire, I truly don't know! She was here. Then Matho left, I guess to squeal on me, and I went out to kill a tree, and when I came back she was gone. As for who she was, I didn't catch her name. I thought she was just one of the camp followers."

"You or Matho thought that?"

"I thought that when Matho brought her here."

Lucien turned to Vitala. "You want to question him?"

Vitala leaned forward eagerly. "What did she look like? Was she Kjallan or Riorcan? How old was she? How tall?"

"She was Kjallan," said Protus. "About your age, maybe, or a little older. Kind of short. Big here," he said, cupping his hands at his chest.

Vitala turned to Lucien. "That could be Ista."

Lucien nodded. Vitala followed him out of the stuffy tent into the cool night air, where Matho waited, along with a small audience of curious spectators. Tribune Quincius stepped forward. "What's the situation, sire? I heard you might have found an assassin."

"There might be one loose in the camp—we're not sure. Pass the word among the soldiers. We're looking for a young Kjallan woman, not one of the usual camp followers, big-chested and a few inches shorter than Vitala. No one is to attack her, but report any sightings immediately."

"Yes, sire. And . . . ?" His thumb gestured toward Protus.

Lucien frowned. "Twenty lashes."

Quincius saluted and turned to give orders to his subordinates.

"You don't believe Protus's story about being framed?" asked Vitala.

"Not a word of it," said Lucien. "What now? Shall we walk the whole camp, and you try to sense her?"

Vitala nodded. "I think so. I—" She blinked as something fell suddenly into her hand. Without thinking, she grabbed it, but it stabbed her finger, and she released it with a hiss of pain. She looked down to see her own Shards, ward-broken and released from their hiding places in the Rift, raining from her fingers. Biting back a curse, she grabbed the nearest one from the air, then dropped to hands and knees to scoop the others out of the dirt. Dead Shards, every one of them, their death spells released and lost forever. Only a wardbreaker assassin, someone with the same training as herself, could have done such a thing.

Vitala stood, clutching the Shards, and cried out, "She's here! Close by!"

"The assassin?" asked Lucien.

"Yes." She started to relax her mind to sense the assassin—*Ista. It has to be Ista*—but stopped. It was too dangerous. Maybe Ista hoped Vitala would do that; then she could shoot her or rush her with a sword while Vitala's mind was focused on sensing wards.

Soldiers sprang into action all around her, their movements chaotic and disorganized. Lucien was shouting something, the bodyguards had drawn their weapons, and everyone was running about.

"Don't attack her—she's dangerous!" cried Vitala.

"I found her!" cried a voice behind her.

Vitala whipped around, looking for the source of the voice. Gods, what perfect cover this was for Ista—hundreds of nearly identical tents in all directions, with only the open road that passed through the center of the camp providing a reference point. "Where? Don't touch her."

"I've got her!" cried the voice.

Vitala scraped her sword from its scabbard. She grasped the hilt in both hands for better control and power, and raced toward the row of tents where the voice had come from.

"Vitala!" cried Lucien.

She ignored him. As she ran, she waited for another shout from the unknown soldier to help her locate him more precisely, but it never came. And when she rounded the row of tents and entered the more open space of the road, she saw why. He was on the ground, twitching away the final moments of his life.

A breath of wind tickled her from behind, and she turned just in time to meet the sword that sang toward her. She knocked it away with the flat of her blade and countered with a thrust to her enemy's midsection, pushing her back. Her guess had been right—it was Ista. Her fellow assassin circled warily in a hanging guard stance.

"Whore," Ista spat. "Traitor."

Vitala adopted high guard and sized up her opponent. No visible weapons except for the sword—she'd probably stolen the blade from the man she'd killed. Good. It would not be the right weight or size, though it was slender enough for her to handle. Ista would have Shards too, but there was no time for Vitala to ward-break them; she'd just have to keep her distance to prevent Ista from using them. "Did Bayard recover?" she asked.

"Yes, no thanks to you."

Ista made a high thrust at Vitala's neck, which Vitala easily parried—not a serious attack. Ista was feeling her out. Vitala had never beaten Ista in the training room, but the last time they'd sparred had been three years ago. Vitala had a slight height and reach advantage, and she'd improved a lot in those three years.

Soldiers from White Eagle were beginning to reach them, but they didn't know what to do. They hung back, watching and awaiting orders.

"Bayard said it was a mistake taking you on, that you were never a proper assassin," said Ista.

"He's such an ass."

"He meant it." Ista tilted her blade upward, shifting into high guard, and aimed a brutal stroke at Vitala's shoulder. Vitala parried it, feinted high, and attacked low, but Ista's blade was there to meet it. The strength and speed of Ista's blows surprised her—her old rival had lost nothing during her years in the field. Vitala pressed hard with another feint followed by a flurry of blows. None of them landed, but she forced Ista to take a step backward.

Vitala smiled. "I seem to be better suited for it than you are."

Ista returned to hanging guard. Vitala knew well the vulnerabilities of that stance. She struck from middle guard, forcefully beating Ista's sword point off to the right so that Ista's wrists were twisted. Then she followed up with an attack to the left shoulder. Ista, still untangling herself, could not parry, but she leapt aside to avoid Vitala's sword point.

Then something exploded in Vitala's ear.

For a moment, Vitala had no idea where she was or what was happening. Ista was on the ground, screaming soundlessly as blood welled from her leg.

Vitala spun around. Lucien was behind her. She smelled acrid smoke and followed it to its source: the barrel of Lucien's pistol. "Why'd you shoot?" she cried. She could hear a little bit out of her left ear, but not at all out of the right.

Soldiers raced toward Ista.

"No, no!" Vitala shouted, but her voice sounded hollow and distant. "Don't touch her! She's still dangerous."

The soldiers hesitated, but only for a moment. Then they moved forward again.

"Obey her!" barked Lucien. "Stay back."

Quickly, Vitala relaxed her mind, saw the nine contact points that held Ista's remaining Shards, and broke them one by one, forcing the dead, useless Shards to spill into Ista's hands. Then she kicked the sword away. "Now you can grab her."

A soldier came forward and picked up Ista.

Lucien said something she couldn't make out, and the soldiers reluctantly dispersed. Vitala stood where she was for a moment, staring at the pool of Ista's blood as it soaked into the ground. Lucien took her by the arm and led her gently away.

Vitala followed Lucien into the infirmary tent, holding a hand over her right ear. It throbbed slowly. The pain built steadily and agonizingly until it reached an excruciating climax, then there was a moment of relief, and the cycle began all over again.

The infirmary tent was smaller than its more permanent counterpart on the command terrace at headquarters, but large enough to hold six cots, five of which were empty. The sixth held a sleeping soldier. Someone laid Ista down on one of the empty cots.

Lucien was giving orders. She couldn't hear them very well, but the infirmary staff leapt into action. A pair of Healers ran to Ista's side, pushed away her syrtos, and revealed the bullet wound, a near-perfect circle in her thigh, red and pulsing blood. One of the Healers placed his hands on her leg and closed his eyes. Vitala stared.

A hand on her shoulder pulled her aside. Lucien's mouth moved. She heard only the faintest echo of his speech, as if he were standing on the far side of the camp, not right in front of her.

"I can't hear," she said. And when that didn't seem to register, "Gods curse it, Lucien, I CAN'T HEAR."

Lucien patted her shoulder, nodding acknowledgment, and directed her to sit on a cot. Soon a third Healer laid his hands on her and murmured something. She couldn't feel the magic, but the pain began to recede, each throb a little less powerful than the last. She was startled to discover the infirmary tent was quite loud, with lots of people talking over each other and shouting orders.

"Better?" asked the Healer.

"Yes, thank you." She glanced at Ista's cot, which was surrounded by people. Lucien walked up. "You didn't have to shoot her," said Vitala. "I was going to win that fight."

Lucien shrugged. "I saw my opportunity and I went for it. You said she was the best assassin in your enclave."

"I said she was the oldest, not the best."

"Longest surviving, I figured that meant the best. And let me guess. You were the young upstart with something to prove?" He smiled, which irritated her.

"Gods, I don't know why I'm trying to explain this to

you," she said. "Do you realize you nearly destroyed my hearing? What if you missed and shot me by mistake?"

"I'm a war mage. I never miss. And why didn't you just shoot her yourself?" He indicated the pistol still tucked into Vitala's belt.

Her cheeks warmed as she realized how much easier that would have been. "I didn't even think of it. Once I turned and parried that first stroke, everything was instinct." She lowered her voice to a whisper. "What are you going to do with Ista? You can't interrogate her—she'll use her deathstone."

"What do you think we should do?"

"Send her home." Vitala bit her lip. As much as it worried her to let a dangerous enemy go, there really was no other way. "The Obsidian Circle will reconsider allying itself with you once they learn you're freeing villages. This would be a bad time to antagonize them by killing one of their best assassins."

Lucien's brows lowered. "She came here intending harm. And she killed one of my men."

"I know," said Vitala. "Let the Circle feel the debt."

He grimaced. "Very well. I was thinking along those lines myself, but I wanted to make sure I wasn't losing my mind—since when has Lucien Florian Nigellus ever spared the life of a murderer? We'll send her back with a message for the Circle. But what happened to you? Were those your Shards spilling out of your hands?"

"Yes." She winced as if she'd stepped on a spinebush thorn; in the excitement of battle, she'd forgotten about the Shards. She opened her hands to look for them, but they were gone. Probably lying in the dirt somewhere. "She disarmed me. I did the same to her, but she can get more Shards from the Circle. I can't."

"Can my people help you recast the spells if we find the Shards?"

"Maybe. It takes a Healer and a Warder, which you have, but I don't think Kjallans know the techniques. I don't know them either."

"When things settle down a little, we'll try. In the meantime, I'll have some men search for the Shards." He glanced at Ista's cot. "I think they're finished with her." The crowd around Ista had thinned. He walked over to her, and Vitala followed.

Ista was sitting up. Her clothes were bloodstained and her skin was pale as sea spray, but clearly she was out of danger.

"Are you strong enough to travel?" asked Lucien.

Ista regarded them with an air of mulishness and said nothing.

"This isn't an interrogation," he said. "We're letting you go. I just want to make sure you won't fall off your horse three steps out of the camp."

Ista's skeptical eyes moved from Lucien to Vitala and back again. "I'm strong enough to ride. May I have some water?"

Lucien nodded to a nearby soldier. "Fetch water. Food, too." He pulled a folded letter out of his pocket and handed it to Ista. "Read this."

Grudgingly, as if she were doing him a favor, Ista unfolded the paper and read. "It's orders. You're to decimate the villages of Tinst, Echmor, and Rynas."

"Those orders are from the usurper Cassian. We've already been to Tinst, and we didn't decimate it—we liberated it. A horse will be prepared for you tomorrow morning. I'd like you to ride to Tinst and see for yourself what my people did there, and then return to your Circle.

Tell them we're not your enemies, and they should call off these assassination attempts."

Ista's forehead wrinkled.

"It's true," said Vitala. "I wouldn't have joined Lucien otherwise. He's not here to harm Riorca. He's here to free it."

Ista regarded them with a mixture of scorn and disbelief. But it didn't matter whether she believed Lucien's words; she'd be a fool to turn down the offer of a horse and clemency. Her curiosity would very likely send her to Tinst as ordered.

A soldier arrived bearing a waterskin and some strips of dried spinefruit and stockfish.

"Camp rations," said Lucien. "Nothing fancy, but it's what we eat when traveling."

Ista didn't seem concerned about the quality, nor should she be; the Circle, like all of Riorca, lived austerely. She drank deeply from the skin and bit off the end of the dried fish.

"You'll stay the night here, under guard, and ride out in the morning. Understood?"

Ista nodded.

"That man you killed," added Lucien. "His name was Jovius. He was twenty-three years old, an only son from Ingdan. His mother's a weaver. She sent him a hand-woven blanket every winter."

"How tragic that he was placed in harm's way," said Ista. "And just think, if your country was not so intent on occupying and exploiting mine, he would still be alive."

"I take your point," said Lucien. "But Jovius was not your enemy. You just killed one of the men trying to free your country. Good night."

21

In the morning, Ista was dispatched, without ceremony, on horseback to Tinst, and the battalion marched on to Echmor, another dead village, which they freed in the same way they'd freed Tinst. Lucien repeated his speech and theatrics, including burning the supposed orders from the usurper. After an evening's celebration, they moved on to Rynas.

In Rynas, a live village, there were no slaves to free, but Lucien spoke to the people and described what he'd done in Tinst and Echmor. Then he announced that they would no longer be required to pay tributes to Kjall, and another village had been converted to his side.

Later that evening, an exhausted rider rode into the encampment, covered head to toe with red dust.

Lucien welcomed him. "Antius. You have word?"

"We have the signal tower at Emwar Pass, sire," said Antius.

"Good," said Lucien. "Rest up, and I'll send you back to headquarters with orders for our signalers."

When the scouts had left and Vitala was alone with Lucien in the command tent, she said, "That's good news. Now you can countermand the decimation orders." After all, if White Eagle had received decimation orders, in all probability so had the other battalions. While Lucien's battalion was freeing villages, other battalions might be decimating them.

"I'm not going to countermand them. It's not the best use of those signal towers, and, besides, it will look suspicious."

Vitala gaped. "Lucien, you *must* countermand those orders. If you don't, Riorcans will be murdered by the thousands. You said you were going to help Riorca. If you want my support, if you want the Circle's support—"

"Vitala, let me finish," he said. "If I countermand the orders, it won't stop the decimation. In fact, it will probably make things worse."

"Why would it make things worse?"

"Because of something else I'm doing. Let me explain." He called to the door guards, "Pass the word for Quincius."

The tribune arrived minutes later and, at a gesture from Lucien, sat down at the command table.

"Do we still get our supply shipments on the fifth day of the soldierspan?" Lucien asked.

"Yes, sire," said Quincius.

"And it's the same for the neighboring battalions, is it not?" He leaned over the map and pointed. "Blue Lion, to the west of us, here. Orange Oak, to the southwest, here. Blue Wolf, east of us, here. Are these positions correct?"

"Yes, sire."

"I want you to call up three prefects and assign each of them one of those shipments. Have each of them work out a plan for quietly intercepting it. They mustn't leave any witnesses. I'm going to send the commanders of Orange Oak, Blue Lion, and Blue Wolf signals from Cassian saying that he's suspended the shipments due to lack of imperial funds."

Quincius laughed. "Very good, sire."

Lucien nodded. "Choose your men for their intelligence and discretion. Have them work up plans this evening and present them to me tomorrow morning."

"Yes, sire."

After Quincius had left, Vitala slumped in her chair. "All right, you're going to make the battalions angry with the usurper while securing supplies for White Eagle, but I don't see what that has to do with the decimation orders. If you take away the battalions' food, they'll steal from Riorcan villages."

"One thing you may not be aware of is that those supply shipments include the soldiers' pay. Imagine for a moment that you're a soldier in Blue Wolf. First you're given orders to decimate a village. Then those orders are rescinded and you're told *not* to decimate the village. Then you're told you won't be getting fed or paid this month. How do you react?"

"I wring my commander's neck," said Vitala.

"Yes, well, how do you react if you don't want to wind up on a stake?"

"I see what you mean. The man who's angry at his boss hits his wife, who slaps the child, who kicks the dog. The soldiers, who can't take out their anger on the usurper or on their commander, will take it out on Riorca, possibly by carrying out the recently rescinded decimation order. And stealing food. But won't they do that in any case?"

"They'll want to exact revenge on the usurper for not paying them, so whatever he last ordered them to do, I think they'll avoid doing," said Lucien. "Including decimation."

"That's risky," said Vitala. "There's no telling what the soldiers will do when denied food and money."

"Conveniently, I'll have extra food and money on hand to offer them."

Vitala laughed. "Come on! You can't believe they'll fall for that—won't they figure out it was you who stole it from them in the first place?"

He grinned. "I won't tell if you won't."

"Where else could it have come from?"

"It doesn't matter," said Lucien. "A Kjallan soldier's loyalty is to whoever provides the tetrals. I'll have White Eagle at my back, and I'm their legitimate emperor. Remember that the usurper has lied to them about the Circle killing me, and my very existence is proof of that."

"Gods help you if they find out you've been lying to them too."

"Indeed," said Lucien.

"And, just like that, you'll have three more battalions at your disposal?"

He shrugged. "There are details to work out. But yes. Just like that."

The days and weeks that passed were heady and dizzying for Vitala, as Lucien's plans began to bear fruit. False signals were sent out, supply trains intercepted, and White Eagle marched from village to Riorcan village, where Lucien gave his speech and liberated the populace. Gifts arrived at White Eagle's encampment—salt cod, goat cheese, wooden carvings, a tiny sack of gunpowder that someone had hoarded in secret for years.

Lucien wanted to seek out the Circle and open negotiations, but Vitala advised him not to. Better to let the Circle come to them.

So Lucien opened negotiations with the leaders of Blue Lion battalion. He ascertained that the soldiers were incensed at the usurper for having denied them pay and supplies, and offered to remedy the situation. When the leaders hesitated, he faked a signal from Cassian demanding a series of random personnel changes: promotions and demotions among the officers that made no sense at all and infuriated them. Soon afterward, they accepted his offer to address the troops of Blue Lion.

The men of White Eagle were openly jubilant about meeting up with the other battalion. Many of them had friends in Blue Lion whom they hadn't seen in years. Supply carts were loaded high with food and wine— after stealing six supply shipments, White Eagle had more than enough to go around—and the march to Blue Lion's grounds was a happy one, with many smiling faces.

The mood at Blue Lion's encampment was quite different. The disgruntled atmosphere was evident not only in the soldiers' faces and in the camp's lack of cleanliness, but also in the whipping posts newly erected in the center of the camp.

The commanding tribune had managed to assemble the soldiers, and Lucien mounted a podium to speak. He moved slowly, emphasizing the action of his wooden leg and crutch rather than downplaying them as he usually did.

"Thank you for tolerating the extra time it takes me to get up here," he began. "As you can see, I've made sacrifices in the service of my country."

Applause began, light at first, but it grew louder and louder. Vitala smiled. Lucien had his moments.

He held out his arms for silence. "I come to speak to you today about a very important matter: the crimes of a man named Cassian." The crowd booed the name; some men shouted and threw clods of dirt at the nearby battle standards that, judging by the stains on them, had seen some abuse already. "What are the crimes of this

Cassian? Let me name them. First, he has, through vile and underhanded means, forcibly removed from the throne the rightful Emperor of Kjall and called him dead. Do I look dead to you?"

"No!" the crowd answered.

"Second, he has blamed this crime on Riorca and ordered the execution of thousands of innocent men and women to assuage his guilty conscience. Soldiers, I ask you: is this the act of an honorable man?"

"No!"

"Third, through his incompetent mismanagement of government and his personal greed, he has betrayed the men most important to the survival of the empire itself—you, the fighting men of Kjall!"

The crowd roared its anger.

"He has denied you much-needed supplies." Lucien ticked points off on his fingers. "He has denied you food. He has denied you your *well-earned pay*. I don't think this is any way to treat Kjallan imperial soldiers."

The soldiers shouted agreement. More clods of dirt flew through the air toward the battle standards.

"You have wives and children, mothers and fathers and sister and brothers to support. That is why I have come here today. You must have your wages, and I shall pay them out of my own personal coffers—"

The shouts of the soldiers became so deafening that he had to pause for a moment, patting the air with his hands in an effort to quiet them.

"Gentlemen, I am only giving you what you are owed. This is your due for the fine service you pay our empire. I don't ask for your thanks, but I do ask for your help. Cassian is no emperor. He is a usurper, a criminal who must be brought to justice. Join forces with me, and we will take back Kjall from betrayers and thieves."

Cheers rose as he stepped down from the podium, and Vitala had little doubt that Blue Lion would soon be joining forces with White Eagle.

Though Vitala had spent almost her entire life in Riorca, it was only now, traveling with Kjallans, that she truly became acquainted with her country. With White Eagle, she marched from one end of it to the other, through dark, mossy forests, red-dirt badlands where little grew but dry brush, and the frost-limned foothills from which one could hear the Great Northern Sea crash angrily against the cliffs. It was a beautiful, austere country, and her heart swelled with joy to know it at last.

Lucien often sent pensive looks in the direction of the iron-gray waters, and she knew why. He feared an attack by sea. When Orange Oak battalion had joined him, he'd gained control of two Kjallan warships, but two would not be enough.

"I hate to say it," he commented as they crossed through Nacuny Pass on their way to some of the villages on Riorca's northern coast, "but we're lucky Mosar wiped out the Kjallan fleet in the last war. The most the usurper will be able to raise is about eight warships."

"You think he's figured out what's going on in Riorca by now?"

Lucien nodded. "The reports coming in from the mainland sound unusually dull. I suspect the usurper knows I have the signal towers. I'm not worried about him sending troops by sea. He can't transport enough that way, and we'd just retreat inland. But he could wipe out the Riorcan fishing fleet."

Vitala bit her lip. "And then we'd have no salt cod."

"Exactly," said Lucien. "The men might cheer that

news at first, but I'm sure they'll wish for their salt cod when they begin to starve."

"Can't we outfit the Riorcan fishing vessels with cannons?"

"We could if we had cannons." Lucien frowned. "Or ammunition. Which brings me to another point." He pulled a folded piece of paper from his pocket. "We've heard from the Circle."

She took it from him eagerly, but as she absorbed its contents, her enthusiasm faded. She handed it back to him. "You have to decline this. I'm not taking you back into one of the Circle's enclaves, not after what happened last time."

He looked pained. "I need the Circle, and I can't wait much longer. I'm completely blind to what's going on south of the Riorcan border."

"You may need the Circle's intelligence, but the Circle needs your army even more," said Vitala. "Send them a counteroffer. Tell them to meet you on White Eagle grounds, and I'll bet you truffles to red dirt they'll accept."

Lucien stuffed the paper back in his pocket. "I hope you know what you're doing."

22

The Obsidian Circle sent three enclave heads into the White Eagle encampment to negotiate a settlement. Two of the men were unfamiliar to Vitala; the third was Bayard, and he was leading Flavia on a rope leash. Vitala locked eyes with him the moment he rode in, careful to conceal her excitement at seeing the dog, even though Flavia was pulling at the leash and swinging her tail so enthusiastically her whole body wagged. Vitala looked all three men over with a wardbreaker's eyes, searching for traps—hidden Shards, hidden anything—but she found nothing.

"Vitala," said Bayard stiffly as he entered the command center.

"Bayard," she replied in the same tone.

"And Emperor Lucien," said Bayard, extending his hand.

Lucien, too savvy a negotiator to even glance at Flavia, clasped wrists with him. "It's a pleasure to welcome the Obsidian Circle into my camp. Even if you did try to kill me a few times," he added without humor.

Bayard pulled out a topaz on a gold chain and offered it to Lucien. "Sir, we would like to return your riftstone."

Lucien glanced at it quizzically. "That's not my riftstone."

"Ah." Bayard raised his eyebrows at Vitala.

She smiled.

"Well, the dog seems to believe she belongs to you," said Bayard, handing the leash to Lucien.

Lucien nodded, passing the leash to one of his guards with instructions to take her someplace where she wouldn't disturb the proceedings. He sent a happy wink to Vitala.

Bayard continued. "You know me already—my name is Bayard. My companions are Asmund and Gulli. We each command an Obsidian Circle enclave."

Lucien gestured for them to take their seats at the table. "And you know Vitala, formerly an Obsidian Circle assassin, now my trusted adviser. And this is Tribune Quincius, who commands White Eagle battalion."

"We're pleased with the work you've been doing here in Riorca," said Bayard. "Freeing villages, relieving them of tribute payments. This work is compatible with the goals of the Obsidian Circle."

"I'm happy to be of assistance to my Riorcan allies," said Lucien.

"Your actions have attracted the attention of Emperor Cassian back in Riat."

"He is no emperor, but a usurper," said Lucien.

"Very well," said Bayard. "Nonetheless, the actions you are taking endanger Riorca. The usurper will send troops, far more of them than you have been able to muster. If you lose this war, Riorca will pay the price for it."

"If I lose this war, I will pay for it personally, with my life."

"And do you believe he will be satisfied with taking only yours?"

"No," said Lucien. "But never forget, no man has more at stake here than I. Before I turned these battalions to my side, Cassian had already ordered them to decimate Riorca. If Riorca is to be punished no matter what it does, let us choose the course of action that gives Riorca a chance to win its freedom."

Bayard smiled. "Your thinking mirrors ours."

Asmund, a burly blond with his long hair tied back at the base of his neck, spoke up. "Emperor Lucien, we propose an alliance between yourself and the Obsidian Circle. We have much to offer you: a vast intelligence network encompassing the whole of Kjall, trained assassins who can target key military figures and destabilize the enemy's forces, and influence throughout Riorca that can solidify supply lines for your troops. We want you to win this war."

Vitala smiled. Lucien was properly expressionless, but he had to be salivating.

"And what does the Circle ask in return?" asked Lucien calmly.

"Several things," said Bayard. "The first is immunity. Any so-called crimes committed by the Obsidian Circle against the Kjallan Empire must be forgiven—they were acts of war, no longer relevant now that we are allies. Furthermore, should this war be won, we require a role in the new government of independent Riorca—"

"Let me stop you," said Lucien. "Riorcan independence is not politically viable if I wish to hold on to my throne. What I propose is an end to slavery in Riorca and an end to tributes, but Riorca must remain under Kjallan rule. It would be treated as any other Kjallan province and ruled by a provincial governor."

"Riorcan independence is the primary goal of the Obsidian Circle," said Gulli. "We cannot compromise on that point."

"If you cannot compromise, you will walk out with nothing," said Lucien.

Vitala spoke up. "What if we were to guarantee, in writing, that the provincial governor of Riorca would always be a Riorcan?"

"How do you define *Riorcan*?" asked Asmund. "Someone born in Riorca?"

"No," said Bayard. "Obsidian Circle. Riorca will remain under Kjallan rule, but the governor of Riorca must be always be chosen from the ranks of the Obsidian Circle."

Lucien sent Vitala a barely perceptible, questioning look. It was clear to her what Bayard was up to. He was thinking ahead and reenvisioning the Circle as a ruling dynasty for Riorca. She didn't care for it, not one bit, but they needed the Circle's support and they had to give them something in return. After all, what was the Circle going to do after the war was over, when a resistance movement was no longer needed—disband and fade away? She nodded her acceptance.

"Done," said Lucien. "The governor will be a member of the Obsidian Circle."

"We need to set this in writing," said Gulli.

Soon all four men were speaking at once. Someone grabbed for paper and an ink pot. Vitala smiled, knowing the horse trading would go on all night.

Lucien's eyes swam as he stared at the page. They had it all down in writing, how power would be shared among Kjall and Riorca and the Circle if they won this impossible war. What time was it, anyway? Late o'clock. The sun would rise soon.

Vitala, at least, had the sense to get some sleep. She'd crept off to bed a couple of hours before and was dreaming now, probably. The agreement would please her. He'd snuck in a clause just for her—the Circle had agreed to rearm her with ten new Shards to replace the ones Ista had taken.

"Emperor, there's one more thing," said Asmund.

Lucien had found Asmund to be the most reasonable of the three Riorcans. He almost liked the man. "The papers are already signed."

"This isn't part of the official agreement," said Asmund, "but we'd like you to take a Riorcan wife."

Lucien blinked. *A wife?*

"You see," said Bayard, "writing this down is well and good, but some of us find it a little suspicious that you developed an interest in liberating Riorca only after you were deposed and suddenly needed people to supply and shelter your army. Who's to say that after you recover your throne, you won't stab us all in the back?"

Lucien glared at him. "Because I don't do that sort of thing."

"We're only seeking assurance that your commitment to Riorca is a lasting one," said Asmund. "Why not a marriage? It's a permanent union—a symbol of the permanent coming together of Kjallan and Riorcan interests."

The request would have been unreasonable were it not appealing to him on its own merits. He hadn't meant to act so soon, but . . . well, why not? "I'll marry Vitala. If she'll have me."

"The problem with Vitala," said Bayard, "is that she does not look Riorcan."

Lucien's eyes narrowed. "She doesn't qualify because her hair's too dark? Vagabond's breath, she's an Obsidian Circle assassin! No one could be more Riorcan than that!"

"Her credentials are impeccable," agreed Asmund.

Bayard shook his head. "You know and I know what she is, but when she stands next to you, she looks Kjallan.

She is not, in fact, full-blooded Riorcan. She's half-and-half."

"She's as Riorcan as they come. I don't care who sired her or what she looks like."

"Choose someone else," said Bayard. "Anyone with the Riorcan look. If you want someone from the Circle, we have many who would suit, including some fine beauties lovelier even than Vitala—"

Lucien shook his head. "It's Vitala or it's nobody."

"Emperor—"

Lucien picked up the packet of carefully inked papers. "It's Vitala or it's nobody."

"I think Vitala is a fine choice—" began Asmund.

Bayard's cheeks flushed with anger. "Emperor, may I speak with you privately?"

"You have something you can't say at this table?"

"Yes, I do. Emperor Lucien, I have known Vitala since she was a little girl," said Bayard. "There is nobody in the world who understands her as well as I do. I'd like to share with you a few things before you make this decision."

The word *no* was on the tip of Lucien's tongue. He reflexively loathed Bayard. The man obviously didn't want this marriage to happen, and was going to come up with some sort of objection to it, probably one based on lies. But Lucien was pretty good at sorting out lies from truth, and Bayard *had* known Vitala for a long time. Wouldn't it be better to hear the man out now than to wonder, later on, what he had to say?

"Very well," said Lucien. "My bodyguard stays, but I'll hear you."

Rather than repair to another room, Lucien stayed put while Quincius and the other two Riorcans headed to their sleeping quarters. When they'd cleared out, custom dictated that Lucien should offer Bayard wine, but he made no move to do so. The snub seemed neither to surprise nor perturb Bayard.

"Emperor, do you know exactly what Vitala is?" asked Bayard.

"Of course I know," said Lucien.

"She's a whore."

Lucien's ears rang as blood rushed to his head. He found himself half rising from his chair. "You will not insult her again, or I'll have you thrown out of this tent."

"It's the truth, and you know it."

"She sells sex for money—is that what you're claiming?"

"Not for money," said Bayard. "For political advantage."

"She slept with men to assassinate them. She did it for love of her country. You're wasting my time if you think you can shock me with that."

Bayard leaned back in his chair. "It doesn't bother you at all that the woman you want to marry sleeps with men and kills them during the sex act?"

Of course it bothered him, but if he'd come to terms with it, what business was it of Bayard's? "Past tense, Bayard. She *used* to do that. I've killed people too, up close and personal. And I've slept with other women before Vitala. I'm not going to judge her for things I've done myself."

Bayard's eyebrows rose. "You're a very tolerant man. But there's something else."

"So far you've only told me things I already know."

"Does Kjall train assassins?" asked Bayard.

"A few," said Lucien.

"Have you been involved at all in their training?"

"No."

"But you work with soldiers. Men who kill for a living."

"That's a vast oversimplification of what soldiers do," said Lucien.

Bayard waved his comment away. "You're probably aware that some soldiers who experience combat develop problems. Nightmares, intrusive memories."

Lucien froze. Bayard could not know about those memories. There was no possible way. "What do you mean, *intrusive memories*?"

"Hard to describe," said Bayard. "Those who have them say they're like a dream—a nightmare, rather—experienced while awake. As if they're transported from the present into another time and place."

Lucien swallowed. *Could* Bayard know? He was, after all, Obsidian Circle. He had access to the largest spy network on the Kjallan continent. "I've never heard of such a thing. Sounds like madness."

"It is rather like madness. Your soldiers never experience this?"

"No." Which was a lie. Some soldiers did go mad and had to be executed or sent home, and some even shot themselves. But those cases were an embarrassment. They were kept quiet, and Bayard didn't need to know about them.

"It is not uncommon among our assassins," said Bayard.

Lucien met his eyes. "Are you saying Vitala has this problem?"

"I don't know for certain. But we find that the assassins who have trouble with their practice kills are the most prone to it. And Vitala had trouble with her practice kills."

"Practice kills—what are those?"

"Before we send an assassin out on her first mission, we have her kill a few captive soldiers to make sure she will not hesitate when it comes time to dealing the fatal blow. The first one's quite easy; the soldier is tied up and she just has to finish him off with her Shard. The later ones are harder. They more closely mimic an assassination scenario."

"And Vitala had . . . what sort of trouble?"

"She made the kills, but with reluctance. One of the kills seemed to traumatize her."

Lucien shook his head. "I think I'd be more concerned about the trainees who *weren't* reluctant."

"You'd be wrong," said Bayard. "Those are our best assassins."

"I'm glad I'm not marrying one of them."

"The point is, the most reluctant assassins are the most prone to madness. The day Vitala broke you out, I thought she'd already succumbed. I thought she'd gone mad and rebelled against the Circle, and that's why I tried to shoot her."

"She was rational then, and she's rational now."

"I realize that, but this madness has a way of lurking, of hiding away for years, until for no apparent reason it emerges. If you marry Vitala and win this war, she will be the Empress of Kjall. What if it afflicts her in later years? Can you afford to have a madwoman on the throne?"

Lucien snorted. "This is the most ridiculous argument I've ever heard. I shouldn't marry Vitala because someday she *might* go mad? Look, anything *might* happen. I might eat some bad fish tomorrow and die, and then the usurper will win the throne by default."

"But that's not likely. This is."

Lucien folded his arms and leaned back in his chair.

There were certain things Vitala didn't feel ready for, because of her ugly experience with Remus, but that was understandable given what she'd been through. She'd get over that in time. She wasn't *mad*. Besides, madness didn't come from combat or assassination experiences—if it did, only soldiers and assassins would experience it. But housewives went mad. Children went mad. No, it had to be evil spirits that caused it, or the corrupting breath of the Vagabond. Why else did they toast the Vagabond at every full moon, saying "Great One, pass me by"? Why else did his tribunes always encamp their armies outside the forests rather than within them, where the spirits were?

Breezily, he waved his hand. "In that case, she'll be the Mad Empress of Kjall. It'll give the people something to talk about."

"I don't think you're taking this very seriously," said Bayard.

"I'm taking it exactly as seriously as it deserves," said Lucien. "So, how do I propose to her? Do Riorcans use a go-between like we do in Kjall?"

Bayard bristled. "The Riorcan delegation hasn't agreed to this marriage—"

"Look." He rustled the papers on the table. "You're the only one from the delegation who objects to my choice. The papers are already signed, and I'm proposing to Vitala. If you don't want to help, I'll get the information from Asmund."

Bayard huffed an exasperated sigh. "To propose, you send her an . . . there is no word for it in your language. An *iskele*."

"What's an *iskele*?"

"It's a carved wooden box. You have to carve it yourself, and you put inside it something that she will recognize as from you. The idea is that when she receives the box, she knows she's received a proposal of marriage. When she opens it up, she knows who is proposing by what's inside."

Lucien wrinkled his forehead. "What do people usually put inside?"

"Anything that will make her think of you and you alone. There are stories about men who—well, never mind. Just make sure she doesn't mistake the proposal as being from somebody else. And keep it simple."

"How do I get the box? I can't carve wood."

Bayard gave him a scornful look. "A Riorcan who cannot carve a simple wooden box is unworthy of marriage."

"Fortunately," said Lucien, "I'm not a Riorcan."

23

By the furtive looks and shy smiles Lucien and the Riorcans had been sending her all day, Vitala could tell something was up—something besides the agreement they'd hammered out last night, which was groundbreaking. That was all right; she had a secret too, something she'd been privately working out with Asmund. When Asmund summoned her for a conference in his tent, she thought it would be about that, but instead he handed her a carved wooden box.

Tears stung her eyes. Though she'd never seen an *iskele* before, she recognized it at once. "Who's it from?" she asked, remembering belatedly that the whole point was to figure that out herself.

Asmund gave her a gentle smile. "Open it and see."

Her first thought was Lucien. But he knew nothing of *iskeles*, and how could he have carved the box? She turned the box over, studying it for clues. Could it be from anyone else? She didn't think so. Finally, she opened it.

There was a Caturanga piece inside, a cavalryman. Definitely Lucien, though the cavalryman was an uncharacteristically humble choice. Why not a more powerful piece, like the Tribune? Perhaps in this proposal he felt humble, because he wasn't sure she would accept him.

She wasn't sure she would accept him either.

"Well," said Asmund. "Who's it from?"

"Lucien. But how did he carve the box?"

Asmund winked. "I helped him."

She began to tremble, a reaction that began deep inside her body and slowly spread to her fingers and toes. How to answer Lucien? She wanted to say yes, except . . . that answer involved obligations. If she married Lucien, she would be expected to consummate the marriage, and ultimately to produce an heir. Could she do that?

"And do you accept him?" asked Asmund.

"I—I don't think I can," she stammered.

Asmund's face fell. "Do you not like the emperor?"

"I like him very much, it's just . . ." She trailed off. How could she possibly explain this? It was too intimate a subject, and she barely understood it herself.

Asmund waited patiently for her objections, and when they did not come, said, "Could you tell me your reasons? This marriage would be very beneficial to Riorca and to the Circle. If Lucien wins this war, you will be Empress of Kjall. Think of that—a Riorcan empress! And your son would be emperor after Lucien. You and your children would be advocates for Riorca long after this war is over, and Riorca needs such advocates."

"I understand. But can't he marry another Riorcan woman?" She winced as she said it—her skin crawled at the idea of him marrying someone else—but what else could she do? Lucien needed an heir, and if she couldn't provide one, someone had to.

Asmund looked surprised. "He will have none but you."

Vitala's throat felt thick, and her eyes moistened.

Asmund took her hand. "Is he cruel, Vitala? Is he a harsh man?"

"Gods, no."

He swallowed. "Is there something about him you're not telling me?"

"No." She shook her head. What was she thinking— let Lucien marry another woman? She would lose him forever, to someone who would never understand him or love him like she did. What sort of coward was she?

Yes, the young soldier haunted her, but who was she to give up on the man she loved after experiencing a single vision, one that hadn't even lasted very long? She needed to conquer this. She was an assassin of the Obsidian Circle; she had killed seven men. The young soldier was but a ghost; he was no match for her. She would banish him from her head, or at the very least find a way to cope with his presence. She would do it for Lucien, for her country, and for herself. Forcing her lips into a smile, she said, "No, there is nothing. I was only startled by so grand a proposal. I accept. Let Kjall and Riorca be united, as Lucien and I are united in marriage."

In the command tent, Lucien greeted her with open arms, and Flavia spun in a happy circle. "Did I do it right, the *iskele*?"

"You did it right," she said, entering the warmth of Lucien's embrace. "I mean, as far as I know. There aren't a lot of marriages in the Circle."

He sat down, pulling her onto his lap, and kissed her. "Please tell me the Circle didn't bully you into accepting my proposal."

"I would never have let them."

"Are you all right with ... you know, the wedding night?"

A shiver ran through Vitala. "Yes. I mean, I know it's been a problem. But I'm ready now."

He angled his head toward the tent flap that led to the bedroom. "*Right* now?"

She mock slapped him on the arm. "On our wedding night."

He rolled his eyes. "How very Riorcan of you. We Kjallans don't wait," he teased. Then added soberly, "Are you sure?"

Her voice grew soft. "I'm sure. I have to conquer this."

"We'll conquer it together. You tell me what you need, and I'll help you. All right?"

"All right." Forcing some brightness into her tone, she said, "When's the wedding?"

"Five days hence. I hope you're not expecting a big imperial to-do, because under the circumstances—"

"Oh no, I wasn't expecting anything big," said Vitala. "I'm still stunned you would take a commoner to wife."

"I think you know why I chose you," said Lucien.

"You needed a bodyguard?"

"Pah," he said, tracing her lips with his finger. "Gods help me, I'm marrying for love. How my father would disapprove! Still, there *are* political benefits to this match, and if I marry a Riorcan, I have no choice but to marry a commoner." He squeezed her arm, softening any sting his words might carry.

She nodded, not offended. Riorca had once had a ruling upper class, but the Kjallans had wiped it out. From what she'd heard, this was no great loss, as the old royals had been violent and oppressive. Their extermination would have been a favor to the Riorcan people had the Kjallans not simply inserted themselves in their place. If Riorca won its freedom, it would get a new start. As empress, her voice would help shape the new Riorca as a freer, happier nation—if she could tame the Circle and its dynastic ambitions.

"But I promise you," Lucien said, "if we win this war, we'll have another wedding later, a proper one, with a guest list of five thousand people and oceans of flowers and I don't know what."

Vitala laughed. "If you say so. It's not important to me."

"It's important to the Kjallan people," he insisted.

The map on the command table caught her eye. It had new figures all over it and wooden pointers and scribbled notes on paper. "What's all this? Did the Circle share its intelligence with you?"

He stood, pushing her off his lap. "They did."

"And now you know where the usurper's forces are?"

"I do, and they're on their way. They aren't unified yet; he's having to bring in forces from both sides of Kjall." He grabbed a pointer. "See, he's got troops here, here, and here. Unfortunately, Riorca is damned near indefensible; there's no single pass where we can cut him off. I haven't decided yet whether we should try to keep his army split or allow it to mass up. If I keep it split, that could hamper his communications, but then I have to fight on multiple fronts." He tugged at his earlobe. "Much to think about. I'll probably keep it split in the short term."

"How many battalions is he sending?"

"There are a couple we're not sure yet are involved, but it looks like fourteen at best; sixteen at worst."

"Fourteen to sixteen battalions? Against our six? Three gods, Lucien, what are we going to do?"

He stared down at the map. "We'll have to be very clever, that's for sure."

"How can clever win against odds like that?"

"Well," he muttered, "I said *very* clever."

*   *   *

In the morning, Vitala rode south with Lucien to Jasah Pass, through which the usurper would soon march several battalions. For this scouting mission, they'd left the troops at the encampment and brought only Quincius and a number of junior officers. And Flavia, who loved nothing more than an all-day expedition. From the top of a weedy hill, they surveyed the pass while Flavia bounded through the brush.

"The problem," said Lucien, "is that there's no real choke point. If we try to hem him in at the road, there are too many ways he can go around."

"No way to block the alternate routes either," said Quincius.

"There's a saying: 'One cat at the hole can keep a thousand mice at bay.' But where can we find such a hole?"

Flavia stopped dead in a patch of thick grass, her ears up and alert. Vitala followed her gaze to the thread of blue snaking its way through the dusty hills. "What about water? Cassian's men have to drink. Would ambush points along the river be more effective?"

Lucien's eyebrows went up. "Maybe." He pointed to a distant hill. "Let's go over there. We'll have a better vantage point."

The river turned out to be rather more promising than the pass itself. Having wound through these lands for countless generations, it had carved its own canyon, and was at the moment running rather low. There were few access points where one could descend to water level. Vitala grabbed hold of Flavia to keep her from heading down into the canyon. Lucien and his officers located several places where bowmen and muskets could set up on the far side of the river so that they had a height advantage, good cover, and an escape route.

"I like this." Lucien shot Vitala an approving glance. "I like it a lot. We won't be able to inflict huge losses on them, but if they can't break up our ambushes, they'll have to divert to the Aleor River east of here, and that will put them off schedule and frustrate the usurper's plans. Even if they do break up the ambushes, our harassment will frustrate them, force them to ration water, and cut down on troop morale. And our own men will be at almost no risk at all."

"Pardon me if this question is impertinent, sire —" began a prefect from Orange Oak.

"Speak freely," said Lucien.

"Why are we so concerned with troop morale? It seems to me we should focus on inflicting real losses, and, as you say, we won't be able to do that here."

"I respect your question, prefect. The reason is that most wars are won or lost based on which side first loses the will to fight. I intend it to be the usurper's side that gives up first."

"Yes, sire." The prefect's head bobbed.

"We already have an advantage in that this war involves Kjallans fighting Kjallans. The usurper's battalions won't like the fact that they've been sent to kill their brothers in arms. Our men don't like it either, but they're not the aggressors. It makes a difference."

As the junior officers left to mark ambush points and escape routes, Tribune Quincius whispered conspiratorially to Lucien, just within Vitala's earshot, "You think you're going to win this war based on soldier morale?"

Lucien shrugged. "I'll win it any way I can."

24

Days later, the combined encampment of six battalions had begun to look like a patchwork blanket. Centuries from each battalion had left to harass and delay the usurper's approaching troops at Jasah Pass and other locations. Once they returned, Lucien would move the combined army to a more defensible location, but that location was still undecided. Since he was the one being pursued and attacked, he had the advantage of being able to choose where the battle would take place. Unfortunately, every site had drawbacks. Some offered the possibility of being flanked, a grave concern when the usurper's army so outnumbered his, while others left him vulnerable to attacks by sea or severed supply lines, also serious threats.

While they awaited the return of the absent troops, they held a wedding.

It was an informal affair, but with six partial battalions of soldiers present, plus one gold-and-white dog, extraordinarily well attended. Had the location been up to Vitala, she would have chosen a high ridge with the Great Northern Sea pounding the cliffs in the background, but to include all the soldiers, they held it in a great open field. Each century was in military dress, with flags and pennants, standing in formation behind its centurion. Together, the centuries formed a circle around Vitala and Lucien and the officiating chaplain.

The ceremony was a blur to Vitala. She remembered placing the garland over Lucien's neck and receiving her own from his trembling hands. She remembered the needle biting into her upper arm as it administered the marriage tattoo. She remembered drinking wine, in turns, from a shared cup, the one Riorcan tradition they had incorporated into the wedding. The rest was a haze of half-forgotten words, the rolling of her stomach, and the thousands of eyes upon her.

The battalions followed the ceremony with their triple salute: the hurrahs with the foot stomping, the sword clanging, and the musket shooting. Carried out by three times as many men as before, it was thrice as loud and thrice as intimidating.

A feast would have been customary at this time, but given the nearness of war and the paucity of supplies, the supply officers had deemed it infeasible. So instead Vitala headed back to the command tent with her new husband, passing by row after row of cheering, catcalling soldiers, smiling and blushing all the way. When they arrived at the tent, they found a private feast had been left for them.

"Gods, that smells good," said Lucien as they entered, lifting the lid off the tray. "Are you hungry?" He removed the garland from around his neck and set it on the table.

"No. I wish I was." She took off her garland too, her fingers shaking with nerves. "I have a gift for you," she stammered.

Lucien blinked. "You do? I'm sorry, I didn't get you anything."

"I didn't expect you to," said Vitala. "This was something special I had the opportunity to acquire. And I'm not sure you'll like it, actually."

"Well." Lucien chuckled. "You make me so eager."

She pulled the cloth-wrapped package out from under her bed and set it on Lucien's lap.

His eyebrows rose at the size and weight of the object, which occupied his whole lap. He began to unwrap it, exposing a length of polished wood. "A weapon?" he asked. Then he pulled it free. "Oh." It was a wooden leg, quite different in style from the one he wore. Instead of a padded hollow carved into the wood at the top of the leg, there was a stiff leather cuff, large enough for him to fit his entire stump into and adjustable. The leather was bolted to the leg itself, made of a wood not so fine as that of his current leg, but equally smooth and glossy. The leg's curved contours led to a hinged ankle and a foot that, while not a replica of the human form, provided good traction and distribution of weight. There were no straps at all. For its size, the device was surprisingly light-weight.

Lucien bit his lip. "You know I tried many legs before settling on the one I have."

"Not one by a Riorcan craftsman," said Vitala. "Please try this one."

He sighed. "Don't be offended if I don't like it." He removed his old leg and slid his stump into the leather cuff of the new one. "How did you get it fitted?"

"I got the numbers from your tailor," said Vitala. "The man who made this leg for you says he'll adjust it once you've tried it on. It will probably need fine-tuning."

"How odd that there are no straps." Lucien regarded the device morosely, as if reluctant to stand and disappoint her.

"He said you wouldn't need them. The cuff will keep the leg on all by itself." Vitala took him by the arm and lifted him to his feet.

Lucien wobbled for a moment and winced.

"Is it hurting?"

"Yes." Lucien reached down and adjusted the cuff. "That's better. It pinched."

Vitala felt herself deflating. "I'm sorry. It's no better than the others—"

"Give it a moment." Clinging to her arm, he took one tottering step forward, then another. He flashed her a grin, and hope surged; her insides melted like candle wax. He reached down and made another adjustment to the cuff, then let go of her arm and walked all the way around the room. "Look! No crutch."

Vitala stared. Such an ordinary thing, a man walking, but she'd never seen Lucien do it before, not without a crutch.

Lucien took a second turn around the room, faster this time. "How did your craftsman get it so light? Is it hollow inside? Most of them feel like you're dragging a cannonball around."

"I believe it is hollow. You can ask him yourself—his name is Braesi."

"Send him to me, because I want to give him a medal. This is a world of improvement." He tentatively jogged a couple of steps on the leg, then came back, grinning infectiously. "I wonder if I could— Say, do you know this one?"

There was no music, but he grabbed her by the waist and swept her into the unmistakable rhythm of the "Carousel Waltz." Giggling, she followed his lead. It was a slow, uncomplicated dance. Even so, he was clumsy and awkward; she'd certainly known better dance partners. But as they wheeled and turned, she felt his confidence growing. His steps grew bolder, his turns sharper. His fingers tapped the rhythm on her hip, and in her head she imagined the keening of the violin and flute. When they came to the part where he was supposed to lift her in the air, he paused, uncertain, and they both laughed. "Perhaps that would be taking things too far," he said.

"I'm glad it's working," Vitala murmured into his chest.

"That Braesi," said Lucien. "I want to kiss him. No. I want to kiss *you*." He lifted her chin and pressed his lips to hers, tasting her, savoring her like wine.

This is it, Vitala thought. But the shiver of fear that ran through her paled next to the wave of heat that pulsed through her body, warming her from the inside out. She loved Lucien. She wanted him. And the time was right.

"You know what?" murmured Lucien into her mouth. "I think we should find out just how much weight this leg can bear." He swept her legs out from under her, and she laughed madly as she found herself struggling in his arms, swaying a bit as he tried to balance.

"This will end in disaster. I can see it," she teased as he tottered unsteadily forward.

"Shush," he said. "I'm a war mage. I see things coming. Like the floor."

His balance improved as he carried her into the bedroom and laid her on the bed. She held out a hand to him. He took it, and she pulled him down atop her. While he went to work on the belts of her syrtos, she reached down to the artificial leg, loosened the cuff, and gently removed it. She rubbed the place where it had been. They were the walking wounded, she and Lucien. His broken place was on the outside, and hers was on the inside. If he could learn to cope with a missing leg, she could learn to cope with her visions.

If such thoughts preoccupied her, they did not preoccupy her partner. He'd succeeded in freeing her breasts and had cupped one in his warm fingers.

"You could be making better use of that hand," he added.

She looked up at him. "Where do you like to be touched?"

"Anywhere," he breathed as he kissed her. "Everywhere."

She reached up to his loosened syrtos and pushed it off his shoulders. He had a beautiful body. Her fingers trembled a little as she reached up to stroke his neck and back. He sighed with pleasure, encouraging her, and she relaxed.

Gods, this is working. I'm not afraid. Even as she thought it, she knew it wasn't entirely true. Beneath the heat of her desire was a cold pit of terror—the young soldier could make his appearance at any time—but she was keeping it at bay. If she could keep it there for the length of this encounter, perhaps all would be well.

"Are you all right?" asked Lucien, his voice honey soft in the darkness. He kissed his way down her neck, down her breasts, and she knew from experience where he was going. She felt a sharp throb of desire from below, but as much as she wanted what he offered, she wanted even more to get through this before any visions could take over and spoil things.

"Yes," she said. "But I think we should try . . . you know." *Intercourse.* Why couldn't she say the word?

"You seem tense to me. I'm not sure you're ready." Instead of working his way farther downward, he settled in beside her and pulled her into his arms. One of his fingers stroked her breast, sending jolts of fire through her as it passed over her nipple.

"It's your wedding night."

"*Our* wedding night," he corrected. "I have no doubts I'll end up satisfied, and there's no need to rush things. We'll have a whole lifetime together. If Cassian doesn't kill us."

"But you need an heir."

"Three gods! Not right this moment."

Vitala pulled him close and kissed him, pressing her eyes shut to stop the sting of tears, overwhelmed with the love she felt for this man. But Lucien didn't understand. Allowing more time to pass would not make things easier. Indeed, she would likely only become more anxious if she allowed the problem to fester, and, worse, continued to mislead Lucien about its nature. Her visions had not diminished in severity over the years. If they could be overcome at all, she would have to fight her way through them. And she feared that might not be possible.

"Lucien," she said, "I appreciate your patience more than you can imagine, but I have to conquer this, and it cannot wait any longer."

"Then tell me how I can help you."

"Enter me now. Before I think too much about it."

"If that's what you want." He checked her for readiness, and his hand came away slick. With a twist of his body, he was atop her, and he pushed himself inside.

"Gods." The young soldier's eyes fluttered closed as he penetrated her. His dark hair, overlong, fell across his brow. She could feel his energy, his excitement, his masculine strength. His mouth found hers and kissed it eagerly. "Who are you?" he asked. "Tell me your name."

She said nothing. She lay still, submissive, waiting for her moment.

He sighed with pleasure, his hips moving. "You're so

beautiful. Say something," he begged. "Are you a prisoner here too?"

She remained silent and motionless beneath him.

He smiled sadly and twirled a lock of her hair around his finger. "I don't understand. You offer yourself to me, but you won't talk. Have they cut out your tongue?"

"Vitala. Can you hear me? Vitala!"

The soldier was gagging, choking, his whole body seizing. Foam burbled from his mouth. Vitala's stomach lurched. She tried to fling the soldier away, but his hands had tightened and locked around her arms. She was caught in his embrace.

His frantic words came out as sharp little huffs of breath. Then the convulsions began in earnest. He thrashed atop her. She squeezed her eyes shut, but felt every moment of his suffering, every frantic kick, every spasmodic movement, every frenzied gyration of his heart. Bloody froth leaked from the corners of his mouth; warm urine soaked her thighs.

Finally she wrenched herself free of him and fled to the far side of the room, where she huddled in a corner. When his body finally lay still, she wept.

"Vitala, for gods' sake, can you hear me?"

She blinked. She was staring at a solid gray wall.

"Should we restrain her, sire?"

Vitala turned her head, startled by the unfamiliar voice. It was one of Lucien's bodyguards. Two of them stood in the doorway, watching her. She was, for some reason, crouching by the wall—and, oh, gods, completely naked. Lucien was naked too, sitting up in bed, but he'd pulled a blanket around himself. What had happened?

They'd been in the midst of coitus. She blushed furiously.

"I think she's coming around." Lucien's voice trembled. "Do you hear me, Vitala?"

"Yes." Her voice sounded strange. Distant.

"Thank you. You may go," Lucien told the guards.

They bowed and left.

"What happened?" asked Lucien. "Why did you scream?"

"I screamed?"

A pause. "You don't remember?"

Vitala shook her head.

"What *do* you remember?"

Vitala took a deep breath. Her heart throbbed so wildly, she feared it would leap out of her chest. "We were— We were making love. And then I was ... somewhere else. Next thing I remember, I was here, crouching by the wall."

"You don't remember screaming?"

"No. I ... I don't think I was conscious. How did I get here?"

"Like you said, we were making love. And your eyes did this funny thing; they went all glassy, like you weren't there. I tried to talk to you, but I don't think you could hear. And then you started screaming. I got off you, but you kicked me and ran to that spot by the wall, still screaming, and the guards came. By then you were crying, not screaming anymore. We kept trying to talk to you, but it seemed you couldn't hear us."

Vitala felt her cheeks and found the wetness there. She climbed shakily to her feet. "I'm sorry," she whispered.

"I've made women scream in bed before, but never like that," said Lucien.

Fresh tears started, and she placed a hand over her eyes.

"Sorry," said Lucien. "Bad time for a joke. It's just that lots of people must have heard, and by tomorrow rumors will be all over the camp."

Vitala's head throbbed. "We'll get an annulment—a divorce—something."

"Three gods!" Lucien blinked at her in shock. "Where did that come from? Tomorrow we'll talk about this, figure out what happened, and fix it. Right?"

Vitala closed her eyes and flopped down on the bed, exhausted and drained.

"Talk to me," said Lucien sternly.

Vitala gritted her teeth. The young soldier's face appeared in her head, unbidden. *Say something.*

"Kiss me," Lucien ordered. "Promise me we'll talk this through in the morning, when you're feeling better. Promise me you're not going to give up just because we've had a setback."

"I promise," she murmured, and when he leaned down, gave him a peck on the lips.

Anything to quiet him for now.

Though sleep came easily to her addled mind, the soldier strode through her dreams, making each of them a nightmare with his bloody froth and convulsions, until blessed unconsciousness eluded her and she found herself staring at the roof of the tent, listening to Lucien's quiet, even breathing beside her. She rolled out of bed.

"You all right?" he mumbled.

"Chamber pot," she said.

He turned over and fell back asleep.

The two door guards peered at her curiously as she emerged from the command tent. One of them reddened a little, and she recalled these were the men who'd seen her after the screaming episode. "Yes, Empress?" one of them said.

"Have my horse brought round."

The guards exchanged glances. "Does the emperor know—"

"You have orders, sir," she snapped. "Obey them."

A Riorcan forest by night might have frightened a lesser being, but Vitala was beyond fear. The clawlike branches in the nighttime fog could not intimidate her, nor could the rustling of leaves, the hooting of owls, or the bark of a badger. Vitala had too many nightmares inside her head to worry about the ones on the outside. Besides, she was in no danger. One of the guards was tailing her. He was keeping well back, but she could hear his horse's hoofbeats.

Her chestnut mare stepped restlessly in the soft dirt, neck overarched with anxiety, a faint sheen of sweat glistening along her shoulder blades. "Shh," Vitala soothed, and the horse calmed at her touch. Would that Vitala herself could be so easily reassured.

Her official kill count as per the Circle was seven, but she had, in fact, killed ten men. It was one of the three others, one of the men who didn't count, who haunted her. She didn't even know his name. He had marked her, taken up residence in her mind like a ghost. She supposed she deserved it; after all, she'd killed him, and this was a fitting revenge.

The chestnut snorted beneath her. She looked up and spotted a glimmer of light peeking at her from between the trees. Sunrise. Time to turn around and go back?

No, not yet.

25

In the early evening, she was nearing the encampment when a search party, probably alerted to her location by a magelight signal from her tail, finally intercepted her. "Empress," said the prefect in charge of the group, "the emperor has been searching for you. I'm to take you directly to the command tent."

She shrugged. "I was headed there, anyway."

The ride to the command tent was quiet and somber; some of the soldiers stole glances at her, but no one spoke. She dismounted, someone took her horse, and she entered the command tent, head high, ready for the inevitable confrontation.

Lucien stood as she entered, a teacup and saucer still in his hands. He was red-faced and practically vibrating with fury. "Do you have any idea what this day has been like?"

"Spare me the lecture, Lucien."

"Do you have *any idea*?"

She sighed and sank heavily into one of the command center chairs. "I suppose it's been about as pleasant as mine."

Something sailed past her, and she jolted in surprise as the teacup shattered against one of the wooden beams behind her, followed shortly by the saucer.

"It's *all over the camp*," Lucien roared. "It's *all over*

the camp about how I tortured you so horribly in the marriage bed that you screamed like a staking victim and ran off in the dead of night. They think I'm a sadist, a deviant, a violent-tempered monster!"

Vitala stared, astonished, at the tea dripping down the walls. "And you're doing such a fine job disabusing them of that notion."

"You promised we would talk about this!" said Lucien. "If you had stayed, we could have made something up to quell the rumors. But when you ran, that was it. I nearly had the guards whipped for letting you go."

"They were only following their empress's orders."

"Then I regret giving you an official rank!"

She shrugged. "I renounce it. We'll get the marriage annulled. It was never consummated, anyway."

He looked stricken. "Vitala, you cannot mean that."

She felt the tears starting and lowered her head.

He crossed the room to her. She realized he was moving without his crutch, that he must be wearing the artificial leg. He waved his hand, and by the sounds of movement, she understood the guards were leaving the room. Then he knelt by her chair and took her hand. "The marriage was consummated."

She shook her head. "No. You did not . . . spill your seed."

He smiled crookedly. "How do you know? You weren't conscious."

"You couldn't have. The way you described what happened—I know you would not have continued like nothing had gone wrong."

"I say I did, and I'm the only credible witness. The guards will attest that you were insensible. I say the marriage was consummated; therefore it cannot be annulled."

She let out her breath in exasperation. "Then we'll get a divorce. Kjallans do that all the time—"

"I will not grant you one. The husband can divorce the wife, but the wife cannot divorce the husband. Did you not know that?"

"No. I never studied Kjallan marriage law. I never thought it would apply to me!"

He made a clucking sound with his teeth. "You ought to have looked into it."

"There's a third option: murdering you in your sleep."

Lucien grinned. "Gods, you're giving me such a cock-stand." He got up from the floor and sat in the chair next to hers. "Tell me what happened last night."

"There's no point," she said. "I can't stop it from happening."

"How do you know you can't stop it?"

"Because I'm not conscious when it happens. I have no control," she said.

"Are you implying this has happened *before*?" he cried.

Vitala bit her lip. Time for honesty. "It has."

"But I thought—didn't this have something to do with Remus?" He looked stricken. "When could it have happened before?"

"I never said it had anything to do with Remus. I know you assumed that, and I encouraged that assumption."

"No, you said it outright. You said something happened in the tent that night."

"Something did. I had a vision in the tent that night, but it was interrupted when Remus and the others showed up."

He paused, and his brow wrinkled. "A vision? I think I remember. Your eyes went all strange—I thought it was because you heard the noise outside. Explain. What was going on inside your head?"

"No point explaining. You realize I can't sleep with you, right? This marriage you're so nobly trying to preserve—it would be a sham, a mockery. I cannot give you an heir."

"You're giving up too easily. One bad experience and you're finished? What happened to the woman who said she wanted to conquer this?"

"Let's pretend for a moment that we sleep together tonight and everything goes fine. I don't have any screaming fits that make the camp think you're a sexual deviant. Do you think that means the problem is solved?"

Lucien bit his lip.

"Of course it isn't solved," she said. "It could happen again the night after, or at the next Vagabond moon, or a year from now. That fear will hang over us always, and because of that, we'll never truly be able to enjoy ourselves. Coitus will be a chore, something we hope to get through without a disaster. That's my reality, Lucien. It will always be my reality, but it doesn't have to be yours. Don't you realize I'm trying to help you?"

"You're making assumptions," said Lucien. "You think this will never get better, but maybe it will. Maybe each episode will be weaker than the last, until it fades away entirely."

"Or maybe they'll get *worse*. When I'm having one of those episodes, I'm not myself. Next time, I might do more than scream and cry. What if next time I summon a Shard and attack you?" It was possible. More than possible. Clearly, some of her actions in the vision were echoed by her real self. Theoretically, she could disarm herself and get rid of her Shards, but in the middle of a war, that didn't seem like a good idea.

"I'm a war mage. I'm not easy to kill."

"Lucien, I *specialize* in killing war mages." She'd thought about it at length during her ride, and concluded that she simply couldn't take the chance. Fear and discomfort were one thing; losing control was another. "I'm sorry. I won't go to bed with you again."

"Vitala—"

"You must divorce me. I love you, and I wish it didn't have to be this way. But there can be no more middle-of-the-night screaming. I apologize for humiliating you."

His cheeks reddened. "Look, I'm sorry I lost my temper. Let the soldiers make up stories. It doesn't matter what they think—"

"I'm going back to the Circle," said Vitala. "That's what I came here to tell you."

Lucien gaped at her, momentarily speechless. "Please tell me this isn't because I threw the gods-cursed teacup."

She smiled sadly and shook her head. "I made my decision while I was out riding. Think about it. You don't need my protection; there are no assassins after you. You've got the battalions well in hand—you are the military strategist, not I. I cannot be your wife without failing spectacularly. I have only one skill, and with the Circle I can put that skill to use." *Killing people,* she thought bitterly. *My sole talent.*

"You're the Empress of Kjall! And you do not have only *one skill*—" he began.

Someone knocked loudly on the door. "Sire!"

His brow tightened in annoyance. "Is it an emergency, Quincius?"

"Yes, sire," came Quincius's voice.

Lucien gave Vitala a stern look. "Do not move. I'm not finished with you." He called out, "Come in." As

Quincius entered, he reached for the teapot and an unbroken cup and saucer. "What's the news?"

"A fleet's been sighted in the Great Northern Sea."

Lucien froze in the middle of pouring. "Soldier's hell."

"They're not Kjallan ships, sire. They're Mosari."

After a moment of stunned silence, Lucien leapt to his feet, wobbling a bit on the new leg. He hurried unevenly to the door, with Quincius on his heels. "Three gods, man, if that's who I think it is—"

"Who?" said Vitala. "Who do you think it is?"

Lucien pointed an urgent finger at her. "Do *not* leave!" He called to the door guards, "On pain of excruciating death, do not allow the empress to leave the command tent!"

"What's going on?" cried Vitala, rising from her seat.

But both Quincius and Lucien were already out the door.

26

Lucien burst back into the command tent. "Pack a day's supplies. We're riding out."

Vitala stood up, startled. "Right now? It's getting dark."

"All the more reason to hurry." He slap-thumped into the bedroom.

She stepped outside to whistle up Flavia, who had the run of the camp. Moments later, with the dog at her side, she followed Lucien into the bedroom and found him yanking clothes out of a chest and tossing them on the bed for his batman to pack. "What were the ships?"

"They're carrying my cousin Rhianne and her husband, the king of Mosar. We've spoken by signal relay, and I must see them immediately—they've come to help us. You'd better start packing, or you'll have nothing to wear." He ogled her for a moment. "Of course, that has possibilities."

Sighing, she went to her own trunk. "Why do we have to go to them? Can't they come here?"

"My dear Vitala, I love you, but ships cannot travel on land."

She raised a hand to slap him. "You know what I mean!" But the smile he lobbed in her direction was so joyous, so full of buoyant energy, that she lowered her hand and went back to picking out clothes. "Isn't this a bad time to leave the army? The usurper's forces aren't far away."

"Quincius will remain here, in charge, and I'll be in touch with him by signal. Once I've spoken to King Jan-Torres and determined our course of action, we'll move the battalions. Besides . . ." He rose to his feet and seized her around the waist, hugging her fiercely. "This will be *fun*. We've been hearing and smelling the Great Northern Sea for ages. Don't you want to get up close where you can *taste* it?" His kissed her neck.

Laughing, she pushed him away. How strange: a moment ago he'd been in the worst of moods and now he was happy again, but she wasn't the one who'd brought about the change. His cousin Rhianne had done it. Irrational as it was, she found herself jealous. "I said I was going back to the Circle. This doesn't change that."

"But if you meet with the Mosari leaders first, you'll have actual intelligence to carry back. Won't you?"

"I suppose so." She glanced at him sidelong. Not long ago, he'd been arguing with her vociferously on this subject.

A corner of his mouth turned up in a sly smile as he grabbed Flavia and hugged her about the shoulders, then dug deeper in his trunk. That Caturanga head of his was at work, scheming as usual. Whatever plan he'd dreamed up this time would likely prove a disappointment, but she was glad, at least, to see him back to his old self.

They packed only the bare minimum and were off at once. A baggage train would follow them with more supplies and a larger party of soldiers. For now, they rode in a vanguard of twenty horsemen and galloped through the entire remaining hour of daylight, pausing only twice to rest the horses.

Traveling among the soldiers, Vitala began to realize

how badly she'd damaged Lucien's reputation. The men watched them closely. Time and again, she saw them whisper to one another and look at her with pity, or at Lucien with revulsion. Lucien bore it well, but was not blind to it. While they rested the horses at a walk, he stared straight ahead, his mouth a thin, hard line.

What could she do to fix this? She couldn't explain to the soldiers what had happened in the bedroom that night; it was too intimate, and it wasn't anyone else's business. She didn't owe them an explanation. And if she told the truth, would they believe it? The rumors probably sounded more plausible than the reality. By now any explanation she or Lucien tried to make would have *cover-up* written all over it.

Let them figure this one out. She kneed her horse close enough to Lucien's that her leg brushed against his, then leaned over in the saddle and kissed him on the lips. His eyes opened wide, but he lost no time in returning the kiss and slipping a hand behind her neck to deepen it. The murmurs of idle conversation behind them suddenly ceased, leaving behind only the rhythmic thudding of hoofbeats. Oh yes, she and Lucien were being watched very closely indeed.

Two days of hard travel brought them to the coastal village of Tovar. Long before the village came into view, they saw the masts of the Mosari ships peeking above the cliffs. Then they rounded the hillside and the harbor came into view. The ships towered over the Riorcan fishing boats like antlered stags among field mice. Their hulls were broader and their bows rounder than Kjallan ships. Carved wooden animals decorated the rails. Though under assault by the unruly waves of the Great Northern Sea, they bobbed in a stately, dignified manner.

While Lucien and his men inquired as to whether the Mosari royals were ready to receive them, Vitala went out on the pier. The little Riorcan fishing boats were delightful to watch. Navigated by oars and a single sail, these tiny vessels, carrying four to six men each, ventured out into waves twice their height, braving rockstrewn passageways as they headed out to sea. Only the incredible skill of the sailors kept them from capsizing. One man in the front of each boat seemed to be in charge. He kept watch for rocks and currents and yelled orders to his crew, who hastened to obey. Watching their frenetic movements, Vitala's heart surged, full of love for her brave, capable countrymen.

Someone called her name, and she turned to see Lucien beckoning. After a last, longing look at the fishing boats, she left the pier and joined him.

"They're ready for us," he said.

"Did you say the king was sick?"

"He was," said Lucien. "Seasick—these waters would do it to anyone. Rhianne says he's feeling better now. Is that Flavia?"

Vitala turned to the shoreline. Last she'd seen, Flavia had been running up and down the beach, tugging bits of driftwood out of the sand.

"No, in the water." Lucien pointed.

"That little brown dot?" She could hardly believe it. Flavia was so far out in the ocean, swimming against the waves, that she could barely make her out. "She's way out there, and the water's so cold!"

"Look at her handle those waves. She's absolutely fearless."

"She has no idea of the danger. What if she drowns?" Vitala whistled, but Flavia didn't seem to hear her.

"I don't think she'll drown," said Lucien, but he

grabbed a stick and hurled it with magically enhanced strength all the way out to where Flavia was swimming. It landed with a splash, and Flavia's ears went up. She swam for the stick, seized it, and headed for shore. When she emerged from the water, she shook herself off and paraded about, looking pleased. "What a swimmer!" said Lucien. "She's a natural."

Vitala held her tongue. She was more convinced than ever that Flavia was Riorcan bred. What Kjallan dog, bred for the balmy lakes of the south, would, on a lark, brave the frigid waters of the Great Northern Sea?

Lucien took her hand. "Let's go in. Don't mention to Rhianne that you once tried to assassinate me. It's not something she would understand."

"All right," Vitala said, bemused.

Lucien led her into the decrepit town hall, which needed a paint job and a new roof. Vitala spotted a large dog prowling the open space within. No, not a dog—it was a great cat, dark brown in color and brindled with black stripes. The creature bared its huge yellow teeth, and Vitala stopped short. A rumbling at her side alerted her to Flavia, whose muzzle had wrinkled into an unaccustomed growl.

"Quiet," snapped Lucien.

Flavia fell silent. The cat eyed them briefly, then turned away. A second cat, slightly smaller but with the same coloration, slept on the floor.

Three men and a woman awaited them. Vitala picked out King Jan-Torres by the four-strand gold necklace he wore around his neck. Though not a large man, Jan-Torres had a calm confidence about him that made it clear he was the one in charge. He was colorfully dressed in the Mosari style, but with a Riorcan cloak thrown about him for warmth. Most astonishingly, there was an animal perched on his shoulder, a sleek, furry, weasel-like creature with rust-and-white fur and intelligent black eyes.

The two other men, both physically imposing and well armed, she took for bodyguards or military officers. A brindlecat sidled up to one of them and rubbed against him. The woman had to be Rhianne. Though paler-skinned than the others, she was darker than the typical Kjallan, no doubt an effect of the tropical Mosari sun. Strands of gold streaked her walnut-brown hair. Her syrtos was Kjallan in its cut and style, but gauzy and multicolored, an apparent compromise between Kjallan and Mosari modes of dress.

"Lucien!" cried the woman. "Are you *walking*? Without a crutch?"

Lucien glanced down at the artificial leg and scowled. "It pinches like a gods-cursed—"

"Three gods. I can't believe it!" Rhianne flung herself into his arms with enough impact to knock the wind out of him. "The things you don't mention in your letters!"

Vitala swallowed the lump in her throat and told herself, *I am not jealous of Lucien's cousin.* She caught the King of Mosar watching her calmly but intently.

"Three gods," murmured Lucien. His hand was on Rhianne's belly, and Vitala realized with a start that the woman was pregnant. "Speaking of things not mentioned in letters . . ."

"I wanted to surprise you," said Rhianne.

"How far along?" asked Lucien.

"Five months."

"What are you doing sailing halfway around the world?" cried Lucien. "You should be at home! Send your husband on errands like this."

With a tight-lipped smile, Jan-Torres stepped between

Lucien and Rhianne. "We decided it would be better for her to come along." Vitala was surprised to hear him speak the Kjallan language fluently.

"Jan-Torres. Your Majesty," said Lucien, extending his hand. "A pleasure."

The two men clasped wrists, their movements stiff and guarded. They circled each other like a pair of wolves with their hackles up.

"Lucien," said Rhianne. "You haven't made introductions." She turned to Vitala, her eyes bright and friendly. "Who is this lovely young lady?"

Lucien hurried back to Vitala, grabbed her hand, and pulled her towards the Mosari royals. "This is my wife, Vitala, the Empress of Kjall."

Rhianne's mouth fell open.

"Before you say anything about leaving that out of the letters," Lucien added hurriedly, "the wedding was three days ago."

Rhianne beamed at Vitala with a smile so wide it forced tears out of the corners of her eyes. "Lucien's wife. Three gods." She reached for Vitala's hand. They clasped wrists, and then Rhianne, apparently unable to resist, pulled her into a full-body hug. "I'm *so* glad to meet you, Empress. Please take good care of my cousin. He's a good man, but if he gets carried away with anything, talk to me. I know a few tricks for dealing with him." She winked.

"Yes, Your Majesty," Vitala choked out, half-crushed by the hug and aching with guilt. Rhianne didn't know, of course, that she was Lucien's wife in name only, that she had asked for a divorce and would soon flee to the Obsidian Circle. No point bringing it up now.

"Emperor." Jan-Torres had a rich, powerful voice, one that instantly commanded the attention of everyone in the room. "You seem to have landed yourself in a bit of trouble."

"I'm afraid so."

"Shall we discuss it?"

"Absolutely, Your Majesty."

Rhianne released Vitala from the hug but clung to her hand. "While they talk business, why don't you and I go for a walk? We have much to discuss."

Vitala hesitated, wondering what she could have to say to this woman.

"Stories about Lucien," Rhianne confided in a mock whisper. "Would you like to hear about the time he learned how to make explosives and blew up the door to his brother's room?"

"Rhianne, you are not telling her that!" cried Lucien.

Vitala smiled. "Yes, Your Majesty. I'd like that very much."

27

Not since he'd last seen his father had Lucien felt so inadequate. He and King Jan-Torres were roughly the same height and weight, but as they strode down the hallway together, Lucien felt like the other man was twice his size. Jan-Torres was the man who, under attack by vastly superior Kjallan forces, had boldly invaded the city of Riat, held the empire in a choke hold, and deposed Lucien's father, granting Lucien the throne. He'd also run off with Rhianne, though Lucien didn't hold that against him, since his cousin had gone enthusiastically.

And three gods, she's pregnant. A smile played about his lips, disappearing as he thought back to his own depressing situation—a wife who'd rejected him after a single night in the marriage bed. Yet another way in which he compared unfavorably. There were no children in *his* future.

"We can talk in the bedroom," said Jan-Torres beside him. "Best place for privacy."

"I knew you were fond of me, but not *that* fond," said Lucien.

Jan-Torres did not respond. What did Rhianne see in him, anyway? He was so serious, so somber. Lucien found himself wanting to provoke the man just to see if he could get a rise out of him.

Jan-Torres's bodyguard opened the bedroom door and allowed the two of them inside. Lucien was instantly embarrassed. The room was small and the furniture shabby. Some country he was running. "I'm sorry about the accommodations," he said. "If I had the means, I'd put you up in the style you deserve."

"Don't worry about it." A corner of the king's mouth quirked upward. "I'm no stranger to hardship."

Lucien snorted. He had no doubt of that; before ascending his throne, Jan-Torres had once posed as a slave in the Imperial Palace to spy on Kjall. Spreading a map out on the bed, Lucien placed markers showing the location of his and the usurper's troops.

Jan-Torres set his ferret on the floor and smiled as the creature scampered gaily about, sniffing along the walls and corners. "First things first," he said. "I cannot provide you with ground troops. My own armies are depleted after the last war."

"I understand," said Lucien, though it was a crushing disappointment. Mosari ground troops would have been a huge asset. The brindlecats that accompanied their war mages would have struck terror into Cassian's soldiers.

Jan-Torres leaned over the map. "Aren't you outnumbered?"

"A bit," said Lucien.

"More than a bit!" said Jan-Torres. "Look, I don't give two tomtits who rules your country. Coming here was Rhianne's idea. She's concerned about you and Celeste."

"Has she heard from Celeste at all?"

"She has."

"What did she—"

"It's family business, so I'll let Rhianne speak to you about it."

"You should care who rules my country, Jan-Torres.

Have you considered what it will mean if something happens to Celeste?"

"Rhianne will be distraught," said Jan-Torres. "She loves the two of you."

"It's bigger than that. Imagine for a moment that I am killed in battle, and Celeste dies without producing an heir for the usurper. This is not an unlikely scenario, especially if Celeste takes her own life. Who in these circumstances is the legitimate heir to the throne?"

Jan-Torres blinked in surprise. "Three gods. The baby."

Lucien nodded. "If male, the child Rhianne carries, *your son*, will be heir to the Kjallan throne. As such, the usurper will perceive him as a threat, and you've seen what that man does to people who stand between him and what he wants. "

Jan-Torres smiled wanly. "Then I shall pray for a daughter. I despise Kjallan politics, Emperor. Your court is a pit of snakes."

Lucien snorted. "And I have fangs of my own."

Jan-Torres scanned the map. "What are your plans, Emperor? You cannot fight the usurper from your current position. He will flank you."

"If you are not providing me with ground troops, Jan-Torres, what are you offering?"

"Support by sea," said Jan-Torres. "Ten warships that outclass anything of Kjall's."

"Very well." Lucien took the markers representing his six battalions and moved them all to Blackscar Gulch. "Here's what I propose: I shelter my forces within the gulch. The mouth is narrow. We can hold the usurper's forces at the mouth and prevent him from using the full advantage of his numbers."

"There's more than one entryway. He will come

through here and flank you." Jan-Torres pointed to Stonemaw Pass.

"He will try," said Lucien, "and the war will be won or lost at Stonemaw. I'll station two battalions at the mouth of Blackscar Gulch and three at Stonemaw Pass. Meanwhile, I'll split the last battalion into small groups and send it behind the Usurper to destroy his supply lines. If we can hold them at the gulch until the soldiers lose the will to fight, we'll win. But if the Usurper's forces break through . . ."

"What about your own supply lines?" asked Jan-Torres. "You'll be cut off in the gulch. No way in or out."

"That's where your fleet comes in," said Lucien. "I had considered and rejected this plan earlier because of the supply line problem. But do you see this?" His finger traced the blue line of the Ember River from the ocean to Blackscar Gulch. "We don't need overland supply routes. We can ship everything by water."

Jan-Torres raised an eyebrow. "You want my warships to act as shipping barges?"

"One or two of them, yes, to ferry supplies from coastal villages to the river mouth," said Lucien, growing excited as the possibilities of the plan took hold. "The rest will guard the river mouth. Then we'll have a system of barges going up and down the Ember. It's perfect, do you see? The Usurper cannot sabotage it! But we can sabotage his supply lines all we want."

Jan-Torres smiled. "It's not a bad plan. I'll speak to my ship captains, and we'll discuss details at dinner."

"Thank you, Your Majesty."

The King of Mosar sat in a wobbly chair and leaned back, lacing his fingers behind his head. "Tell me about your wife. Is she a Kjallan like yourself?"

"Half Kjallan, half Riorcan. She's from the Obsidian Circle."

"Obsidian Circle? What's that?"

"A Riorcan resistance movement. A network of spies and assassins."

Jan-Torres blinked. "You married a spy?"

"An assassin."

He laughed. "I wish you every happiness."

"Thanks," said Lucien, annoyed.

"Emperor," said Jan-Torres. "Say nothing further to Rhianne about how she should have stayed home because of the pregnancy."

"As you wish. Obviously, she's here now, and there's no going back until your fleet leaves. But you should have said something at the time. I know she loves to travel—"

"Lucien," Jan-Torres broke in. "It's her second pregnancy."

"Her *second*?" Lucien's eyes widened as he imagined a baby already at home in Mosar—and then he realized that if a child had been born, Rhianne would have said something in her letters. Something fluttered briefly in his chest and turned to pain.

"She miscarried," said Jan-Torres. "When we learned of her pregnancy, we were on the verge of leaving on a trip for Inya. I talked her into staying home, and while I was gone, she lost the baby."

"Not because she stayed home!"

"Of course not. It was the Vagabond's will, nothing more. But I told myself that if she got pregnant again, I wouldn't ask her to stay home. Whether the baby lives or dies, she will be with me. She will not be alone in her grief. Do you understand?"

"Yes, Your Majesty." Lucien lowered his eyes. He

might not be fond of Jan-Torres, but there was no question that the man loved his wife. And with Rhianne pregnant for the second time . . . well, it was clear they weren't having any difficulties in the bedroom. Why couldn't he have that with Vitala?

Lucien's troubles faded the moment he saw Rhianne. Once again he marveled at the bulge in her belly. He was going to be an uncle! Or something. What did children call their mother's cousin, anyway?

"Lucien." She folded him into a hug.

Her touch drained away his tension, turned him to butter. No one could calm him the way Rhianne did. Vitala, he hoped, would eventually be the woman whose presence made his muscles unknot, but they didn't fully trust each other yet. They needed more time.

Rhianne pulled back and studied his face. "Will you go walking with me, cousin? There are some things we should discuss."

"Of course."

Trailed by a handful of discreet guards, they took a trail of switchbacks leading up the hill and found themselves on the high cliffs overlooking the sea. Rhianne walked right up to the edge, watching the waves break against shards of black rock. She sighed. "This is my first visit to Riorca. I had no idea it was this beautiful."

"It's an awful country," said Lucien. "Underpopulated, run-down, poor as dirt."

"I meant the landscape. But as for the rest of it, whose fault is that?"

"Not *mine*," he snapped.

She sent him a chiding look. "That was my point."

He sat down on a rock. "So, the baby. What do you think it is—a boy or a girl?"

"I don't know."

"Aren't women supposed to just know?"

"I don't." Rhianne sat beside him. "Lucien, can you win this war?"

He shrugged. "It's going to depend on a lot of things."

"You realize we can evacuate you to Mosar. You and Vitala and whoever else we can find room for."

He sighed. It was a tempting offer, but there was no way he could accept it. "I've got to see this through. After all, what about Celeste? You can't evacuate her."

"I know, but better one of you than neither. If you change your mind, the offer's open."

He nodded. "Jan-Torres told me you'd heard from Celeste."

Rhianne made a face. "I have. I brought the letter so you could see it." She pulled a folded piece of paper from a pocket and held it out to him.

Lucien read. The letter had definitely been written by Celeste—he recognized her handwriting—but the things she said were all wrong. She wrote of her grief at Lucien's death and her happiness in marrying Cassian, but the words were empty and vacuous. Where was her wit? Where were the asides she always wrote in the margins? Frowning, he handed the letter back to Rhianne. "This is not her. Someone forced her to write this."

"That was what I thought," said Rhianne. "And I'm trying not to think about what else he may be forcing her to do."

Lucien shifted uncomfortably on the rock.

She nudged him. "So, tell me about your wife. How'd you meet her?"

"You just spent hours talking with her and that subject never came up?"

"I want to hear about her from your perspective. What was it about her that attracted you?"

"She's beautiful."

"So are lots of women. What else?"

He bit his lip. "She's strong. She's brave. She can fight like you wouldn't believe. And she's an amazing Caturanga player—"

Rhianne rolled her eyes. "Caturanga! Now I know your reason. You finally found a woman who will play that silly game with you."

"Vitala *gets* Caturanga, truly gets it. She won the tournament in Beryl, you know. She beats me two games out of three."

"And your fragile ego can handle this?"

"My ego's not fragile. She used to beat me in *every* game. I'm getting better, though. You watch. By next year, I'll have turned that around." *If we're still married a year from now. And the usurper hasn't killed us all.*

"You married her because she can beat you at Caturanga."

"Did I mention she was beautiful?"

"For what it's worth, I like her a lot," said Rhianne. "I think you chose well. I spoke with her a long time. She's prickly on the outside, but underneath, she has a good heart. In that respect, she's a lot like you. You practically married a copy of yourself, which, given your ego, is probably a good thing."

Lucien snorted. *Married a copy of myself. How silly.*

Rhianne's eyes were teasing. "You disagree?"

"She has both her legs, unlike me," he pointed out.

"How did you meet her?"

"She won a Caturanga tournament, and I invited her to the palace to play."

"And she's from the Obsidian Circle? A covert organization?"

Lucien shrugged. "Everybody has to come from somewhere."

"What was she doing playing Caturanga if she's part of a covert organization?"

"She's entitled to a hobby. Don't you think?"

"Hmm. I think you're keeping something from me."

He glanced up, checking the position of the sun. "Sadly, this visit will be too short for me to go into all these details."

She scowled. "I hate it when you act like this."

"Good thing you're not Vitala. She has to put up with it all the time." He uttered a silent prayer, mustering his courage. "Cousin, you have to help me. I'm losing Vitala."

"Losing her? What do you mean?"

"She wants a divorce."

Rhianne's mouth fell open. "But you've been married only three days!"

"It was a rocky three days."

"Please tell me you didn't lose your temper with her!"

"I may have thrown a teacup."

"Lucien!" she scolded.

He scowled. "Not *at* her. It's not about the teacup. It's about . . . this is embarrassing. You have to promise not to tell anyone about this, especially Jan-Torres. Promise?"

"All right, I promise."

"Then here goes." With much awkwardness, much halting and backing up, he explained what had happened on their wedding night. "Have you ever heard of anything remotely like that? A woman screaming in the middle of the sex act because, I don't know, her mind had gone somewhere else?"

Rhianne looked dumbfounded. "No. Never."

"Thanks. You've been a big help." Sighing, he rose to his feet.

"Wait." She grabbed him by the arm. "Have you talked to her about it? About exactly where her mind went, what she saw?"

"I've tried, but she always changes the subject and says there's no point discussing it because it can't be fixed."

"Well, that's no help. Do you think she'd be more comfortable talking to me about it? A woman?"

"I doubt it. The thing is, I think she's right about it being unfixable. I think I even know what's happening."

"What, then?"

He sat back down. "Do you remember that dinner party with the Bromidus family where I left the room and never came back?"

"Yes. Florian was so angry."

"I told you I was sick, but that wasn't the reason. Do you remember when I lost my leg?"

Rhianne grimaced. "How could I forget?"

"I never told you all the details about that. The story involves a patch of lemon balm plants. So now I avoid anything that smells of lemon balm. That night at the dinner party, the cooks served lemon balm tea along with the second course, and when I smelled it—"

"It reminded you. Of course! Why did you never tell me? I knew you hated lemon balm tea after coming back from Riorca, but you never said why."

"Rhianne, it's more than just being reminded. I've never told anyone about this before. But there's this fellow from the Obsidian Circle, name of Bayard. He told me that their people sometimes suffer from what he called intrusive memories—these are like nightmares that happen when you're awake. You can't control them; they're a form of madness. He warned me that Vitala might suffer from them, but when he mentioned it, I realized I had them myself. Sometimes when I smell lemon balm tea, or lemons, actually, I don't just remember what happened back then, I *relive* it."

"What do you mean?"

"In my head I go back there and reexperience it again and again. I thought I was going mad, but if I avoid lemon balm, I don't have any problems. And, for the most part, lemon balm is easy to avoid."

"So, you think Vitala experienced one of these intrusive memories?"

"Yes! During sex, which makes some sense given her history. The problem is, just like I avoid lemon balm tea, she believes she must avoid sex. And I understand why she feels that way. I just . . . don't want her to give up so easily."

"Have you told her any of this?"

"Only that I don't want her to give up."

"Well, there's your mistake. Tell her all of it."

He shook his head. "It will only reinforce her feelings on the matter. I never conquered the problem; I only avoided it."

"Lucien, your wife is not a Caturanga board. You can't strategize and manipulate and tell her only what you want her to hear. You tell her *everything*. If you won't do that, then it's your own gods-cursed fault if you lose her." Rhianne looked bemused. "What a sly creature she is. We talked for hours, and she said nothing of this. Mostly she spoke of how much she loves you."

A flicker of hope lit in his chest. "Maybe she changed her mind about the divorce."

Rhianne shifted on the rock, placing a protective

hand on her belly. "I don't think so. There was an under-current of grief to her words. I sensed at times she was on the verge of tears, which I attributed to fear of the usurper and his army, but now I wonder if this was her way of saying good-bye. She was singing your praises to me, telling me things she might have been uncomfortable stating to you directly. Maybe she hoped they would work their way back to you."

"I'd better get back." He headed for the trail.

Rhianne got up from the rock and picked her way toward him. "Why the hurry?"

"Vitala could run off at any time. It's one of her irritating habits."

Rhianne took his arm. "Promise me something."

"That I'll talk to her?"

"Yes. Regardless of your feelings on the matter, I think you're more likely to succeed with Vitala if you tell her what you told me about losing your leg. Open up to her, and she may open up to you."

"Fine," he said. "But I'm only humoring you. After all, you're pregnant and you'll probably get all emotional if I refuse."

He dodged her incoming slap easily, then grinned, walking backward down the trail just fast enough to stay out of her range. Gods, he'd missed Rhianne.

28

Vitala had been eating cod since their arrival in Riorca, always dried or salted, but at the feast that evening, the fish was fresh off the boats, fried with tiny black mushrooms, and more delicious than she could have imagined. The Mosari provided some delicacies from their ships: tropical oranges, tart and juicy, and a bitter drink of shaved chocolate. During dinner, Jan-Torres and Rhianne acted as translators between Lucien and the Mosari ship captains, who argued and gestured over maps. Meanwhile, brindlecats prowled beneath the table, and seabirds squawked from their perches on the backs of chairs. The presence of the animals was exceedingly strange, but she was beginning to accustom herself to Mosari customs. Mosari mages focused their magic through animal familiars instead of through riftstones, so the creatures accompanied them everywhere.

When Vitala had heard enough of Lucien's plans to have something worth carrying to the Circle, she slipped out. A bodyguard followed her, but she left him behind a closed door on the pretext of using a chamber pot, and escaped out the window. A quick trot down to the stables, and she was struggling with her mare's bridle. She had the bit in place and was pulling the straps over the animal's ears when she heard movement outside the stable. The bodyguard, perhaps? She ducked beneath the stall door.

The door opened, and she heard a familiar *slap-thump, slap-thump*. Lucien, gods curse him. She bit her lip in exasperation as the footsteps came closer.

His head appeared over the stall door. "Going for another midnight ride?"

She straightened, as if nothing were amiss, and buckled the throatlatch. "I told you I was leaving."

"You weren't going to say good-bye?"

"You'd have made it difficult for me."

He leaned over the stall door. "Should I have made it easy?"

She opened the door, pushing him out of the way, and led the mare out. "I'm sorry. I know it's wrong to run away, but I couldn't face you. I still can't." She picked up a saddle pad from the shelf.

Lucien snatched the saddle pad from her hand. "Stay one more night."

"I can't keep putting this off."

"Just this once."

"You said that last time. Give me the gods-cursed saddle pad."

He clutched it to his chest. "You want it? Take it from me."

Vitala sighed. He was too strong; she'd never wrestle it away from him. "Why one more night?"

"I want to talk."

"We've already talked."

"I know, but . . ." His face screwed up as if he'd bitten into something unpleasant. "About something else. I want to tell you about my brother. How he died."

"I already know how your brothers died." She blinked. "Which one?"

"Mathian."

"What does his assassination have to do with anything?" Despite her protests, he'd piqued her curiosity. All three assassins who'd targeted Lucien and Mathian had been killed in the attack. Only Lucien himself knew exactly what had happened.

"Stay and you'll find out."

"Are you just trying to make me too curious to leave?"

"No." He paused, and his eyes lit. "Is it working?"

"I'm not sure."

Lucien drew his sword and pressed the blade against the saddle pad. "Stay one more night, or I cut this saddle pad to pieces."

Vitala laughed in spite of herself.

"I'm a war mage. I never miss," he added.

"You win. Spare the poor saddle pad." She led the mare back into the stall and unbuckled the throatlatch. "But you have to tell me about the assassination."

Without enthusiasm, he said, "I will."

The bed in their town-hall room sagged like a sway-backed mare. Someone had piled extra blankets on it, which was good, since even heat-glows couldn't keep away the chill of a Riorcan night. Vitala stripped down to her chemise and burrowed under the blankets, shivering. Lucien joined her, wrapping her in his warm body. "So, what do you know about the assassination attempts against me and my brothers?"

"Our assassins were supposed to target each of you separately, but, for some reason, after the successful hit on Sestius, they attacked you and Mathian together."

"Yes. That was by accident. Mathian was supposed to travel alone that day, riding out to the tower to speak to our dear father by signal relay. To his annoyance, I joined him at the last minute, hoping to air some grievances about our Riorcan policy."

"Wouldn't Mathian have brought a bodyguard?"

"Oh yes. He did bring one, and so did I. I think the assassins, not expecting me to be there, mistook me for another bodyguard. I wasn't in imperial dress."

Vitala nodded, sympathetic to the assassins, who probably hadn't seen Lucien in person before that day. She was lucky she'd been presented to Lucien at the palace rather than having to pick him out of a crowd.

"We were in the foothills of southern Riorca," said Lucien. "Wild country, rocky, lots of places to hide. I had been rehearsing my speech in my head, the one I meant to give to my father, when I heard a wet thud and looked around in time to see Mathian hit the ground with two arrows in him. That's how to kill a war mage, if you want to take notes. Lie in wait and fire three arrows at him from three different directions. Mathian must have known the arrows were coming, but he couldn't dodge all of them at once.

"The bodyguards ran to help Mathian, who was screaming and obviously still alive. I think that's why the assassins didn't come out of hiding at first. If they'd struck Mathian dead in that first volley, they could have run. Why stick around to fight the bodyguards? But they hadn't killed him, not yet, so they hesitated, trying to determine if his injuries were fatal. In those moments of delay, I spurred my horse in their direction.

"I found the first assassin behind a rock. With my height advantage from horseback and room to maneuver, I made short work of him. By then, the other two assassins had emerged and were fighting with the bodyguards, trying to get to Mathian. I hurried to join the fight. Vespillo went down before I got there—"

"Vespillo?" asked Vitala.

"My bodyguard at the time, Soldier's Peace be upon

him. When I arrived, it was two of us against two, all war mages. Your assassins, they fight well, but they're weak at high blocks. I got past the guard of one of them and half decapitated him. As for the other . . ." Lucien's mouth twisted.

"What about him?" prompted Vitala.

"I don't recall, exactly. From that point, the memory is hazy. I think I'd been struck, a blow to the leg. Hard to say exactly when I was hit, since in the heat of battle I don't feel pain, and there was so much blood I didn't know who it all belonged to. Bruccius, the other body-guard, went down next, and somehow I slew the final assassin. That left me the last man standing, but when I took a step toward Mathian, the leg injury caught me and I fell, so there was no one standing. From the ground, I assessed Mathian's wounds. One arrow protruded from his side; another from his back. 'Help me up,' he said, and I tried, but he was limp and useless. He had no feeling in his legs.

"There was nothing I could do for him. If I could have lifted him onto a horse, he might have had a chance, but such a thing was impossible. He asked for water, and I gave him some, but after a moment I pulled the skin away. We hadn't meant the trip to be a long one, and our supplies were scanty. I might need every drop of water we had to get home myself, and no amount of water was going to save Mathian.

"When I moved away, he began to panic. He begged for help, and I ignored him. I tried to catch a horse, but they wouldn't let me near, not even my mare, who'd taken a carrot from my own hands every gods-cursed morning. I suppose I smelled too much of blood. So I crawled about, collecting supplies, while Mathian be-rated me. He accused me of betraying him so I could steal the throne, of taking my anger out on him over the long-past insults of childhood. You're aware there was no love between us when we were young?"

"I'd heard you didn't get along."

"Both my older brothers bullied me back then, and Rhianne and I retaliated by playing tricks on them. But that's ancient history, of no importance now. The assassins had no supplies on their persons. They'd hidden them somewhere, and I would never find them. When Mathian's tirade had run its course, he began to cry, and I realized I couldn't just leave him there. What if there were other Obsidian Circle agents about? He could fall into their hands. And if the Circle didn't get him, the wolves and scavengers might. So I went back, and I slit his throat."

"Gods, Lucien."

"So now you know my secret, the one I've never told anyone, not even Rhianne. Mathian didn't die at any assassin's hand. He died at mine."

"I wouldn't say he died at your hand. That was a mercy killing."

Lucien pulled her closer. "And yet, if he'd had help, he might have survived. I just couldn't get him that help. I still wonder sometimes if . . . well, if on some level I wanted him to die. And if that influenced my decision."

"I don't see how it could have, if there was only one reasonable option to choose from. How did you get back to camp?"

"I never made it," said Lucien. "I crawled for a day, maybe two, and then I collapsed in a bed of plants, unable to continue. They were lemon balm plants, Vitala. I'll never forget that smell, the tang of the lemon balm and the stink of my rotting leg. I couldn't stop thinking about Mathian and the horror of opening his throat. I lay there a while—days, maybe. Then, next I remember, I was in the infirmary tent back at camp, with my lower leg amputated. A search party had found me. But they never found Mathian and the others, though I showed them where the attack took place."

"They were eaten by wolves," said Vitala. "You made the right decision."

"We assumed the Obsidian Circle had found them."

"No, my people never did. Although if they had found Mathian while he still lived . . . Well, he'd have been better off with the wolves."

"I don't know, Vitala. I've had many occasions to examine the decision I made that day with a clearer head, and I'm not certain I did the right thing. He had a chance, and I took it from him."

Vitala shook her head firmly. "I'd have made the same decision."

His mouth quirked. "Somehow I'm not entirely reassured by that. But I'm glad someone knows now besides me. It's been a hard secret to carry."

Vitala fell silent, marveling at Lucien's trust. His claim to the imperial throne could be compromised if his detractors knew he'd killed his elder brother. Cassian would certainly have made much of it. "So, now I know why you hate lemon balm tea."

"Do you remember that field I made us go the long way around, just north of Tasox? There was lemon balm growing by the side of the road."

"And you didn't want to be reminded. It makes sense to me now."

He sighed. "Vitala, it's more than that."

"How do you mean?"

"It's more than not liking lemon balm tea. It's hard to explain, but sometimes when I smell lemon balm, I go back to that time, the day of the attack, the aftermath, the days spent lying in those crushed plants. I don't mean I just think about it. I mean I feel as if I'm *literally there*, reliving the event. I can't control it. It happens, and I sort of . . . lose myself."

Vitala's throat suddenly constricted. He *relived* the incident? Wasn't that just like what happened to her? Her heart throbbed, its pace increasing until she could hear the blood rushing in her ears. "Lucien—three gods—I think I know what you're talking about. It happened to me."

His voice was soft. "What's happened to you?"

"I've relived a past incident like that. The other night, in the marriage bed. *That's what happened.*"

"Tell me."

His voice was gentler and less surprised than she'd expected, and she realized he'd already guessed it. He'd known that what had happened to her in the marriage bed was analogous to what had happened to him when he smelled lemon balm tea. Why hadn't he said anything before? Perhaps he'd been too ashamed—it couldn't have been an easy story to relate. For that matter, she didn't especially want to tell hers. But now that he'd shared with her, it seemed only fair. Besides, if he understood what was happening to her, maybe he could help. "I was fourteen when I killed for the first time."

"Was that a practice kill?"

"Yes. How do you know about those?"

"Bayard said something. He was trying to talk me out of marrying you."

Vitala snorted. Somehow the knowledge that Bayard had tried to prevent this marriage made her more inclined to make it succeed. "He's such an ass. What did he say about my practice kills?"

"That you were reluctant to carry them out."

"Well, that's true." She took a deep breath. "The first time, the man was tied up and gagged. He was a Kjallan soldier, a patrolman who'd strayed too close to the enclave. I was to use my Shard on him. I was hanging back; I remember this terrible cramping in my stomach. Bayard had to yell at me and threaten me to get me to make the kill, and I finally stepped forward and did it. The second time, I was a year older. The man was loose in a room, weaponless, and I was armed with a knife and a sword. They threw me in the room with him, and my job was to come out alive. That was the easiest of my practice kills, because he immediately tried to take the weapons from me, and I fought back, so even though it was an execution, I just went through the motions like in the training room, and it felt like self-defense.

"The third was two years later, and . . . that was the difficult one." Her throat tightened again, and she paused for a moment, trying to calm herself. Lucien rubbed her back. "This man, another Kjallan soldier, was locked in a small room and left there for a few days. He was given food and water, as if we were going to keep him prisoner, but the Circle does not keep prisoners. I was sent in, unarmed and dressed in a light shift. My orders were to seduce and kill the soldier as I would a war mage. He was tied up, so I could have killed him outright, like the first man, but my superiors wanted me to practice the technique I would be using in the field. They were watching from a hidden window.

"By the way he stared at me, I could tell that of all the things he'd expected to happen to him—torture, interrogation, execution—having a young, skimpily dressed woman enter his cell was not one of them. He was lying on the bed with his wrists and ankles bound. I walked over and untied him. I had no knife, no weapons at all, so undoing the knots was painstaking work. He questioned me endlessly as I worked. Who was I? What was I doing here? Why was I untying him? I didn't say a word, and I'm sure he believed I was Kjallan—a fellow prisoner, perhaps, who'd come to aid or comfort him. When I finished the last knot, I kissed him. And then I started to undress him.

"I can't imagine what he was thinking. He'd been expecting to be killed or interrogated, and here was this young woman who untied him and wouldn't say a word, but apparently wanted to make love to him. He didn't resist. He was quite cooperative."

Lucien's arm moved suddenly, bumping her, and he muttered a quick apology. His muscles were hard, she realized, knotted up with tension.

"I'll skip the details," she said. "What struck me was how young he was—no more than seventeen, I think. He was handsome. Indeed, he was almost a younger version of you, very sweet and gentle."

"I'm not sweet and gentle," grumbled Lucien.

"I think you are," said Vitala. "He kept telling me how beautiful I was, though I never said a word back to him. I could feel his beating heart next to mine as he . . ." She swallowed. "I did what I'd been trained to do. You've seen my death spell in action. It's not a pleasant sight, and I was literally attached to him—his hands locked around me as the paralysis took effect, and in the early stages of his death throes he was also . . . in me. You know. When I finally freed myself from his grip, I fled to the far side of the room. And I had the strangest experience. It was like I left my body. I was on the outside, looking down at myself as I cowered in a corner, staring at his shuddering, dying body on the bed."

She crammed her fists into her eyes as if to physically press back the tears. "I have no memory after that point. Someone must have come and fetched me." She took a deep breath.

Lucien was still for a long time. His hand on her back had gone motionless.

She let the tears come. "So, now you see why I can't—"

"Three gods, Vitala," choked out Lucien. "I'm sorry. That sounds worse than what happened to me."

"For you, it's lemon balm tea. For me, it's—"

"I know." He hugged her face to his chest. "But wait. You killed seven men after that incident. Weren't some of those—well, for lack of a better term, sex kills?"

"Yes, two of them. Remus and one other man, a sort of practice mission I was assigned before I went after you."

"So why didn't you have this problem with them?"

"I don't know." She wiped her eyes. "Probably because they didn't remind me of that young soldier at all. They were much older. They didn't look like him, they didn't act like him—"

"Wait," said Lucien. "So the whole problem is the way I look? What you're saying is we could solve this by putting a sack over my head."

Vitala sobs turned to a surprised, choked laugh. "I don't want you to put a sack over your head!"

"But we could," he insisted. "If that's what it took."

"Maybe. I don't think it's entirely visual. I know it is partly, because I've had ...'events'... based merely on seeing someone who looked like that soldier. It happened to me in the Imperial Palace with one of your door guards."

He stared at her. "You slept with one of my door guards?"

"No, no. I just saw him in the hall, and that was enough to trigger it." She reached up and stroked his face, pushing back the hair that drooped over his forehead. "You look like the soldier, but not exactly. Your hair and face are similar, but I remember him having peach fuzz on his chin, and you don't." She ran her hand over the rough stubble. "I think you don't look similar enough to cause a problem just by my looking at you. But in a bedroom situation, combined with all the other sensations—touch, sound, smell—that's when it happens."

"You might have said something."

"I'm sorry. I was ashamed. I didn't think you'd react well to hearing that I see images of another man when I'm with you. It's not something I want to happen or that I can control, but until you told me your story, I didn't think you'd understand."

"I don't like it," said Lucien. "But I understand. It seems the real problem is—well, how should I say? When the man enters you. That's what caused the event."

She shuddered. "Yes. And I don't think that was visual at all, because I had my eyes closed."

He was silent for a moment, thinking, his fingers idly stroking her back. "Am I correct in assuming Remus entered you?"

"Yes, but it was ... completely different. He was rough. I was dry. It hurt."

He sighed. "Well, I don't think the solution is me hurting you."

"No."

Again he paused to think. "But you don't have a problem when I use my mouth or my hand."

"No. But I can't give you an heir that way—"

"Shh." He squeezed her in gentle rebuke. "It's too early to be worrying about heirs. My point is that we know at least one way to avoid your visions. We may find other ways."

"But, Lucien . . ." How could she explain this to him? She was so limited. He had made her an empress, but she couldn't do this simple thing that virtually any woman could do. He wouldn't be happy with her long term, couldn't be. He was normal, and she was broken. "You deserve more," she choked out. "You deserve *better*."

"This is what's really bothering you. Isn't it? You think I'm unhappy with you."

"If you're not now, you will be. I'm not normal."

"No, you're certainly not normal," said Lucien. "You're extraordinary. You're beautiful and smart and deadly, and I love you. And if you've got some problems, remember I'm a Caturanga player. I view those as *challenges*."

"Lucien—"

"Look," he said, grabbing her hand and placing it on the stump of his missing leg. "Am I normal?"

She rolled her eyes. "You get around fine. It's not a big deal."

"Not a big deal?" He snorted. "In Kjall, a nation that worships physical perfection? Do you know how many of my legati laugh at me behind me back? Do you have any idea what my father used to think of me?"

"I'm sorry—I had no idea. It's never bothered me."

He kissed her. "I know it doesn't bother you. You've never reacted to my weakness with anything more than curiosity, and I love you for that. We made a deal before. I propose we make another."

"What sort of deal?"

"We're neither of us flawless. You accept my broken parts, and I'll accept yours."

"But I've already accepted—"

"Shh," he said, unbelting her syrtos. "So have I. Makes it all the easier. Doesn't it?"

"What are you doing?" His tongue found her nipple, and she gasped.

"Sealing the deal. No more words, love, unless you're screaming my name."

"I don't scream your—" She bit her tongue, because he was doing that thing with his fingers that she loved.

"Don't lie, Vitala. Yes, you do."

Early the next morning, Vitala watched the small encampment spring into action. Lucien had signaled Quincius and ordered him to march the bulk of the army to Blackscar Gulch. Now the small contingent of troops that had accompanied them to the coast was packing up; they'd be off by midday. She and Lucien had a final breakfast with Jan-Torres and Rhianne.

"Empress," said King Jan-Torres. "May I speak with you privately this morning?"

"Of course, Your Majesty."

She and the king of Mosar retired to a small office off the great hall, which seemed to have been raided of its furniture; it contained only a single chair and a flimsy desk. Jan-Torres bade her sit and fetched a chair from another room, then took a seat beside her. He seemed less intimidating today than yesterday, and she realized it must be something he could turn on and off as he desired.

"I hear you're considering returning to the Obsidian Circle," he said.

Vitala bit her lip. Had Lucien told him that? Perhaps Lucien had told Rhianne and she'd passed it along. "I was, but not anymore."

"I understand you and Lucien are having problems,"

he said. "I don't know the details; you two will have to work them out. But something Rhianne said struck me, and I wanted to speak to you about it. She said you felt useless in the role of empress and believed you could best aid the war effort by taking up your former role of assassin."

She nodded. "Lucien and I are getting along better now. But it's true: my role as empress is an empty one. We don't rule a country yet. We rule an army, and that army has a chain of command I have no business inserting myself into. Besides, my knowledge of strategy is confined to Caturanga. It has little real-life application. It's not as if this war is going to be easy to win, so why waste my talent on being a figurehead? One more assassin could shift the balance."

He smiled and said nothing.

"You agree with me?"

"Not at all. Empress, I recognize what you're going through. Most of my officers go through it when first promoted to a captaincy. You've been a doer all your life, someone who accomplishes things through direct action. But now, in this less-active role, you feel useless."

Vitala nodded.

"But you're not doing nothing—far from it. You were the one who rescued Lucien and brought him to Riorca, and when your superiors at the Obsidian Circle didn't share your vision of a productive alliance, you broke him out and helped him gather an army. This alliance between Riorca and Lucien's forces came about entirely because of you."

She flushed, pleased at his praise, but she had to correct him. "The army part was all Lucien."

Jan-Torres nodded. "You did your part, and he did his. Remember that you are a symbol to both Kjallans and

Riorcans. You and Lucien, united in marriage, are living, breathing proof that former enemies can work together for a shared cause. What would it mean to those Kjallans and Riorcans if you were to suddenly abandon them?"

"I wasn't going to abandon them. I'd be helping the war effort."

He shook his head. "Now that you're a figurehead, you have to consider the *appearance* of what you're doing. Running away makes it look like you've given up. What kind of message does that send your people?"

Her shoulders sagged. "That I think things are hopeless."

"War is psychological, Vitala. Your role is not to *do*, but to *inspire*. Work out your problems with Lucien in private. But in public, stand by his side. Show your people that you will not give up on them. You must hold this coalition together."

Vitala swallowed the lump in her throat. "Yes, sire."

Through the town hall's thin walls, she heard a centurion barking orders, calling soldiers to attention. The king of Mosar cocked his head to listen. He stood, took her hand, and lifted her from her seat. "Your people are ready. Go on and take back your country."

29

From the top of the ladder, Vitala poked her head over the partially completed stone wall. A gust of wind surged up the canyon, whipping her hair about her face. She clambered onto the wall and stood, staring out onto the rocky bleakness of Stonemaw Pass. Once a river canyon, it was now dry and dead, with only a few wilted spinebushes raveling up from the cracks.

Lucien stepped onto the wall beside her, snugged an arm around her waist, and said, "What do you think?"

"The men are making good progress."

He nodded. "Every day counts." He pulled her in for a kiss.

She wrapped her arms around him, sighing with contentment.

A shuddering boom startled her. Lucien's hand tightened around her waist, and she turned to see an avalanche of rocks tumbling into the gorge. A cloud of dust and pulverized stone drifted silently upward on the tongues of the wind. Just another pyroglycerin blast, clearing space and providing raw materials for the walls that climbed a little higher each day. Two of the five were already complete. Above them, crude towers and shelters were also taking shape, as well as rockfalls that could be released onto the enemy soldiers.

Similar preparations were in progress at Ashfeld, the

southern pass. The gulch where the battalions were now encamped could be reached only through one of the two passes or by traveling up the Ember River from the ocean. The Mosari fleet guarded the river mouth, and if Lucien's troops blocked both passes, the usurper would find it difficult to inflict much harm on them.

"Sire," someone called from below.

Vitala looked down at the messenger standing in the bottom of the gorge.

"What is it?" Lucien called back.

"The boat's arrived, sire."

Lucien grimaced. "Obsidian Circle," he said to Vitala. "You'd better come along."

Bayard, accompanied by only Asmund, didn't even look at Vitala as he entered the command tent, but she pulled him aside for a moment, anyway. "Did you make the inquiries I asked you to make about Flavia?"

"Who?" He blinked in confusion.

"The dog."

Bayard shook his head. "I've more important things to do, Vitala."

"If you're meeting with people, anyway, it doesn't hurt you to ask an extra question. If for no other reason than to honor the memory of our agents who died in Tasox."

"I'm sorry. It never crossed my mind." He moved away.

"Gentlemen," said Lucien, clasping wrists around the table. He took a seat, and the others followed. "What's the news?

"Our news is over a week old," said Bayard. "Cassian has retaken enough signal towers to make them unreliable, and travel by barge is slow."

"Understood," said Lucien. "Slow intelligence is better than no intelligence."

"Cassian's forces have torched the villages of Tanim, Quattan, and Bluas," said Bayard. "There were no survivors."

A chill settled in the pit of Vitala's stomach.

"I'm sorry to hear that," said Lucien.

Asmund huffed angrily. "Your troops were supposed to prevent these abuses, yet here they are, holed up in the gulch. Why have you gone to ground like a coward?"

"The usurper has more than twice as many troops as I do. I cannot face him in open battle."

"What good are your troops if they will not fight?" demanded Asmund.

"They will fight," said Lucien. "But only in a situation where they can win."

Bayard spoke up. "How many more Riorcans must die before that happens? We cannot supply you forever."

"I do not think it will be much longer," Lucien said. "He will come after me."

Vitala cleared her throat. "Gentlemen, the emperor is right. I'm as disturbed as anyone about the loss of the villages, but to come out of the gulch and face the usurper in open battle would lead only to a certain loss. Just as in Caturanga, some sacrifices must be made in order to achieve victory."

"Is that what those villagers are?" said Bayard. *"Sacrifices?"*

Asmund fumed. "Why is it that whenever sacrifices are called for, it's always Riorcans who are offered up?"

Vitala folded her arms. "There will be hardships enough to go around when the usurper's army arrives."

"This is a difficult loss," said Lucien in his gentlest tone. "But we have no choice. We must face the usurper where I can neutralize his advantage in numbers. Right now he's making a tactical error. He hopes to draw me out and is probably trying to locate and cut off my supply lines. But he doesn't know we're supplying by river, and his reluctance to attack is working to our benefit. We've nearly succeeded in walling off both entrances to Blackscar Gulch."

"And what if he never comes?" said Asmund. "What if he sweeps across the whole of Riorca, leaving death and ashes behind him?"

"He won't," said Lucien, "because dead villagers pay no tribute. Once he realizes I cannot be lured out of the gulch, he will come after me."

The Riorcans sat for a moment in disgruntled silence.

"Is there anything further?" asked Lucien.

"Yes," said Asmund. "Cassian is leading the invasion personally."

Lucien sat up straighter. "He's in Riorca? Did he bring Celeste?"

Asmund nodded. "Our spy has not actually seen her, but we're told she's with him."

"Can she be rescued and brought here?"

Bayard and Asmund exchanged looks.

"I don't see how that would be possible," said Bayard. "We have no ability to rescue people. Instead, I propose that we attempt to assassinate Cassian."

"Your assassin could also retrieve Celeste."

Bayard flicked a glance at Vitala and shook his head. "Our assassins are not trained for that. We wanted to ask you, since presumably you understand the mind-set of Kjallan soldiers, would assassinating Cassian end the war?"

"Hard to say," said Lucien. "There are four legati in his army who might attempt to seize power if Cassian died. Of those, Dignus and Sorio are loyal to Cassian but they despise each other; they won't join forces. Titillian would support me if he knew I were alive, and Getha is a wild card. None has solid support from the enlisted men or a clear advantage over the others. This is one reason we need to get Celeste out. If Cassian died, there would probably be a string of murders and possibly outright civil war as those four men maneuver to be her next husband. On the other hand, if she were gone, nobody would have a way to legitimize himself as emperor. Have you been circulating those rumors, as I asked?"

"Yes," said Bayard. "Not only has the rumor that you're alive and commanding the troops in Riorca taken root, but the usurper is also trying to quell it. Right now any enlisted man who speaks your name gets ten lashes, and, of course, that's just convincing everyone that the rumor must be true."

"In that case, if you assassinate Cassian and get Celeste out, I believe the war will end. Titillian should have the most support from the enlisted men."

Bayard nodded. "We'll attempt the assassination, but it's a long shot. We normally prepare for high-profile assassinations years in advance. Did you know Vitala was assigned to you at the age of thirteen? She had a full seven years to learn your habits."

"I cannot thank you enough for sending her to me," Lucien said dryly. "What about extracting Celeste?"

Bayard shook his head. "I can't promise that. The assassination itself will be very difficult, especially since we know so little about Cassian and his weaknesses. In fact, it would be easier . . . Well, we'll do our best."

Vitala spoke up. "Bayard, I should be part of the assassination team—"

"It will be easier if what?" interrupted Lucien.

"Nothing," said Bayard. "If we had more information."

"It would be easier if your assassin killed Celeste along with Cassian, to prevent her being used once more as a pawn," said Lucien. "That's what you were about to say."

Bayard shook his head. "That's not what I was about to say."

Lucien's voice grew quiet. "If your assassin kills my sister, you can forget the Circle's sweet deal. I'll stake the lot of you."

Bayard glared at him. "And just how successful have you been at quelling the Circle in times past?"

"Maybe I just needed more motivation," said Lucien.

"Gentlemen," said Asmund. "Of course our assassin will not harm Celeste."

"I should be part of the assassination team," said Vitala.

"And do what?" cried Lucien, looking horrified. "Seduce Cassian?"

Vitala shook her head. "It doesn't have to be done that way. In fact, it probably won't be. For an assassin to gain intimate access to a man of that rank takes years, and we don't have that kind of time. We can infiltrate as camp followers, but emperors don't sleep with whores. They have other options."

"If it's not to be done by seduction, why send a woman at all?" said Lucien. "Send a group of men, like the ones who took my leg."

"It must be women," said Vitala, "because they can infiltrate the camp."

"Vitala has the right of it," said Bayard. "But she cannot participate in the operation. She's no longer an Obsidian Circle assassin."

"I have the skills," said Vitala. "No other assassin in the Circle has ever successfully targeted someone so highly placed."

"You never killed your target," said Bayard.

"She could have if she'd chosen to," said Lucien. "But I agree. The empress cannot be risked on such a mission."

Vitala laid a hand on Lucien's arm. "Whom do you trust—me or some nameless assassin? I wouldn't harm Celeste. I'd go out of my way to rescue her. I don't know any other Obsidian Circle assassin who's performed a successful rescue mission."

Lucien looked stricken. "Don't you understand? I can't risk you *both*."

"She's not going," said Bayard.

"I concur," said Lucien.

Vitala sat back in her chair, fuming, as Lucien and the others discussed the logistics of the proposed assassination. She'd promised Jan-Torres she wouldn't abandon her position as empress, but this would be no ordinary assassination. This mission could end the war! It wouldn't be an easy task, to be sure, but was anything worthwhile ever easy?

"What sort of man is Cassian? What are his weaknesses?" asked Bayard.

"He's ambitious. Combative," said Lucien. "Not especially loyal. I know little else."

"What about his sexual proclivities?"

Lucien swallowed, looking suddenly nauseous.

"Must you ask him that?" Vitala snapped. "Cassian forced his thirteen-year-old sister into marriage."

"I'm sorry if this conversation is disturbing to the emperor, but it's very important," said Bayard.

"I don't know his sexual proclivities, as you put it,"

said Lucien. "What have your spies seen, as far as he and Celeste?"

"You mean, is he fucking her?" asked Bayard. "We don't—"

"You cull!" cried Lucien, rising from his seat, his face hot and flushed. "Is that how you speak about the Imperial Princess?"

"My apologies, Emperor." Bayard's half-hidden smile, contrary to his words, made it clear he was delighted to have provoked such a response.

Vitala took Lucien's hand and stroked it with her thumb until he had calmed enough to sit back down.

"The answer is, we don't know," Bayard continued. "We don't have spies that close. What we're trying to find out is if he can be tempted into some kind of liaison. Vitala is correct that high-ranking men usually aren't interested in common whores, but if he has a weakness, some way he can be tempted . . ."

Lucien shook his head. "I don't know of one."

"In that case," said Bayard grimly, "I hope your army is prepared for war."

30

A horn blast startled Vitala from sleep.

Lucien leapt out of bed and began throwing on his clothes.

Vitala sat up and looked around the dark bedroom. She didn't feel too groggy; it was probably around dawn. "What's going on? What does the horn mean?"

"It means our scouts have sighted the enemy," said Lucien.

Vitala's stomach fluttered. The weeks of waiting were over. Later that afternoon, as the enemy drew closer, Lucien took Vitala up one of the towers near the southern pass for a look. The entire horizon was orange, as if she viewed a dazzling sunset, but the effect was no trick of the light. It was the uniforms of Cassian's men. Her throat tightened as she finally grasped the enemy's numbers. "Are they attacking us only here, not at Stonemaw Pass?" Lucien had stationed half his army here at Ashfeld and half at Stonemaw. The walls and fortifications were complete at both sites.

"He's split his army. See? Count the battle standards," said Lucien. "I'm sure the other half is on its way to Stonemaw."

She stared at him. "That, on the horizon, is only *half* his army?"

*   *   *

The fighting began at sunset. A pair of bodyguards escorted Vitala to her tent, while Lucien remained near the front lines to command his troops. Vitala lay awake all night, terrified by each blast of the cannons.

When she stepped outside the tent and stared toward the horizon where the battle was taking place, the distant flashes of muskets and artillery told her nothing at all of how the battle progressed, only that the armies were fully engaged. Twice she heard the thundering of a rockfall released onto the enemy, and many times she thought she heard screams. But who was doing the screaming?

After dawn, the sounds of fighting died down, and Lucien arrived at the tent, exhausted and reeking of gunpowder. "The walls held," he told her shortly, and collapsed in his bed without undressing.

Later, after they'd both rested, he explained further. The fighting had been bloody on both sides, but the rockfalls claimed many casualties, and the usurper, not expecting fortifications, had not brought enough artillery to break through the walls. "He has withdrawn," Lucien said, "no doubt to regroup and bring in more cannons. This time of quiet shall not last long."

He was right. The fighting began anew that evening.

Your role is not to do, but to inspire.

Vitala wandered among the wounded in the Healers' tent, wondering how anyone could provide inspiration in a place like this.

The south side of the tent was by far the worst. Here the men whom the Healers hadn't yet treated lay moaning on makeshift cots, grimy and reeking of blood. Healing magic took time to work, and the battalion's few Healers were overwhelmed. Aides rushed about, bandaging wounds, trying to keep the men alive long enough to be saved by the Healer. But many of the men on the cots lay all too still. Last night a man burned along his left side had expired before Vitala's eyes while she held his hand.

She stroked foreheads, wrapped bandages, and sat at bedsides. When she couldn't bear the stench of death any longer, she moved to the northern side of the tent, which held recuperating patients whom the Healers had already attended. Some soldiers, after treatment by a Healer, could get up and return to the front. Others could not. A Healer's magic could mend almost anything, but it couldn't re-create a shattered arm or restore lost blood. Some of these men were merely weak and would recover in time; others were missing a leg, an eye, half a hand. Still, there was no blood here and no wound fever. These men weren't in pain, but in some cases they had to adjust to a new reality.

She spent half an hour sitting by the bedside and stroking the arm of a man who appeared intact but couldn't stop weeping. She wasn't sure why, and he wouldn't say.

"Empress," called someone behind her.

She gave the weeping man a final pat and turned. The man addressing her lay in a cot; the bottom half of his left leg had been amputated. *Like Lucien,* Vitala thought with a wave of pity. She sat down beside him. "How are you feeling?"

"Do you remember me?" he asked.

All at once she recognized him. "Kryspin!" He was the man who'd shown her around the White Eagle encampment. Gods, that seemed so long ago. She stiffened as she remembered how chilly Kryspin's demeanor had become when he'd learned she was Riorcan.

"Look," he said, pointing to his leg. "I'm like the emperor now."

"I'm so sorry. How did it happen?"

Kryspin shook his head. "Don't remember."

Vitala nodded. She got that answer a lot.

"But if the emperor can get by . . ." He smiled weakly. "I figure I can too."

"Of course you can." She considered taking his hand. Most men seemed to welcome it, but Kryspin . . . well, he'd been pretty obvious in his dislike of Riorcans. There was a longing look in his eye, though, and she could hardly treat him differently than the others. She took his hand, which was clammy. "You're cold." She grabbed the blanket at the foot of the cot and pulled it over him.

"Thank you, Empress." He closed his eyes.

Vitala couldn't help herself. "You don't mind anymore that I'm Riorcan?"

He cracked an eye half-open. "You're not Riorcan. You're White Eagle."

She smiled and smoothed the hair back from his brow. What was she really—Kjallan, Riorcan, Obsidian Circle, White Eagle? She was all of those and none of them. "I know a fellow who makes wonderful wooden legs. He made the emperor's. When the war's over, come and see me, and I'll have him make one for you."

"I'd like that," said Kryspin. "Then I'd be just like the emperor."

The war became a siege. While Vitala spent most of her days in the Healer's tent, Lucien split his time between Ashfeld and Stonemaw passes, riding between them as needed. He was a hands-on commander, always involved in something, whether it was to set up an ambush or rockfall, exploit some weakness in the enemy's line, or deploy a new tactic. Most evenings he came home to Vitala, but sometimes that was not possible.

"They've brought in more artillery, but the walls still hold," he said on the eleventh day of the assault, yanking off his boot and turning it upside down. A collection of pebbles spilled onto the floor. Blackscar Gulch had once been the center of Riorca's mining industry. Maws of long-abandoned caves gaped from the cliff walls, and flat shards of rock, the detritus of the old mines, were everywhere. They got into one's clothes, one's boots, one's blankets. "We inflicted heavy losses on them today."

"I'm glad to hear it." Vitala pushed Lucien into a chair, brushed the dust from his syrtos, and massaged his shoulders.

He turned and gave her a lopsided grin.

Gods, that was all it took now. He smiled, and all her blood flowed south. It was delicious, a promise of pleasure soon to come. After all, why shouldn't they enjoy each other while they still could? The usurper could break through at any time.

"Have you heard anything from the Circle?" she asked.

"No," he said, reaching for the belt of her syrtos.

"Nothing about the assassination? What about poisoning the enemy's water? They said they would do that."

"No. Nothing at all." He reached up and kissed her, long and slow.

"Nothing about—"

"Shh," he said, kissing her again. "I don't want to talk about the Circle right now."

31

The cliffside shelter had walls, shielding them from incoming arrows, but no roof. The rain fell in sheets, plastering Vitala's hair to her face, dripping off her cloak, swirling about her feet, and carrying off the little rock shards by the hundreds. She squinted at Lucien, who, in the company of his fellow soldiers, was effortlessly drawing back a longbow. He loosed the arrow, and she tried to follow its progress as it plummeted toward the enemy forces in the gorge. She lost it in the driving rain, along with the other arrows in the volley.

"Do your arrows always strike their targets?" she asked as he nocked another arrow. "Because of your war magic?"

"I wish, but no." He drew back the bow, aimed, and loosed. "It doesn't operate at this range. I can't even *see* individual targets. So much for never missing."

She stared down at the gorge, narrowing her eyes to try to pick out detail. The visibility was awful. From their shelter on the cliff, the enemy forces were no more distinct than swarming ants. The rain, which had punished them for days, had not deterred the usurper's forces from attacking. Today the enemy forces were bashing the walls with cannons and harquebuses. Lucien's bowmen were targeting the cannoneers. They could not damage the cannons themselves, but picking off the men who operated them was nearly as effective.

Lucien shook his head, spraying raindrops everywhere, then mopped his face in exasperation. "Gods curse this weather! It will be the death of us all."

Two days later, Lucien returned to the command tent in the early afternoon, pale and shivering and bedraggled, like a cat who'd fallen into a lake.

"Are you all right?" Vitala took his hand to draw him inside, where it was warm and dry.

He stayed put, refusing to be pulled out of the entryway. Perhaps he feared that if he had even a taste of comfort, he wouldn't be able to resist it. "I'm not coming in. I have a mission for you."

She stared at him. "What mission? Have you heard from the Circle?" She grabbed her oilskin cloak off a peg and flung it over her syrtos. Flavia, stir-crazy and eager for an outing, ran to her side.

"No. I want you to deliver a letter. Leave Flavia here."

"A letter?" That sounded odd. "Has something happened?"

"I'll tell you on the way," he said, and pulled her outdoors.

He led her down to the river, which was muddy and bloated to twice its usual size. Four soldiers were sitting in a boat, bailing it and looking rather like drowned rats themselves.

"Here." He handed her an oilskin pouch. "There was a flood in Stonemaw Pass. It destroyed two of our walls—"

"Three gods, Lucien! Our walls are down?"

"I want you to take this letter to my cousin Rhianne and apprise her of these events," continued Lucien. "The details are in the letter."

"But what can Rhianne possibly do about it? What can anyone do? Are our troops holding steady?"

His voice was flat. "I want Rhianne to know, and you're the only person I trust to get this letter to her."

"Wait a minute. Is this about delivering a letter, or is it about removing me from danger?"

"You have orders, Vitala," he said firmly.

"Gods curse those orders. Deliver it yourself!" Furious, she grabbed him by the front of his syrtos and shoved the oilskin pouch into it. "You get on that boat, and *you* take it."

"I can't," he said softly.

"You're the emperor. You can do whatever you want."

"No, I can't. Vitala, please just do this."

"I will not!" she cried. "If you're going to stay here and die with your men, then I'm staying too. I'm their empress."

"I'm not planning on dying. We're fighting back, but it's imperative you get to safety," said Lucien. "You could be carrying the heir to the throne."

"I'm not carrying any heir, and you know it!"

Lucien turned his head and gestured, but the gesture wasn't aimed at her. She followed his gaze, and four soldiers materialized from behind the trees. Gods curse him, he'd set up an ambush.

Vitala drew her pistol, but one of the soldiers knocked it away so quickly she could barely see his hand moving. *War mage,* she realized. With a touch of her mind, she released a Shard and grasped it in her fingertips. One of the men seized her arm. She whipped her hand around, ready to stab him, and saw his face. *"Quincius?"*

He nodded. "I'm sorry, Empress. I have orders."

She couldn't kill Quincius. She couldn't kill any of these men. She dropped the Shard, and the soldiers grabbed her. Two of them bound her hands behind her back.

Lucien stepped forward and tucked the oilskin pouch into her syrtos. "I love you, Vitala."

"Gods curse you!" she called back as the men led her to the boat and seated her in the bow. Lucien watched from shore, his head bowed.

Quincius released the mooring line. He and the other officers stayed on shore, while the four soldiers in the boat rowed to speed their progress downstream. As Vitala floated down the swollen river, Lucien's form dwindled, but he never took his eyes off her. It was only when he'd disappeared from view entirely that she wished her final words to him had been something else.

The following morning, the rain finally stopped and the boatmen untied her wrists. There was nowhere she could run to, not with the boat in the middle of the frigid river. She curled up in the bottom of the hull, feigning sleep, and pulled out the oilskin pouch. If Lucien thought she wasn't going to look at the letter, he didn't know her very well. Besides, after tricking her like that, he deserved whatever he got. She pulled the letter out of the pouch, slipped a fingernail under the wax seal, and opened it.

Dear Vitala, the opening read.

She almost laughed out loud. All right, he *did* know her well. Though the letter appeared short, there was a second page underneath the first. She flipped up the first page to see the second, which opened, *Dear Rhianne.* Vitala went back to the first.

> *Dear Vitala,*
>
> Shame on you! I knew you would not be able to resist reading this. By now you will know that a flash flood tumbled down the canyon in Stonemaw

*Pass and destroyed everything in its path — soldiers
from both sides, and, most devastatingly, two of
our walls. I've reinforced our troops at Stonemaw,
but you are too much the Caturanga player not to
realize that this is a bad turn of events. I shall have
no peace of mind until I am certain you are out of
danger. I'd have sent Flavia with you, but given her
extraordinary swimming ability, I couldn't be certain she would stay in the boat. You will see in the
other letter that I have asked Rhianne to take you
on board her ship. If the war is lost, she will evacuate you to Mosar. I know this plan does not please
you, but if you love me at all, you will comply. If
the usurper's forces break through and death
awaits me, I shall face my fate bravely, knowing
that the woman I love survives. Please grant me
this small measure of peace.*

Yours now and forever,

Lucien

Vitala stared at the letter until the loops and whorls
swam before her eyes. Then she read the one addressed
to Rhianne. There were no surprises; it explained the
situation and requested that Vitala be evacuated.

She lay quiet for a long time, thinking and occasionally wiping away tears. Then she refolded both letters
and slipped them into her pocket.

When they arrived at Tovar, Vitala spotted several Mosari ships slipping up and down the coast, patrolling the
river mouth. Three other ships remained in the harbor,
and as her boat approached them, Vitala saw they were
damaged. Sailors were up on the yards, replacing torn

sails and splintered spars. One ship had lost its main-mast.

She'd expected to be taken to one of the ships, but it turned out Rhianne and Jan-Torres were on land, still in the town hall. The soldiers handed her off to the Mosari guards, who led her inside. Her arrival had interrupted Rhianne's and Jan-Torres's lunch.

"Empress!" Rhianne's eyes lit with sudden pleasure, then turned worried. "Is Lucien all right? How goes the war? For over a week, we have heard nothing."

Vitala took a deep breath. "Lucien is fine, but the storm dealt us a nasty blow, same as it did to your ships."

"A Kjallan fleet happened to those ships," said Jan-Torres. "But never mind. What's happened in the gorge?"

"We had walled off the Stonemaw and Ashfeld passes and were holding the enemy soldiers at bay, but a flood knocked down part of the wall, and now the enemies will be coming through."

Rhianne and Jan-Torres exchanged stricken glances. "Did he send you here so we could evacuate you?" asked Rhianne.

"No, Your Majesty. He needs me to carry an urgent message to the Obsidian Circle. I've come to request a horse, supplies, and some local currency."

"Why you?" asked Jan-Torres. "Anyone could deliver that message. Why send the empress?"

"On the contrary, Your Majesty, the Circle is famously difficult to locate. I am the only one capable of reading the signs and finding an enclave."

"Did he send a letter explaining this?" demanded Jan-Torres. "He should have sent guards to accompany you!"

"He could not have sent guards. The Circle executes all Kjallans who come too near their enclaves."

"When you are *allies*?" Jan-Torres shook his head. "Surely not."

"Come and sit with us," said Rhianne. "You must be famished. Have some lunch, and you can tell us more."

"With all respect, I cannot. I must be off immediately."

"Absolutely not," said Jan-Torres. "Sit down. You must give us a better explanation than this."

"Janto," said Rhianne soothingly, "I'm sure she has her reasons."

"Your Majesty, please," said Vitala. "Lucien's life may depend on this mission."

"Then I'm sure you can explain why—" began Jan-Torres.

Rhianne placed a hand over her husband's, and he fell silent. "Of course we shall provide you with what you need," she said.

Half an hour later, Vitala was galloping south on a fine black mare with provisions and a bag full of tetrals.

32

Infiltrating the usurper's encampment took almost no effort at all; young women like Vitala were more than welcome. She'd expected to pay a substantial rent for tent space, but half the tents were unoccupied, so she got it for a pittance. She was also able to buy a syrtos in the proper style for a camp follower—shorter, light, and gauzy—as well as a furred cloak to throw around it for warmth. Food prices, however, were five or six times the norm. No wonder so many women had left.

After securing accommodations and changing into her new clothing, she bought some ridiculously priced "pork" on a stick that tasted like no pork she'd ever eaten and wandered the camp to get a feel for the place. How should she approach this task? She needed to reach Cassian, but gaining entry to the officers' pavilion would not be as easy as infiltrating the camp. The pavilion was well guarded. Camp followers weren't allowed inside.

A pair of rank-and-file soldiers propositioned her as she walked, but she turned her back on them. She needed an officer with access to Cassian. And if she found one, how was she to proceed from there, when she knew nothing about Cassian himself? How different this was from her original mission! She'd studied Lucien for nearly a decade before trying to approach him.

"Three gods!" cried a woman behind her. "Vivian, is that you?"

A tingle of familiarity ran down Vitala's spine. She turned just in time to catch Ista, who rushed into her arms.

Ista squealed and hugged her. "What happened? Was the action too slow in White Lion? Why do you look so dumbfounded? You can't be surprised to see me."

"No, of course not." Vitala blinked. She'd never seen Ista "on" before; it was startling.

Ista slipped an arm around her waist and led her from the crowd. "You must stay with me. I've got a fabulous tent, lots of space. Just ignore the bitch next door. The men here are wonderful! I'll introduce you to some of my beaux—there's more than enough to go around." She nattered on, talking of nothing, until they reached a large red tent with strings of beads hanging over the entryway. Ista parted the beads to go inside and dragged Vitala after her.

Vitala glanced around the tent. They were alone. "What's going on?"

Ista put a finger to her lips.

Vitala leaned forward to whisper but was interrupted by a muffled wail, which emanated from the adjacent tent.

Ista pounded on the tent wall. "Shut it, you old bitch!"

The wailing intensified.

"Gods, she never stops." Ista rolled her eyes.

"Why are the food prices so high?" asked Vitala, feeling that was a safe subject to discuss even if they were being spied upon.

"Not enough to go around," said Ista. "Whatever you get your hands on, eat it quickly, because the battalion leaders may come through and confiscate it for the soldiers. The good news is lots of women are leaving. The bad news is there have been women attacked, even killed. Sometimes the men don't pay enough for what they ask for, or don't pay at all. And good luck to you if you try to seek redress."

Vitala nodded, biting her lip. "And how is the war going?"

"Better," said Ista. "For a while, we weren't getting anywhere. The rebels had walled themselves into a gulch and our men couldn't get through, but then we had a stroke of luck. A flash flood knocked down a couple of walls and drowned a few centuries of soldiers, and now we're advancing steadily. We'll probably have to pack up and move the camp again tomorrow. Have you heard the rumor that the rebel troops are commanded by the old Emperor Lucien?"

"I thought Emperor Lucien was dead," Vitala said carefully.

Ista shrugged. "Maybe he is and maybe he isn't."

Vitala chafed with frustration. She had so much to ask Ista, and no privacy in which to do it. "Are your friends still here, or did they clear out when the food prices went up?"

The wailing next door intensified, and Ista punched the side of the tent a few more times. "Shut it!" she cried.

"We could go to my tent," said Vitala.

Ista shook her head. "It'll be as bad there, most like. My friends are gone. But now *you're* here. We can look after each other. We'll have fun together!"

So the Circle had presumably sent a team of assassins. And all of them were gone except Ista? What had happened?

"There's a junior officer I'd like to introduce you to," continued Ista. "His name is Glavius, he's very handsome, and he always pays. I'm meeting him tonight. You should meet him too." There was a gleam in her eye that told Vitala this meeting was important.

"That sounds wonderful," said Vitala.

Ista lowered her voice. "Let me tell you what to do."

"Izzy, you got company already?" The young officer poked his head into the tent, rattling the beads. "You know what I said—" His eyes found Vitala, and he fell silent.

Ista grinned. "I *do* have company. I was thinking we'd have a little extra fun tonight. Did you bring what I asked?"

The officer stepped all the way into the tent. He was a big man, tall and well muscled. He pulled a bottle of wine from his syrtos and held it up enticingly. "Of course." He eyed Vitala appreciatively. "What sort of extra fun did you mean?"

"This is my sister Vivian. She likes a good time too. Don't you, Vivian?"

Vitala wrinkled her face into a pout. "It smells in here."

"Vivian, who cares?" Ista turned to the officer. "She's new to camp life, not used to it yet. But she and I used to have a lot of fun together. Vivian, this is Glavius. Isn't he the most handsome man you ever saw?"

Vivian looked him over and nodded, giving him the ghost of a smile. "But it smells. And that old bitch never shuts up." As if on cue, the woman next door started wailing again. "I couldn't possibly have fun *here*. You two do what you like. I'll leave you to it." Vitala stood and headed for the tent-flap door.

"Vivian," protested Ista.

Glavius stepped in front of the door, blocking it.

When she paused in front of him, he lifted her chin and examined her face. He smiled. "What if we went to another tent?"

"They all smell bad," said Vitala.

"I know one that doesn't," said Glavius.

"Where?" said Vitala.

"In the officer's pavilion. My own tent."

Ista gasped. "You would take us *there*?"

Glavius shrugged. "I think we can relax the rules this one time. The rebels are in retreat, and the camp's going to pick up and move tomorrow. Why shouldn't you ladies move a little early? Vivian's right. It *does* smell in here."

"Vivian, say yes," said Ista. "The officer's pavilion is so much nicer than here."

Vitala gazed adoringly into Glavius's eyes. "Yes."

The officers' pavilion was on high ground, surrounded by a makeshift fence and guarded by uniformed soldiers. Some of the guards looked like they wanted to say something when they saw Vitala and Ista at Glavius's side, but after a look at his insignia and blood mark, they bit their tongues.

Inside the pavilion, Vitala passed a junior officer who looked right at Ista's chest, then at Glavius with a raised eyebrow.

"Prisoners to be interrogated," said Glavius.

The officer grinned, his eyes bright. "Need help?"

"Nah."

As they walked, Vitala analyzed the layout of the pavilion. The tents were of different shapes and colors and sizes. The size of each tent, she inferred, was a function of rank, with the larger tents reserved for the more senior officers. One tent, located in the center of the pavilion, towered over the others. That one must be

Cassian's. Her heart beat faster. She and Ista were getting close.

Glavius's tent was one of the smaller ones, red in color. Two battle standards leaned against each other at the entrance; a human skull dangled from one of them. Vitala softened her mind to check for wards and found an enemy ward across the doorway. Before she could ward-break it, it fizzled away into the Rift. Ista had broken it first.

Inside the tent, Glavius tidied up a little, grabbing clothes, a helmet, and a mail shirt off the backs of chairs and his cot and tossing them haphazardly into a leather-bound chest. He grinned and uncorked the wine, then sat in a chair and bade them sit together on his cot. "Let's play a game," he said. "For each swig, you have to take something off." He handed the bottle to Vitala.

Vitala tilted the bottle, blocking the opening with her tongue so that only a little wine leaked into her mouth. Then she removed one of her belts and passed the bottle to Ista. The officer watched her every move, his eyes shining. As the game continued, she glanced around the tent and at the cot. The cot wasn't large enough for three people. What was Ista planning? What role was Vitala intended to play? Glavius seemed to like being in charge, so their best bet might be to follow his lead for now. Ista would make her move when she was ready.

Vitala took another pretend swig from the bottle. After several rounds, she'd removed her two belts, her cloak, and her shoes. There was nothing left to do but take off her syrtos, so she did so, stripping down to her chemise. She shivered, and her nipples tightened. Glavius stared at her chest.

"Glavius, dear." Ista drank from the bottle and removed her own syrtos. "You know mine are better." She brandished her ample chest. "And it's no fair taking off things like your sword and your pistol. Look at all those clothes you've got on compared to us. Take off something that counts."

He grinned and pulled down his trousers. "Like this?"

"Yes, exactly like that," said Ista, as he drank deeply from the wine bottle.

His gaze moved from one of them to the other, and he licked his lips. "So, do you ladies often do this together?"

"Indeed we do, sweetie," said Ista.

"Say." His eyes lit. "Do you ladies ever ... you know ... with each other?"

"Glavius, we're sisters. That would be incest."

"Oh. I suppose you're right."

"So it's one at a time, love. I'll go first." Ista peeled off her chemise, revealing creamy white skin.

Glavius stood and moved toward her, but Vitala caught the barely perceptible hand gesture Ista had sent her.

"No, me first." Vitala pulled off her own chemise, shivering as the cold air tickled her bare skin.

Glavius goggled at her, then at Ista. "Maybe both of you could, um ..." He turned to the cot, which could barely fit two people, let alone three. "Hmm."

Though disrobed from the waist down, he was still wearing his unbelted syrtos and a mail shirt and undertunic. Ista removed the syrtos and began pulling the mail and undertunic over his head. Vitala stepped forward to help. Lying against his lightly furred chest was his riftstone, the topaz of a war mage.

"I go first," crooned Ista, meeting his lips with hers as they emerged from the shirt. She led him to the cot and he followed, unresisting.

Vitala trailed after them, feeling awkward, but if Ista

was going to take the lead on this, she wouldn't object. Not that she would hesitate to sleep with this man if that was what it took to save Lucien, but she certainly didn't relish the idea. And what if she had one of her "events"?

Glavius climbed atop Ista and, as far as Vitala could tell, penetrated her almost instantly. Ista moaned. Vitala assumed she was faking, but it was hard to tell; Ista was an awfully good actress. Vitala turned away and waited, having little desire to watch or even think about what they were doing. It reminded her too much of those awful practice sessions. After a time, Glavius's breathing grew heavy, his movements stronger, jerkier, which meant the end was near. Vitala swallowed uncomfortably.

He grunted, and the cot began to shake. Vitala heard the sounds of a struggle and forced herself to look, in case Ista needed help. Glavius was shuddering in his death throes, and Ista was trying to squeeze out from under him. "Get him off," she choked.

Dry-mouthed, Vitala rolled the twitching Glavius off the bed.

"Gods, he's like an ape." Ista scrambled off the bed and grabbed a blanket, which she used to wipe off Glavius's sweat and spittle.

Vitala stared at Glavius. He wasn't dead yet.

"What are you doing—daydreaming?" snapped Ista. "Get dressed."

Vitala tore her eyes away from the living corpse. "Doesn't it bother you?"

"What—killing this sapskull?" Ista pulled on her chemise, then her syrtos.

"Killing anyone. Doesn't it give you nightmares?"

"Anyone who'd let himself get suckered like that deserves what he gets."

Vitala picked her syrtos and chemise off the floor and began to get dressed. "What happens now?"

"I don't know. I got us into the pavilion. Now you'd better come up with some ideas. Whatever we do, it'll have to wait for morning. There are too many officers here now, resting in their tents."

"Won't Cassian be away in the daytime, along with his officers?"

"Probably, but we could have a look around his tent, maybe set up an ambush."

"You don't think this can be done by seduction?"

"No. He's not interested in whores. There's a woman who goes to his tent most nights, a mistress he's known for a long time. I doubt we can impersonate her, so we're looking at something more straightforward, like putting a sword through his gut." Ista went to the first of Glavius's two leather-bound chests, opened it, and rifled through it. "Clothes. Hmm." She went to the second, but it wouldn't open. "Find the key."

Wrinkling her nose, Vitala went to Glavius's corpse — he was dead now — then realized she wouldn't find anything on a naked body. She found his clothes and fished through the pockets. "Here." She handed Ista a ring of keys.

Ista opened the second chest and whistled. "Guess who's a weapons aficionado." She lifted a couple of beautiful, high-quality pistols from the chest.

"Too noisy for this kind of work," said Vitala. "But nice in case of emergency."

"Agreed." Ista took one pistol for herself and gave the other to Vitala, then resumed looking through the chest. She set a couple of lesser-quality pistols on the ground, then several swords and knives. "Oh, look." She pulled out several wine bottles and set them on the ground. "Make him look like a drunk, will you?"

Vitala uncorked the bottles one at a time. She poured their contents over Glavius, then stashed the empties around the tent, making it look like he'd drunk himself into a stupor. When she finished, the whole tent reeked of alcohol, and Ista had amassed a pile of weapons next to the chest. Vitala selected a sword and a pair of throwing knives from the pile. Ista brought out a selection of poisons she'd hidden in her clothes, and they coated the knives with a paralytic. It would have no effect on a war mage like Cassian or Glavius, but it should work beautifully on anyone nonmagical they came across.

"We're going to have to sleep in here, aren't we?" noted Vitala. "With the corpse."

"Yes, unless you have a better idea," said Ista. "He's my kill, by the way. I was working on him before you arrived. Don't you even think of claiming him!"

"Of course. He's your kill."

Ista nodded, satisfied. "You sleep. I'll take first watch."

33

Vitala was startled out of the quiet of her early morning watch by a thundering roar that shuddered through her body. Had the storm returned, or was it a cannon? Moments later, there were answering booms, accentuated by the staccato crackle of musket fire.

She ran to the cot and shook Ista. "Wake up."

Ista rose silently, armed and clothed.

The camp began to rouse. Vitala heard shouts, movement, footsteps.

"Glavius!" The voice came from just outside the tent. Vitala slipped behind the cot and covered herself with the blanket. Ista ducked behind a chest. There was a rattling sound. Vitala flinched, wondering what it was, and finally figured out it was the skull banging against the battle standard. "Wake up, Glavius. We're under attack!" A pause. "Glavius?" The tent flap opened. The voice, closer now, was full of scorn. "Gods, Glavius." The tent flap closed and the footsteps ran off.

Vitala stood up from behind the cot.

"Are Lucien's forces attacking the pavilion?" whispered Ista.

"No, those cannons are distant," said Vitala. "I'm sure the officers are being roused so they can help at the front lines. I think Lucien's making some kind of desperate push."

"Could be an opportunity for us," said Ista.

Vitala nodded. She and Ista waited in the tent while the camp emptied. When the sounds of activity faded, Vitala poked her head out the tent, ascertained there was no one watching, and emerged with Ista behind her.

The grumbling and groaning of the cannons sounded horribly near as they worked their way toward the imperial tent, but Vitala knew from experience that they were farther away than they seemed. *How far?* she wondered. Wherever the action was, Lucien was probably close by. He could be within walking distance. Of course, with thousands of hostile troops in between the two of them, the physical distance didn't matter at all.

Two guards stood in front of the imperial tent.

Vitala peered at them from behind a weapons rack and grimaced. "Legaciatti."

"Yes and no," whispered Ista. "Most of the Legaciatti are dead, killed during the coup or afterward during the purge. Cassian has been assigning ordinary soldiers to Legaciatti positions."

"Really?" Vitala brightened. "Then these might not even be magical."

"They might not be," said Ista. "But we shouldn't assume."

"I don't think we should kill them," said Vitala. "It leaves too obvious a calling card."

They crept around to the back of the tent, where they found more guards. These she and Ista dispatched with the poisoned knives. From the outside, the tent appeared to have the same shape as Lucien's old imperial tent, the one she'd burned. Assuming it was also the same on the inside, she worked out where the bedroom would be and crouched in the dirt along its back wall. Vitala began cutting a slit near the floor of the tent. The leather was thick, and she strained with the effort. Ista shoved the guards' bodies up against the tent wall and kept watch. Vitala had dulled the first knife and switched to a second by the time she'd opened enough of a gap that they could slip through.

She peeked through the opening. It was indeed a bedroom. "I don't see anyone."

"Go in," said Ista. "We're still clear outside. I'll shove the bodies in after you."

Vitala pocketed her knives and squirmed headfirst through the small opening. She was just tugging her hips through when something landed on her head.

She bit her tongue to keep from crying out and fought silently, twisting to free her trapped shoulder. She flung the weight off of her, surprised at how light it was. She turned and located her attacker, a boy with a knife.

He launched himself at her, swiping inexpertly with the knife. Vitala dodged the blow and caught his hand. She applied pressure to the wrist, making him drop the weapon, then scooped it up herself. She grabbed her assailant and held the knife to his neck, but it wasn't a boy at all. Her attacker had long hair and a delicate, feminine face. She'd been fighting a teenage girl. *Celeste.*

I should put down the knife and let her go, Vitala thought. But no, that was a bad idea—she needed to explain herself first, or the girl might summon the guards. *I should put down the knife and let her go.* The thought recurred, forceful and persistent. And strange. Nonsensical. Vitala blinked in confusion. Then something rose in her, so virulent she almost vomited, and shoved the thought from her mind as if it were a foreign invader. In the moment of clarity that followed, she realized that was exactly what it had been. Celeste, like most Kjallan noblewomen, was a mind mage.

"Nice try," she said, keeping her voice low, "but I'm magical. Your tricks won't work on me."

"Who are you?" squeaked the girl.

"Believe it or not, I'm the Empress of Kjall," she said. "Lucien sent me." A pang knifed through her; looking into the girl's black eyes was like looking into Lucien's, and she missed her husband terribly. But there were differences. Celeste's hair was lighter than Lucien's, and she had a sprinkling of freckles across her cheeks. Where had those come from? Vitala didn't know Lucien's ancestry beyond a couple of generations. Did his line carry foreign blood?

Ista squeezed in behind her and gasped. "Is that Celeste?"

"Yes," said Vitala. "Get the guards' bodies in here."

"What's going on?" hissed Celeste—but quietly, as if she didn't want the guards out front to hear.

"I'll explain in a moment," said Vitala. Then, to Ista, "Get the bodies."

Instead Ista launched herself at Celeste.

"No!" cried Vitala. She flung herself at Ista. Spying a poisoned knife in Ista's hand, she grabbed it, forcing it away from Celeste's neck. Celeste squeezed herself out from under the two of them and scrambled away, and Vitala and Ista crashed to the ground, wrestling over possession of the knife. Ista kneed Vitala in the crotch, a tactic that didn't accomplish much, and Vitala, unable to free up a fist to strike with, elbowed Ista in the face. She had a height and strength advantage. Grunting with the effort, she used that advantage to maneuver the knife blade to Ista's throat. "Yield," she whispered. "Or I finish this mission alone."

Ista let go of the knife and stared up at Vitala. "We have to kill her. Don't you understand?"

"You're mad," growled Vitala. "I am not killing Lucien's sister."

Pounding footsteps approached. Vitala froze with the knife in her hands and turned to see the two guards standing in the doorway, weapons drawn, ready to attack. Celeste moved to intercept them. Though only half their size, she faced them down.

"Everything's all right," said Celeste. "You may go back to your posts."

The guards stared at Vitala and Ista. There could be no question that they were aware that intruders had broken in, and yet their eyes whirled with foggy indecision. "You're certain, Empress?"

"I'm certain," said Celeste. "Return to your posts."

The guards turned to leave, and Vitala shuddered. Mind magic was the creepiest thing she'd ever seen.

"I can call them back at any time," said Celeste, with a pointed look at Ista. "So you'd better not touch me again."

"Your guards are no threat to us," Ista sneered.

"We're not here to kill you," said Vitala. "At least I'm not. I'm here on Lucien's behalf, to assassinate Cassian and get you out of here. Is Cassian here now?"

"No, he's gone to the front," said Celeste. "Why do you call yourself empress? And how could Lucien have sent you when he's being held prisoner?"

"He's not being held prisoner. Here, you'll want proof." She fished through her pockets and found the letter he'd written her. "He and I were married not long ago."

Celeste read the letter and wrinkled her brow in confusion. "How can this be? Where is he?"

"He's leading the rebel army."

Her eyes widened. "How did he get there? Did he escape?"

"Yes. I helped him escape."

Celeste looked more confused than ever, but handed the letter back. "That's his hand; I'd know it anywhere. But I don't understand how he got away. Also, according to this letter, he didn't send you here. He wanted you evacuated to Mosar."

"I interpreted his words somewhat creatively."

Celeste peered at her. "How does he even know you? I've never seen you before."

"You have, but you don't remember. I can't tell you the whole story right now," said Vitala. "Lucien is alive, but you're right: his army is losing. We must end this war before his troops are overrun, and the only way to do it is to assassinate Cassian. Will you help us?"

"I would," said Celeste. "But you can't kill Cassian. He's a war mage. If it were possible, I'd have done it already."

Ista broke in. "Celeste is right. It's not possible to kill Cassian, not with only two of us. That's why Celeste has to die instead. She's the one who makes his claim to the throne legitimate. Without her, he is nothing. If Celeste cares about her country, even she must agree with me."

Celeste gaped at her.

"We came here to kill Cassian!" cried Vitala. "I would never have agreed to come here and murder Lucien's sister."

Ista smiled grimly. "Plans change. What's more important to you: the life of one girl or the future of your entire country?"

Vitala shook her head, refusing to view the conundrum as a math problem. "Killing Celeste won't save Lucien, and it won't save Riorca. Cassian is too well entrenched as a leader to be thrown out just because Celeste has been killed."

"You don't know that," said Ista. "Besides, what choice

do we have? We can't kill Cassian. It takes three trained warriors at least to challenge a war mage. We have two."

Celeste swallowed. "I'll help you."

"You are not a trained warrior," snapped Ista. "You're a little girl."

"The reason you need three people is you need him distracted," said Celeste. "I can't fight, but I can distract him."

"How?" said Vitala.

Celeste shrugged. "I could make him angry at me."

"No good," said Ista. "You might distract him initially, but once he realizes he's being attacked, he'll ignore you and focus on us. Then we'll die and he can punish you at his leisure."

Celeste's cheeks colored.

"We're here to kill Cassian, not the princess," said Vitala. "You know as well as I do that if you kill Celeste, the deal between Lucien and the Circle falls apart and we have nothing at all—no peace, nothing." She turned to Celeste. "When will Cassian be back?"

"Probably when the battle is over."

"And when the battle is over, will his officers return too?"

"Most of them."

"We need him alone," said Vitala. "Is there a way to get just Cassian and not the officers?"

Celeste was silent for a while, thinking. "Well . . . I could fake a suicide attempt or illness. But if he came back at all, he'd probably bring a Healer with him."

"We'd rather not have the Healer," said Vitala. "We need him alone. Let's come back to this problem later. What about the guards out front? I take it they're non-magical, if they're susceptible to your magic?"

"Yes," said Celeste.

Vitala nodded. "Can you use your magic to keep them out of the fight? I'd rather not kill them, as it makes our presence here too obvious, but I don't want them adding to our difficulties when we fight Cassian."

"I can neutralize them, yes."

"Could you make them fight on our side?" asked Ista.

"Probably," said Celeste. "But they'd be confused and wouldn't fight well."

Ista grunted. "Never mind. They'd be a hindrance. Look, if you could control these guards all along, why didn't you just leave? Why stay here and help the enemy wage war against your brother?"

Celeste bristled. "I was *helping* my brother. If I left, Cassian would have killed him!"

"An empty threat," snorted Ista. "He's been trying to kill Lucien all along. That's what the war is about."

"No." Celeste violently shook her head. "The war is about the Riorcan rebels. Cassian was holding Lucien prisoner. He would have killed him if I tried to run away." She looked at Vitala. "But you helped him escape, and now he's with the rebels?"

"I helped him escape during the initial coup. He was never Cassian's prisoner. The rebels aren't rebels at all; they are Lucien's supporters." One of the final Caturanga pieces clicked into place. Now she knew why Remus and the others hadn't killed Lucien right away. Their orders were to deliver him to Cassian, who would secretly hold him prisoner and use him as leverage over the imperial princess. When Lucien escaped capture, Cassian had been forced to improvise.

"But I *saw* him," insisted Celeste. "In a prison cell."

"Not up close, I'll bet," said Ista.

Celeste looked uncertain. "Not up close, but it was Lucien. I'm sure."

Ista rolled her eyes. "You saw a fake. Cassian tricked you. Foolish chit, you fell for the oldest trick in the book!"

"Leave her alone," snapped Vitala. "She's only a child."

"A sapskull of a child, who played right into his hands."

Celeste looked stricken.

"Never mind," said Vitala, taking Celeste's hand and squeezing it. "He tricked the entire country, not just you. Be easy. Lucien is free, at least for now, and if we can assassinate Cassian, he will stay that way."

Celeste swallowed. "I can get Cassian to come back alone."

"How?" asked Vitala.

"I'll send him a message. 'I know about Lucien.' That should bring him back in a hurry."

"Won't he bring backup?" asked Ista.

"Why would he? He's not afraid of me. My magic can't touch him, and he's twice my size. He'll just threaten me, beat me perhaps, and tell me I'm stupid."

"Send your message," said Vitala.

From her hiding spot, Vitala heard hoofbeats gallop to the tent entrance, followed by a dusty thump as someone dismounted. The footsteps came closer and became less muffled, suggesting that whoever it was had entered the tent, unchallenged by the guards. It occurred to Vitala that she didn't actually know what Cassian looked like.

"Celeste, what's this about your brother?" The voice was deep, suggesting a man of some size. "Have you been listening to the camp rumors?"

"They're not rumors." Celeste's voice shook.

Vitala winced from her place of safety behind the curtain. The girl had been so strong, so resilient, up until this point, but now she appeared to be cracking. Cassian must terrify her. If only she could hold herself together a few minutes longer . . .

The footsteps crossed Vitala's position, and the voice continued. "Idiot girl. They *are* rumors. Your brother is in my custody, not leading any rebel army. You have seen this with your own eyes."

"You lied. You showed me a look-alike."

"Then why haven't you run, my darling?"

Celeste gasped in surprise and fear. Vitala guessed that Cassian had grabbed her; their voices were very near to each other.

The deep voice fell almost to a whisper. "No answer? Never mind, then. I know why you haven't run—because you don't truly believe this nonsense about your brother. You repeat these silly rumors for no other reason than to provoke me. Stupid, ugly girl."

"No—my lord." Celeste's breath was coming in terrified gasps; she wouldn't last much longer.

"You realize I have no choice," said Cassian. "It's ten lashes for any enlisted man who gives voice to the rumor. I can hardly make an exception for my empress, who ought to be setting an example for her people."

Celeste made no reply. Instead, there was a rustle of clothing, a brief struggle, the sound of a blow as it landed, and a grunt of pain from Celeste.

That's my cue.

Vitala sprang from the curtain. Ista was a half a breath ahead of her, running at Cassian, her sword point barreling toward his heart. Cassian was almost too late to respond. Just in time, he flung the girl aside and turned. His own blade leapt from its scabbard to block Ista's attack. Vitala hurled her throwing knife, aiming it at the middle of his back.

His body contorted impossibly and the knife scraped by his side, tearing a gash in his syrtos. Knocked askew, the blade flew across the room, thumped against the tent wall, and fell to the ground. Cassian howled, but though Vitala saw blood, the wound didn't hamper his movement. Celeste scrambled behind a couch for safety.

Vitala drew her sword, and not a second too soon. Cassian was upon her, having knocked Ista off balance with a flurry of blows. He whipped the blade at her again and again. She parried the strokes, but each parry came a little slower than the last—he was too fast, too strong—and all that saved her from a devastating follow-up blow was Ista, who struck at him from behind, forcing him to swing around. Vitala recovered her stance, took a breath, and stabbed at Cassian's back. He whirled just in time to block it and, with a snarl of contempt, aimed a heavy slash at her midsection that took every ounce of her strength to knock away. His blade flew up again, and she jumped back. Pain seared her thigh. The wound felt deep and serious, but her leg could still bear weight.

Ista leapt back in and pulled Cassian off Vitala before he could follow up with a blow to the chest. They played him like a pair of crows harassing an eagle, drawing him from one of them to the other, scrambling over chairs and end tables as the fight progressed about the room. Cassian was elegant, she realized, a superb fighter with skills that went beyond the enhancements of his war magic. Not only did he see her blows coming; he picked all the right countermoves. For all their skills, she and Ista were losing.

Ista bled from wounds on her cheek, arm, and gut. Her blows looked weaker and weaker. Cassian drove her relentlessly backward. Though light-headed, Vitala struck at him, trying to pull him off her. He turned just enough to parry Vitala's blows and drive her away, then struck again at Ista, who stumbled backward, tripped over a chair leg, and crashed to the ground. Cassian turned back to Vitala, grinning in triumph. He lunged, stabbing his blade at her chest.

Vitala knocked it aside, but her hands trembled on the sword hilt. Her vision darkened. She shook her head, trying to clear her mind, but the flurry of blows that came at her was overwhelming. She could not possibly get past his defenses. Ista struggled to her feet, but she didn't look strong enough to pose much of a threat.

With a grunt of impotent rage, Vitala summoned the last reserves of her strength. She raised her weapon, arms shaking, to block another blow. Ista stabbed desperately at Cassian's side. He turned to face her, then screamed in pain.

Ista's blade hadn't connected. Neither had Vitala's. Instead, Celeste clung to Cassian's back like a monkey. He flung her off. Where she had been, a knife protruded from his back. Cassian staggered. Vitala leapt toward him, swinging her sword. His face contorted in agony as his movements shifted the dagger in his back. He was slow with the parry, and she slipped past him to bury her blade in his shoulder. Ista's sword impaled his gut. Gasping, Cassian slid to the floor. Taking no chances, Vitala yanked her blade free and cut his throat.

She slid to the ground, too weak to stand, and dropped her head between her knees.

"Bandage that leg," grunted Ista, slicing off a strip of Cassian's syrtos and handing it to her.

Vitala wrapped the cloth tightly around the gash in her thigh. It was bad, but she felt she would survive if the bleeding stopped. Her eyes found Celeste, who crouched, white-faced, in a corner of the tent. "You all right?" she called.

Celeste nodded.

"So," panted Ista. "Whose kill was that?"

34

While Ista freed one of the tent poles and sharpened one end, Vitala, weak from blood loss and still sitting on the floor, directed Celeste to fetch a quill and paper and write:

> *The gods hate false emperors. See here the fate of a man who lied to his countrymen and claimed honors and titles that did not belong to him. My brother is alive. He commands the battalions in Blackscar Gulch, which fight not in rebellion, but to preserve the integrity of the empire. I order you to cease hostilities at once, request a parley, and place yourselves under the lawful command of Emperor Lucien.*
>
> *Imperial Princess Celeste Florian Nigellus*

"Wrap that leg again," said Ista. "It's still bleeding."

"Just a little," said Vitala, but she cut another strip of fabric and wrapped it tighter.

"You sure you can stand?" asked Ista.

Vitala nodded.

Celeste directed her tame guardsmen to fetch horses from the stables. Then the four of them, minus Celeste, whom Vitala asked to wait outside with the horses, staked Cassian in the middle of the tent. When it was done, Vitala did not turn her back on the grisly sight but directed her full gaze upon it, committing it to memory. Before they left, Vitala used a knife to pin the freshly inked letter to Cassian's chest.

Though Lucien could not be far away, he might as well be on the other side of the Great Northern Sea, for all it mattered. Vitala and the others could never pass through the hordes of hostile soldiers that stood in their way. To return to White Eagle, they would have to go back the way Vitala had originally come, first leaving the battalion, then riding north all the way to the coast and catching a supply boat south along the Ember River. Too weak for such a lengthy journey, Vitala consented instead to accompany Ista to the nearest Obsidian Circle enclave, taking Celeste with her, since she didn't trust the girl in anyone else's custody.

The enclave was unfamiliar to Vitala and she didn't know a soul, but a few of the enclave members knew Ista. The staff welcomed them. Upon hearing what had transpired in the camp, they dispatched a messenger to bear word to Lucien.

Vitala was taken immediately to a Healer, who repaired the wound in her leg, but she remained listless and weak. Only time would fix that.

For once, Vitala didn't mind lying around and resting. She'd done all that she could do for Riorca and for Lucien, at least for the time being. Celeste was hidden away, out of reach of any ambitious Kjallan looking to crown himself Cassian's successor, and Lucien was quite capable of sorting out the aftermath of the assassination. Celeste, trusting no one but Vitala, stayed with her constantly, which, to Vitala's surprise, she found to be a comfort. She liked the girl. Celeste bore a slight resemblance to her brother, whom Vitala missed terribly, and whatever Celeste had been through with Cassian, Vitala felt it gave them a certain kinship.

"Do you want to talk about it?" Vitala asked once. Celeste was ostensibly composing a letter to her brother, but the girl's quill had not scratched the paper for quite some time, and the look on her face was distant and troubled.

Celeste startled, dropped her quill, and picked it back up. "Talk about what?"

"Cassian."

Celeste turned away. "What is there to talk about? He's dead."

"Do you want to talk about what happened when he was alive?"

"No." Her quill scratched on the paper. An inkblot scarred the page, and she cursed.

"Perhaps not with me," Vitala said gently. "Perhaps you'd like to talk to your brother."

Celeste snorted and set down the quill. "Talk to my brother. What a lovely idea. *No*." She wadded up the ruined piece of paper and dropped it on the floor.

"No one will make you, of course," said Vitala. "But your brother is an understanding man, more so than perhaps you realize. He cares about you. Do you know he went to war with Cassian almost entirely because of you? And he's helped me with some problems of my own. I've had some problems related to . . . well, sort of like what you might have been through with Cassian."

Her eyes flashed with anger. "And what is it you think I've been through?"

"I'm not sure," said Vitala.

"I know what they say about me," said Celeste, gratingly. "Don't think I don't hear it."

"Your brother has problems too," said Vitala. "Wounds that never healed."

Celeste threw her a look of contempt.

"I'm not saying it's the same," added Vitala. "But ask him sometime about how he lost his leg. You might be surprised at the story he tells you." A lift in Celeste's brow told Vitala she'd piqued the girl's curiosity. Figuring it would be unwise to provoke Celeste any more than she already had, she left it at that.

The enclave's spies reported in frequently, keeping them apprised of events. Cassian's officers had called for a cease-fire and parley. Lucien did not agree to the parley immediately, perhaps suspecting a trap, but after a few days of confusion and delay, it finally took place. At that meeting, the officers pledged fealty to Lucien under the sage flag, and the war came to an end.

Some days later, Vitala received a letter from someone she'd never heard of. He introduced himself as the leader of a distant Obsidian Circle enclave and wrote:

> *It has come to my attention that you are in
> possession of a Northern Sea Retriever by the
> name of Flavia, previously looked after by Hanna
> and Glenys of Tasox. Flavia is one of few
> individuals remaining of this valuable breed,
> which our ancestors once used to hunt ducks and
> seabirds on the wild northern coast. These
> retrievers were nearly destroyed by Kjallan
> soldiers, but some of our countrymen smuggled
> the best ones to safety, and we have preserved the*

*bloodline in secrecy ever since. Flavia is
particularly valuable because she is female and
descended from an exceptional maternal line, and
we respectfully request her immediate return. She
is to be bred on her next heat to a dog in Worich.*

    *Alternatively, if you have become attached to
Flavia, we offer you the opportunity to be her care-
taker, provided you are willing to breed her as directed.*

The letter went on to provide details. Vitala smiled. The
enclave leader had some nerve, dictating terms to the
Empress of Kjall, and he seemed not to be aware that
Flavia was Lucien's dog as much as her own. Still, if not
for the enclave's efforts, Flavia's ancestors would never
have survived to produce her. Vitala would honor their
wishes. She and Lucien would become Flavia's caretak-
ers and have her bred to the dog from Worich.

And wouldn't Lucien be surprised when she told him
all this?

Lucien sent word to the Circle requesting the return
of Vitala and Celeste. His army was still encamped in
the gulch and would remain there for another week at
least, attending to funerals and the burning of bodies.
Vitala still felt too weak for the journey, but Celeste was
well enough, and Vitala urged her to go. The enclave
escorted Celeste to a secure location where she was
handed off to a combined party of White Eagle and Mosari soldiers.

Vitala felt the loss keenly. Once again, she was left all
alone. But Celeste's escort returned with a surprise for
her—a letter from Lucien. She opened it eagerly and
read it in the privacy of her room:

Dear Vitala,

Please rejoin the battalion as soon as you are able; I miss you terribly. The story of your exploits has been told to me, and I find it astonishing. I look forward to the day you can relate it to me yourself. Until then, take care of yourself. Thank you for the gift of my sister.

Much love,

Lucien

She pressed the paper up to her nose and inhaled deeply, hoping to catch a trace of Lucien's scent, but she breathed in nothing but the musty smell of paper. If only he'd written more! Why had he been so brief? Perhaps he'd disliked the thought of Obsidian Circle spies reading his words, for there was no doubt they would have done so before passing on the letter. Yes, that had to be the reason. What did he mean when he said he found her story astonishing? Was he proud of her for assassinating Cassian, or horrified?

Never mind how Lucien felt. If what she'd done bothered him, he would get used to it, damn him, because the memory of her accomplishment never failed to bring a smile to Vitala's face. Her mission was complete. She'd assassinated an emperor. Maybe it wasn't the emperor she'd originally been sent for, but so what? That was a minor detail.

Someone knocked on the door.

"It's open," she called, looking up from *The Seventh Life of the Potter's Daughter.*

Ista came in. "Are you well enough to ride?"

"Depends on the distance."

"Your emperor and his army are marching for home," said Ista. "They're out of the gulch now, and they'll pass within a few hours' ride of the enclave tomorrow morning. An escort will be arranged for you, if you think you can ride that far."

Vitala looked up. "I can ride that far, yes." This was it, then—back to Lucien and her new role as the Empress of Kjall. Good-bye to the Obsidian Circle. Her stomach fluttered. Was it excitement she was feeling, or fear? "Thank you, Ista. This couldn't have happened without you."

Ista smiled cynically. "I know."

"What will you do now?" asked Vitala. "With Riorca and Kjall at peace, there is little need for assassins. Would you like a position in the palace? Most of the Legaciatti are dead. Lucien and I will need to establish a new intelligence network. You could head it up. "

"Palace life isn't for me. And what do you mean, there's no need for assassins?"

"Riorca is free, and I intend to make sure it stays that way."

Ista snorted. "You've too much faith in that husband of yours. Kjallans are Kjallans. They're always going to want a free ride on the backs of Riorcan labor, and they'll take it if we roll over and let them. Besides, what about the Riorcan slaves in Kjall? You think your precious emperor is going to free them, when he has promised them nothing? You go fight the Kjallans your way, in the palace, and I'll fight them here at home."

Vitala sighed, conceding that Ista was at least partially correct. Lucien wasn't the only man in Kjall with power—and even he might need a stern reminder from time to time that the Riorcans needed to be treated fairly. "Very well," she said. "But don't forget we're on the same side. And if you change your mind, let me know." She held out her arms, hoping to draw Ista into a hug.

Ista accepted the embrace and hugged her back stiffly. "If you change *your* mind and decide to be an assassin again, let me know. But I can see why you'd rather not. After all, while you're not bad at it, you'll always be second best."

Vitala rolled her eyes. "I'd better go. I think Riorca's too small for the both of us."

As her mare crested the top of the hill, Vitala spotted the battalion. A long, thin serpent of soldiers, mules, and supply wagons humped its way over the hills and valleys. The battle standards, glorious flying eagles against the blue and orange, glittered in the sunshine. Her heart leapt at the sight.

She searched for the head of the column, but it was hidden behind the next hill.

She clucked to her horse and galloped onward, leaving her escort behind. Heads turned at the tail of the column and eyes widened. The men whispered to their fellows ahead of them, and word of her arrival spread through the troop column like a snake's undulation.

The wave disappeared over the rise. After a few moments, three horn blasts in quick succession called a halt. Hot and dusty soldiers turned to face her as she flew past them at a gallop, racing for the head of the column. Some soldiers bowed to her, others saluted with a thumb to the chest. She nodded to a few that she knew by name, but she wouldn't stop, not until she saw Lucien.

Another horn blasted, then Quincius's shout carried over the hills. "White Eagle salutes the Empress of Kjall!"

A thousand Kjallan boots struck the ground. "HUR-

RAH!" shouted the soldiers, their voices full-throated and powerful. Vitala's mare shied, almost unseating her. She reined the animal to a halt and turned to face the battalion with a tight throat.

Their swords clashed against one another in unison. "HURRAH!"

Then came the shattering blast of muskets. "HUR-RAH!"

She hardly knew how to respond. What was one supposed to do when saluted by the battalion? She stayed where she was, trembling and wiping tears from her eyes.

A trio of riders appeared over the rise ahead. In the middle was Lucien, astride a magnificent black warhorse. The loros, recently restored by the Obsidian Circle, glittered on his chest. On his left rode Celeste, and on his right Quincius. Between the horses trotted a fluffy, recently bathed Flavia.

Lucien reined up in front of her, and she leapt off her horse to meet him. He dismounted, landing on his artificial leg, and in a few paces they were in each other's arms with the gold-and-white dog bounding happily around them.

"You are the world's most disobedient wife. Do you know that?" Lucien crushed her in an embrace and tucked her tearful face into his chest. Softer, he said, "Gods, woman. You saved us all."

She wrapped her arms around him, suddenly feeling that even skin-to-skin contact wouldn't get her close enough to this man. "I couldn't have done it without Ista and Celeste."

"So I heard." He pulled away enough to look her in the eye. "I couldn't be prouder of you and of Celeste. But don't ever run off again." He kissed her, rough and possessive.

Dizzy at the taste of him, she wished they didn't have the entire battalion as an audience. If she could, she'd drag him off to a tent right now. She grinned up at him with a gleam in her eye. "Are you going to punish me later?" she whispered.

He grinned back at her. "Absolutely."

"There was something I meant to say on the river-bank," she said. "At the time, I . . . forgot to say it. I meant to say I loved you too."

"I knew that already," said Lucien.

Dimly, she became aware of the soldiers' applause and catcalling, growing louder and more boisterous by the minute. These were her people, she realized. Never before had she felt so accepted, so valued. Not in her parents' house, not in Riorca, not in the Obsidian Circle.

It had finally happened. She'd come home.

35

His flesh moved against hers deliciously. Vitala shivered with delight and burrowed into the sheets, dragging the emperor with her. He kissed his way down her neck, toward her breasts, and she stiffened in anticipation—she was so sensitive there. Her back would arch, and he would have no mercy as he drove her to greater heights of pleasure.

"Lucien," she whispered.

"Mm?" he grunted.

He found her nipple. She hissed, muscles contracting. "I think it's time to try again."

"Try what?" He tongued her some more, grinning at her response.

"You in me."

He rolled off her, his playfulness gone, and propped himself on his side. He stroked her cheek, looking her in the eye. "Are you sure you're ready? You only just got back. And we'd have to wait for the fertility wards to wear off before you could get pregnant, anyway."

"But I'm a wardbreaker." She relaxed her mind and located the tinge of purple swirling through Lucien's body. She followed it to the contact point and, with a tweak of her mind, released it, sending the magic back into the Rift. She found her own ward and did the same. "There. You're ready now, and so am I."

"You didn't *do* anything."

"I did. You just can't see it." He looked impressed, but Vitala shivered in fear. Releasing the wards was the easy part.

He pulled her close, stroking her back in a way that was more soothing than erotic. "I've been thinking about this for a while, and I have an idea," he said.

"What's your idea?"

"Well—the episode you told me about, with the young soldier. What position were you in when he made love to you? Was it you on the bottom and him on top, face-to-face?"

"Yes."

"And that's the position we were in when you had your event."

"Yes."

"So I thought maybe if we try another position, we might avoid the problem."

Vitala blinked. She'd never thought of that before. "What position did you have in mind?"

"Do you have a favorite?"

She winced with embarrassment. "I don't know. I've never tried any other."

He stifled a laugh. "You Riorcans are so conservative. Well, a from-behind position might be our best bet, at least in the beginning. That way you won't see my face, so there won't be a visible trigger. I'll show you what I mean. Don't panic; I'm not going to do anything." He rolled her onto her side and positioned himself behind her, grasping her around the shoulders. "You see?"

It felt strange to have Lucien behind her for something so intimate. "I don't know. I want to see you." She turned in his arms and stroked the stubble on his chin.

"It's better than you think. A lot of women love this

position—you get deep penetration. And my hands are free, so I can do this." He fondled her breasts.

"I want to see you," she insisted. "At least this first time. Is that possible?"

"Well, we could try putting you on top." He rolled onto his back and pulled her on top of him, positioning her arms and legs. He raised his eyebrows questioningly.

She swallowed, tamping down her fear. It was very different from what she'd done with the young soldier. "Let's try this."

He lifted her a little and placed his erection directly beneath her. She needed only lower herself onto him. She did so partially, supporting herself with her hands, and he slipped halfway inside her. She jumped, a little startled. "Gods."

"*Gods* is right," he gasped.

She lowered herself the rest of the way, until she was essentially sitting on him. She swallowed, waiting for the madness to take her, but nothing happened. "Lucien, it's working," she said, jubilant. Then she realized it felt good, him being in her.

"Yes." His voice was tight. "Now when you're ready, just move. In your own time—no rush." He reached for her face, framed it in his hands, and drew her downward for a kiss.

She leaned over him, brushing her nipples against his chest. He tasted clean and masculine. His hands roamed along her back and shoulders, and she relaxed, simply enjoying the sensations: Lucien loving her, kissing her, filling her.

She discovered she was moving. She'd made no conscious decision to move, and yet it was happening, anyway, her body responding to the sensations in a way that women's bodies had responded since the gods had whispered the first breath of life into them. She experimented, trying one form of movement and then another, until she found one that made her dizzy with pleasure.

Lucien's breath quickened and she watched him, loving the way his face contracted. He was moving now too, his rhythm matching and accentuating hers. He reached between them and touched her, finding the little nub that always sent her pleasure skyward, and she moved, delirious, until their bodies convulsed, one after the other. They rolled over and lay in each other's arms, side by side, still joined, their sweat mingled together.

I may have conceived Kjall's heir, she realized. It wasn't likely, but it was possible. And if not? Well, she'd be doing this again. Many, many times. And maybe that other position was worth trying too.

She lay on the bed boneless, devoid of energy, but inwardly she was exultant. Lucien had been right. Her problem *was* fixable. Well, maybe not fixable, but it could be worked around.

"You are a brilliant, brilliant man," she murmured.

"Mmph," he said sleepily. "At the moment, I haven't a single coherent thought in my head."

She kissed him. "I don't think I fully appreciated the benefits of marrying such a clever fellow."

"And to think, if the Obsidian Circle hadn't sent you to kill me, we never would have met. At least, not for very long." He closed his eyes. "Wake me in half an hour and I'll show you some more positions."

She nestled her head into the crook of his shoulder. "Just remember, you're not out of danger yet. If you break your promises to Riorca, I'll still kill you."

His eyes cracked open. "Keep talking dirty to me, and I may not need that half hour." He propped himself on an elbow and stroked her cheek. "So, what will you do to me if I keep my promises?"

"Make you a very happy man."

He wrapped his arms around her and grinned. "Now, *that's* what I want to hear."

Read on for a look at the next book in
Amy Raby's Hearts and Thrones series

SPY'S HONOR

Available from Signet Eclipse in October 2013.

The guards dragged open the double doors, and Rhianne swept into her cousin's sitting room. "Is the council over? I need your fifteen tetrals."

Lucien whirled on his wooden leg, jumpy as a winter partridge. He wore his imperial garments, the silk syrtos and the thin, jeweled loros that marked him as the son and heir of the Kjallan Emperor. His dress suggested he'd only just returned from the council or was about to head out again, since he never wore the loros in his private chambers except to receive important visitors. Rhianne could not blame him. As the emperor's niece, she possessed a similar garment and found its weight onerous. Lucien, whose left leg had been amputated below the knee and who walked with the aid of a crutch, probably liked it even less.

He glanced at the door. "This is a bad time."

She could see that it was. Lucien had neither retreated to his Caturanga board for a war game nor settled on one of the many chairs and couches in his finely appointed sitting room to read one of Cinna's treatises on battle tactics. He seemed to be standing in the middle of the room, waiting to receive someone, and the someone he'd been waiting for had not been her. She glanced back at the door, but aside from the guards, she and Lucien were alone. "I only need the tetrals. Hand them over and I'll go. We can talk later."

Lucien frowned. "This business with the money—it has to stop."

Rhianne straightened her shoulders. He'd never balked over this before. "But we agreed to it. Fifteen tetrals from each of us. And besides—"

"There are more important things going on right now." Lucien's eyes went anxiously to the door. "And I can't afford to upset him any more than I already have."

"Who? His Royal Unreasonableness?"

Lucien grimaced. "We should stop calling him that."

Rhianne smiled sadly. Lucien was trying so hard to grow up, and he seemed to forget sometimes that she, three years senior to his tender age of seventeen, already had. And she wasn't leaving without her tetrals. "How am I supposed to come up with the full amount if you don't kick in your share? When you've got an obligation to somebody, you don't walk out on that obligation because something else came up—"

"It's not just me," snapped Lucien. "Your name came up at the council meeting."

"Mine?" She couldn't imagine why. It was a war council, and why should anyone, in the context of talking about the war with Mosar, bring up the emperor's niece? She was royal, but from a side branch of the family with a somewhat questionable pedigree. She wasn't important the way Lucien was.

"Well," thundered a voice from the doorway, "if it isn't our yapping dog from the War Council."

Rhianne, recognizing the deep tones of her uncle, the emperor, sank into a welcome curtsy. She glanced at Lucien long enough to see him steel his face and bow to his father.

"Emperor," said Lucien coolly.

Now she understood why Lucien was off-color. He and Florian were about to have a fight, and in these frequent and unavoidable conflicts, Lucien, the subordinate figure, always came off worse. She ought to have left when Lucien had told her to. "I'm sorry to intrude," she said. "I'll leave you to your privacy."

"No, no," said Florian, his eyes on Lucien. Though the emperor and his heir were cut from the same cloth, the resemblance one noted on first glance was superficial. They shared the same black hair, black eyes, and aquiline profile, but Florian was broader and taller by several inches. Florian reminded Rhianne of an eagle with his sharp eyes, craggy nose, and severe face. His elder sons had looked like stamped woodcut copies of him, but Lucien and his sister, the two youngest, with their slighter builds and finer features, resembled their late mother. Lucien was handsomer and smarter than his father, but Florian had never forgiven him for losing his leg to a trio of Riorcan assassins or for becoming his only choice of heir when the assassins had also murdered Lucien's elder brothers. "Stay," continued Florian. "I should like to hear your opinion. I should like to know what you think of a son and heir who openly criticizes his father's strategic decisions in a Council of War."

Rhianne winced. "Well, without knowing the particulars—"

"Father," Lucien broke in, "it is a *private* council, and its purpose is the discussion of strategy. If the council members cannot speak their minds—"

Emperor Florian backhanded him hard across the face. Lucien cried out, and his crutch clattered to the ground. Bodyguards, both Florian's and Lucien's, stiffened, ready for action, but nobody touched the pair.

"The *Legati* are there to speak their minds," hissed Florian. "*You* are there as a courtesy. *Your* purpose on the council is to agree enthusiastically with everything I say. Is that clear?"

Lucien nodded. Limping on his wooden leg, he recovered his crutch and straightened his syrtos. His hand moved instinctively to his face, a protective gesture, but then dropped back to his side. Florian tolerated nothing he could interpret as a sign of weakness.

"Rhianne understands. Don't you, my dear?" said Florian. "We have enemies, and to protect ourselves, we must present a united front. Family solidarity. Isn't that right?"

"Absolutely," said Rhianne. "But when Lucien led White Eagle battalion in Riorca, he was regarded as a brilliant military tactician. If the War Council isn't the right place for his ideas to be heard, perhaps they should be heard somewhere?"

Florian laughed. "You were right the first time when you said you needed to know the particulars. This idea of your cousin's was practically treason. He wants us to call off the war with Mosar."

Rhianne turned to Lucien, who grimaced without meeting her eyes.

"I don't call that brilliance. I call it cowardice," said Florian, turning to Lucien. "And I will not hear it from you again. Is that clear?"

Lucien nodded.

"Speaking of family, it's time to expand it," said Florian. "Rhianne, you shall marry."

A shiver crept up her spine. Marry? Most of the men were away at war. She hadn't met anyone she desired to marry. And then there were practical considerations. Marrying would almost certainly take her away from the

Imperial Palace, and then who would deliver the tetrals? Certainly not Lucien, the way he'd been talking. "Well, I . . . I haven't met anyone yet."

Emperor Florian waved his hand. "I have a husband in mind for you: Augustan Ceres, commander of our forces at Mosar. When he finishes the military operation, I plan to offer him the governorship of the island, and you shall be his bride."

"I'm to be a war prize?" She glanced sidelong at Lucien, whose eyes were downcast. He'd already known.

"Not a war prize. A governor's wife!" said Florian. "You've always wanted to travel to foreign lands. Now you shall, to Mosar."

"I've never met Augustan."

"Easily remedied," said Florian. "I shall summon him back to Kjall long enough for a brief engagement before he returns to the front."

"And if I don't like him?"

"You will," said Florian.

Rhianne supposed if she didn't, he'd smack her like he had Lucien until she changed her mind.

"Now, if you'll run along, I have a few more things to discuss with your cousin," said Florian.

Rhianne walked numbly toward the door.

"One moment," called Lucien, swinging rapidly toward her on his crutch and wooden leg. When he reached her, he whispered, "We'll talk later," and slipped something into the inside pocket of her syrtos. She could tell by the clinking sound that it was the fifteen tetrals.

COMING OCTOBER 2013

FROM

Amy Raby

SPY'S HONOR

The Hearts and Thrones Series

Rhianne, the beautiful and headstrong princess of Kjall,
is stunned when the Emperor betrothes her to Augustan,
the Kjallan general leading the invasion of Mosar,
a rival nation.

Janto, Crown Prince of Mosar, has come to Kjall in secret
to seek information about Kjall's war strategy. With his
shroud-mage gift of invisibility, he slips easily through
Kjall's Imperial Palace as a garden slave—until he captures
the attention of Rhianne, who hears him speaking Mosari
and requests that he tutor her in his native language.

Soon a forbidden romance buds as Rhianne shows him
that Kjall is not so different from Mosar. But Augustan's
return to Kjall, and Janto's mission to find the elusive
Mosari spy, will prove perilous to their love.

Available wherever books are sold or at
penguin.com

facebook.com/ProjectParanormalBooks

S0457

ALEXIS MORGAN

MY LADY MAGE

A Warriors of the Mist Novel

Oppressed by a cruel guardian whose dark magic
threatens to destroy her people, the beautiful and
courageous Merewen calls upon the legendary warriors of
the mist—those cursed by the gods and summoned only
when a champion is needed and the cause is just. In
Gideon she finds more than a champion, and in his arms,
more than protection. However, their enemies are fighting
with a power darker than anything they imagined, and
should Gideon fail, she will lose everything she holds
dear—including her heart.

**"Plenty of mystery, action, and passion to keep
you flipping pages well into the night."
—Fresh Fiction**

Available wherever books are sold or at
penguin.com

facebook.com/ProjectParanormalBooks